KU-618-318

HELEN GRANT

WISH
me
DEAD

PENGUIN BOOKS

PENGUIN BOOKS

Published by the Penguin Group
Penguin Books Ltd, 80 Strand, London WC2R 0RL, England
Penguin Group (USA) Inc., 375 Hudson Street, New York, New York 10014, USA
Penguin Group (Canada), 90 Eglinton Avenue East, Suite 700, Toronto, Ontario, Canada M4P 2Y3
(a division of Pearson Penguin Canada Inc.)
Penguin Ireland, 25 St Stephen's Green, Dublin 2, Ireland (a division of Penguin Books Ltd)
Penguin Group (Australia), 250 Camberwell Road, Camberwell, Victoria 3124, Australia
(a division of Pearson Australia Group Pty Ltd)
Penguin Books India Pvt Ltd, 11 Community Centre, Panchsheel Park, New Delhi – 110 017, India
Penguin Group (NZ), 67 Apollo Drive, Rosedale, Auckland 0632, New Zealand
(a division of Pearson New Zealand Ltd)
Penguin Books (South Africa) (Pty) Ltd, 24 Sturdee Avenue, Rosebank,
Johannesburg 2196, South Africa

Penguin Books Ltd, Registered Offices: 80 Strand, London WC2R 0RL, England

penguin.com

First published 2011
001 – 10 9 8 7 6 5 4 3 2 1

Text copyright © Helen Grant, 2011
All rights reserved

The moral right of the author has been asserted

Set in Sabon by Palimpsest Book Production Limited,
Falkirk, Stirlingshire
Printed in Great Britain by Clays Ltd, St Ives plc

Except in the United States of America, this book is sold subject to the condition that it shall not, by way of trade or otherwise, be lent, re-sold, hired out, or otherwise circulated without the publisher's prior consent in any form of binding or cover other than that in which it is published and without a similar condition including this condition being imposed on the subsequent purchaser

British Library Cataloguing in Publication Data
A CIP catalogue record for this book is available from the British Library

ISBN: 978-0-141-33770-8

www.greenpenguin.co.uk

MIX
Paper from
responsible sources
FSC® C018179

Penguin Books is committed to a sustainable future for our business, our readers and our planet. This book is made from paper certified by the Forest Stewardship Council.

For William Grant

EAST RIDING OF YORKSHIRE L.I.S.	
9016411429	
Bertrams	04/12/2012
	£7.99
BEL	TEE

CHAPTER ONE

The funny thing is, I never even meant the first one. I had nothing against Klara Klein, nothing at all. It was Max who started it, with his plan to visit the witch's house.

There were six of us: Max and Jochen, both of them tall and well built, but Max sprouting a head of unruly dark hair while Jochen had blond curls; Izabela, who had slightly exotic looks and an accent, both inherited from her Romanian mother; robust, dark-haired Hanna, who went through her life with her chin out; wiry, compact Timo, who had been my boyfriend for three years; and me, Steffi Nett, the shy blonde one. Six of us, but as usual it was Max who came up with the plan.

I knew it was a crazy idea, just the same as it was a crazy idea to go skinny-dipping in the Steinbach dam that time, or steal stale pastries from my parents' bakery kitchen to see who could eat the most. Max and Jochen were always egging each other on. It was a pattern that had started when we were in kindergarten together and it showed no sign of changing. When Max and Jochen are both in their nineties and sitting side by side in easy chairs in the old people's home at Otterbach they will probably still be putting each other up to all manner of idiocy, stealing each other's hearing aids and trying to peer up the orderlies' skirts.

I can recall the precise instant when this particular scheme occurred to Max. It was the last night of April and the first dry evening of a wet week. We were waiting in the snack bar on the Orchheimer Strasse, all six of us, because Jochen had decided that he couldn't do anything unless fortified with a *Currywurst* beforehand.

I was standing at the big plate-glass window, staring out. There was a red sports car idling at the other side of the street, a streamlined monster with gleaming bodywork. I didn't need to look closely to see who was behind the wheel, but I did anyway. Kai von Jülich. Blond, blue-eyed and staggeringly gorgeous. Wealthy too; I didn't know anyone else in Bad Münstereifel whose parents could have bought them a car like that, even Max, whose family were very well off. Kai was only a year or two older than me, but he might just as well have come from a different planet.

I realized with a start that Kai's head had turned. He was looking towards the snack bar and had almost certainly seen me gazing out at him. Instantly I turned away, my face burning with embarrassment. To my relief, no one seemed to have noticed my confusion. Timo wasn't even looking my way; he was looking at Izabela instead.

Max was lounging against one of the tables, idly looking at the calendar on the wall of the bar, with its large glossy illustration of a motorbike, and jiggling one denim-clad leg in impatience. Suddenly he said, 'It's Walpurgisnacht.'

'So what?' said Timo.

'So we should . . .' Max paused and considered for a moment. 'We should go to Rote Gertrud's house.'

'Rote Gertrud?' asked Izabela. Not having been born in the town, Izabela had not grown up with the tale of Red Gertrud, the Witch of Schönau.

Max expanded on the theme as we left the snack bar, Jochen having collected his curried sausage. 'Rote Gertrud, the witch, right? Only not an ugly old bag like they normally are. She's supposed to have been . . .' He broke off and outlined an hourglass figure with his hands. 'You know, hot. She had a house way out in the middle of the forest, right off the track, where nobody ever goes. This was three hundred years ago.'

'Four hundred,' said Timo.

'Three hundred, four hundred, who cares? Whatever,' said Max. 'Anyway, get this. The house is still there. They burned the witch but they left the house standing, and it's still up there, in the woods. And since it's Walpurgisnacht, when the witches are supposed to fly, we should go up there and see if Rote Gertrud is flying too.'

'That's a –' began Timo, and I was pretty sure he was going to say *crap idea*, but Jochen interrupted him.

'What? That place in the Eschweiler Tal? You're crazy.' There was no mistaking the admiration in his voice. He took an enormous bite of *Currywurst*, and not for the first time I wished that he would learn to chew with his mouth closed. 'What're we gonna do up there? Hold a black mass or something?'

Max looked at him as though he had just invented the Theory of Relativity. He slapped Jochen on the back. 'Genius. That's *exactly* what we're going to do.'

'We *are*?'

'Course we are.' If Max saw the glances Hanna and I

exchanged, with much rolling of the eyes, he chose to ignore them. 'We're going to have a black mass and call up Gertrud's ghost.'

'Isn't that a seance?' asked Izabela. She had her arms around her slender body, hugging herself; it might have been for warmth, but I thought she looked apprehensive.

Max was unperturbed. 'Black mass, seance, whatever it is, we'll do it.'

'It'll be pitch dark up there and the ground'll be wet,' objected Timo.

'So?' Max shot him an evil look. 'Got a better idea?' He gestured towards the posters taped to the snack-bar window. 'Want to go to the jazz night at the old people's home?'

Having demolished all audible opposition, Max led the way to the car. Timo was walking a little apart from the rest of us, his face a mask of resentment. He knew he had been checkmated. Izabela took the opportunity to drift over and speak to me, appearing at my elbow like a thin, dark-haired wraith.

'Steffi? The Eschweiler Tal, isn't that where that guy who did all the murders is supposed to have put the bodies?'

I knew exactly whom she meant. Everyone in the town knew the story, though we didn't talk about it much: it was like the scar of some horrible wound, healed over but still visible, something which gave you trouble on damp mornings but was otherwise best ignored.

'One of them,' I said reluctantly. 'I think they found the rest in a house in the town.'

Actually I did not just *think* this, I knew it for a fact, and like everyone else whose family had been in the town at the time, I could have pointed out the house itself; I could have named the killer. But Izabela's family had moved to Bad

Münstereifel afterwards; to them the story of the killer who stole the town's children from the streets was a newspaper article, a bloody tale as gruesome and as remote from everyday life as the legend of the eternal huntsman who roamed the Quecken hill.

'Do we have to go there?' she said in a low voice.

With her pale skin and strands of dark hair falling over her face, she might have been Snow White, begging the huntsman not to take her into the depths of the wood.

'Max is right,' cut in Hanna from behind us. 'What else are we going to do?' She gave Izabela a playful shove. 'Come on. Maybe it'll be fun.'

Izabela looked at me. I shrugged – and the die was cast.

Perhaps if I had sided with her, if the three of us girls had insisted on doing something else, we might not have gone to Gertrud's house at all that night. We might never have tried to raise Gertrud's ancient spirit, we might never have hit upon the plan of asking it to carry out our commands, and maybe all the things which happened afterwards would never have come about at all.

I've told myself since then that I couldn't have done anything differently. Wasn't I the shy one, the one who couldn't even make *Realschule*, let alone the very academic *Gymnasium*, because I was too timid to say a word in class? The one who was studying to be a baker because she couldn't find the right words to tell her parents that it was the last thing on earth she wanted to do? It would have been almost impossible for me to speak up, to change the way the evening went. That's what I tell myself now, when regret becomes too bitter – I just couldn't.

CHAPTER TWO

So now there we were, sitting in the brooding darkness on a couple of tree trunks that were soft and slimy with wet moss, and bolstering our courage with a stomach-churning mixture of drinks, Bitburger beer and miniatures of Kleiner Feigling, a fig vodka, left over from *Karneval*. Rote Gertrud's house was somewhere close by, hidden in the tangled undergrowth and overshadowed by ancient beech trees.

I remembered my sister, Magdalena, bringing me here one afternoon when I was a kid, maybe eight or nine and still at primary school. I could not recall why we had done it. She must have been left in charge of me, and when she made up her mind to come here she had to bring me along. But as to why she had wanted to come at all, that escaped me. Now I came to think of it, it was a strange place to bring a child, and it could not have been easy to get here. We must have cycled, although she would have had to nag me like mad to go that far. Why had we gone there? It was a mystery.

They called Gertrud Vorn the Witch of Schönau even though she lived most of her life in the house in the forest. Supposedly she was born in the village of Schönau, to the south of Bad Münstereifel; at any rate, the Münstereifelers were keen to disassociate her from their town. They called her Rote – Red – Gertrud not because of the long auburn hair she had, but because her hands were literally and figuratively stained with blood – the blood of innocents. She'd lured away and murdered two children, Hans Schmitz and little Löttchen Bär. For this she was dragged from her house by a mob of angry citizens howling for retribution and burned to death on a bonfire. They say the fire went out three times because the Devil, the witch's master, blew out the flames. More likely it was because the fire was too hastily built and more firewood had to be added to keep it going. Gertrud took an hour to die, during which time she shrieked 'like a devil' and fought in vain to escape. She screamed her innocence until her smoke-scoured lungs gave out.

After Gertrud's death, no one cared to take the stones from the walls or steal the timbers from the roof, which was why the house remained, crumbling slowly in the depths of the woods. The witch's house.

'So,' said Max eventually, breaking the silence. 'Are we going on?'

He swung the torch around so that the beam danced over the damp tree trunks and sagging bushes. Black shadows leapt and scurried, my imagination unwillingly transforming them into imps and goblins circling just outside the borders of the light.

'Do we have to?' asked Timo. In the torchlight his lean face looked pinched and resentful.

'No point in coming all this way and not going into the house,' said Max glibly. 'Who's coming?'

I felt in the pocket of my jacket for my torch. As I stood up, I realized that the little bottles of vodka had had more of an effect than I thought and I staggered, my head thumping. The light from Max's torch seemed to wink at me, as though it were the revolving beam of a lighthouse. It was nauseating, the light flashing in time to the throbbing of my head. I closed my eyes for a moment to shut it out.

Stumbling through the bushes with the others, I had a faint nagging sense of anxiety, but it was almost drowned in the false courage of the vodka, a distant signal like the black box of a crashed plane beeping away under a mile of icy seawater. I switched on my torch but I couldn't keep the beam level. People kept bumping into me, shoving me, and the bushes clutched at my clothes with thorny hands. I fell over a tree root that twisted unseen across my path. My heart pounded as I fought back the image of hands reaching up from the spongy earth, trying to grasp me.

'This is it,' said Max suddenly, and stopped short so that we were suddenly all jostling each other.

In the feeble torchlight I could see a wall rising up in front of us, speckled with black growths like the tarnish on an old mirror and seemingly featureless. For a moment I wondered stupidly where the door was and then I realized that we must be at the side of the house.

'Come on,' said Max, and vanished round the corner, leaving us to follow as best we could over the trailing brambles and broken chunks of stone which were strewn over the ground.

The front of the house was in a considerably worse state than I remembered from my childhood visit. There was a hole in the wall so large that I could have stepped through it. Max ignored this and went for the doorway, which was little better than a hole itself, the door long gone and the lintel sagging alarmingly. At the last moment he turned and put his torch under his chin, shining it upwards to make himself look like Dracula. With his saturnine looks and the yellow light deepening the hollows of his face, the resemblance was a little closer than I cared for. We all laughed, but the laughter sounded tinny in my ears and I was beginning to feel little prickles of nervousness. I stopped short at the threshold and peered inside.

If it hadn't been for the precarious-looking stone chimney, it could have been anything: a store, a cowshed. There was no sign of comfort, nothing to show that this had ever been a home. The walls had a scored and pitted appearance. Stones littered the floor, which was blanketed so thickly with the rotten leaves of the previous autumn that it was impossible even to say whether there were boards or flagstones. The moving torch beams picked out the rusting remains of beer cans, the glint of abandoned bottles. Reluctantly I stepped inside.

'What do we do now?' Izabela asked.

She was hugging herself against the cold, her dark hair falling over her face. In the torchlight her dark eyes were like pits and her lips almost blue; she might have been mistaken for the witch herself, or some bloodsucking wraith in the sorceress's pay. *Stop it*, I thought. *Your imagination's working overtime.*

'Hey, Max, don't we have to take our clothes off or something?' said Jochen.

'You can forget about that right now,' said Hanna promptly. 'It's freezing and you're a pervert.' She listened to Jochen's complaints for a moment, only a pucker at the corner of her mouth betraying her amusement. Then she said, 'OK, let's get on with it, whatever we're going to do.'

'We're going to call up Rote Gertrud,' said Max. I heard the sound of liquid swilling around, followed by a contented sigh. 'And then . . .' He paused for a moment, seeking inspiration. 'Then we're going to tell her to . . .'

'Give us more beer,' suggested Jochen.

'You're going to summon up a ghost and ask it to give you *beer*?' said Hanna under her breath.

'No,' said Max. 'I'll tell you what we're going to do.'

His face loomed at us out of the chilly darkness, unnaturally sallow in the torchlight. He no longer looked like the old familiar Max; he looked like a ghoul. Involuntarily I stepped back, stumbling against Hanna in the dark.

'We're going to kill Klara Klein,' said Max.

I looked at him. 'You're joking,' I said.

Klara Klein – the folk singer – was the local celebrity, or had been, when our grandparents were young; she seemed to have been around forever, and indeed she still drew ageing fans to the town from all over Germany. The idea of wishing her dead was something akin to cursing the Tooth Fairy or the Easter Bunny: faintly sacrilegious and almost certainly ineffective.

'No, no, it's a great idea,' cut in Jochen. 'It'd be a public service,' he went on in the rapturous tone that meant that he was deep in the clutches of an entirely new idea. 'I bet there are people in Bad Münstereifel who'd give us a *medal* for getting rid of her.'

'What about the fans?' asked Hanna ironically.

'All dead. Or they will be soon,' said Max airily. 'They must all be a hundred, at least.'

This was an exaggeration, but it was certainly true that the ranks of Klara Klein fans were thinning out these days, and most of the surviving ones were in a state of decrepitude. Not that Klara herself – 'Little Klara', as she was known – was any spring chicken. The famous folk singer resembled nothing so much as a Gila monster in a blonde wig and dirndl. She lived alone in a very large mansion near the village of Mahlberg. The house was designed to look like an oversized Swiss chalet. I had seen a photograph of it in *Freizeit Revue* and it had a row of edelweiss flowers the size of car tyres carved on to the wooden facade.

I wondered if she were there now, hatching some terrible new song about blue gentian flowers and everlasting love, oblivious to the fact that her doom was being plotted in the dark woods on the other side of the town. It should have been funny, but somehow it wasn't.

All the same, I said nothing. I listened queasily to Max and Jochen discussing the best way to go about summoning up Gertrud's ghost. Jochen said that they should say the Lord's Prayer backwards but Max said no, that was for calling up the Devil. Both of them sounded a little drunk, and the conversation would have roamed back and forth interminably but for the shriek which suddenly froze us all where we stood. I glanced around me wildly and realized that Izabela had vanished.

CHAPTER THREE

'Izzi?' I felt a moment of panic before I heard her voice speaking quietly in the darkness.

'I'm here.'

I looked down and could just make out the dim shape of Izabela hunched on the mulchy floor. Relief washed over me, but still I wished she would stand up. There was something indefinably sinister about that crouched posture, something that made her look a little less than human.

'There's a hole in the floor,' she said. 'My foot went right into it.'

'Are you all right?' I glanced around nervously, imagining subsidence, hidden pits awaiting to engulf the unwary.

'Yes. But there's something here, in the hole. I'm trying to get it out but it's wedged in.'

I squatted on the floor, squinting at Izabela in the dark, trying to direct the wavering beam of the torch so that I could see what she was doing. Now that I was close to the ground I could detect the odour of rot. Of decaying leaves and sodden wood, and something appallingly sweetish underneath, the scent of decomposition. I wondered whether some woodland creature had crawled into the space under the floor and died. I marvelled at Izabela's temerity, rummaging around in there with her bare fingers.

'I've got it,' she said suddenly, and drew something out of the hole. She stood up, clutching it in one hand, brushing the clinging dirt from the legs of her jeans with the other.

'Show Papa,' said Max, pushing past me.

He held up his torch and we all looked to see what Izabela had found.

It was a rectangular object, perhaps twenty centimetres long, and I thought it was all of one colour, although in the dim light it was hard to tell. The surface had a strange pitted texture, which I realized must be carving, though very worn; the thing was clearly very old.

'It's a box,' said Izabela. She was running her finger along a join I had not noticed.

'A money box?' asked Max.

'Be serious,' said Izabela. 'There's something in it, I think, but it's not money.'

She shook the box and we heard a faint slithering sound as something light moved back and forth inside it.

'Well, open it, then.' Max sounded impatient.

Don't open it, I thought. *Put it back.* If there were something inside the box, it was there for a reason. Someone had put it there and wedged the box into the hole in the floor of the deserted house because it was not meant to be found – not meant to be opened.

Izabela turned the box over in her hands and I saw that her fingers were stained with something dark and sticky. For a sickening moment I imagined that they were slick with blood, before I realized that it must simply be mud from the box's grave under the floor. *Fool*, I told myself.

Eventually Izabela located the catch on the front of the

box. It was rusted and stiff and it took her a moment to undo it. As she opened it we all craned forward.

'A piece of paper.'

I could hear the disappointment in Max's voice, though what he could have expected to find in this heap of decay and dilapidation it was hard to say. Izabela was unfolding the paper.

'Give me the torch, Max,' she said.

There was a long silence.

'Well?' said Hanna eventually. 'Is there anything on it? What does it say?'

'It says . . .' Izabela paused. '*J.M., die before 12.11.*'

'J.M.? Who's J.M.?'

'It doesn't say, Max,' said Izabela quietly. 'There's nothing else on the paper, just that.'

I shivered. The effect of the fig vodka seemed to have worn off; all of a sudden I felt stone-cold sober and slightly sick. 'And "12.11"?' I said, though I thought I knew the answer.

'December eleventh,' said Hanna at my shoulder. 'Or maybe December 2011, or November 2012.'

We all considered.

'Let's go home,' said Izabela suddenly. 'Let's put this back and go home.'

'Come on, Izzi –'

'Max, it gives me the creeps. I don't want to stay here, OK?' She stuffed the paper back into the box and closed the lid. Her hands moved swiftly, as though she could not wait to replace the box in the hole, and in the torchlight her face had a tight, strained expression that made her seem much older than her years. The look of someone holding back the **floodgates of fear or grief.**

'It's just someone's idea of a joke,' said Max.

'It's not funny.'

'Don't be a spoilsport, Iz.'

'I'm not.'

'Look.' Max's voice became silky, persuasive. 'We didn't come all the way up here for nothing. We're going to hex Little Klara.'

'I'm sorry, Max, I just want to go home,' said Izabela tremulously.

'She's right, Max. It was a crap idea anyway, coming up here,' said Timo.

I noticed he had an arm around Izabela's shoulders.

'Timo!' Now Max was starting to look nettled.

Next to me, Hanna gave a heavy sigh. 'Look,' she said, 'if it's such a big deal, let's just do it and go. OK?' She glanced at the rest of us. 'I'm not stripping off and dancing round a fire, though, you can forget that.'

'No need,' said Max. His good humour was returning now that it looked as though he might get his own way. 'We can do the same as whoever. The person who wrote that note in the box.'

'The stripping off sounded better,' said Jochen.

'Later, Jochen, later, if you can persuade anyone to watch you,' said Max, patting him on the shoulder like a benevolent uncle. 'Look, this is the real thing, right? Someone's been up here already and put a hex on this J.M., whoever they are.' He ran a hand through his untidy dark hair. 'Let's put one on Little Klara.' He flashed us a grin, and not for the first time I thought what large white teeth he had, great slabs like polished tombstones. When Max smiled you found yourself wondering if he wanted to bite you.

15

'Fine,' said Hanna in a flat voice, a voice that said *let's get this over with*. 'Who's got paper?'

All of us started to say that we hadn't got any paper with us, obviously, because who takes a notebook on a drunken night-time ramble through the woods? But then I slid my hand into the back pocket of my jeans and discovered that I had a flyer for an evening of live music in a local bistro, and scrawled across the bottom of it in an enthusiastic but unruly script was a message that was meant for me only. Hastily I folded the bottom couple of centimetres back and tore them off. Then I handed the rest to Max. 'Here.'

'Pen?' said Max in the self-assured tone of a brain surgeon asking for a scalpel.

This time it was Izabela who silently held out the required item.

'Who's going to write it?' asked Max.

Izabela simply shook her head.

'No point in my doing it,' said Max. 'Rote Gertrud wouldn't be able to read it. Here, Steffi, you do it.' He saw me put up a hand as if to ward him off. 'Come on, don't be wet.'

Unwillingly I took the pen and paper from him, tucking my torch under my arm. I knew he had asked me to do it because he thought I was the least likely to say no, even if I didn't want anything to do with the whole scheme. For the thousandth time I found myself wondering why other people found things easy to say, when I seemed unable to speak my mind. It was as though the words were all there, ready inside my head, like a group of jostling kids on the high diving board, daring each other to jump; but at the last minute they just couldn't do it.

I put one foot up on a piece of broken stonework so that I could use my knee as a surface to write on. I spread the paper out and uncapped the pen.

Max stepped close to me, so close that I could smell onions on his breath. He trained the wavering torchlight on the paper. 'Go on,' he said.

I wrote: *Klara Klein, die by 5.10.*

CHAPTER FOUR

I held up the piece of paper so that they could all see what I had written by the light of Max's torch. Then I folded it twice, carefully. Max had taken the box from Izabela, who relinquished it with obvious relief, as though it contained fishing maggots or a dead creature starting to decompose. He raised the lid.

I looked at the note already inside the box, the one wishing death upon the unknown J.M. For a moment I thought about removing it, but really I was reluctant to touch it at all. In the end I just dropped my own piece into the box. There was a click as Max closed the lid.

'Is that it?' asked Jochen. He sounded disappointed.

'You should say something, Max,' said Hanna, but she didn't sound particularly enthusiastic.

Even though tomorrow was the first of May, the night was still surprisingly chilly. I guessed Hanna was thinking about going home and warming up. It was an attractive idea, even if in my case the cost of sitting by the living-room fire was probably a monologue about baking from my father.

'Steffi?'

Izabela was nudging me. She held out a hand; on my

other side Timo was also fumbling for my hand with cold fingers. When all six of us were holding hands in a ragged circle, I looked down and saw that Max had placed the box in the middle. There was something so ludicrous about this that I smiled to myself in the dark, but the smile curdled on my lips as I thought about the message I had scrawled on the paper inside.

I suppose I mostly imagined someone coming to the ruined house, finding my note and recognizing the handwriting. Common sense said that this was highly unlikely – impossible, even – but if they did I could imagine the fuss that would ensue. I was not even sure that there wasn't some law against putting a wish for someone's death into writing. Did it count as a threat, I wondered?

It never occurred to me to think that the writing itself might *do* anything, that it might cause the ancient and wealthy Klara Klein to collapse over her late-night mug of cocoa, or make her aged heart burst the next time she hit the top note in 'Geh' aus mein Herz'. It was a piece of paper in a tatty old box. It was harmless – or so I thought.

Max cleared his throat. 'Rote Gertrud,' he began in a sonorous tone. Someone smothered a snigger. 'Hear our . . .' He paused. I suspected he had been about to say *prayer*, but had thought better of it. 'Request,' he finished eventually.

Izabela's fingers felt cold in mine. I felt her move restlessly, shifting her weight from foot to foot, and guessed that she liked this entertainment as little as I did. But we both knew it was useless arguing with Max. The sooner he put the hex on Klara Klein, the sooner we could leave the ruined house and make our way back to somewhere warmer and drier.

19

'Rote Gertrud,' intoned Max again.

'Are you there?' cut in Jochen in a spectral voice.

It was intended to make us laugh, but this time nobody did. Then there was silence, and we could hear the movement of the wind through the branches of the trees surrounding the house. I strained to listen for a voice, even a faint one, whispering a reply, but all I could hear was the creaking of timber.

Nervously I glanced towards the nearest of the empty window frames, but there was nothing to see outside. Beyond the limited range of the torchlight everything was inky black. Even if someone had been standing right there outside the window, just a couple of metres away from where we stood, I doubt I could have seen them. But who would be there on such a dark night, here in the woods?

The witch.

As soon as the thought occurred to me I tried to stifle it, but it was too late. Already in my imagination she was there, silently watching us. Rote Gertrud. I thought of pale skin, as white and translucent as the inside of an oyster shell; two eyes blazing with dark fire; a great fall of hair the colour of copper, of fox fur. But Gertrud had burned. Perhaps the thing which lurked there was dreadful to see, a burnt stump with a withered tuft of hair sprouting like poisoned weed from the charred scalp, the eyeholes dark pits.

My mouth was dry. I tightened my grip on Izabela's hand.

Max appeared to be oblivious to the dark and decay. 'Rote Gertrud, strike down Klara Klein,' he said, and laughed. Then he glanced quickly round at the rest of us, his eyes glittering. 'Come on, say it.'

'Rote Gertrud,' we mumbled unconvincingly.

'Strike down Klara Klein,' insisted Max.

'Strike down Klara Klein,' we parroted.

Timo was a beat later than the rest of us and he was still speaking when we heard a rustle in the bushes outside, followed by a snap. Izabela gave a little scream.

'What was that?'

'Calm down,' said Max. He let go of the others' hands. 'Just a fox or something.'

We listened. There was another sharp snap and then the sound of something moving away heavily through the undergrowth, the bushes springing back behind it.

'It's bigger than a fox,' said Izabela in a thin voice.

'A deer,' said Max, but he made no move to go and look. 'Or a wild pig.'

'Or Rote Gertrud,' said Jochen. His voice was mocking but there was no real humour in it.

'Crap,' said Max shortly. He ran both hands through his hair so that it stuck up in untidy clumps. 'This was a stupid idea.'

None of us pointed out that it was he who had suggested it.

'Now we're all agreed about that, can we go please?' said Hanna, shifting restlessly.

For just a moment I saw Max cock his head to one side. I could have sworn he was listening, trying to tell whether the thing which had moved so noisily through the bushes outside had gone or not. It was then that I realized he was as rattled as the rest of us.

'OK,' he said.

Once the decision was made, he didn't waste any time. He made for the crumbling hole which represented the door

21

and the rest of us followed him. We left the box lying in the middle of the floor. Max had forgotten it already and no one else cared to pick it up. I was the last out and I watched Timo help Izabela over a pile of stones, leaving me to struggle over them as best I could.

I saw Izabela's eyes turn to me and I made a play of swinging my torch around, as though making one last sweep of the deserted house. It looked as forlorn and dilapidated as ever. Perhaps a bright fire had once burned in that hearth, warming the house and gilding everything with a soft light, but it was utterly impossible to imagine it now. I thought the house was a dank smelly hole and I promised myself that I would never visit it again.

That was only one of the promises I made to myself that I later broke.

CHAPTER FIVE

The next day was Saturday, generally the bakery's busiest day, when tourists mingled with the regular customers. Normally my parents let me sleep in on Saturdays. My father could never understand why I would prefer to lie in bed when I could be up and about in the bakery, inhaling the heady perfumes of yeast and rye flour, but my mother said I was a growing girl and needed the sleep, although I was now a couple of centimetres taller than she was. When she said this, I had the uncanniest feeling that she was still thinking of me as the child I had once been, that she had not really *looked* at me for years. Not, perhaps, since my sister, Magdalena, had left.

On that particular Saturday, however, I had to be in the bakery by eight thirty in the morning. One of the regular Saturday staff had telephoned to say that she was sick and couldn't come in, and I was to stand in. As I dressed in the green dirndl and frilly white blouse that served as a waitress's uniform, I sent up a silent prayer that Kai von Jülich would not come into the bakery that morning. It was unlikely, since he and his friends probably had something considerably more exciting to do than sit alongside the town's senior citizens and eat apple strudel to the strains of

'Edelweiss' (instrumental version). All the same, it would be doubly humiliating to be seen working while he was undoubtedly playing, and I was looking distinctly waxen from the effects of the Kleiner Feigling.

Our flat occupied the floor above the bakery. At eight thirty-five I let myself out of the flat's front door, went downstairs and found myself in the narrow passage leading to the seating area. It was a very plain corridor, windowless and unadorned by pictures. It reminded me of the stark backstage area in a theatre. Step through the door and you would find yourself in a place quite as flamboyant as a stage set, with enough potted plants for an entire production of *The Jungle Book* and canned folk music drifting through the air like some kind of poison gas, sickly sweet and stupefying. Generally I hated the moment when I stepped into the cafe and into the clutches of the dozen or so old harridans who would inevitably be sitting there, lips pursed and chins up, because their morning coffee and slices of cream gateau hadn't reached the table within two nanoseconds of their placing an order. Today, however, I would have been pleased if I had been able to go straight into the cafe, even if it had meant coming face to face with an entire coachload of superannuated Klara Klein fans, all screaming for a cooked breakfast at the tops of their creaky old voices. It was not to be, however; someone was blocking the way. With a sinking feeling, I recognized the beefy figure of Achim Zimmer.

Achim, my father's assistant, was dressed in his baker's whites and was lounging against the wall in an attitude of contrived carelessness. He had a cigarette in one large pink hand and a plastic lighter in the other.

I hated Achim's hands. He had the delicate fair skin of the natural redhead, easily sunburnt or chapped by the wind. On some people this might have had a porcelain beauty, but Achim was too solid for that. There was nothing ethereal about him; he was Hercules executed in Meissen porcelain. In summer he reminded me of a boiled lobster, with his reddened skin and pale eyes. But it wasn't the repulsiveness of their appearance that made me dislike Achim's hands. It was the fact that they wandered wherever they liked.

Achim had clearly left the kitchen on the pretext of taking a break to smoke, but there was no sign he intended to go outside. I wondered whether he had known that I would be working this morning and that I would be coming down at this time. Whether he had waited for me on purpose. He looked up as the flat door closed behind me and gave me a jovial nod. I saw him slide the lighter into his pocket; the cigarette also vanished somewhere inside the baker's jacket. The two big, waxy-looking hands moved and I saw that he was actually rubbing them together, which only enhanced the impression of an evil troll gloating over his next victim.

I wondered whether I could concoct some excuse to go back into the flat, but a glance at my watch showed that I was already late. I hesitated as usual, and as usual I was lost.

'*Guten Morgen*, Steffi,' Achim said in an over-familiar tone. He had an insinuating expectant air about him, managing to convey without words the conviction that it was I who had planned this meeting and not he.

'*Morgen*,' I muttered.

I looked longingly past him at the door to the cafe. There

was only one way to get there and Achim was standing right in the middle of it.

'Won't you say, "*Morgen*, Achim"?' he asked me, with a nauseating attempt at a beseeching expression.

I said nothing. If Hanna had been in my place, I knew she would have said something which would have taken that leer off his face. But I stood there, dumb and paralysed as always, every word which came to mind as useless as a coin on the tongue of the dead.

'I didn't hear anything,' said Achim.

I bit my lip. Was he ever going to drop it? I eyed the space between Achim and the wall, estimating my chances of slipping past him without further annoyance. Achim was about thirty, but he had the belly of a man ten years older, pregnant with beer and *Wurst*. It slowed him down, but it also made him a formidable obstacle.

I made myself speak up. 'I have to go to work.'

'I'm not stopping you,' said Achim, but he didn't move a centimetre.

The passage was so narrow that to be a real gentleman and let me pass entirely freely he would have had to flatten himself against the wall like a gunman in an action movie. Of course there was no question of that. Between that straining belly and the wall there was so little clearance that I fully expected I would be squeezed through the gap like a lump of dough going through the rollers of a pastry machine.

I thought about trying to push past Achim and the inevitable necessity of coming into actual contact with him. I also thought about my mother, waiting impatiently behind the counter, and of my father leaning out of the kitchen with his brown hair turned salt-and-pepper by the dusting of flour in it, wanting to know where the devil Steffi had got to.

'Dad's calling you,' I said as loudly as I could.

Achim gave me an unpleasant smile. 'No, he isn't.'

I took a deep breath. 'Dad?' I called at the top of my voice. 'Did you want Achim?'

The smile melted into an ugly sneer, but Achim took the point. Before my father had time to come out of the kitchen, Achim opened the connecting door himself and lumbered inside, not without giving me a backward glance which clearly telegraphed, *I'll see you later.*

I slipped through the door into the cafe, vowing that I would come downstairs with my mother every day from now on. As the door swung shut behind me I did my best to look calm, smoothing down my apron and trying to breathe deeply and slowly.

'What's the matter with you? And where have you been all this time?' said my mother, who was passing with a tray laden with coffee cups and dirty plates. She paused for a moment, regarding me with her lips slightly pursed. I guessed that I was looking pink in the face and dishevelled, whereas she had not a single blonde curl out of place.

'Sorry,' I said.

'The coffee machine is playing up again,' added my mother. 'God knows we could do with a new one. I need you downstairs on time, Steffi. I can't do everything myself.' She shook her head. 'Frau Lanzerath on table six wants another hot chocolate with cream and a *Nuss-striezel*. I know she normally has a *Plunderteilchen*,' she added, as though I had been about to argue, 'but not today.'

'Yes,' I said.

27

I went behind the counter and picked up a plate. Out of the corner of my eye I could see restless movement to the left, which meant that Frau Lanzerath was working herself up into a state of red-hot impatience. Still, it was not Frau Lanzerath and her irritating manners that preoccupied my mind as I slid the yearned-for *Nuss-striezel* on to the plate. It was Achim and his clammy hands.

It was a shame, I thought, that our attempt to wipe out Klara Klein by witchcraft was just a game, that it couldn't possibly have any effect on real life. If it had been genuinely possible to strike someone down by leaving a note for Rote Gertrud, I wouldn't have chosen Klara Klein for my victim at all. It would have been Achim.

Chapter Six

It was not until Tuesday morning, the Tuesday after our trip to Gertrud's house, that the news broke. On Monday I had been at the college in Kall, filling my head with more unwelcome information about the science of baking. This was a process which always made me feel like the unwilling recipient of brainwashing in a totalitarian state. Study, work, home, all seemed to be pushing me in the same direction. One day in the distant future I would be standing in the Werther Strasse outside the cafe, wearing the hated dirndl and watching a man on a ladder painting AND DAUGHTER after KONDITOREI NETT on the facade. There would be no escape then; I would be stuck in Bad Münstereifel forever. In my very worst nightmares, a middle-aged Timo would be standing next to me with a proprietorial air and I would have his ring on my finger. If that happened, I thought, I would not care how soon I gorged myself to death by comfort-eating the cream cakes.

The Tuesday morning was bright and sunny, and from my post behind the glass counter displaying the day's gateaux I had a clear view out of the bakery's front window. Across the street, on the other side of the River Erft, was an enormous May tree, fixed outside one of the half-timbered houses. The multicoloured crêpe streamers danced in the breeze. Someone, some girl perhaps the very same age as I was, had got up on May morning and looked out of her bedroom window to see the tree waiting there, a gesture of true love. I sighed. Timo would never have thought of such a thing, not in a million years. Not that I wanted him to, I told myself. What I wanted ... I slid my hand into the pocket of my apron and felt the piece of paper folded there, the paper with the ragged edge. Could I stretch out my hand and take what I wanted? Could I summon up the courage to do that?

From this dismal reverie I was awakened by my father coming in through the bakery's front door with a thick bundle of newspapers in his arms. The bakery sold them in the morning alongside the breakfast rolls in paper bags and the Styrofoam cups of coffee.

'Late,' my father was grumbling. 'We'll never sell even half of these now.' He put the stack of papers down heavily on the nearest table. 'Steffi, can you put these out? Not that there's any point now,' he added as he stumped off towards the kitchen.

I didn't look at the papers for at least another half an hour. A large group of customers came in and opted for the full works: sliced ham, smoked bacon, boiled eggs, buttered rolls, coffee with cream, coffee without cream, rosehip tea, apple juice. They kept me running backwards and forwards so busily that when another customer came in and asked for a newspaper with his morning roll I directed him to the stack on the table without so much as glancing at it myself.

'Sad, isn't it?' the customer said, brandishing the paper as he took the bag containing his order.

'Yes,' I said automatically. My head was still full of the previous order. Someone had asked for a *latte macchiato* and I had given her an ordinary *Milchkaffee* by accident, a disaster of titanic proportions judging by her expression. I hastened to make the *latte* and spilt half of it down my apron. I had to leave the other two staff to hold the fort and make another *latte* while I went to get a clean apron. Still I did not look at the newspapers.

When I got back the *latte* had been delivered and peace restored, but another large group had come in. This time they were foreign, and since they spoke no German and I spoke no French, it took a long time to serve them. By the time I had worked out that a *pain au chocolat* was a *Schoko-brötchen* the little clock which hung behind the counter was chiming nine thirty. I wiped my hands and had started moving around the counter to tackle the stack of newspapers when the front door opened and Izabela came in.

Instantly I was struck by how terrible she looked. Izabela was always pale – she had the dark hair, the pallid skin and ice-blue eyes of Snow White. Today, however, she had an almost greyish tinge to her face. With her dark hair straggling over her shoulders, she reminded me of nothing so much as a drowned girl, face and limbs bleached white by the icy water. As I stood by the counter staring at her, she stumbled forward, her hands outstretched as though she wanted to clutch on to me. I glanced swiftly around the cafe. To my relief, my mother was not in sight; I guessed she had gone into the kitchen. I went to Izabela, not knowing what to say, conscious that whatever this was, it could not be good news.

'Have you heard?'

I started to ask her what she meant, what I was supposed to have heard, and then the words died on my lips. Standing this close to her, I was level with the table where my father had dumped the stack of newspapers. All of them were copies of the *Kölner Express*. Glancing at the headline upside down from where I stood, I could pick out the two capital Ks in the glaringly large type.

I had the strangest feeling in the pit of my stomach, a dropping sensation as though I had taken a step on to ice, innocently thinking that it was solid ground, and gone right through. I moved away from Izabela and reached for the newspaper at the top of the pile, flipping it around to read the headline properly. Even before I had done so, I knew what it said.

KLARA KLEIN DEAD.

CHAPTER SEVEN

I am a quiet person, a shy person if I am honest, but I am not stupid. It would have been very easy to crumble at that moment, to scream or to become distracted, as Izabela was. I knew that if I did any of those things I was lost. My mother would be back in the cafe at any moment and she would ask questions. Probably she would go and fetch my father, and he would ask questions too; they might insist I went into the kitchen, away from the avid gaze of the assembled customers, so that they could question me the better. Even if I managed not to tell them anything, they would be suspicious. Trying to discuss anything with my parents was like arguing with an unholy partnership between a prosecuting lawyer and a Jesuit priest. With this in mind I bit back the hysterical babble that came to my lips.

I put the paper back on the pile. I looked down at my own hands smoothing the front page, straightening the stack of papers so that they looked tidy again. I felt as though I were observing someone else doing this. Then I turned to Izabela.

'Go and sit outside at one of the tables,' I told her. My voice was surprisingly calm. I spoke firmly too; the fear that Izabela might drop some incriminating words into the waiting ears of the customers was enough to give me a little courage for once. 'I'll come out,' I added, seeing her hesitate. Still she did not move, so I gave her a gentle push, and then she stumbled slowly back outside as though sleep-walking.

My heart was thudding in my chest, so violently that it was almost painful. *The witch*, I thought. *The wish we made – the witch has granted it.* The idea was dizzying. I made my way very carefully back around the counter, walking slowly because I felt so unsteady that I was really worried I might trip. I could feel the gaze of dozens of pairs of eyes on me, like insects crawling over my bare skin. All the same, by some miracle nobody called me over – nobody wanted to order another coffee or pay the bill at that precise moment. I was able to retrieve an order pad and pencil from their place by the till and carry them outside without hindrance.

Izabela was sitting bolt upright at one of the outside tables. I wondered whether I looked the same as she did: white and wild-eyed with shock. If so, there was no way it would escape my mother's notice.

'I don't want anything,' said Izabela when she saw me with the pad.

'I can't just stand out here chatting. Have a Coke or something.'

'I'm not thirsty.' She looked stricken. 'I feel awful. I feel like we killed her.'

'Shhhh.' I couldn't help looking around to see if anyone was listening, even though I knew this must make me look as though I were up to something suspicious. 'Izzi, this can't possibly have anything to do with – you know.' My voice was steady but my stomach was churning as though I were standing on the deck of a ship on a stormy sea.

'But, Steffi –' Izabela was shaking her head. 'It's so – don't you think it's too much of a coincidence, what we did on Friday night and now this?' She put her hands up and pushed the dark mass of hair back from her face. 'What are we going to do if someone finds out?'

The sheer absurdity of this brought me back to myself. I looked around at the street, at the view that was as familiar to me as the lines on my own hands. The sun was shining, the pansies and primulas in the window boxes made bright splashes of colour on the monochrome facades of the half-timbered houses. Two doors up from the bakery the bulky figure of an old woman in a floral housecoat was bent over her broom, sweeping vigorously. Everything looked reassuringly normal. Bad stuff happens everywhere, even in neat little towns like Münstereifel; nobody thought otherwise, not since those murders a decade before. But people don't die because someone puts a hex on them. They die because they don't see the lorry coming when they step out into the road, or they have something malignant growing inside them, or they are simply so weighed down with years that one day their heart just gives out.

That cold feeling that had been stealing over me, a churning mixture of fear and guilt and the dread of being found out, began to recede like an ebbing tide.

'Nobody's going to find out,' I said, 'because there's nothing to find out. We were just messing about. It was just a game.'

All the same, I thought, *it might be worth going back to Gertrud's house and removing that note from the box.*

There was a hard little tapping sound. I turned and saw a wrinkled visage like the face of an old and very ugly tortoise glaring at me through the bakery window over a barrier of silk flowers and ornamental tea-light holders. Even if my mother didn't come out in a minute or two and scold me for chatting to a friend while customers were waiting, it looked as though the customers themselves would do it.

'I have to go in,' I said.

'Steffi –'

'We'll meet up with the others this evening, OK? Look, Izzi, this is mad. We didn't do anything.'

Izabela looked at me, her blue eyes wide. She didn't look reassured at all. I thought she was on the verge of panic. She looked the way I thought a person might look if they were sitting at the wheel of their car, afraid to turn around and see what it was that they had run over, the thing that had disappeared under the wheels with a thump that was at once hard and yet horribly yielding.

'Izzi,' I hissed. 'We didn't *do* anything. We were just messing around. It's a coincidence, all right? It's just not *possible* that it was anything else.'

'She died, Steffi,' said Izabela, and the flat tone she used sent a chill through me all over again. 'We wished it and she just dropped dead.'

I dared not stay any longer. I put the pad and pen into my apron pocket. 'Look, I'll just get you a Coke, OK?'

I hurried back into the bakery. I was itching to get my hands on the newspaper, to read the details of Little Klara's death from beginning to end. If I could have found a quiet corner for even two minutes I would have liked to call

36

Hanna too, to hear her sensible voice telling me what I had just told Izabela, that it was all a coincidence. Predictably, however, the moment I reappeared inside there was a babble of voices calling for me to bring the bill, to refill a coffee cup, to bring another pastry, a glass of water, a cake fork ... They kept me busy for a full twenty minutes, running to and fro, and when I finally carried Izabela's Coke outside she had gone.

CHAPTER EIGHT

She just dropped dead. Much later, when the details of Little Klara's death had seeped out, as they are prone to do, especially in a small town like Bad Münstereifel, I discovered that this was not strictly true.

At first, given the circumstances of Klara's death, the police didn't release any information at all. Then Klara's agent issued a statement saying that Little Klara had died peacefully at home. He was almost as old as Klara had been, white-haired and venerable-looking, but that didn't stop him from rushing on from announcing Klara's death to plugging her latest CD, which he described as her 'memorial'.

The unfortunate truth was that Klara Klein had met her maker face-down in a plateful of cherry streusel.

When Klara was a young woman, she had been marvellously slim, with such famously slender legs and ankles that she had sometimes been known as 'the doe of the Eifel'. As the years went by, the effects of passing time and a weakness for patisserie had made Little Klara at least twice the woman she used to be. Had she not been considered a national treasure, someone would surely have pointed out by now that if she resembled any traditional woodland creature, it was not so much a doe as the female of the species *Sus scrofa*, also known as the wild pig.

Little Klara was as fond of cheesecake and *Sahnetorte* as the next woman, but her especial weakness was for cherry streusel, a confection of sour cherries, flour, eggs, cinnamon and an alarming quantity of butter and sugar. On the evening – or perhaps morning – of her demise (depending on the accuracy of the estimated time of death) she had cut herself a simply enormous slice of cherry streusel from the tray in her refrigerator and carried it through to the living room, where she had seated herself on her well-padded sofa. Pictures of Little Klara in magazines such as *Freizeit Revue* or *Das Goldene Blatt* always showed her dressed in a traditional dirndl, even for the housework which it was fancifully suggested that she did herself. However, away from the cameras, Klara swathed her not inconsiderable bulk in a long ruffled nightdress of peach-coloured chiffon and a matching bedjacket.

Comfortably seated on the sofa with the cherry streusel set out invitingly on the coffee table in front of her, Klara had picked up the remote control and switched on the television. When the body was eventually found, the television screen was blank and silent; Klara had been watching a video at the time of her death and the tape had run to the very end and stopped. The videotape was still in the machine, of course. It was a very old recording of Klara's greatest hits, along with footage of her wandering through forests and alongside rivers, clutching a single red rose to her bodice.

Some time between Klara turning on the video and the tape reaching the end, the years of smoking and eating too many cakes had brought her down, as surely as a pack of dogs taking down a deer. As she leaned over the coffee table with a cake fork in her hand, her abused heart had given out. Klara had fallen forward on to – indeed into – the cherry streusel, the fork with a chunk of streusel on it dropping from her lifeless hand. As her heavy features settled into the crushed streusel with the finality of rubble settling after a building's demolition, a lone sour cherry hit the floor tiles. After that, there was no movement in the room other than the images of Klara's younger self on the television screen, and some time later those stopped too.

On Monday morning, around about the time I was climbing on to the bus for Kall, my heart heavy at the prospect of a morning of baking theory, Klara Klein's cleaning lady had turned up at the Swiss chalet with its bloated edelweiss carvings and had been unable to get in. Klara had not given her a key of her own; she was too suspicious or too private a person to allow anyone free access to her house. So the cleaning woman had stood there on the wooden porch ringing the bell, and then she had knocked, and eventually she had tried to look in at a window. The curtains were closed, which was unusual, but she was able to peer through the narrow slit between them into Klara's living room. The view of Klara's chiffon-clad corpse was largely obscured by the bulk of the sofa, but at the side of it one plump hand was just visible, motionless on the floor.

The cleaning lady, panicking, called the local police in Bad Münstereifel, and it was not long before the interested residents of Mahlberg saw a blue-and-silver police car with its blue lights flashing passing through the village. It was shortly followed by an ambulance, but the police were the first to reach Klara's house.

One of the two policemen on duty that day was Herr Wachtmeister Tondorf, the oldest of the small group of policemen stationed in Bad Münstereifel. A decade before, it was Herr Tondorf who had discovered the body of the town's one and only serial killer. Very little had occurred in the interval, however, and Herr Tondorf was now looking forward to his impending retirement, which he intended to spend trout fishing and listening to his extensive collection of *Karneval* CDs. When he arrived at Klara Klein's house and saw how things lay, he gave a heavy sigh; in his opinion he was getting too old to shoulder down doors. He stood back and invited Schumacher, his partner, to do it.

Schumacher had also been present the day Herr Tondorf discovered the killer's body. He had been younger then; now he was approaching middle age and becoming stout. A decade before, he had been easily dominated by his older partner, and nothing much had changed. Schumacher was never going to rise very much higher in the regional police; he simply lost his head too easily.

Now it was Schumacher who forced his way into the house, with Herr Tondorf close behind him. Barely pausing to take in the opulent but rather sentimental decor or the row of golden discs on the wall, they charged over to the coffee table where Klara's body lay like a fallen colossus, streaks of red cherry juice staining the collar of the peach-coloured chiffon nightdress and the side of Klara's face where it was visible under the gilded tangle of her hair.

Blood was what it looked like, blood and some indefinable but unmistakably pulpy pale substance – the two cops didn't even want to *think* what that might be. Clearly, they thought, violence had been done. Little Klara had been bludgeoned to death in her own living room.

At this point Herr Tondorf may have become aware that his heart seemed to be pounding raggedly, that there was a dull ache in the left side of his body. If Schumacher had been looking at him, he might have noticed a greying pallor to the older man's face. But Schumacher wasn't looking at Herr Tondorf's face. He was staring with horrified fascination at something which lay on the floor tiles, a soft red spherical object, its incarnadine hue matching the stains on the peach-coloured gown.

As he watched, Herr Tondorf's large and highly polished black shoe came down with a horrid finality on the red sphere, crushing it so that dark streaks of fluid shot out on all sides. Herr Tondorf, conscious of moving more slowly than usual, hindered by the strange numbness which seemed to be creeping over him, began to raise his foot to examine the thing he had trodden in.

At that moment Schumacher, in an ecstasy of horror, shrieked out, 'Her *eye*! You've trodden on her *eye*!'

When the ambulance crew entered the house a mere ninety seconds later, they found two casualties. For Klara Klein they could do nothing. Herr Tondorf was alive, but only just; he had suffered a massive heart attack and was slumped against the side of the sofa, while Schumacher, green-faced, was trying to loosen his superior's collar. The paramedics got Herr Tondorf into the ambulance, still alive but glassy-eyed and unresponsive, like some great beached fish, and closed the doors. The sour cherry was still stuck to the bottom of his shoe.

CHAPTER NINE

'We have to go back there,' said Max.

'No,' said Izabela and I simultaneously.

Hanna said nothing, but I saw her looking at Max as though she were appraising him.

We were sitting on a wooden bench opposite the ice-cream parlour – at least, we three girls were sitting on the bench; Timo and Jochen were sitting on the low stone wall which ran along the side of the River Erft, and Max was on his feet, pacing restlessly up and down as usual. He looked like a general addressing his troops – or, I thought, taking in his tigerish grin, like an evangelist just getting into his stride.

I wondered whether Max had been so sanguine when he first heard the news of Klara Klein's death. If he had been shocked, he had recovered by now. Looking at the nervous energy he was expending, the way he was almost buzzing with it, I understood something quite clearly: this was the best thing that had happened to Max in ages. He was not going to let it go.

In the warm sunshine of a spring evening, with early tourists wandering past, it was hard to believe that our night-time visit to Rote Gertrud's house had been anything but a piece of tomfoolery, and yet a tiny sliver of doubt remained in all our minds, a doubt which created a kind of dark excitement in the pit of the stomach. Max was thriving on that excitement, like an engine running on high-octane fuel.

I knew that Max, like me, was never going to get out of Bad Münstereifel. He had an indifferent *Hauptschule* qualification and a future all mapped out for him in his father's car dealership on the edge of town. And yet Max had this unquenchable conviction that there must be something more, that there must be excitement and drama and danger, and that he should be in the middle of it, the hero of the story.

Now he had stopped in front of the bench and was hanging over us like a vulture on a branch. 'Look,' he was saying, 'it's a coincidence, right? It's *probably* a coincidence. So no harm done. Little Klara was probably going to bite the dust anyway. But –' his eyes widened and he spread his hands out, encompassing us all – 'suppose it *wasn't* a coincidence?'

'Max –' began Izabela, but there was no stopping him.

'Suppose Rote Gertrud *did* have something to do with it? We'd be mad not to try it again.'

'We'd be mad to mess with it,' grumbled Timo at my right shoulder.

'Scared?' said Max in a mocking voice, looking at Timo with raised eyebrows.

'Of course not.' Now Timo sounded nettled. 'It's just a rubbish idea.'

'You *are* scared,' said Max, and his grin widened.

I listened to the pair of them arguing with each other, but my mind was elsewhere, back in that evening when I had trudged down from Gertrud's house in the dark, slightly drunk and sick to the stomach, promising myself that I would never go up there again. I was thinking about the box we had left lying in full view on the decrepit floor of the house – the box with a note in it, a note in *my* handwriting. Again, common sense told me that nobody could trace the note back to me, but then I began to imagine ways in which they might be able to. Suppose someone had seen Max's car in the Eschweiler Tal? Suppose that same person was one of the other visitors who had undoubtedly been inside Gertrud's house, leaving a trail of beer cans and food wrappers behind them? I was still not sure whether I could get into trouble of any sort, even if someone positively identified my handwriting. I imagined that the note could be seen as some kind of death threat, not that we had posted it in Klara Klein's letter box or anything. All the same, I thought I would feel a little happier if I could retrieve the note and tear it into little pieces. Maybe burn it, to be sure.

'I think we should go,' I said suddenly, and they all turned to stare at me.

'You see?' said Max triumphantly. 'Even Steffi's got more guts than you have.'

Jochen slid off the wall. 'OK, let's go.'

'Now?' asked Hanna.

'Why not now?' said Max. 'Or do you want to wait until it gets dark?'

Nobody answered that. Max pulled the car keys out of his jeans pocket and hefted them in his hand so that they jingled together. 'Come on, then.'

CHAPTER TEN

'This is a totally stupid idea,' grumbled Timo as we struggled our way uphill through the clinging undergrowth. 'I don't know why we're even doing this.'

He had not stopped complaining since we set out, all six of us crammed into Max's car as usual. All the same, he had not missed an opportunity to be all over Izabela, I noticed. With four of us in the back of the car there was barely room to breathe, but I didn't think that was the only reason Timo had his arm along the back of the seat behind her, his hand dangling casually above her left breast. I didn't bother to challenge him about it. Two strands of emotion twisted around each other inside me like snakes. One was indignation; the other was relief.

Now, as I picked my way between brambles and tree stumps, I found myself wondering why I didn't just tell Timo it was over between us. Was I condemned to spend my entire life in stasis, like an insect in amber, existing but never going anywhere? I wanted more than a safe job in the family bakery and a relationship that had become little more than a habit. I wanted to get out of Bad Münstereifel. To escape.

I was so absorbed in these gloomy thoughts that I barely

noticed that we were approaching the ruined house until I was almost close enough to touch the grey and lichenous wall. It looked little better than it had at night-time. There was a dank, desolate air about it, the dark growths on the stonework as ominous as grave mould on dead skin. We made our way along the side of the house, as we had that first night, and it was not until we turned the corner and came to the gaping hole in the front wall that we had a clear view of the interior.

'*Ach, du Scheisse,*' said Max.

Beside me I heard Izabela inhale sharply. She stopped dead in her tracks and would not have gone into the house at all if Jochen hadn't pushed her forward, jostling her in his attempt to see what Max was looking at. Then I heard him swear too under his breath.

The six of us stood there, arms hanging limply by our sides, mouths open, eyes round, staring at the walls. The first time we had come to the house, it had been dark, even the moon shrouded in clouds. Now, with nearly two hours until sunset and the spring sunshine still bright, we could see what had been invisible the first time.

The walls were covered with writing. Not graffiti, at least not in the normal sense of the word; no enormous spray-painted names in wild colours or crude cartoons. Writing, in dozens, maybe hundreds of different hands, some of it large and straggling, some of it small and cramped, scratched or painted on to the rough stone walls.

Even before I stepped up to the wall to read some of the legends scratched there, I knew what I would find. *J. Fuchs, die by 05.06. Peter S., die by 12.98. A.H., die by 07.87.* Some of the inscriptions were very faint, almost obscured by weathering and lichen. I leaned close to the stonework, screwing up my eyes to try to make out what was written there, and with a sense of shock I read *H.D., die by 10.43*.

Did it really mean *1943*? I ran my finger over the worn and pitted stone, searching for the faintest and oldest inscriptions. Someone had written *1941* in black paint, although the rest of the message, if there had been one, was long since gone. And here, low down on the wall, as though the writer had tried to hide them, were three numerals: *917*. If they were really the remains of *1917*, then they had been there for almost a century.

They weren't all curses. There were messages pleading for love, messages asking for good health. Some of the older inscriptions simply said 'return'; I thought perhaps they were from the war years, written by mothers and wives and sweethearts, desperate for loved ones to come home safely.

There weren't just scratched messages either. In half a dozen places I found scraps of paper, folded into tiny squares and thrust into cracks in the walls. I pulled one of them out, feeling slightly squeamish, as though I were touching something best left undisturbed, but there was nothing to read. I could see a bluish blur where letters had been, but moisture had seeped into the paper and the ink had run.

Even Max was silent as the six of us stared at the walls. None of us said a word and outside the house there was not even the sound of a bird singing. And yet I thought that Gertrud's house was an unquiet place. It teemed with the distant voices of all those who had scratched their words laboriously on the stone, their messages of desperation and love and hatred. I thought that if I strained my ears I would hear them, the buzz and crackle of anxious voices, radio signals from the past. I looked at the walls and I felt cold. Did it even matter whether I believed in the witch or not? It looked as though the whole town did.

'This place gives me the creeps,' said Timo eventually.

'No kidding,' said Hanna ironically.

A broad smile crossed Max's face. 'People,' he said in his most expansive voice, 'it's *supposed* to give you the creeps.' He turned, taking in every angle of the densely inscribed walls. 'What would be the point of coming here otherwise?' He looked at Jochen. 'Right?'

Jochen shrugged. 'So, what are we going to do?'

'I'm not wishing anyone dead,' said Izabela suddenly. Her face was very pale but it had a stubborn expression, a hardness which made me think of white marble.

'Izzi.' Max sounded as though he were talking to a little child. 'We're not going to wish anyone dead.'

'Then what are we going to do?'

'We're going to try a little experiment.'

CHAPTER ELEVEN

Perhaps it really started there, with Max's experiment. Klara Klein was a fluke, after all; we had just been fooling about when we put the hex on her. It was something to do on a dull evening in a town where nothing was happening, nothing for anyone our age, anyway. We could just as easily have decided to go bowling in the alley at Schönau or to hang out at Max's house, an enormous white villa paid for by the car dealership, with a well-stocked drinks cabinet that Max's parents never bothered to check. Klara Klein just got in the way somehow, as though we had been a bunch of young kids playing with someone's father's hunting rifle and had accidentally shot a passer-by. We didn't really intend anything to happen to her.

Now it was different. Logic said that a few words scrawled on a piece of paper couldn't hurt someone, yet here was Klara Klein as dead as a stone. It shouldn't be possible and yet it was so. And now Max wanted, in a parody of scientific technique, to test the application of this apparent power. *It can't work – but suppose it did?* seemed to be his line of argument.

He found the carved box which had been hidden in the hole in the floor. It was still lying where we left it; evidently no one had been to the house since our first visit. He undid the catch and raised the lid. Before Max could react I put my hand into the box and grabbed the paper. Without bothering to read it, I tore it into tiny pieces. When I was satisfied that nobody could possibly piece the message together again I opened my hands and let them go, like a fall of paper snowflakes. Max didn't try to stop me; he seemed amused at my alarm.

Weren't there two *pieces of paper in the box?* I thought suddenly as the white scraps drifted to the ground. I stared at them. Was it possible that one piece of paper had been inside the other and I had torn them both up? If not, which one remained? It was too late to tell now, I realized with a shiver. With a sense of vague unease I tried to dismiss the matter from my mind and concentrate on what Max was saying.

Max's plan was that we should write another message. At Izabela's insistence, nobody was to put a hex on any other person. Max accepted this quite mildly. More problematical was the matter of what we should actually ask for. Jochen's and Max's ideas all seemed too stupid to me – wishes for expensive motorbikes and holidays and dates with people they had never even met, models and actresses. Timo refused to say what he would wish for. Hanna claimed not to have any ideas at all. Izabela was so fearful of the whole thing that her suggestions were far too vague and general to be of any use; she would have wished for world peace if Max had let her. As for me, I had wishes of my own, but not ones I was prepared to share with Max and Jochen.

'Why don't we *all* write something?' suggested Hanna in the end.

'We've only got one piece of paper,' objected Max.

'We'll tear it up,' said Hanna firmly.

She took the paper and folded it carefully, then tore it down the folds. There was enough for one strip of paper each, but we only had one pen between us, so we had to take turns.

Max went first, of course, writing with a great flourish. The pen was passed from hand to hand and last of all it came to me. I looked down at the piece of paper. *It doesn't really matter what you put*, I told myself. *Because it's not going to happen anyway. The Klara Klein thing, that was just a coincidence*. Still, I wondered what I would write if I knew my words really would come true. My grip on the pen felt slick, as though my fingers were damp with perspiration.

'Come on, Steffi,' said Jochen, peering over my shoulder.

'Can't you think of anything?' asked Hanna.

There was a curious emphasis to her tone, insinuating yet sympathetic, that brought warmth to my face. I wondered if she knew what was in my mind, if she could read my thoughts in my hesitation. I kept my head down, not meeting her eye.

You have to put something, I thought, and at that moment my mother's words floated through my mind: *The coffee machine is playing up again – God knows we could do with a new one . . .*

Five hundred euros, I scrawled quickly. I was surprised how satisfying it felt putting the words down on paper. *Don't be stupid*, I told myself. *It can't possibly work*. All the same, it was pleasant to imagine my mother crooning with delight over a new coffee machine. It was something to put in the balance against my guilt-inducing lack of devotion to the bakery.

I folded the paper in two and then folded it again, although there was nothing to hide. I handed it to Max.

'Are we going to say something, the same as we did last time?' asked Hanna.

She was watching Max, her arms folded. Perhaps, I pondered, she was attracted to him. But Max would never look at Hanna, with her dumpy figure and predilection for jeans and worn-out sweatshirts. *Stop it*, I thought. *She's your friend.* Nevertheless, I hoped that I was wrong, that she wasn't interested in Max at all, because I was terribly afraid she was doomed to disappointment otherwise.

Max eyed her back, his stance casual. Then he shrugged. 'If you like.'

'Can't we just go?' asked Izabela.

Inevitably, that decided the matter. Max shook his head. 'Got to do it right.'

Reluctantly we joined hands. 'Rote Gertrud . . .' intoned Max.

I put my head back and focused on the sky above, clear blue beginning to deepen as day moved to twilight. I didn't want to be in this place, with its mean little messages scrawled everywhere like bitter whispers heard in corners, with its burden of yearning and hopelessness and malice. I could feel the weight of other people's desires – Max's, Timo's, Hanna's – and the silent clamour of the inscribed walls. It felt too much like my life: the family bakery, the future my parents had mapped out for me.

Five hundred euros, I thought. *If it works, what else could I wish for?*

CHAPTER TWELVE

On Friday I worked in the bakery kitchen. The aim of my studies, as my father frequently reminded me, was for me to be able to run the bakery one day, not simply dispense apple strudel and coffee to the elderly customers. Once or twice a week I would get up when my father did, when it was still pitch dark outside, even in summer, and help him run the machines that mixed the bread dough. There was a great oven for the larger loaves, like a stack of shelves, close together and radiating a heat that was glorious in winter and torture in summer. There was a smaller one for the rolls, with a conveyor belt that carried them along like a row of fat ducks at a fairground shooting range.

On the whole I preferred the kitchen to serving in the cafe itself. Generally I worked there on Achim's days off, so there was little chance of running into him. I was spared the dispiriting experience of hours spent under the customers' critical eyes and I didn't have to wear the hated green dirndl.

On the other hand, the white baker's jacket which I wore had the legend *Magdalena Nett* embroidered on the breast pocket in green silk. Whenever I put it on I had the uncomfortable sensation of stepping into dead man's shoes. I had tried asking my father for a new one, but the answer was always the same: 'We're a small family business and we can't afford to waste.' Once he added 'Magdalena' without thinking, and when I stared at him he snorted and asked me why I didn't get on with my work.

I was thinking about that this morning as I went to the cold store to fetch another tray of uncooked bread rolls. It could so easily have been different. It could have been Magdalena standing here, shivering in the chilly air, manhandling trays of rolls. I looked at them with distaste, puffy little hemispheres of pallid dough sprouting in the dark like great mushrooms.

It was *meant* to be Magdalena, not me, that was the thing. Magdalena was the one who had been going to take over the bakery. I was the afterthought, the also-ran. The accidental heir. When it came down to it, everything about me was accidental. My mother had been twenty-five when Magdalena was born; when I arrived she was thirty-six. She said I was a 'surprise', but I thought she was being euphemistic.

I closed the door of the cold store with my elbow and went back into the main kitchen with the rolls. Another hour and the morning's work would be finished. My father would go to bed and sleep until mid-afternoon. I ought to do the same, but I rarely did. I relished the hours of freedom, even if I spent them yawning and rubbing my eyes. Sometimes I met Timo, or Hanna and Izzi, if they were free, but quite often I went off by myself, to walk along one of the woodland tracks which surrounded the town, or sit in a quiet spot under the medieval walls. Then I would look up at the open sky and formulate complicated plans for escaping the town – plans which always ran aground on the simple fact that there was no one else to take over the bakery when my parents retired.

Magdalena, I thought. She was hardly a person to me now, more an idea. What would it have been like to have a *real* sister? *If she were here now*, I thought, *even if she refused to have anything to do with the bakery, at least I could talk to her. At least we could share the problem.*

'Post,' said my mother, bustling into the kitchen, blonde curls bouncing, her shoes with the edelweiss flowers on the toes clicking smartly on the tiled floor. She looked at the fan of letters in her hands, looked again and said, 'There's one for you, Steffi.'

I was mildly surprised at that. Hardly anyone ever *wrote* to me, not a letter anyway. An email or a text, yes – but nobody I knew bothered with pen and ink and paper and envelopes. It might be a letter from the college, I supposed, but it didn't look official, and the envelope was the wrong size. I put down the tray and held out my hand.

'I don't know who it's from,' said my mother, musingly.

When I said nothing, but continued to hold out my hand, she put the letter into it with slightly bad grace. She looked at me for a moment and then she turned her attention back to her own letters.

I turned the envelope over. The address had been typed on to a sticker. Whoever had sent the letter had addressed it to STEFFI NETT, which struck me as a little strange. When the college or the doctor's surgery or anyone else sent me an official letter, it was always directed to *Frau Stefanie Nett*. Officialdom never called me anything as familiar as Steffi. And there was no stamp. I wondered whether someone had delivered it by hand.

The envelope felt thick, as though there were several sheets of paper inside, or perhaps something folded several times.

I glanced at my mother, then tore the corner of the envelope, just enough so that I could peep inside.

It took me a few seconds to realize what was inside. I must have inhaled sharply or made some movement, because my mother looked at me.

'What is it?' she asked.

'It's nothing,' I managed to say.

'Are you sure?' She was looking at me quizzically.

'Yeah. Some of my friends are just . . . messing about.'

I jammed the envelope into the pocket of my baker's jacket. I had no intention of opening it right up in front of my mother. 'I have to . . .' I couldn't think of anything plausible to say. In the end I just turned on my heel and fled back to the cold store.

I didn't close the door completely. There was an inner handle as well as an alarm, but even so I didn't like to feel shut in. I turned my back on the door in case my mother tried to follow me inside. Then I fumbled the letter out of my pocket and tore it open, the whole length of the envelope.

The contents spilt out, tumbling through my trembling fingers. I knelt to gather them up, the wad of euro notes that had been stuffed inside. There were a lot of them – they were mostly fives and tens – but I knew even before I started counting them. *Five hundred euros*.

CHAPTER THIRTEEN

That afternoon I went up to the woods to walk by myself. At home, there was my father, filling the flat with his snores, and there was also the risk that Max, Jochen or one of the others would drop in. I had to think and I had to do it alone.

The moment I'd counted the money I realized that things were not going to be so easily settled as I had imagined. I could not give my mother five hundred euros without questions being asked, and no immediate explanation sprang to mind. I had no way of earning so much extra money, but if I said I had found it she would insist I take it to the police station. If I told her it had been delivered to me she would ask who had sent it, and to that I had no reply.

I had turned the envelope over and over, checked it inside and out, but there was no note, no return address, nothing except my name and address, and those were typed, not handwritten. I folded the envelope into a tiny fat square and slid it into the mobile phone pocket of one of my bags. The banknotes I rolled together and shoved into my jeans pocket, as deeply as they would go. I dared not leave them lying around.

I left the bakery and walked up to the old spa building,

then took the well-worn footpath up the hill. I had taken that path many times when I was younger; in autumn the brambles were always thick with juicy blackberries and the hedges so high that a child could gorge itself to its heart's content, far from reproving adult eyes. I rarely met anyone there and today was no exception, but it was a relief when I had reached the top of the hill unseen. I crossed the road and turned up the little cut-through to Gut Vogelsang. Within five minutes I was in the forest.

There was a little-used track I knew which was almost grown over with brambles and weeds. I went up it, following the vague traces of ruts long covered with a blanket of rotting leaves. Eventually I came to a fallen tree. There I sat down and put my head in my hands.

Was it a joke? That was the obvious answer. It had to be one of the others playing a trick on me. Any of them could have returned to Gertrud's house afterwards and read the notes we had written. None of us had signed them, but my handwriting was easily distinguished from Hanna's bold hand and Max's untidy scrawl. *But five hundred euros ...* Nobody could afford to use that sort of money playing a trick on someone. Not even Max, whose parents were really wealthy; Max's father, a self-made man, was determined that his children should be the same and was not free with his cash.

So who had sent the money? If it wasn't one of us, that left two possible options, the second of which was so bizarre that I hardly even wanted to consider it. First, someone outside the group could have sent it. Someone could have seen us going up to Gertrud's house; they could have gone inside after we had left and found the slips of paper with our scrawled messages on them. It was stretching credulity, though, to think that they could have worked out which was mine and decided to send me the money I had casually requested. Why would anyone do that? Five hundred euros – that was a lot of money to anyone. If you were rich and wanted to give your money away, why not give it to charity instead, or to one of your own relations? Anyway, rich philanthropists didn't spend their time hanging out in dank woods, standing in the undergrowth with dark glasses on, clutching a bag of banknotes, waiting for potential beneficiaries. It was ridiculous.

The other option – that was the one my mind kept skirting around. I knew it was impossible, insane even to consider that Rote Gertrud might have anything to do with the money. *For goodness' sake*, I reminded myself, *it arrived in an envelope with a typewritten address. Dead witches don't* type *things*. An image rose unbidden into my mind, of the spirit of flame-haired Gertrud rising from the detritus of her house, floating unseen into the town and descending upon some unsuspecting person, sliding herself into them, working herself into each limb, each finger, as though she were putting on gloves, and then –

No. The idea was ludicrous, something out of a trashy film. I groaned with frustration. There was no explanation that felt right. I put my head back and stared up at the pine trees towering skywards, the patch of blue sky visible at their crowns.

It *had* to be one of the others. But I still couldn't see how any of them could have laid hands on five hundred euros just to play a joke on me. Unless they had somehow clubbed together to do it – and that was another place I didn't want to go, the thought that my friends would conspire like that to trick me. The idea of them huddling round, grinning and whispering, plotting together to make a fool out of Steffi – gullible, unsuspicious Steffi – chilled me. *No*, I told myself. *It's too much money to find for some stupid joke, even if they clubbed together. How could they be sure that they would get the money back again? Suppose I denied ever receiving it?* None of it hung together, but it seemed the most plausible explanation. The question was what was I going to do about it?

Shall I deny receiving it? That thought remained, nagging at the back of my mind. Suppose the others asked me whether my wish had been granted and I said no? If they were really behind the delivery of the money, they would have to admit it, or else lose their money altogether. Of course, I thought, I had no idea what anyone else had wished for, or whether any of them had got it. On the whole I thought this was unlikely; rather, someone had picked me out as the most gullible, the most likely to fall into the trap.

A feeling of hot resentment was brewing up inside me, a bubbling cauldron of poison. I imagined the five of them sitting in the snack bar, talking about what they had done, laughing at me. Max slapping the table, slopping everyone's drinks, guffawing.

Steffi's the only one dim enough to believe it. That was what they would say. *Steffi the mouse.*

Won't she be mad when she finds out?

What's she gonna do, Max?

Nothing, same as always.

I slid my hand into my jeans pocket and drew out the roll of notes. *I could tell them I asked for fifty and that fifty was what I got.* I fingered the notes, thinking. It could work. If the rest of them were in it together, if this was their idea of a joke, they'd soon stop laughing when they realized that four hundred and fifty euros of their money had vanished. I would watch their faces very carefully when I told them. I would watch to see who flinched, who blanched at it.

And if this was more than some stupid trick, if by some unimaginable and miraculous coincidence *everyone's* wishes had come true, well, I would still have my story to contribute. I had asked for money and I had got it. The amount was immaterial.

I shivered, hugging myself. It was a bitter thought, that my friends might be ganging up on me, plotting behind my back to make me look a fool. I knew that I was never going to be the most popular girl in town, the one everyone swarmed around, wanting to be friends with her, wanting her on their arm. I was too shy for that. But it was quite another thing to consider that the friends I did have were laughing at me. I looked down at the crumpled banknotes and felt my mouth tightening into a hard line. I would watch their faces when I told them about the money; I would watch them well.

Chapter Fourteen

On Friday evening I usually went out with Timo, but when I stumbled back into the bakery, weary from roaming through the woods and sickened by the dark and suspicious thoughts that were running incessantly through my brain, my mother greeted me with the news that he had telephoned to cancel. I patted my pocket; no mobile phone. I must have left it in my room.

'Did he want me to ring back?' I asked.

'He didn't say so,' said my mother.

She had been bagging up the leftover rolls and buns but she stopped what she was doing to look at me. I could see the question that was coming: *Is everything all right?*

What would she say, I wondered, if I said, *Here's five hundred euros. Now you can buy the new coffee machine you wanted.* I was almost tempted to do it.

Instead I simply said, 'OK,' as breezily as I could, and escaped before she had time to quiz me. As I ran up the stairs, I wondered idly what would happen if I tried to call Izabela. Would *she* know anything about Timo's sudden lack of interest in me? At any rate, I decided, it was for the best. If I met Timo this evening he would be bound to ask me about my wish, and I didn't want to talk about it to any of them until we were all together. I wanted to make sure that nobody was forewarned.

The issue of what to do with the five hundred euros was eating at me. When I came to think about it, there were half a dozen other things my parents could have used as well as a new coffee machine; the bakery did well enough but we were hardly rich. I longed to hand the money over – but how to do it, that was the question. Could I add it to the till at the end of the week? Or put it in a new envelope and deliver it anonymously to my mother? I thought of going to the bank and simply paying it into the bakery's account, but if my mother noticed the unexpected deposit she would ask questions, and if anyone at the bank remembered me paying the money in I would have some explaining to do. The one thing I didn't consider was telling the truth; it was simply too bizarre. So I carried the money around in my pocket and tried desperately to think what to do with it.

On Saturday we met at Max's house on the Ashford Strasse. It was one of the smartest streets in Bad Münstereifel, running directly up the side of the hill at such a steep angle that climbing it on foot felt like mountaineering. There was something apt about this, as though in scaling it you attained a rarefied atmosphere not felt elsewhere in the town. The houses were all enormous; the Müllers' was so large that you could have fitted two of the bakery inside it. It had four garages, housing Herr Müller's gleaming top-of-the-range cars. This evening one of them was empty because he and his wife had gone off somewhere in the BMW.

I rang the bell and heard it echoing in the cavernous interior. As I waited, I stared about me, taking in the polished perfection of the white-painted front door (Max's mother employed an army of cleaners, although she didn't work herself) and the carefully manicured shrubs which stood in enormous ceramic pots on either side of it. Everything about Max's house screamed money.

It could be Max, I thought. However stingy Herr Müller was with his cash, anyone who lived in a place like this had to have access to greater funds than the rest of us could dream of. Five hundred euros was nothing to the Müllers. They probably had that much lying around the house in cash, just in case Frau Müller needed to tip her manicurist or something.

The door opened. Hanna was standing there, clad in jeans and a sweatshirt as usual, her dark hair falling untidily over her eyes. Was it my imagination, or was there a question in the way she looked at me? I did my best to look nonchalant. The five hundred euros were still in my jeans pocket, since I dared not leave them lying around at home. When I moved I could feel them, like a knot in the fabric, pressing against the top of my leg.

'Hi,' I said, stepping into the house.

When I went into the living room the others were there already, lounging around on Frau Müller's white leather sofas in a way that would have made her bleached-blonde hair stand on end, had she been there to see it. Timo was sitting next to Izabela, I noticed. They all looked up as Hanna and I came in. The sensation of all those eyes on me was daunting. I wondered whether they had been talking about me before I arrived. Eight o'clock, we had said, but I had arrived exactly on the hour and yet they were here already. Had they been sniggering together over the trick they had played on me? Deliberately I kept my expression neutral. I caught Timo's eye and thought that he made the very faintest movement with his shoulders, as though shrugging.

'Steffi, at last,' said Max.

'It's only just eight,' I said.

'Well, we said seven thirty,' said Max.

No, you didn't, I thought, but I simply shrugged. 'I'm here now.' I went and perched on the padded arm of one of the white leather chairs. Somehow I felt reluctant to sit on the chair itself, to sink into the yielding comfort of the cushions. I felt I would be putting myself at a disadvantage.

As usual it was Max who took the lead. He didn't waste any time either. He stretched his arms out along the back of the sofa and tilted his head, then said in an ironic voice, 'So, anyone's wish come true?'

I waited for them to turn to look at me, but nobody did. I said nothing, waiting.

'Nope,' said Jochen.

'Told you so,' said Timo. 'There was no way Heidi Klum was ever going to come to Bad Münstereifel anyway.'

'Izabela?' said Max.

Izabela shook her head.

'Hanna?'

I was watching them narrowly, studying each of their faces as they replied. I saw the same expression every time – a mixture of faint disappointment, boredom and expectancy as they looked at each other. There were no meaningful sidelong glances, no knowing smirks. Either they were all brilliant actors or there was nothing going on between them.

Eventually Max turned to me. 'Steffi?'

There was a perfunctory tone in his voice; by this time he

wasn't expecting to hear anything surprising. In another moment, when I had told him that nothing had happened, he would lose interest in the whole thing. It would be yesterday's news, totally uninteresting, buried as deep as last year's rubbish, while he would be free to pursue some new hare-brained scheme. I paused and licked my lips. Max wasn't even really looking at me; he was waiting for me to rubber-stamp the failure of the plan so that he could move on. The moment stretched out. Hanna's face turned towards me.

'Yes,' I said.

'Yes?' repeated Max stupidly.

'Yes, it worked,' I said quietly.

'What? *No* . . .' said Max.

His face was slack, his eyes wide. I was watching him very carefully and I saw no hint of amusement, no sign of dissemblance. He appeared to be genuinely shocked. I glanced at the others. Timo had missed the exchange altogether; he was looking at Izabela. Everyone else looked stunned.

'What did you wish for?' asked Jochen.

I looked down at my hands. 'Fifty euros.'

'Fifty euros . . . ? And you *got* them . . . ?' Max sounded dazed. 'You should have asked for a thousand. Ten thousand.'

'*How* did you get them?' asked Hanna.

I guessed that she was thinking what had not yet occurred to Max, which was that this might have nothing to do with Rote Gertrud's house at all, this might be nothing more than coincidence. Fifty euros was a not insignificant amount for us – you wouldn't want to lose it, to have it drop out of your pocket in the street – but it wasn't a fortune. It wasn't an impossible sum of money to come by all of a sudden. A generous relative might send you that much for your birthday, you might get it for working an extra day.

I shrugged. 'The money arrived in the post. Well, it was in the postbox anyway. There was no stamp on it. Just an envelope addressed to me.'

Silence. The others pondered this.

'You're joking, right?' said Max.

I shook my head. 'I've still got the envelope at home. But the address was typed. There's no return address or anything.'

As I looked at the ring of astonished faces I began to feel an unpleasant sensation in the pit of my stomach, a restless seething like maggots in a carcass. I thought they were all genuinely astounded by what I had told them – which meant that none of them had sent the money. But if none of them had sent it . . .

'It *has* to be a joke,' said Izabela nervously. 'One of you did it, right?'

There was a clamour of denials.

'Someone else, then,' said Max. 'Someone found the pieces of paper at Gertrud's house. It has to be that. Someone's playing tricks on us.'

'Who?' asked Hanna. 'We didn't see a soul up there, Max. You know we didn't.'

I said nothing. They were simply rehashing things that had already gone round my head a hundred times. I still had that horrible feeling, the crawling, slithering feeling inside me. Max wasn't play-acting. I *knew* he wasn't. He looked as shocked as the rest of them.

'Why her?' he said suddenly, turning to look at me. 'Why Steffi's wish and not anyone else's?'

'Maybe she's making it up,' said Jochen, talking about me as though I wasn't sitting within a metre of him.

'I'm not,' I said.

'Show us the fifty euros, then.'

I pushed my hand into my jeans pocket and was fishing for the money before I realized that if I drew the whole wad out, everyone would see that it was much more than fifty euros. I hesitated, suddenly feeling my face burning. I guessed that I was blushing and knew that this would make me look guilty. The realization made things worse; now I felt as though my cheeks were on fire. I plucked at the rolled-up notes with my fingers, praying that I could fish out the right amount. Eventually I succeeded in withdrawing a little clutch of notes. I held them out.

Max took them from my outstretched hand and quickly riffled through them. 'There's only forty here.' He sounded accusatory.

'Hang on.' I dug into my pocket again and managed to separate one note from the others, praying that it was a ten. As I drew it out, I saw to my relief that it was.

'Fifty,' I said. I dared anyone to contradict me.

Jochen whistled. For a moment everyone simply stared at the cash in Max's hand.

'No,' said Timo eventually. He shook his head.

'Yes,' said Max. He looked at me.

I nodded slowly.

'You know what this means?' said Max, and he sounded almost ecstatic. 'We have to go back up there. To Rote Gertrud's house. We have to go up there and try it again.'

CHAPTER FIFTEEN

'No, Max,' Izabela was saying, and I could hear a catch in her voice, as though she were about to start crying, actually crying.

It was Sunday afternoon and we were crammed into Max's car again, all six of us. Max was driving us up the bumpy track through the Eschweiler Tal, on the way to Rote Gertrud's house. It had not rained for some days and the mud had hardened into ruts which made the car lurch and bounce unpleasantly.

'I really don't want to go back there,' Izabela continued in a pleading voice.

Timo had an arm around her and was making a show of comforting her, but he wasn't trying to talk Max out of going. I suspected he was as intrigued as the rest of us. In truth I felt sorry for her. I guessed it was not just the thought of the witch's house that was upsetting her; it was being railroaded by Max again. It irritated me too, but I was not sorry to be going to Gertrud's house. After what had happened, I knew I would have had to go there again anyway, to try it out once more. To wish for something I really wanted.

And I would rather go up there with the others than by

myself. It had been bad enough the first time, when it had been pitch dark and we had all been rather drunk, but the second visit had chilled me. Standing inside those four walls with all those messages of hate and desperation scrawled upon them had been like standing at the epicentre of an electrical storm: you could almost feel their bleak power crackling in the cold air. No, I didn't want to be there on my own.

Out of the corner of my eye I could see that Timo's head was close to Izabela's. I wondered whether he would dare kiss her while I was sitting next to them. Perhaps it should have upset me, the fact that he had moved on without bothering to talk to me about it, but actually I was glad. I had plans of my own, something I wanted to wish for which did not include Timo. This just made it easier.

Max braked with unnecessary abruptness and pulled the car over to the side of the track. I was the first out of the car, and while the others were extracting themselves from the cramped space, I went to look at the gap in the bushes which led to Gertrud's house. I was no tracker, but I wondered whether there might be any clue as to whether someone else had been up to the house – an obviously broken branch or recent footprints. But I could see nothing to indicate that anyone ever went into the woods this way.

The next moment Max was pushing past me, taking the lead as usual, Jochen at his heels like an eager lieutenant. Timo and Izabela followed. Izabela was still protesting in a plaintive voice. Timo murmured something to her and then took her hand in his.

As Hanna followed them she turned to look at me, a sympathetic question in her dark eyes. I smiled at her, deliberately not understanding, then looked away. I put my head down and started up the hill, looking at the ground rather than at Hanna or the others. Through the shrivelled remains of last autumn's leaves, green shoots were springing up like tiny hands supplicating the sky. By summer the whole area would be a tangle of overgrown bushes and weeds and it would be more difficult to reach the ruined house. Assuming, I thought, we were still visiting it by then. The next experiment might fail and then perhaps the whole thing would peter out. I listened to my own breath rasping in and out as the gradient steepened, and wondered whether I would be relieved or disappointed if that happened.

As the crumbling grey shape that was Gertrud's house came into sight, I felt a strange lurch in the pit of my stomach, a rolling sensation that was somehow dreadful and pleasurable at once, like the feeling of riding a roller-coaster. There was something about those scarred and lichenous walls, the blank side of the house like an eyeless face, that made me want to turn tail and run back down the hill to the safety of the car. At the same time I felt an almost irresistible compulsion to go inside, a nagging urge that thrummed to the beat of my heart and the blood pumping through my veins. I was curious, yes; I was dying to know whether a further attempt would be successful, whether my next wish would be granted as easily as the first. It was more than curiosity, though; there was a dark pride in the fact that it was *my* wish that had been granted. *I* had been chosen, as surely as if the witch herself had materialized in front of us, her flaming hair swirling about her, and laid a slender hand upon my shoulder. Something had distinguished me and I was strangely satisfied by it. Perhaps I had more in common with Max than I thought. I wanted to be the heroine of the story for once and not just a bit part.

Climbing through the gap in the wall, I did my best to focus on the others and not on the inscriptions which screamed silently from every surface. As usual, Max and Jochen seemed to fill the available space with their bulk, all broad shoulders and loud remarks, shoving each other and guffawing.

'Timo . . .' Izabela was saying, in a reluctant voice, as though she were resisting something.

I pretended not to hear.

'Max . . .' Hanna had to repeat his name several times before she had his attention. 'Are we going to get on with this or not?'

'Right,' said Max, snapping to attention with mock seriousness. 'Who's got the paper?'

Hanna was digging in her pocket. 'Are we going to agree what to write this time?' she asked.

Max shook his head. 'Same procedure as last year,' he quoted in English, then reverted to German; a single line from *Dinner for One* was the limit of Max's foreign-language skills. 'The way we did it last time, it worked. So we do the same again.' He reached for a piece of paper. 'We all write our own stuff. Nobody looks at anyone else's.'

'So how do we know –' began Timo.

– *whether anyone's wish comes true?* I finished in my head. I could see the answer coming: *We'll check the papers*. The obvious next step would be: *Let's see the papers from last time, then*. And if the others did that, they would see that mine didn't say *fifty euros*.

Before it could occur to anyone to do so, I slipped behind Max and Jochen and stooped to retrieve the box. It felt cool and slick in my hands; I suspected the wood was damp with last night's dew. I struggled with the catch, eventually managed to get it open and raised the lid. Quickly I rifled through the scraps of paper inside. Max's untidy scrawl, Izabela's neat hand . . . I was turning all of them over, looking for my own handwriting, and then I was counting them, and my heart was thumping.

Five. There were five pieces of paper in the box. Count them again. Check the ground. Could one have fallen out? As I fumbled with the box, it slipped from my fingers, turning as it went so that the scraps of paper fluttered out.

I knelt swiftly and began to gather them up, counting under my breath. There were really only five.

'Steffi?' said Hanna's voice close to me.

I didn't look around. 'There are only five pieces of paper,' I said.

For a moment she said nothing. I could hear her breathing as she leaned over me.

'You must have missed one,' she said at last.

'No,' I said.

I stood up and found myself the focus of five pairs of eyes.

'Whose is missing?' asked Izabela. Her blue eyes were round with dismay.

'Mine.'

I held out my fist, the papers crumpled inside it, but Izabela shook her head, stepping quickly backwards.

There was a silence.

'Look,' said Max eventually, 'so what, OK? It doesn't change anything. Maybe someone took Steffi's piece of paper.'

'Who?' asked Izabela.

Max shrugged. There was no possible answer to that question, unless he chose to pluck one out of the air.

'I really don't like this,' said Izabela suddenly. She looked at each of us, her expression anxious, lips quivering, like a child begging for reassurance from its parents. 'I want to go. I want to go *now*.'

'Shhhh,' said Hanna in a mild voice. She wasn't even looking at Izabela, I saw; she was looking at Max, and her eyes were bright. I saw the tip of her tongue appear and move slowly along her upper lip, leaving it wet and shining. 'Write something, Max,' she said softly.

Max stared back at her and then his face slowly broke into a grin. 'Pen,' he said, without looking round, and Timo put his own pen, a tatty plastic ballpoint, into Max's hand. Max was still looking at Hanna with that grin on his face as he wrote on the slip of paper. He finished with a flourish and folded the paper tightly. Then he passed the pen back to Timo. The paper remained firmly clasped in his fist.

When it came to Izabela's turn she tried to refuse the pen. She looked at it as though it were some pernicious drug that Max was handing around, and kept her hands by her side. Max didn't bother to argue with her. He simply stood in front of her, holding the pen out, until she gave in and took it with a very bad grace, handling it as though she were a child on a zoo visit who has just been given some repulsive live thing to hold. The pen slashed irritably across the paper; I suspected that she was wishing never to come back to Gertrud's house again.

Now Timo was writing and I fleetingly asked myself what he was wishing for. An unimaginably long time ago, he had wished for me, but now he no longer wanted me. I looked at the top of his mousy brown head as he bent over the paper, wondering what was passing through his mind. In another moment he would be passing the pen to me, as I was the last. I would have to think of something to write.

Of course, I knew what I was going to write. I had known it even before we came here today, even before Max announced that we were going to do it. If Max hadn't insisted on returning to the house together I would almost certainly have made my way here on my own in the end. The temptation would have been simply too much.

It wasn't pique, the thought of Timo and Izabela together, that made me want this thing. I was dying to know whether my wish could possibly come true. Five hundred euros was a lot of money, but it was still only money. Money can be borrowed, or taken from a savings account, or stolen. But people – and more specifically, one particular person – that was another matter. Perhaps it would really take witchcraft to make a person do what you wanted them to do – to make them think and feel the way you wanted them to.

Silently I took the pen from Timo's outstretched hand. I turned away, to hide what I wrote from the others' eyes. I put my foot up on a block of stone, as I had the night we wished Klara Klein's fate down on her, and wrote the words using my knee to rest on. Then I folded the paper very tightly and put it into the box that Max was holding.

Max gave me a wolfish grin and for an appalling moment I thought he was going to remove the paper and read it. But then he closed the box and fastened the catch, and I was able to breathe again. My gaze followed the box as he placed it almost reverentially on the ground. I hardly listened to the rest of it, the address to Rote Gertrud; I thought about the contents of the box instead, how they reminded me of a message in a bottle, floating away from us to who knew where. I thought about the tightly folded scraps of paper inside, with six different wishes on them. But mostly I thought about my own wish: *Kai von Jülich*.

CHAPTER SIXTEEN

If I had hoped for an instant response to my prayers I was doomed to disappointment. On Monday morning I was at college in Kall and if Kai dropped in at the bakery I was not there to serve him. I was listening to a seemingly interminable talk about food hygiene, but my thoughts were elsewhere. I was wondering whether Kai would come into the bakery and whether he would be looking out for me. *Suppose it really happens?* I thought. The very idea made me feel slightly light-headed. *Will he come in specially to see me, or will he just come in anyway to get his usual order, catch sight of me and suddenly it will hit him?*

I could feel my cheeks burning and hoped that I was not blushing. *Get a grip*, I berated myself silently. *It's not going to happen. The five hundred euros – a real person sent those, whatever their reasons. But nobody can make Kai von Jülich fall in love with me.* All the same, I couldn't resist the temptation to indulge in a few daydreams, ones in which Kai's face was very close to mine, and I was drinking in the glorious radiance of those golden good looks, basking in the gaze of those heavenly blue eyes.

By Tuesday morning I was in such a state of anticipation that I was distracted. The inevitable happened and two minutes before Kai and his friends came into the bakery I spilt a customer's coffee all over the floor at the back of the cafe. While I was on my hands and knees like Cinderella, mopping it all up with a cloth and apologizing for the fourth time, Kai had been and gone, served by someone else.

On Tuesday night Achim called in sick, so on Wednesday I worked in the kitchen with my father. Another day at college, on Friday I was in the kitchen again, and then the week was over.

On Friday evening I dragged myself up the stairs to the flat, put the white coat with *Magdalena Nett* on the front pocket into the wash and shut myself in my room. I felt miserably disappointed and, worse, I felt stupid. I flung myself on the bed and gazed with distaste at the contents of my room – the battered dressing table covered in bottles and jars, the faded duvet cover with a pop star design which had seemed desirable when I was fourteen but now looked ridiculous, the posters tacked up to hide the sentimental-looking floral wallpaper my mother had chosen. I was old enough to vote, old enough to be married – and yet here I was, with no space of my own other than this little girl's bedroom, no future prospects other than one day receiving my father's secret recipe for the perfect *Florentiner*.

I fumbled in my jeans pocket and pulled out the crumpled euro notes which were still stuffed in there, as I had not been able to think of a better hiding place, or a solution to the question of how to pass the money on. If I hadn't been holding the notes in my hands I would have thought the whole thing was a dream. The delivery of the money was still a mystery, but clearly it was some sort of joke, the work of some all-too-solid person, nothing to do with Rote Gertrud's house or the witch herself. Well, now the joke was well and truly over. I shoved the cash back into my pocket and lay on the bed, fixing my eyes on the ceiling. *Nothing is going to change*, I thought, and my heart was heavy. *Nothing is going to change.*

CHAPTER SEVENTEEN

I did not work in the bakery again until the following Tuesday morning. The weekend had passed in a kind of dull haze. Hanna had phoned me to ask whether anything had *happened*, putting particular emphasis on the last word, and I had told her that it had not. It occurred to me that it might be prudent to return to Rote Gertrud's house on my own in the next few days, to remove the piece of paper with my writing on it from the box before someone else had a chance to see it. I could imagine Max and Jochen chortling over it, or Timo wrinkling his nose at it. The thought was intolerable, and yet I felt so low and apathetic that I could not summon up the energy to do anything about it, not yet at any rate. When Hanna asked if I was coming out with the rest of them, I pleaded a headache, and it was not far from the truth. My head was full of dull, heavy, miserable thoughts, all tangled together like great dumb animals shut in a stall, kicking the doors and each other, unable to get out. I had not realized how much I had pinned on this, the idea that somehow my wish might really come true.

By the time Tuesday morning came round and I was due behind the counter of the bakery again, I had talked myself into a steadier state of mind. As I smoothed down my apron over the skirt of the hated green dirndl, I thought that I might even be able to face Kai von Jülich quite cheerfully, were he to come in for his ham and egg roll. Nobody would be able to tell from my face what my hopes had been, or how they had been dashed.

All the same, I almost jumped when the street door opened and the little bell jangled. When I looked up my heart was in my mouth. But it was not Kai von Jülich. It was someone else I knew, as tall as Kai but unmistakably different. Leaner, more angular, scruffier, with thick hair the colour of burnished copper and brown eyes whose gaze seemed to dance over everything, never still for a moment. He reminded me irresistibly of a red squirrel.

'Julius,' I said under my breath.

He was glancing around him, checking to see whether there were any other customers demanding my attention, whether my mother was lurking around in the vicinity. Satisfied that the coast was clear, he came right up to the counter.

I didn't have time to ask him what he had come for; he plunged straight in without a preamble, without even greeting me.

'Steffi, I've come to ask you if you've changed your mind.'

'Julius –'

'Tell me you've at least thought about it.' He put both hands on the counter and leaned towards me. 'You got my note – the flyer?'

'Yes.'

Julius waited for me to go on. Put on the spot, I panicked.

'I can't do it. I'm sorry.'

'Why not?'

He didn't sound annoyed, just interested. That was the thing about Julius: he always acted as though he thought I were the most fascinating creature he had ever seen. Since I was unused to this kind of attention it had something of a mesmeric effect. I always found myself weakening and was obliged to dredge up reserves of self-will to resist him, whether it was a favour he wanted – or a date.

'I have to get up at two thirty on Friday,' I said. 'I'm working in the kitchen. By the evening I'll be worn out.'

Julius studied me for a moment, and I was sure I felt myself reddening under his gaze.

'Come on, Steffi,' he said eventually. 'Please. Gina's blown us out. She's crap anyway, you know she is. She sounds like Klara Klein on helium. You'd be a million times better.'

'I wouldn't,' I said, but I was wavering. I bit my lip, glancing covertly to the side to check my mother was still occupied elsewhere. 'Really,' I said, but he wasn't giving up.

'Your voice is way better than hers,' he insisted. 'I've heard it. School choir, remember? You were brilliant.'

I almost caved right in when he said that. Nobody ever called me *brilliant*. To my parents I was the also-ran, the second daughter whose interest in the family business was disappointingly insipid. At school I had been too quiet to attract any comment, good or bad. Even Timo had given me up after three years without a second thought. The lure of being thought *brilliant*, of having an actual talent that others might admire, was irresistible.

I desperately wanted him to persuade me – and perhaps he might have, only at that moment the little bell which hung by the door jangled vigorously as someone came into the bakery. I turned to look and froze. It was Kai von Jülich.

'Ah . . .' I seemed to have been struck with some form of facial paralysis. I was gaping away like a fish, unable to get a single word out.

'A customer,' said Julius.

He shrugged and took a few steps back to let Kai approach the counter. Then he drew out a chair from one of the little tables and to my dismay he sat down to wait, his long legs sprawled out in front of him.

I flapped a hand at him, trying to get him to leave, but he was looking away, towards the window. *Go, go*, I thought desperately. Having Julius overhear everything Kai said, and seeing me blush and stammer like an idiot, would be bad enough, but suppose this really *was* the moment I had been hoping for, suppose Kai had come to ask me out, he might see Julius sitting there and think he was more than a friend. *Well, isn't he?* said a voice in the back of my mind. *It's not just your voice he's after, dummy*. Amid the urgent desire to usher Julius out of the bakery I discerned a twinge of guilt, as though I were somehow betraying him. But that was ridiculous; we weren't even going out.

By now it wasn't just my face that was warm; the entire exposed surface of my skin was tingling hotly with deep embarrassment. I suspected I was glowing like a lava lamp. It was all I could do to stand there and face Kai, instead of bolting for the safety of the kitchen.

Kai glanced at Julius as he came in, but instantly disregarded him. Fortunately the bakery was almost empty, otherwise for the second time that morning the avid customers would have been treated to the sight of a young man striding up to the counter and leaning towards me with undisguised intent.

'Steffi,' said Kai.

He didn't bother to say *Guten Morgen* or *Morgen* or even *Hi*. Just my name, pronounced with a lingering relish, as though he was tasting something unbelievably delicious. He looked at me as though he would like to have vaulted over the counter and laid eager hands on me right there among the sesame rolls and cheesecakes.

I just stood still, aware that I was staring at him like an idiot, but unable to think of a single thing to say. This was the moment for the wonderfully intelligent remark, the coquettish riposte, but I was as stiff and silent as a showroom dummy.

'OK,' said Kai, as though I had made some scintillating observation. He didn't seem to notice that I was paralysed with self-consciousness. His gaze flickered up and down me, snagging on the low-cut neckline of the frilly white blouse. I could have sworn he actually licked his lips. 'Friday,' he said.

'F-Friday?' I stammered.

There was a feeling of faint unreality about the whole brief exchange. In spite of the way he was looking at me, my rational mind said that there had to be some unexciting explanation for this. Perhaps he wanted to order something from the bakery for Friday. I could be winding myself up to a pinnacle of expectation just to discover that Frau von Jülich wanted a *Sahnetorte* for a coffee morning.

A fleeting expression passed over Kai's perfectly handsome features, a shadow of impatience at my inability to make any sensible reply. It was gone so swiftly that I wondered if I had imagined it. He leaned a little closer and I caught a hint of aftershave, a scent so intoxicatingly good that I really thought there was a danger of my swooning among the serried ranks of pastries.

'Friday evening,' murmured Kai. 'Just you and me.' There was a meaningful tone to his voice that sent a delicious shiver down my spine. He must have seen the effect of those words – *just you and me* – as a slight smile curled the edges of his mouth. He straightened up. 'I'll be here at seven thirty. OK?'

I found my voice. 'Yes,' I said breathlessly.

Kai glanced around. 'Friday, seven thirty,' he repeated. He didn't bother to lower his voice. 'Don't forget.' Then he turned on his heel and left the bakery. The door banged shut behind him, the little bell jingling wildly.

For a moment there was silence. Then I heard the sound of chair legs scraping on the floor. Julius was standing up. For a moment he stood there, looking after Kai. Then he turned to me. In the sunlight streaming through the bakery window his shock of hair was the brilliant colour of flames, but his face was cold.

'Friday night,' he said.

'I'm sorry,' I said. I hardly dared look at his face. I knew how it looked, as though I had been caught out in a lie. *I can't do it . . . I'll be worn out.*

'No, *I'm* sorry,' said Julius with angry emphasis. He half turned, as if to leave, and then thought better of it. He came up to the counter where I was standing, nervously twisting the hem of my apron in my hands. 'Look,' he said, 'I can't make you come with me on Friday. But Kai . . .'

With an effort I made myself face him. 'What about Kai?' I said defiantly.

My voice was steady, although my hands were still wringing the crumpled fabric of my apron. The way he was looking at me made me feel guilty and unreasonably I retreated into indignation; being angry with him was better than feeling as though I had somehow betrayed him.

If I had been expecting an insulting remark about my taste in men, it didn't come; perhaps he had thought better of it. He sighed.

'He's not like you think,' he said at last. 'He's not . . .'

'Not what?'

I picked up a cloth lying on the inside of the counter, trying to make it plain that I had work to do. Inside I felt slightly sick, as though I had been caught out doing something I shouldn't have.

'He's not a nice guy,' said Julius eventually. 'I know him,' he added.

I held up the cloth. 'I'm supposed to be working.'

'OK.'

He studied me for a moment with a frankness that made my blood boil. I began to feel that if he stood there for a second longer looking at me in that way I would throw the balled-up cloth at him. But then he turned and left the bakery without a word. The door closed and the bell's jingling faded to silence.

Into this abyss fell the distinctive sound of someone clearing their throat. With a sinking feeling I turned to survey the room. I had been right when I thought that the bakery was *almost empty*; almost, but not quite. The seating area was divided up with little trelliswork screens to give the customers a sense of privacy in spite of the limited space. Behind one of these screens someone was sitting. I could see a dark shape lurking there, sufficiently well hidden by the wooden slats that I had not seen it before, but almost certainly commanding a perfect view of the counter where I stood, if whoever it was cared to lean close to the trellis and peer through one of the gaps. Having lived in Bad Münstereifel all my life, I was not naive enough to think that any of its residents would balk at such an act.

'Excuse me,' said a tart voice. It was a voice I recognized.

Oh no. With a creeping sense of horror I stepped out from behind the counter and approached the screen. *Not her.* Of all the people it could have been, lurking unseen in the corner and taking in every single detail . . . *Please, not her.*

I rounded the end of the screen and my worst fears were realized. Sitting very upright on the cushioned seat, with her gnarled old hands folded on the most enormous leather handbag I had ever seen, was Frau Kessel. Her head was tilted back so that the light flashed on the polished lenses of her spectacles, but I didn't need to see her eyes to know that they were filled with knowing disapproval. Frau Kessel was a legend in Bad Münstereifel. They said she could hear a whispered conversation from a hundred metres away and I was not stupid enough to think that she would have missed a word of what had just passed.

I gave her a sheepish grin, the self-deprecating smile of the prisoner in the dock trying to win the jury round but knowing that the evidence against him is too great.

'*Bitte schön?*' I said, resisting the insane temptation to curtsy.

'If you have time, young lady,' said Frau Kessel acidly, 'I would like to pay.'

'Certainly,' I said, hoping that my dismay was not showing on my face. I went back to the counter and fetched the order pad. 'Four euros seventy-five,' I said.

Frau Kessel counted out exactly four euros and seventy-five cents.

'Thank you,' I said.

I watched in silence as she gathered up her coat and bags. There was nothing to say – nothing, at any rate, that would not incriminate me further. I followed her to the door, which I held open for her.

Frau Kessel paused for a moment on the threshold and looked me up and down very deliberately. Then she sniffed and, without a word, stepped out of the bakery and set off down the street.

I stared after her. *What can she do?* I asked myself. *It's a free country. I can spend Friday night with whomever I want. It's not like the bakery was full of customers and I was ignoring them or anything.*

All the same, as I saw her disappear into a shop I realized that there would be mischief. I could count on it.

Chapter Eighteen

The next few days dragged by. As I cleared tables in the cafe or carried trays of poppy-seed rolls around the kitchen I asked myself whether I should go back up to the ruined house in the woods by myself and try to retrieve the piece of paper with my wish on it. In the end I concluded that it was unnecessary. If Kai von Jülich and I were going to be an item everyone would know about it soon enough. Half the girls in town had had their eye on Kai at one time or another; it would certainly cause comment when I appeared on his arm. *However did Steffi Nett get hold of him?* they would all be saying. *Still waters run deep.*

I saw little of the others. Timo and I were ancient history, we never met apart from the group any more. Max and Jochen were spending every spare moment trying to repair some problem with Max's car. Hanna called at the bakery once, to see whether I wanted to meet up on Saturday night. She didn't ask me about my wish and I didn't volunteer any information. I saw Izabela too, briefly; we met in the street one evening and chatted for a few minutes. Izabela was one of the few people I might normally have confided in. She was quieter than the others and less likely to poke fun or threaten to tell the whole town about my date with Kai.

Now, however, there was a certain restraint between us. Neither of us mentioned Timo at all, but he might just as well have been standing between us. I think we were both relieved to part.

I didn't see Julius at all and on the whole I was glad. I told myself that I had nothing to reproach myself with – it had nothing to do with him if I wanted to go out with Kai. All the same, I was content to let the passage of time do what it could for the inevitable awkwardness between us.

Meanwhile I couldn't help luxuriating in imagining the events of Friday evening. I wondered what we would do, where Kai would take me. He had a car, after all – not a dull and relatively old one like Max's, but a sporty one with gleaming paintwork the colour of a fire engine. How people would stare if they saw me in the passenger seat of *that*.

'What's up with you?' asked my mother, hearing me singing as I sped around the flat on Thursday morning, collecting up my things for college.

She was standing by the kitchen sink, neat and compact in her green dirndl, sipping a cup of coffee before starting work. Her voice sounded vaguely disapproving, but she was smiling. Perhaps she thought I had finally done what she and my father were always hoping I would do and given my heart to the world of bakery products.

'Nothing,' I said.

As I walked through the town to the bus stop, that smile was still on my mind. I knew what my parents wanted. I could even see it their way. If I didn't take over the bakery one day, what would happen to it? If in some far-distant time, say 2025, someone were standing outside the bakery on a ladder, not painting in 'AND DAUGHTER' but painting 'NETT' right out, it would break my father's heart.

I knew how much my parents still suffered over my sister Magdalena's disappearance from our lives, although they rarely spoke about it any more. She never phoned, never wrote, and their sorrow had become like grief for the dead. It was almost unimaginable that I should add to their sadness by turning my back on their hopes and dreams. I felt like a wretch just for thinking of it, even as I struggled against their plans for me, longing to shape my own life, make my own decisions.

I was thinking about my mother, and wondering whether she had ever had these restless longings, whether she had ever wanted more from life than her cosy corner of a little town where everyone knew everyone else, when the idea came to me. I had been trying to imagine my mother at my age, with her mother – my grandmother – and suddenly my mind flitted to the things my grandmother had left us. Nothing of very great value – books and ornaments and a few pieces of furniture – but most of it was still stored in the spare room that had once been Magdalena's, awaiting the day when my mother would go through it all and decide what to do with it. Suppose I put the five hundred euros into one of the boxes or vases? I might even volunteer to look through the things myself, and then I could 'discover' the money and hand it over to my mother.

The more I thought about the idea, the more foolproof it seemed. The momentary gloom which had hung over me began to lift; the guilt that had been seeping through me was dissipated by the prospect of doing something which would thrill my mother for once. *Look what Steffi's found*, she would say. *Thank goodness she thought to go through all those old things*. And she would hug me and say, *Now we can finally replace that old coffee machine*.

I bounced along over the cobblestones with my bag swinging from my shoulder and my mind full of joyous images. Let the long-term problems wait. For once I would make my parents happy. And even better, tomorrow I was going to meet Kai von Jülich.

I gave a sigh of delight so audible that a woman walking her dachshund gave me a second look. *Kai von Jülich* was going to pick *me* up. He might infuriate the neighbours by driving that scarlet sports car through the Werther Tor, the great medieval gateway at the north end of Bad Münstereifel – a route that was strictly deliveries-only for most of the time – and parking it right outside the bakery, where everyone would see it. Or – delicious thought – he might come and fetch me on foot, and we would stroll through the cobbled streets hand in hand, Kai leaning close to me every so often to whisper some intimate phrase, while every woman under twenty-five in the town fumed with jealousy.

Optimism sprang up inside me like fireweed burgeoning on scorched ground. In the bright morning light it was impossible to believe that Kai's invitation had anything to do with Rote Gertrud, or with that dank and horrible ruin in the woods. Kai had simply looked at me and seen something new. Perhaps the fact that I had been waiting for him to speak to me had worked its own magic. Perhaps – and this thought was such an enormity that I hardly dared confess it even to myself – he had wanted to ask me out for a long time and had never dared.

If something as fabulous as this could happen, *anything*

could happen, I thought to myself. Perhaps the confidence that always seemed to radiate from other people was not some impossibly unattainable gift but something I could learn to have myself. Maybe I had always had the power within me – I had just never known it.

When I got on to the bus I astonished the bus driver with a cheery *Guten Morgen* instead of scuttling past him with my head down, as I would normally have done. I settled myself in a window seat and watched the streets and then the fields drift past and my heart was light; I felt like singing.

Anything can happen, I thought to myself. Even the prospect of a day at college studying bakery techniques failed to affect my mood. *Things are going to change*, I told myself. *It's already started.*

CHAPTER NINETEEN

It was during that bus journey that I made up my mind. I think it was the moment when the bus turned ponderously into the road where the college stood, a moment that always made my heart sink, as though I were being driven up to Castle Dracula in a horse-drawn carriage. It was not so much the actual studying itself that I dreaded; it was the fact that every day spent learning the science of baking and the properties of half a dozen different types of flour was another link in the chain shackling me to Bad Münstereifel. Once I started work at the bakery full-time, I would never get away. A family bakery is open six days a week nearly all year round and you are up half the night preparing the day's baking, which means early nights every night, forever. What I had told Julius about being too tired to sing for him was based on truth. If I took over the bakery the only music I would be producing at night would be snores.

There must be some way to change this, I thought. *Some way to make my life my own without hurting anyone. I have to try at least.* I stared at the facade of the college as it came into view. *I can't go on like this forever. Better to sort it out now than hurt them later, when it's too late for them to make other plans.*

The morning dragged by. I felt as though I had been booked in for a risky operation: I dreaded the discussion that would inevitably come, but I could hardly wait to get it over with. I knew there was no point trying to talk to my parents while the bakery was still open, so with difficulty I made myself wait for supper time that evening. By then I was fizzing with so much suppressed tension that it was a wonder sparks didn't come arcing out of my fingertips as I set the table.

My father looked tired when he came to supper. In the yellow light of the glass lampshade which hung low over the table his face looked lined and pouchy. The white in his hair was no longer just a dusting of flour from his day's work, I realized with a pang. My father was getting old; in a few years he would be sixty.

My mother had kicked off the shoes with the edelweiss flowers on the toes and slipped on some ancient Birkenstocks, but she was still wearing her green dirndl. I hardly ever saw her in anything else. Max's mother actually wore jeans on occasion, although admittedly they were dazzling white ones usually teamed with high-heeled sandals. I couldn't imagine *my* mother wearing anything like that. I suspected that when she died she would like to be buried wearing that dirndl. She was practically married to the bakery, I thought.

I looked from one tired face to the other and my heart misgave me. Could I really tell them that I didn't want to continue with my bakery training? The voices of self-doubt and fear started buzzing insistently in my head: *You can't do it to them. You'll break their hearts. You can't do it.*

You have to, I flung back at them. *It will be worse if you don't do anything now. If you say you're not taking over the bakery when Dad's sixty-five, what's he going to do then? Say it now.*

I thought of Kai von Jülich, of his fantastically handsome face, the way he had gazed at me over the counter, as though he would have liked to lay hands on me then and there. That was a miracle I had never hoped could come true, proof that life could be surprising sometimes, that things really could change. I cleared my throat.

'Mum? Dad?'

Now they were both looking at me. My father paused with a forkful of potato salad halfway to his mouth, a slightly ironic look on his face. *What's coming now?* Perhaps he thought I was going to ask for a day off.

'I've been thinking . . .'

For a moment I almost couldn't do it, but then I made myself go on.

'I really don't want to go on with college. It's not what I want to do.' I looked at their blank faces. At least they weren't screaming at me. I plunged on. 'I'm really sorry, because I know you want me to take over the bakery, but I don't think I can.'

There was a pause which stretched out so long that I began to wonder if I was going crazy, if I had imagined the entire speech I had just made.

'What do you mean?' said my mother suddenly, her voice rising. 'What do you mean, you don't think you can?'

'Irena,' said my father, cutting across her and raising his hand as though trying to stop a flow of heavy traffic that threatened to mow him down. He put down his fork on the side of his plate and leaned towards me. 'What's brought this on?'

Kai von Jülich asked me out, I thought, although I could not possibly say it. 'Nothing brought it on,' I said as firmly as I could, although even to my own ears my voice was wavering. 'I've been thinking about it for – well, for a long time.'

'And you didn't say anything?' shrilled my mother.

'Irena,' said my father again, and this time he gave her a significant look. He turned back to me. 'Since when?' he asked me. 'A week? A month?'

His voice was quite mild, but I began to suspect that I was treading on thin ice.

'Since before I started college,' I said, looking down at the plasticized tablecloth with its pattern of checks and flowers, unwilling to catch his eye.

'Hmm.' My father appeared to be thinking. He picked up the glass of Pils my mother had set out for him and took a swallow. 'So what do you want to do if you don't stay in the bakery?'

I clasped my hands under the table, squeezing my fingers together, feeling the sharp edges of my nails digging into the skin. 'I'd like to study music.'

'Music?' My father's voice was still perfectly level and reasonable. My mother gave an indignant little snort, but if he heard it he gave no sign. 'And what will you do if you study music?'

'I want to sing,' I said. I put my clasped hands on the table, feeling foolishly as though I were praying for mercy. 'I know it's not easy to make a living from it. That's why I want to study, so I can teach music as well.'

My father sighed. 'Steffi, you graduated from *Hauptschule*.'

'I know. I know it's not enough –'

'You'd need to pass the *Abitur* exam to study music.'

I shook my head vigorously. 'There are a few places that take you if you've graduated from *Realschule*.'

'But you haven't,' my father pointed out mildly.

'I could go back,' I said. 'I could try for the *Abitur* at night school. My school marks were good.'

'Yes, for written work,' said my father.

He didn't bother to say what we both knew, which was that I had ended up in the *Hauptschule* – the least academic type of German secondary school – because I had virtually never opened my mouth in class during my entire time in primary school. For four years I had flitted about the school like a little ghost, with my head down and my shoulders in a permanent hunch. When the class had had to memorize a poem to recite in front of the others I had clammed up, and stood in front of them with tight lips and tears trickling from the corners of my eyes. When the teachers spoke to me I looked at the floor. Even kindly Frau Richter, who ran the music classes, had been unable to give me a mark higher than a 3, because I never said anything in her lessons. At secondary school things had improved a little. By then, however, it was far too late to think of a place at a better school.

'I can do better,' I said, trying not to sound as though I were pleading. 'I really want to try.'

My father put a large hand across the table and touched my clasped hands. 'Steffi, it's a good thing to want to improve yourself. But have you thought how you would manage your bakery studies and the hours in the kitchen if you were trying to study at night too?'

I took a deep breath. 'I wouldn't go on with the bakery course.'

'I know you said that,' said my father patiently. 'But have you really thought about it?'

'Of course I –'

'Suppose you give up the course and go to night school to do your exams – what if you don't get the grades you need? What then?' He shook his head. 'Even if you manage it, there's no guarantee of a place to study anywhere.'

'I still want to try,' I said.

My father sighed. 'Steffi, I don't want to order you to go on with the course.' He shook his head. 'I *can't* order you, in fact. You're practically grown up. But there are other considerations. You're halfway through training. We can't afford to take on another trainee in your place and support you while you study something else. The bakery isn't making enough to do that. I'm sorry, because I don't want to tell you *no* for reasons like that, but unfortunately that's the way it is.'

I didn't reply. I felt as though I were choking on the emotions which warred within me: disappointment, frustration and guilt. I could see perfectly well what my father was saying; if the money wasn't there, it was completely impossible. I had upset my parents and I was no better off than before. In fact, I was worse off, because before I had had hope.

'Look,' said my father kindly, 'your sister, Magdalena, wanted to be an actress, did I ever tell you that?'

I looked up in astonishment. My parents mentioned Magdalena so rarely that it was a shock to hear her name on my father's lips.

'No,' I said.

'She did,' said my father. 'But careers like that – if you can call them careers – singing, acting – they're very uncertain. You probably think it's easy –' if my father saw me open my mouth to protest at that he gave no sign, but simply swept on – 'but for every person who actually makes a living out of being a singer or an actress there are thousands who don't.'

'I don't want to be rich,' I said desperately.

'You may not think you do,' said my father. 'But you have to live on *something*.' He patted my hands. 'You could continue with your bakery course and, if you still think you want to sing, why not join a choir?'

This was both undeniably sensible and deeply dispiriting. But I could not bring myself to assent to it. As soon as possible, I escaped to my room to think.

If I thought that was the end of the discussion, I had thought too soon, however. After supper my father went straight to bed. Within ten minutes the sound of his snoring was droning around the flat. I was sitting on my bed with the little bundle of euro notes in my hands, wondering if it would have made any difference if I had asked for five thousand euros instead of five hundred, or even fifty thousand. Suddenly the door opened and my mother entered the room, so precipitately that I barely had time to stuff the money under my pillow. I saw at one glance that she was livid with fury. She was still clad in the green dirndl and her blonde curls bounced smartly as she burst in, with somewhat the effect of snakes bristling around a Gorgon's head. In spite of her anger she managed to remember to shut the door quietly so as not to wake my father.

'Well, miss,' she hissed. 'I hope you're pleased with yourself.'

I looked at her in astonishment.

'You're breaking your father's heart.'

I could hear the snoring which floated around the flat, vibrating like a bass note. Thankfully it seemed he was not too heartbroken to sleep, though I dared not point this out. In fact, I realized as I looked at my mother's furious face that it would probably be unwise to say anything at all. I had better let her scold me until she ran out of steam.

'Do you know how long he's worked in this bakery?' my mother demanded. 'Thirty years. Thirty years, since he took it over from old Kastenholz.' She paused, her bosom heaving alarmingly in her white frilly blouse. 'Does that mean *anything* to you?' She didn't wait for a reply. 'Well, I'll tell you this, young lady. Don't think you're living off us if you throw it all away to do some ridiculous music course. You can pay your own way.' She snorted. 'I don't think you'll find it so easy then. You can't live off musical notes. You might think about *that.*'

There was a lot more in the same vein. I sat on the bed with my cheeks burning and an uncomfortable consciousness of the roll of euro notes stuffed hastily under the pillow, a mere millimetre out of sight. I did my best to keep my face composed, sensing that if I cried or shouted back it would just make things worse. There was an unstable edge to my mother's fury, as though it were feeding on some inner poison, but eventually her ranting wound down, like the batteries of an alarm clock someone has left to ring and ring.

'Thirty years, all for nothing,' she finished, and in a paroxysm of rage she lifted her right hand as though to slap me. A spasm passed over her face and I realized that she was holding herself back with the utmost difficulty. Then she actually stamped her foot, like an angry child, turned on her heel and stalked out of the room.

After a moment I got up and went to the open door. I looked out, but there was no sign of my mother. Either she had gone into my father's room or she had shut herself up in the kitchen. Carefully I closed the door.

I sat down on the bed again, drawing out the hidden money from under the pillow. *Five hundred euros.* A lot of money, but not enough to live on. I held the notes in my hands, feeling their wrinkled texture, the tiny crumples in the paper. It was like touching skin. *It worked for five hundred euros*, I said to myself. *Would it work if I asked for more?*

CHAPTER TWENTY

Friday morning dawned bright and sunny, but by then I had been up for some hours, helping my father. Sometimes he let me get up later than he did, but that morning he woke me very early with a loud knock on my bedroom door. I suspected that the knocking, like the rapping at a spiritualist meeting, had a message in it. This one was: *It's business as usual.*

I shrugged on the white jacket with my sister's name on the pocket and went downstairs. The memory of the previous night's discussion was still raw, but I consoled myself with the thought of the evening to come. One thing in my life had changed, at any rate: I was no longer doomed to yearn for Kai from afar.

Never had the working day dragged by so slowly. I would look up from my work in the kitchen, where I would be glazing a batch of buns or sprinkling poppy seeds on to a tray of rolls, and gaze hopelessly at the clock. Sometimes it seemed as though the hands were not moving at all; once I went to check that they had not stopped altogether. When at last I was able to go back up to the flat and take off the baker's whites, I was worn out with the anticipation. I decided I'd better take a nap, otherwise I risked spending the entire evening yawning at Kai.

By seven twenty I was downstairs in the cafe, peering out of the front window, hoping to catch a glimpse of him coming down the street. I still didn't know whether he would be bringing the dashing red sports car or not. At seven twenty-five, suffering a crisis of confidence, I dashed to the ladies' room at the back of the cafe to check my appearance in the big mirror. Were jeans too casual? The ones I had on were my newest, and I had teamed them with a jacket and a slightly bohemian-looking shirt which had seemed perfect when I put it on, chic but not trying too hard; now, however, I began to have extravagant imaginings about the type of place a person like Kai von Jülich might frequent. He might take me somewhere really smart, where jeans would look hopelessly scruffy. *Get a grip*, I thought. *It'll probably be the bowling alley in Schönau.* But still my mind ran on, conjuring up images of us in some expensive restaurant, maybe that fancy one on the edge of Euskirchen, with waiters offering to bring me a glass of *Sekt*. I wondered whether I should run upstairs and change.

Outside the bakery, a car horn sounded. As I hurtled out of the ladies' room, breathless and probably pink in the face, I heard it again, loud and impatient. I ran for the door. Through the bakery's front window I could already catch a glimpse of gleaming red. Kai *had* brought the sports car. The bakery door banged shut behind me as I clattered down the few steps into the street.

Kai was sitting at the wheel, looking as usual as though he had just stepped out of the pages of a magazine, blond, bronzed and beautiful. Suddenly I felt almost afraid. He was so good-looking that it was intimidating. Someone like him didn't belong with someone like *me*. Surely the whole thing was a joke? I almost expected him to lower the window and say, *Get out of my way, can't you? I'm waiting for someone important.*

But he didn't. He leaned over and opened the passenger door.

'Steffi, get in.'

I fumbled with my bag, cursing myself for being a clumsy idiot, then climbed into the car, thumping my head on the door frame as I did so. Having made as much of a fool of myself as possible, I was almost too abashed to look at Kai. My attempt at a cheery greeting came out as a hoarse squeak and I subsided into the low-slung seat with my face burning, doing my best to hide behind my hair.

Kai leaned towards me and for a moment I almost flinched back. I could still not quite get it into my head that we were really here together in his car, that it wasn't some kind of mistake. Then he put out a hand and brushed the hair back from my face, twisting the fair strands in his long fingers. The next second he was kissing me.

It wasn't as though I had never been kissed before; Timo and I had been going out for three years. All the same, the passion behind Kai's kissing took me aback. I felt as though I were about to be eaten alive. Nor could I break away with Kai's fingers entwined in my hair. With a distinct feeling of shock I realized that his other hand was moving purposefully across the front of my shirt.

I froze, barely able to breathe, limp in the clutches of the maelstrom inside me, like a drowning person being sucked down into the depths of a whirlpool. Anxiety that one of my parents would step out of the bakery and see me in a clinch of vampiric proportions mixed with a strange excitement. Tentatively I put up a hand and touched Kai's hair. I closed my eyes.

Knocking. Someone was knocking. My eyes flew open as Kai broke the kiss, sitting back in his seat. He was scowling as he reached for his seat belt. I struggled to sit up, following the line of his angry gaze. *Oh no.*

Standing on the cobbles right beside the car was a compact figure firmly upholstered in green wool. Even if that grim and wrinkled face had not been visible from where I sat, I would have known that ugly edelweiss brooch anywhere. *Frau Kessel.* She was raising her knuckles to rap on the car window again. From the expression on her face I imagined she would have liked to throw a bucket of cold water over the pair of us. As pitiless as a searchlight, her gaze moved from my flustered face and dishevelled hair to the front of my shirt. Not daring to look down, I prayed that all my buttons were still done up.

Frau Kessel was gesturing for us to lower the windows. I would just as soon have signed my own death warrant, but sheer force of habit made me reach for the button. At that moment, however, Kai revved the engine and the car leapt forward, pressing me back into the padded seat and forcing Frau Kessel to step backwards rather smartly. As the car sped off down the street in frank defiance of the speed limit, I looked in the side mirror and saw Frau Kessel's stiff and furious form diminishing behind us, like some evil genie vanishing back into its bottle. The old lady would not be so easily disposed of as that, I realized. I could only imagine what mileage she would get out of the scene she had just witnessed. It was lucky for us that the pillory outside the *Rathaus* was no longer in use, otherwise she would have been lobbying for the pair of us to be chained up and pelted with vegetables.

We swept around the town centre, the car rumbling on the cobblestones, and then we were driving out through the gap in the medieval walls. Kai had turned on a CD and the car was filled with the sound of a band I didn't know, something loud and strident, grating voices fighting an insistent beat. It sounded more like the soundtrack to a violent film than the background to a romantic evening, but in a way I was relieved. The incident with Frau Kessel had rattled me and now I couldn't think of a single thing to say to Kai.

Furtively I peeped at him through my curtain of fair hair. He wasn't looking at me, didn't even seem to be aware of me. His eyes were fixed on the road, his profile composed. Only a tightness around the jaw betrayed his irritation at the old lady's interference.

'Where are we going?' I asked eventually as the car reached the edge of the town, but Kai didn't hear me over the roaring and crashing of the music. *It's that place in Euskirchen*, I thought, as we passed the car dealerships and the main road out of Bad Münstereifel lay before us. To my surprise, however, Kai turned left and we sped down a road I knew well. I had been here several times, very recently – only then it had been in the back of Max's car, squashed between Timo and Hanna, and we had been heading for the Eschweiler Tal. For Rote Gertrud's house.

I looked at the street flashing past, and at the road ahead, and I felt the strangest feeling of dislocation, as though I were in a rocket screaming into the sky and the world were dropping away behind me. The car was slowing as we reached the end of the tarmac. Of course. The track which led into the Tal was simply dirt and gravel. It would put a few scratches in that gleaming scarlet paintwork if we drove up it at high speed.

Why have we come here? I wanted to ask. My lips formed the words, but nothing came out. I wouldn't have expected a reply even if Kai had been able to hear me. We were off the script now. My brain told me that it was completely impossible to make someone love you by writing a note to a dead witch in a filthy ruin in the woods. Kai must have wanted to ask me out anyway, that was the logical explanation. And yet here we were in the Eschweiler Tal, closing the distance between us and Rote Gertrud's house as rapidly as Kai's concern for his car would allow. It could not be coincidence, could it? And yet – suppose my scrawled words really had made this happen? How could a relationship born of such impossibility possibly go on?

Perhaps being here in the Tal was part of it, I thought. Perhaps Kai unknowingly felt the lure of that silent grey wreck hidden among the trees. It was not a comforting thought. Everything I knew about bargains made with things outside the rational world suggested that there would be a heavy price to pay.

The car was slowing down again. We were still some distance from the spot where Max had parked the times we visited Rote Gertrud's house. Puzzled, I glanced at Kai. This didn't make sense either. If the ruined house wasn't the lure, what were we doing here? I looked at the track ahead. Although it was a fine spring evening, even warm, there was nobody in the Tal, not even a solitary dog walker or mountain biker. We were quite alone.

Kai pulled in at the side of the track and turned off the

ignition, stopping the music mid-screech. As he turned to me, unclipping his seat belt, I realized that we had not really communicated since I got into the car, not unless you counted fastening on to each other's faces like leeches. The way he was looking at me now caused little prickles of nervousness in my stomach. He didn't look at me the way I had imagined and hoped he would, as though I were an angel descended from heaven. Instead there was a grim energy about him, as though he wanted to jump on me and sink his teeth into my neck. I had a feeling he was about to do more or less that very thing; he was going to kiss me again. Not that I had anything against that – I had wanted to go out with him for ages – but it didn't feel right, sitting here in the car in the deserted Tal, with barely a word exchanged first.

As Kai moved towards me I found myself backing up against the window.

'Um . . . Kai?' I said.

'Mmm?' Kai's face was coming closer and closer, until it filled my vision. At such close quarters it was like looking at him through a fish-eye lens. I was unnerved.

'Why –' I started, and I had to turn my head to one side, otherwise his lips would have been on mine and speech would have been impossible. 'Kai? Why did we come here?'

'What?'

I had the distinct impression he was not listening to me. His hand was on my shoulder. I heard a *click* as he undid my seat belt.

'Why did –'

'Shhhh,' he said, and his hand slid down to the front of my shirt.

I jumped like a startled cat. 'What are you *doing*?'

'What do you think?'

I was stunned by the casual tone of his voice. Timo and I had spent plenty of evenings fooling around when his parents were out, but it had never been like this. Kai wasn't even trying to talk to me, to get to know me. Unbidden, Julius's grim face flashed across my mind. *He's not a nice guy*, he had said. Was this what he meant? Kai was probably used to getting everything he wanted. He was good-looking, he was rich – how many other students had a sports car? Every single girl in Bad Münstereifel wanted Kai. They'd probably do anything to be the one on his arm. Probably not one of them ever said –

'No.'

I had surprised even myself. I put my hands up and pushed Kai as hard as I could, trying to get him off me. For a moment I thought I had succeeded, but then I saw that he was grinning, although there was no humour in his eyes.

'Come off it, Steffi.'

He reached out for me again. I parried his hand with both of mine.

'Stop it.'

This time I saw real anger flash across Kai's face. It was as if I had seen through the handsome exterior to the real Kai beneath. I was shocked by what I saw, as though I had leaned forward to smell the scent of a rose and seen a fat worm come writhing out of it. The next second his expression was smoothed over, although his eyes remained hard.

'What's this crap?' he said.

'You're . . .' I struggled for words, still wondering if I could recover the situation. 'You're going too fast for me.'

'Oh yeah?' Kai's voice was insolent. His hand moved to my hair, snagged it painfully. 'You think?'

'Don't.' I could hear the tremor in my own voice. I was feeling behind me for the door handle, but I couldn't find it. In the cramped space I had no room for manoeuvre.

'Come on, Steffi. You want it.' Kai easily pushed aside the hand I had wedged between us, and reached for my breast.

Outraged, I tried to slap his hand away. I felt a painful yank on my hair and then we were actually grappling with each other. My head snapped back and thumped painfully against the window.

'Stop it! Stop it!'

'Tease.' Kai was holding both my hands by the wrists now and the words which came spewing out of those perfectly moulded lips were as savage as knives slashing at me. 'You asked for it,' he kept saying in between pitiless epithets that pelted me like hailstones. 'You wanted it.'

He's completely insane, I thought, panicking. Since I'd left school Kai had only ever seen me in the bakery, dressed up like Snow White, it was true, but generally wilting like an unwatered plant behind the rows of sesame rolls and slices of cheesecake. I had hardly spoken a word to him other than to thank him for his purchases and yet somehow he seemed to think I had been leading him on.

I did my best to close my ears, but it was impossible to shut out the terrible things Kai was saying. He sounded as though he was quoting from some Devil's list of depravity, under the impression that I had offered him everything on it. There was no time to think how this could be. He was batting at me like an enraged tiger balked of its prey. If we had not been in a confined space with the gearstick between us he would have been actually on top of me. Now he had a hand bunched in the fabric of my shirt, but at least he was no longer holding both my wrists.

Twisting frantically, I managed to reach the door handle and yank it. With my full weight on it, the door opened and I spilt backwards out of it with a savage ripping sound as my shirt tore in Kai's grasp. He still had the sleeve of my jacket in his other hand, but I twisted like a landed fish and somehow slipped out of the garment altogether, hitting the ground with a jarring thud that sent a jolt of pain through my hip.

I staggered to my feet. I was not sure whether Kai would get out of the car after me, but I dared not wait to find out. I abandoned the jacket but made a grab for my bag, which was lying in the dust by the car's front wheel. Then I turned and ran for it.

As I pelted up the track, putting as much distance as I could between myself and Kai, I heard the car engine start again. I realized with a thrill of horror that Kai would have to follow me until he came to a space wide enough to turn the car. I didn't know whether he was angry enough to try to run me down, but I wasn't prepared to risk it. I flung myself at the overgrown bank to the side of the track and scrambled up it on hands and knees, heedless of the brambles which scratched and tore my skin.

I heard an angry roar as the car went past, throwing up a little shower of dried mud and gravel; in his fury Kai had forgotten about the bodywork. Then I was tearing uphill through the trees, my heart pounding in my chest and my arms flailing. I had no sense of where I was going, no aim but to put as much space as possible between myself and Kai.

I ran until my chest was heaving and every breath seemed to scour hotly up my throat. When I could no longer run at full tilt I continued to walk, stumbling on through the knotted undergrowth, shivering in the cooling evening air. As panic subsided I began to take stock of my situation. The shirt I had selected with such care was ruined, ripped from the shoulder to the hem. My exposed skin was already covered in goosebumps. My hip was throbbing from the impact with the ground and my hair was hanging over my face in great clotted hanks. I looked at my outspread hands, which were bleeding from a dozen tiny scratches and streaked with dirt. None of this seemed very important. My physical appearance was just a shell, a hole in a stone for the wind to shriek through. Inside I felt a deadening numbness. *I'm in shock*, acknowledged a distant voice in the back of my mind. There was some comfort in this. If I started to feel again I would be overwhelmed. I dreaded to examine the things that Kai had said to me; it was easier not to think about them.

I looked around me, thinking that I should try to find my way back to the track. I was shivering and as night came on it would get colder. I would have a long walk back to the town.

Where am I? I thought, but the next second I knew. I recognized this part of the forest. Perhaps ten metres away from me, a little uphill, was a fat tree trunk covered with spongy-looking green moss. I had sat on it one night drinking Kleiner Feigling from a miniature bottle, while Max and Jochen horsed around in the dark and Max's plan hung over us with dark foreboding.

I had only to go a little way further and I would be at Rote Gertrud's. The witch's house.

CHAPTER TWENTY-ONE

I wish I could say that as I pushed my way through the undergrowth towards Gertrud's house I was impelled by terror, or desperation, or righteous anger, that I could not help myself. Instead I felt as though something inside me, some vital human part, had turned to ice. My feet carried me onwards, my hands swept the overhanging branches aside, my eyes scanned the uneven ground, but I might just as well have been a robot for all I felt, marching mindlessly on metal claws over the surface of some unknown planet.

I reached the house quickly, rounded the blank wall with its corroded-looking covering of lichen and stepped through the hole in the facade. Every other time I had been here, I had been with someone else; now I was completely alone, and night was coming. There was still enough light to see the scratches and scrawls which clustered on the stone walls like the muffled clamour of the long-dead. I moved among them, the only living thing.

Where was the box? I found it nestling in a cluster of rotting beech leaves and picked it up. I was not surprised when I opened it to find that my slip of paper had gone, the one with the wish for Kai von Jülich on it. Once again, the other five remained. At some point I would think about that, about why it was only *my* wishes which were granted, why everyone else's lay ignored in the box. For now it was enough that the method worked.

I put the open box on top of a chunk of fallen masonry. Then I fumbled for my bag. I had a pen, a cheap one with the bakery's name on it. Finding something to write on was a little more difficult, but eventually I discovered a handwritten receipt from the bookshop in the town stuffed into my purse. The back of the receipt was blank and there was enough space to write the dooms of half a dozen people on it.

I picked up the box and sat down on the chunk of stone. I smoothed out the paper carefully on the lid of the box. I pressed the button at the end of the pen, so that the ball-point sprang out. I felt perfect, icy calm as I did all this, and it was not until the point of the pen touched the paper and danced across it that I realized I was shaking too badly to write. Hot tears were leaking from the corners of my eyes. My hand and arm shuddered with the effort of trying to control the pen. A sob forced its way up from my throat.

Rote Gertrud, do this one thing for me, I thought. *If you hated the men who dragged you out of your house and burned you – help me.* It was irrational, but at that moment I was beyond reason.

The first time I tried to write anything the pen tore right through the paper. By then I was crying loudly and tears were running down my face. It took me a long time to control the pen well enough to write legibly, but in the end I managed it.

Kai von Jülich, die.

CHAPTER TWENTY-TWO

When I finally emerged from the edge of the forest on to the track, it was getting dark and I was so cold that my teeth were chattering. There was no sign of Kai and his ostentatious car apart from a curving mark in the rough surface of the track and a little spray of gravel. I stood and listened before I stepped right out from under the trees, but there was no sound of an engine idling, no human voice or footsteps audible. I found my jacket lying on the ground, one sleeve turned completely inside out, from where Kai had tried to hang on to me, and the shoulder seam parting. There was a dusty tyre mark right across the front of it. I brushed it down as best I could with bloodless fingers and shrugged it on. It was better than nothing but I was still freezing. I shoved my hands into the pockets and began to walk towards the town.

As I walked, I tried not to think about what had happened. In fact I tried not to think at all. I switched off and drifted away from the aching cold and the pain in my limbs and the weary trek ahead. I let the world shrink to the sound of my feet stumbling over the rough surface of the track and the sound of my breathing.

It took some time to reach the place where the track led on to a tarmacked road surface and then to walk the rest of the way into the town. I thought that if I stayed off the main road and kept to the footpath which ran parallel to the railway line, I might avoid meeting anyone. What an observer would make of my tangled hair and torn shirt didn't bear thinking about. I thought I had a fat lip too; at some point during the struggle with Kai I must have bitten it.

My luck held all the way to the Werther Tor. As I limped through it, I could see that the pavement cafe was still open. Rather than parade myself right past anyone who was enjoying a last drink at one of the outdoor tables, I elected to turn right, along the narrow street running along the inside of the town wall. I thought I might walk down the backstreets unnoticed and slip into the bakery without being seen at all. But at that point my luck ran out.

'Steffi Nett,' said a voice I knew and loathed, a voice which positively suppurated disapproval.

Now I thought my legs would give way beneath me. *No*, howled a voice in the back of my mind. *Not her. Why does it have to be her? Not Frau Kessel. Please.* Caught in compromising circumstances, twice in one day – it had to be some sort of record.

'Hi,' I muttered under my breath, keeping my head down, avoiding her eye in the hope that she would not look closely at me. I tried to push past her but she was too quick for me. For someone in her eighties, she was surprisingly nimble. She grasped me by the upper arm, her wiry old fingers digging into the flesh. It was like having a very large bird of prey land on my shoulder, talons outspread for purchase.

'You could have run me over, you two,' she hissed as I tried to pull away. 'Driving like that. There's a speed limit in the town, you know.'

There were any number of replies to that, such as *I wasn't the one driving* and *What business is it of yours?*, but as usual I was unable to articulate a single one. My tongue was as useless as a stone. I shook back my hair and did my best to give Frau Kessel a defiant look, but I knew I had made a mistake the moment I saw her expression change.

Her eyes narrowed behind her spectacles as she took in the rumpled hair, the puffy lip and – horrors! – the rent in the front of my shirt, through which a glimpse of bra was no doubt visible. I grabbed at my jacket and pulled it shut, but it was too late. Those beady old eyes had taken everything in.

'Where is he?' she asked me in glacial tones.

I didn't bother to pretend innocence, to ask whom she meant. Instead I did my best to extricate my arm from her pincer-like grasp.

'I have to go,' I said, cursing my own feebleness. I was up to my neck in it anyway. I might just as well have given her an earful – it couldn't have made things any worse.

'Didn't bother to run you home, then?' said that relentless voice. Frau Kessel leaned closer and I caught a whiff of her scent, sickly sweet and powdery, an old-lady smell. 'I'm not surprised,' she said in a venomous undertone. 'I know it's the modern way. But nobody respects a girl like that.'

She didn't have to spell it out. I wrenched my arm out of her bony grasp and scurried away down the street, clinging to the shadows, the jacket pulled tight around my body. I didn't meet anyone else on the way to the bakery. The backstreets were deserted. It was just evil luck that the one person I *had* run into was the last person I wanted to meet.

When I came into the flat, my parents were in the living

room, watching television. I could see the ghostly blue light dancing on the wall and hear the unmistakable sound of Klara Klein's singing drifting through the air. I guessed they were watching a memorial programme.

'I'm home,' I shouted, but I didn't go into the room. Nor did I wait to see whether they would come out. I scuttled into the bathroom and locked the door behind me. I felt filthy, cold and so weary that I could have lain down on the fluffy peach bathmat and gone to sleep.

With an effort I made myself turn on the shower and while I was waiting for the water to run hot I went over to the mirror to inspect the damage.

I looked as though I had been in a fight, which I supposed I had. The bitten lip had a bee-stung appearance, I had a streak of mascara under my right eye and my hair looked as though I had just got up after a particularly bad night, all of which had no doubt fuelled Frau Kessel's prurient imaginings. I shuddered to contemplate the monstrous thoughts which must have slithered and bumped their way through the cloacal tunnels of her mind.

The shirt was ruined beyond all hope of repair, of course, and even if it hadn't been, I would never want to wear either that or the jacket again. I dragged them off and left them in a ball on the bathroom floor; they would be going straight into the dustbin. Then I stepped into the shower.

I stood there, letting the scalding water soak my hair and cascade over my skin. The water was as hot as I could stand it, but still I was shivering.

I stayed under the shower for as long as I could, but eventually my father banged on the door.

'Are you going to be in there forever?' he bellowed.

I turned off the water. 'Five minutes,' I called back.

I suppose I spent four and a half of those minutes staring at myself in the mirror, in the porthole I had rubbed out of the steamed-up surface. My hair was dripping wet but clean. My lip was still swollen, but now that the smudged mascara was gone, my face didn't look as bad as it had before. What gave me away were my eyes: they looked enormous in my face, bleak and haunted.

I tried a smile but it was a vain attempt. My parents would see at a glance that there was something wrong; there was no hiding it. In the end I spent the last thirty seconds tucking myself into a thick fluffy towel and snatching up my clothes from the floor. Then I opened the door and bolted for my bedroom.

'Bathroom's free!' I shouted, and slammed the door shut. Explanations could wait for another time.

CHAPTER TWENTY-THREE

On Saturday morning Hanna called at the bakery. My mother, who was hurrying between tables carrying a tray laden with coffee cups, directed her upstairs to the flat. I was skulking in the kitchen, having waited until both my parents were down in the bakery before coming out of my room. My lip looked better this morning but I still didn't feel like talking to anyone. Hanna had been knocking for a full minute before I gave in and opened the door.

'Steffi, you look terrible,' was the first thing she said as she walked past me into the flat. 'What happened?'

I didn't say anything. I just walked back to the kitchen, sat down at the table and picked up my mug. The fruit tea I had made myself was cold. It hadn't tasted that good in the beginning; now it was undrinkable. I put the mug down again.

'What's up?' said Hanna. She sat down opposite me and put her elbows on the table.

'Nothing.'

'Come off it, Steffi.'

Kai had uttered those very words. I couldn't help it; a little sound escaped, more a squeak than a gasp. I hugged myself, huddling inside my dressing-gown.

'What?' said Hanna. She put out a hand and touched my arm. 'What is it? Something's happened, hasn't it?'

Miserably, I nodded.

'Did you have a row with your parents?'

'No. It was . . .' I thought. 'It was Gertrud's house. You know.'

'Your wish? It came true again?'

'Yes,' I said in a tiny voice.

Hanna whistled. 'That's *amazing*. But what's the problem? You must have wished for something you wanted, didn't you?'

I didn't say anything.

'What did you wish for?' persisted Hanna. She shook my arm gently, as though trying to wake me from a dream. How I wished that were possible. I would have given anything for the whole episode to have been nothing but a nightmare. 'Come on, what was it?'

'I wanted . . .' I sighed. Everyone would know, sooner or later. If I didn't tell them, Frau Kessel would. 'I wanted a date with Kai von Jülich.'

'No!' Hanna was impressed. 'And did he? Ask you out, I mean?'

I looked down at the tablecloth. 'Yes.'

Hanna whistled. 'He *did*? Steffi, that's – it's unbelievable. When are you going?'

'Last night,' I said. 'We went last night.'

'Wow.' Hanna sat back and stared at me. 'You're not . . . you're not kidding me, are you?'

I shook my head.

'That's . . . incredible,' she said. 'He just came up and asked you out? Did he come here, to the bakery?'

'Yes.'

'So, how was it? Are you going to go out again? This is amazing,' she added, more to herself than to me. She seemed to have forgotten that I was sitting there, looking more like a guest at a wake than someone in the grip of a new romance.

'No,' I said, rather more emphatically than I had intended.

'Why not?'

'Because he's a *pig*,' I blurted out, and promptly burst into tears.

'Oh . . .' For once, Hanna seemed lost for words.

'I'm sorry,' I said, scrubbing furiously at my eyes with the back of my fist. 'It's just . . . he was horrible, Hanna.' I let out a juddering sigh. 'Julius said he wasn't a nice guy, and he was right.'

'Julius?' said Hanna. 'You mean Julius Rensinghof?'

I nodded.

'What's it got to do with him?' she asked indignantly.

'It hasn't got anything to do with him. He was sticking his nose in.' I fumbled in my pocket, looking for a tissue. 'I suppose he'll be glad,' I added bitterly. 'He was right.'

'But what did Kai do?'

'I don't want to talk about it,' I said.

'Sorry,' said Hanna, but although she did her best to look sympathetic I could tell that she was almost bursting with excitement. Another wish come true. Something occurred to me.

'Hanna? What you wished for, did it come true?'

She shrugged her shoulders. 'Not yet, anyway.'

'What about the others?'

'I don't think so. You know what Max is like. It would

have been something so big that nobody could have missed it, and if he actually got it, he'd never be able to keep his mouth shut. Look, this is amazing. I know you had a bad time –'

'A horrible time.'

'OK, a horrible time. But your wish still came true, didn't it? And only yours.' There was awe in Hanna's voice. 'What is it about you? Have you got some sort of power?'

'Don't be ridiculous.' In spite of my tears I couldn't suppress a snort of amusement.

'Wait till the others hear this.'

I opened my mouth to tell Hanna not to say anything, that I regretted telling even her, that I wanted the whole thing forgotten. But then I remembered. *Frau Kessel*. There was no way that she would keep her mouth shut. I might just as well have marched through the streets bearing a placard with my shame written on it in letters thirty centimetres high.

'Hanna . . .'

'That's what I came round for anyway. We tried to call you last night. Nobody knew you were out with Kai von Jülich, you sly thing.' Hanna saw my expression and hurried on. 'So, we're meeting up tonight at Jochen's place. His mum and stepdad are going to the Klara Klein tribute concert at the Heinz-Gerlach Halle.' She wrinkled her nose. 'Max wanted to know if anyone's wish had come true.'

'I'm not going,' I said.

'Come on, Steffi. You've got to.'

'I can't,' I said simply. 'You can tell them what happened if you want. I'm sorry.' I put a hand over my eyes. 'I don't want to see anyone this evening.'

'Timo?' said Hanna significantly. 'You know *he's* not going to care.'

I shrugged. 'I'm sorry. I just can't come.' I shook my head. 'I can't see anyone.'

CHAPTER TWENTY-FOUR

I can't see anyone, I had told Hanna. But by Sunday night I had seen three more of them.

Izabela was the first. She dropped into the bakery on Saturday afternoon. When I opened the flat door to find her standing there I was mildly surprised. We had seen very little of each other since she started going out with Timo. I would really much rather have been left alone, but I hadn't the heart to be unfriendly. I was increasingly coming round to the view that anyone who thought Timo was Prince Charming was slightly deluded, so I had no hard feelings towards Izabela.

'Can I come in?' she said.

She seemed more nervous than usual, as though she thought there was a faint possibility I might jump on her and try to scratch her eyes out or pull her mane of dark hair. I knew that Izabela was quite timid and wondered all the more that she had dared drop in.

'Of course.' I stepped back to let her enter.

As soon as the door closed behind her and there was no danger of anyone downstairs overhearing, she turned to me.

'I just heard,' she said.

'Heard what?'

She wasn't listening. 'I'm really pleased for you. It was kind of odd before. I mean, Timo said you weren't really . . .' She paused. 'Well, he said it was really over, but . . .'

I took pity on her. 'That's OK,' I said. 'It *was* over really.'

'I just feel so much better now,' she said.

'Good,' I said cautiously.

'So did he really come into the bakery and ask you out in front of everyone?'

So that's what this is about.

'Izzi,' I said, 'I don't know what you've heard, but I'm not going out with Kai von Jülich.'

'But –' She looked perplexed. 'I heard he asked you out.'

I gritted my teeth. 'Well, he did. And I went – once. But that's the end of it.' I said the last bit so ominously that Izabela didn't ask me *why* that was the end of it.

'I'm sorry,' she said.

'Don't be,' I said, but I spoke so sharply that her face fell and I relented. 'Look, Izzi,' I said as kindly as I could, 'there's no need to worry. It's fine about you and Timo. And I don't need Kai von Jülich around to be OK with it.'

'All right,' she said, but I could see that she was doubtful. After that the conversation trailed off. I could see that Izabela was dying to talk about Timo but no longer dared to, probably imagining that I was suffering the horrors of heartbreak. I had no particular desire to talk about him either. I was a little piqued at the way the relationship had ended – or rather failed to end. I thought Timo made a very poor sort of love interest, but I could hardly say so.

When Izabela left, it was on the whole a relief. I watched her clatter down the stairs and turn to wave at the bottom. I raised my hand in return and smiled at her, but I had a feeling the friendship had suffered a fatal blow.

CHAPTER TWENTY-FIVE

Later that afternoon I was standing by the railing overlooking the River Erft, throwing chunks of yesterday's stale bread to the mallards which clustered among the weedy stones, and the next thing I knew someone was grabbing at my waist, as though to tickle me.

Kai, I thought, with a cold flash of panic. I whirled around, my fists up as though to beat him off. But it wasn't Kai; of course it wasn't. It was Max.

'Whoa,' he said. 'You going to beat me up, Steffi?' He was grinning.

'I thought you were someone else,' I said crossly.

'I bet you did.'

I looked at Max uneasily. He was a premium-quality bullshitter, I knew that. But it wasn't like him to use that insinuating tone with me. That was something new. And the way he was looking at me, there was something new and not entirely pleasant in that too.

A hideous suspicion began to grow in the back of my mind. Max and Kai von Jülich had never been friends, so far as I knew. Max had attended the *Hauptschule*, as I had, whereas Kai had (naturally) been at the *Gymnasium*, the most academic type of school. But they both lived in the same part of Bad Münstereifel, the same smart street full of white-walled palaces with BMWs and Mercedes parked outside.

Slow down, I told myself desperately. *He hasn't talked to Kai. They're not even friends. Anyway, nothing happened. You got out of the car and you walked home. What's Kai going to tell people about that?*

'You're not coming to Jochen's place tonight, Steffi?' said Max. He was still grinning.

'No.' I shook my head, not wanting to elaborate.

'Shame.' Max was looking me up and down, assessing me.

I shifted uncomfortably from foot to foot. *It's just Max*, I told myself. *He's got the cheek of the Devil. It doesn't mean anything.*

'I have to go in,' I said.

Max's gaze shifted to the half-full bag of rolls I was holding. 'Ducks don't want to eat any more?'

'Bye, Max,' I said.

'Catch you later,' he said, but I was already walking away.

If the conversation with Max made me uneasy, the one with Jochen was worse. He came when my parents were at church on Sunday evening. The bakery was shut, so he rang the outside bell. Like Hanna, he was persistent; when I didn't come down within the first couple of minutes he kept ringing. All of a sudden, it seemed that everyone had to speak to me, very urgently.

'Jochen, I'm not feeling well,' I lied as I opened the door, but he didn't listen. He was already shouldering past me into the bakery.

'We have to talk,' he said.

I glanced out at the street. All it would take to make my life infinitely worse was for Frau Kessel to wander by at that moment and catch me ushering another young man into the bakery, and while my parents were at mass, to boot. But the street was deserted.

I hoped he wouldn't stay long. I had been lying about feeling ill, but now I thought I could detect the beginnings of a headache. I would have preferred to see nobody at all, especially since Max's familiarity the day before. I was beginning to wonder whether there was something about me which attracted unwholesome behaviour as jam attracts wasps.

'I want you to curse Udo,' said Jochen, without further preamble.

I stared at him.

'Udo, you know, my stepfather. Udo the *Arschloch*.'

I knew perfectly well whom he meant. It was nigh on impossible to live in Bad Münstereifel and not know Udo Meyer. He was tall, broad-shouldered and slightly pudgy-looking, with wiry hair and an officious-looking moustache underlining a nose like a beak. He was also the town's champion know-it-all. At any given public event you could be sure that Udo would be on his feet at the very first opportunity, giving the assembled masses the benefit of his superior wisdom in a voice with all the lilting charm of a dentist's drill. After five minutes of listening to it, you were ready to agree with anything he said, just to shut him up.

I could well imagine that living with Udo and listening to his pompous monologues on a daily basis would be enough to drive anyone up the wall. All the same, I needed more than this to go on before cursing anyone.

'Why?' I said.

'What do you mean, why? He's a tosser.'

Jochen sounded impatient. The light from the overhead lamps turned his blond curls golden and for a moment I was reminded unpleasantly of Kai von Jülich. But Jochen was nothing like Kai. Instead of that smooth bronzed skin, he had the pallid sort of complexion which freckles easily and blunt heavy features. Jochen would never have the girls clustering around him the way Kai did.

'Jochen . . .'

'Come on,' he said. 'It works when you do it. I want that stupid *Arschloch* dead.'

'Don't be silly,' I said uneasily.

'I'm not joking.'

'What's he done?'

I saw Jochen's hands ball into fists. 'Bastard. He wants me out. I have to leave home.' His face twisted like a spoilt child's. 'I know what his problem is. He can't stand it if you don't agree with him and his stupid ideas.'

'Why does he want you to leave?' I asked cautiously.

'Because he's an utter jerk.' After a pause Jochen seemed to realize that this was insufficient information. 'He says I have to pay my own way. I told him to stuff it. Mum never made me pay anything before he came along. She ought to stick up for me, but she doesn't. He's got her right where he wants her. I'm not taking it.'

'Jochen,' I said as calmly as I could, 'I can't curse Udo.'

'You have to.'

He looked at me with a mutinous expression in his pale

blue eyes. *He means it*, I thought. It was the same as Max handing me the pen and paper and saying, *Here, Steffi, you do it. Come on, don't be wet.* Everyone just assumed that I would do what they told me to do.

I took a deep breath.

'No, I don't.'

'What? Come on, Steffi.' Jochen eyed me and saw resistance in my expression. An ugly look of disbelief and indignation spread over his face. 'Don't mess me around.'

I was shaking my head.

'You only wish stuff for yourself, is that it?' He sounded really angry. 'Your friends can take any kind of shit and you won't help them out?'

'It's not that,' I said in a low voice.

'Well, what then?'

'Suppose it works?' I said. 'Suppose he really drops dead – like Klara Klein – because I've wished it?'

'That's the point,' said Jochen in a hard voice, as though talking to the terminally stupid. 'It has to be you who wishes it, because it only works when it's you.'

'Udo's never done anything to me,' I said.

'So you're just going to let him fuck up my life?' Jochen sounded ready to burst with indignation and I found myself wanting to back away.

'Can't you talk to him?' I suggested. 'Or talk to your mum? Jochen, I can't just –'

'Talk to him?' Jochen was shaking his head in disbelief. 'What sort of crap is that?'

'I'm sorry,' I told him.

'Yeah,' said Jochen bitterly. 'I'm sorry too. Sorry I even bothered talking to you. You're a loser, Steffi. Maybe it wasn't you at all. Maybe it was coincidence, Klara Klein and the rest of it.' He sneered at me. 'You haven't got the guts for anything.'

If he thought he could taunt me into agreeing to do what he wanted, he was wrong, but no sharp retort rose to my lips. I simply stood there in silence with my head down, as though I were trying to push my way forward through a storm. Finally he gave up.

'Thanks a lot,' he said sarcastically. 'Loser.'

I heard the bell above the door jingle as he pushed his way out of the bakery. Then he was off down the street.

I went to the door and looked the other way, up towards the old brewery. My heart sank. Little knots of people were drifting out from the Marktstrasse and the alley which ran parallel to it. Mass had ended and the church was emptying. I could only hope that no one had glimpsed Jochen's departure from the bakery. If my parents had spotted him, there would be awkward questions. If Frau Kessel had spotted him, my life would not be worth living.

CHAPTER TWENTY-SIX

I did my best to avoid the others for the next couple of days. I couldn't have faced Jochen, and the prospect of any of the others making similar requests was just as bad. I switched off my phone and spent the evenings in my room, but although I successfully managed to avoid my five friends, that didn't stop me running into someone else I knew.

It was Tuesday afternoon and I was serving in the bakery. A large coach party had come in and, judging by their advanced ages, they were Klara Klein fans visiting the town to pay their last respects. I thought that if you added all their ages you would probably have more than a thousand years, which was a dizzying thought: a millennium of broken hearts and edelweiss flowers.

I was just putting a large cup of hot chocolate with cream and a slice of cheesecake down in front of an old woman whose wrinkled face was alarmingly at odds with her head of fanciful Klara Klein-inspired curls when the bell above the door jingled a couple of times. I looked up and saw a tall angular figure clad in a long black coat in spite of the clement weather, a figure I would have known anywhere, even without the shock of brilliant red hair which topped it like the flame of a torch.

Oh no. Julius. After our last meeting I was amazed he had even come back to the bakery. What could we possibly have to say to each other?

I glanced around, hoping that someone else would deal with him, but my mother was taking down a long, involved order for a table of six and the other waitress was nowhere to be seen at all. Reluctantly I went over to him.

'*Guten Tag*,' I said, trying to sound businesslike.

I carried the tray which had held the hot chocolate and the cake in front of me, making the point that I was working. I wondered why Julius had come. Was it possible that some version of Friday evening's events had filtered through to him and he had come to gloat?

'Steffi, can I talk to you?'

'I'm working,' I said desperately.

I rounded the end of the counter and put the tray down, then looked at the display of cakes in the glass-fronted cabinet – the almond *Nuss-striezel*, the honey-sweet *Bienenstich*, the great gateaux laden with strawberries and cherries – anywhere, in fact, but at Julius's face.

'Are you going to order anything?' I said pointedly to the cherry cake.

'OK, a sesame roll. With cheese and ham – and salad.'

I sighed. I was going to have to make the roll from scratch and Julius knew it. It was just an excuse to keep me there at the counter, a captive audience. I reached for a roll and a bread knife.

'Friday was a disaster,' said Julius's voice.

It sounded close, as though he were leaning right over the counter, but I resisted the temptation to look up. I sawed roughly at the bread roll as though I were an eighteenth-century surgeon trying to cut through a bone in the shortest possible time.

'Gina did it and she was terrible. She sounded like a wild sow calling for her piglets.'

In spite of my resolve I was terribly tempted to laugh. Determinedly, I kept my head down.

'It would have been ten times better if you'd been there.'

'Really?' I reached for a smaller knife and opened a pack of sliced cheese.

'How did it go with Kai?'

The knife slipped, cutting a notch in my fingernail. I swore under my breath and examined the nail, using it as an excuse not to answer.

'Are you going to see him again?'

Now finally I was provoked into looking at Julius. I gave him such a scorching glare across the glass counter that it was a wonder the cream on the *Sahnetorte* did not curdle on the spot.

'What the hell has it got to do with you?' I hissed.

It was an effort to keep my voice down; only my consciousness of the presence of a coachload of Klara Klein fans enabled me to do it.

'Nothing, I suppose.' Julius's angular shoulders went up in a shrug.

'Shut up, then.'

I began to hunt for the ham.

'Steffi, we're friends, aren't we?' said Julius.

'Are we?' I snapped.

'Look, Kai . . .'

'He's not a nice guy. I know. You told me.'

'He isn't,' said Julius, and something in his voice made me look at him again.

'What?' I said, although I had a feeling I would rather not know whatever it was he had on his mind.

Julius sighed and ran his long hands through his hair so that clumps of it stood on end, making it look more like a shooting mass of flames than ever. 'He's going round telling people . . .' He paused. 'That you threw yourself at him. That you and he . . .' He didn't finish the sentence; he didn't have to. 'I thought you should know.'

So I can wish him dead? I thought. But I had already done that.

'Telling people?' I said tightly.

It felt as though my throat had constricted; it was difficult to get the words out. My worst fears were confirmed. Now I knew for certain why Max had looked at me the way he had. He wasn't seeing me as shy little Steffi any more, the one who was afraid of her own shadow. He was seeing me as – well, I didn't want to think what went through his mind when he looked at me.

I had forgotten about the roll. Now I picked up a slice of ham with the flat of the knife and added it to the cheese. Never mind about the salad; I just wanted to end the conversation before I died of shame. I was afraid to imagine what Julius thought, whether he was even halfway to believing what Kai was saying.

'Nothing happened,' I said in a low voice.

'Steffi, I'm not poking my nose in.' He didn't say whether

he believed me, I noticed. 'I'm just warning you – as a friend. Kai's got a big mouth.'

I put the finished roll into a paper bag. 'Two euros,' I said to the row of pastries under the glass. I was afraid to look at Julius again.

A minute later the bell jingled and the door swung shut after him as he left the bakery. I stood behind the counter with my cheeks flaming. I was afraid that I might start crying and I really did not want to do that.

Get a grip, I told myself severely. *Kai's a pig. OK. You knew that already. He thought you were going to give him what he wanted, like all his other girlfriends probably do, and you didn't, and now he's getting his own back*. I swallowed, blinking back tears. *Don't react. Don't even think about it. In a week it will have blown over.*

But I was wrong, because the next week Frau Kessel came to call.

CHAPTER TWENTY-SEVEN

She came on the Monday, and I wondered afterwards whether, in her sharp-eyed way, she had noticed that that was one of the days when I was not in the bakery but over at the college in Kall.

Before she came, I had really started to think that perhaps my life might drop back into its old groove. I had met with the others on Saturday night, but it had rained so heavily all weekend that there was no question of any further trips to Rote Gertrud's house, whatever they may have liked. The track along the Eschweiler Tal would be brown and sticky with mud, as alluring as a strip of flypaper.

If I had worried about how Jochen would behave around me, I needn't have bothered. He spoke to me only when necessary, but there was nothing in his manner which would have alerted the others to any possible resentment towards me. He didn't try to get me alone to renew his request either.

Of Kai von Jülich I saw absolutely nothing. He didn't come into the bakery and I didn't even see the gleaming red car in the town. The absence of any news about him was reassuring, however. I had still not made up my mind whether to try to get back to Gertrud's house on my own to remove the curse, but it seemed that nothing had come of it anyway. If it had been Kai who had dropped dead, his magnificent features buried in a plate of cherry streusel, it was inconceivable that the news would not be all over town.

When I came back from college I was not thinking about Kai; I was thinking about the bakery, and my parents, and wondering whether there would ever be a solution to the problem, one that would leave us all happy. I took my mother's indignation and *Well, miss, I hope you're pleased with yourself* less seriously than my father's tired face and calm request that I should *think about it*. It seemed wrong to hurt two people for the sake of one, yet I could not bring myself to say that I would give up all my dreams.

As I came in through the front door of the bakery, swinging my bag off my shoulder, the first thing I saw was Achim Zimmer lurking by the door to the corridor which led to the kitchen and flat. He was partly obscured by a screen covered with swathes of pale green chiffon and artificial creepers which hid the indecorous sight of the door from the cafe users, but he was instantly recognizable from the baker's whites he wore. He stood out like a member of the backstage crew who has accidentally stumbled on to the stage in the middle of a play.

It was never a pleasure to see Achim; passing through the kitchen on the days he was there was like crossing a field with a bull in it. Aside from the general feeling of dislike which welled up inside me whenever I saw him, there was something about the way he was standing that aroused little prickles of suspicion in my mind. His posture was furtive and I guessed that this meant something undesirable for someone.

Achim must have heard the bell over the front door

jingling, because his head turned my way and a slow smile spread over his heavy features. He looked me up and down very deliberately. Achim's habit of eyeing me up was never pleasant; the way his gaze seemed to slither all over me had all the charm of walking close behind a muck spreader. Today, however, there was something especially nasty about it, a smug knowingness which seemed to glisten out of every pore of his pallid skin.

I saw from the corner of my eye that my mother was a metre or two away, on the other side of the screen, talking to someone I could not see. It was probably her presence which prevented Achim from saying anything to me, though it did not prevent him from giving me a lascivious wink. After that he lounged through the door into the corridor and vanished from sight.

I was in no hurry to follow him. Instead I lingered in the cafe, thinking that if I spent a few moments greeting my mother, by the time I went into the corridor Achim would have retreated into the kitchen like a slimy marine creature hauling its tentacles back into a crevice in the rock.

My mother, however, seemed very unwilling to talk, or even to catch my eye. This could not be because she was overwhelmed with customers, since it looked as though the person she was talking to was one of only two visitors to the cafe. The other was a corpulent woman of about seventy whom I recognized as Frau Schneider, a neighbour of Timo's. She had a large cup of coffee and a slice of plum streusel in front of her, but she wasn't taking any notice of either. Instead she was leaning forward with an avid expression on her face, doing her best to listen in to my mother's conversation.

This instantly piqued my curiosity. I had been a denizen

of Bad Münstereifel long enough to know that this meant something significant was occurring, some new name was being painted on to the glorious roll of characters who featured in the town's oral history. I slowed my pace as I approached the spot where my mother stood.

Now she turned around and saw me, and a look of dismay crossed her face. She took a step back and, as she did so, I saw that the customer with whom she had been speaking was Frau Kessel. My mother's gaze went from me to Frau Kessel and back again, and then, puzzlingly, I saw it drop to my midriff.

I looked down automatically, wondering whether I had spilt something down myself, but could see nothing. When I looked up, my mother had turned back to Frau Kessel.

'I think I should prepare your bill, Frau Kessel,' she was saying.

Her voice was very cold and hard, which struck me as odd. At home with my father and me, my mother could be acid-tongued, but with the customers she was always determinedly polite and charming, even with the ones who complained about everything, like Frau Kessel.

Frau Kessel was peering past my mother, her gimlet eyes glittering behind her spectacles. It was impossible not to shrivel under that gaze, like an ant under a magnifying glass in the sun. I recalled the last time we had spoken, the way she had grasped my arm with her skinny claw. The impulse to flee overcame my curiosity. I nodded vaguely at the pair of them and made for the door. To my eternal relief there was no Achim on the other side. Evidently he had vanished into the kitchen, so I was able to escape up the stairs to the flat unnoticed.

I dumped my bag just inside my room and went into the kitchen to scavenge something to eat. I was searching the fridge when I heard the flat door open and close. A moment later there were footsteps and my mother came into the kitchen. She had such a peculiar look on her face that I straightened up and stared at her.

'Who's looking after the cafe?' I asked.

'I've closed it,' said my mother.

I gaped at her. This was completely unheard of.

'Frau Schneider?' I said.

'Gone,' said my mother tersely. 'Sit down.'

I knew I was in trouble, so I elected to sit in one of the chairs on the outside of the table, thinking that if I slid on to the bench jammed up against the wall, I would be trapped with little chance of escape. My mother manoeuvred herself opposite me on to the bench. In her green dirndl and with her face puckered with some disturbing emotion, she looked like Snow White catapulted into middle age and weighed down with worldly cares.

She didn't bother with the niceties, coming straight to the point.

'Steffi, Frau Kessel has just informed me not only that you are pregnant, but that Kai von Jülich has left the town because of it.'

CHAPTER TWENTY-EIGHT

I felt a wave of shock so strong that it was like nausea. I leaned forward, elbows on the table, hands clamped to my face, covering my open mouth. For about a minute I was completely incapable of saying anything.

I think my mother had the sense to realize that Frau Kessel's pronouncements could not always be taken as gospel, but my silence began to alarm her. Her face seemed to sag with the accumulation of her fears, fears that Frau Kessel was not only telling the truth but also going to proceed to tell it to everyone she knew.

'Steffi . . .' she began.

'She's lying,' I blurted out.

I was horrified to see an expression on my mother's face that I recognized as relief. Surely she had not really entertained the idea that what Frau Kessel had told her was true?

'She says she saw you with him,' said my mother.

'She did,' I spluttered, torn between a feeling of towering indignation and the insane impulse to laugh.

'Are you seeing him?'

'No,' I said instantly. I saw my mother open her mouth to question this and added, 'We just went out once.'

I looked at my mother and saw that peculiar look on her

face again. She opened her mouth and then closed it again without saying anything, but the air around us was thick with unarticulated questions which hung over us like poison gas.

'Mum,' I said firmly, 'I didn't sleep with him.'

'I wouldn't dream of asking,' she said hastily, but she didn't look me in the eyes.

'Frau Kessel is just an old . . .' *Bitch*, I was going to say, but I remembered it was my mother I was talking to.

'I know,' said my mother. She put out a hand across the table towards me. 'So there's nothing you want to tell me?'

'No!' I almost screamed. Now I was not just indignant, I was beginning to feel very anxious. If my own mother was carrying on like this, what about all the other people into whose ears Frau Kessel would inevitably pour her poisonous suggestions? I made an effort to lower my voice. 'Look, Mum, I'm not pregnant. I only went out with him once and I'm not seeing him again. In fact I haven't seen him since we went out, so I've no idea why he's left town, but it's got nothing to do with me.' I looked at her pleadingly. 'Now, can we forget about it?'

My mother sat looking at me for several moments, her face grave and thoughtful. I had never seen her look so old. I saw how the grey at the roots of her blonde hair drained the colour from her cheeks, how the corners of her mouth turned down, giving her whole face a melancholy look. At last she said, 'No . . . I don't think so.'

'*Mum* –'

'Steffi!' I saw her face crumple. 'I can't go through this again.' She put a hand to her cheek, rubbing at the skin, as though she were suffering the worst migraine of her life. 'I don't want to see you get hurt, like Magdalena did.'

Now I was staring at her. My parents rarely mentioned Magdalena's departure from the town. It wasn't some kind of *never darken my door again I no longer have a daughter* type of thing. I had the feeling it was simply too painful, a wound that neither of them wanted to reopen.

I was still at the primary school when she went, but even now I remembered her as a teenager, fair-haired like myself and my mother, though her smiling face was becoming blurred in my memory with the passage of time, as an old photograph fades in the light. I suppose when she first left I must have pestered my parents to know why and where she had gone, how long she would be away, whether she would ever come back – but somewhere along the line I had understood that the questions would never be answered, that my parents would prefer me not to ask them at all. My sister had been transformed into an absence; I had become an only child. In time curiosity had faded into a kind of sad emptiness whenever I thought about my sister.

How would it have been, I sometimes wondered, if Magdalena had stayed? If I had had an older sister waiting there for me at the school gates when the boys in my class followed me out, calling me names because they knew I was too quiet and shy to fight back? If there had been someone to share the long afternoons after school, when both my parents were downstairs in the bakery and the hands of the kitchen clock seemed to creep around so slowly as I sat at the table, struggling my way through my homework on my own?

Later, when I was older and the memories of my sister had become fainter, until she was little more than an idea, I had even felt a twinge of resentment. If Magdalena were still here, I would not be the one facing a lifetime making *Florentiner* and *Plunderteilchen*. But by then I had almost given up speculating why and where my sister had gone; it was news to me that someone had hurt her.

I frowned. 'What happened to Magdalena?'

'Frau Kessel,' said my mother bitterly. 'That woman is a menace. A few hundred years ago they would have tried her for a witch and serve her right.' If my mother saw me react to the word *witch* she gave no sign of it. 'She happened to come into the bakery a couple of mornings in a row and saw Magdalena looking unwell. In fact I think Magdi had to go out once when she was serving her.'

I'm not surprised. She'd make anyone sick to the stomach, I thought privately.

'The next thing we knew, people were asking us if it was true that Magdalena was expecting. Frau Kessel had put two and two together and decided that Magdalena had morning sickness, and instead of keeping her surmises to herself she'd gone and retailed them all over town.' Now that my mother had decided to tell me what had happened, the floodgates opened. 'She sees sex and babies wherever she looks, the dried-up old baggage. Sticking her nose in where it's not wanted.'

'Magdalena left because of *Frau Kessel*?' I asked.

My mother nodded wearily.

'But why?' I said. 'Couldn't she just tell people it wasn't true? And anyway, whatever they'd said, if she had just waited, it would have been obvious it wasn't true.'

For a moment my mother didn't reply. She just sat there staring at the table, as though there were some universal truth hidden in the pattern on the plasticized cloth. I looked at her and was appalled to see that her eyes were brimming with tears.

Then she said, 'But it *was* true, that was the thing.'

I was dumbfounded. 'It was true? She really *was* pregnant?'

'Yes.' My mother looked at me now and I saw more than grief in her eyes; there was anguish. 'She was . . . and that old – that old *bitch* guessed it.' The hand which lay on the table curled into a fist. 'She guessed it right away, even though Magdi wasn't showing. And she couldn't keep it to herself. It was too good a story, and what did she care whose life she ruined by telling it?'

'But –' I was struggling with this new piece of information. 'But, Mum, it's not a crime to have a kid before you're married. Maybe it was, back when Frau Kessel was born, in the Dark Ages. But now . . . couldn't Magdalena just have ignored what people said? I mean, they couldn't *do* anything to her.'

'They could make her life very difficult,' said my mother. 'They could make it unbearable.' She gave a strangled cough and I realized that she was trying to choke back a sob. 'And I . . .' she began. 'I didn't know what to do. I know I didn't react the way I should have. I just kept thinking about what people were saying – and I was angry with Magdi for letting it happen. I shouldn't have been, but I was. Angry, and scared for her too. We rowed all the time.' My mother put her head in her hands. 'Your father was angry too. He kept asking her why she hadn't been more careful, why she had to do that in the first place. Said she was too young to get married – and anyway, the boy wasn't the sort of husband you'd want. And Magdi just got quieter and quieter and then she wouldn't talk to us at all.' Now she really was weeping. 'It was our fault she went. My fault. She needed help and I just shouted at her.'

I sat for a moment and watched my mother crying. It was almost too much to take in. My mother very rarely said she was wrong about anything; generally she went through life with a brisk air of self-righteousness. Now I saw that this was a shell, a facade she had erected to conceal feelings that she hardly dared acknowledge to herself. I felt a terrible pity for her, even at the same time as I felt a growing sense of indignation on my sister's behalf.

'So she went away to have the baby?' I asked.

My mother looked up at me with red eyes. 'This is the thing, Steffi. She didn't keep the baby.'

I stared at her, stunned. 'You mean . . .'

My mother nodded. 'She had a termination.'

My eyes were irresistibly drawn to the wall behind her, to the crucifix which hung there. I could barely conceive of the strain it must have put on the whole family, trying to reconcile what Magdalena had done with the line the Church would inevitably have taken. If the news had got out – which it almost certainly would have done when Magdalena's pregnancy, reported all over town by Frau Kessel and undenied by our family, had failed to progress – her life would not have been worth living. My sister had had a choice: to continue with a pregnancy she clearly had not wished for or planned, or to terminate it and have everyone in the town know it. In either case she would be torn to shreds by the town gossips, led by Frau Kessel. And my parents, panicking, had not supported her. And so . . .

'She just couldn't stay,' my mother said. 'She left. Left the town and left us.'

I looked at her haggard face and I could not find it in my heart to blame her. Whatever my mother's failings, it was clear she had paid for them tenfold.

As for Frau Kessel, I felt a hatred so pure that it was almost cold. *She* had wrought this evil in all our lives. If she had managed to keep her prurient suppositions to herself, Magdalena could have made her own decision in her own time; she need never have been hounded out of the town she had grown up in. My parents need never have suffered the pain of losing a daughter as completely as though they had seen her laid in her grave and I might have had a sister there throughout my lonely childhood.

Frau Kessel had not just wrecked our past, I thought; she had ruined the present and all our futures too. If it were not for her, Magdalena might still have been here in the bakery, mixing up dough for *Bauernbrot* and sprinkling poppy seeds on the rolls, while I, like the younger son in a fairy tale, had gone out to seek my fortune in some unnamed place, with nothing much in my pockets but no weight of expectation on my shoulders either, and no fear of letting down the ones I loved. The old witch had cursed us as effectively as if she had really laid a spell on us.

I suppose my mother finally noticed that I was silent. Perhaps she thought I was shocked, or abashed. Petrified at the power the old lady wielded. At any rate, she reached over and grasped my hand, her expression urgent.

'Steffi . . . it was wrong, what Frau Kessel did to Magdalena. I won't ever forgive her. *Never*,' she said with bitter emphasis. 'But . . .' She paused. 'It wasn't right to let her hound someone out of the town. We let her win. I'm not doing that again.'

'I can't just ignore it,' I said furiously. 'Not if she's going round telling people *that*.' I was imagining myself in the cafe, clad in the loathed green dirndl, serving coffee with cream and filled rolls. Everyone's eyes dropping to the front of the dress, as my mother's had, speculating. *Is it true? How far on is she? Did Kai von Jülich really have to leave town over it?* Perhaps some particularly prurient soul would lean right over the counter to get a good look.

'I'm not telling you to ignore it,' said my mother. Her blue eyes were bright, their expression forceful under her knitted brows. 'We have to fight her. This has gone on long enough. She can't go around interfering with other people's lives – ruining them – like this.'

Why not? I thought bitterly. I supposed Frau Kessel was in her mid-eighties now. If her poisonous career had begun when she was a teenager, that meant it had spanned over six decades. Nothing would stop her except the Grim Reaper, and even then I fully expected that she would be dragged off to the Underworld still spouting stories about her neighbours and preparing to sneak on them to Satan. *She ruined my sister's life*, I thought. *She made the town Magdalena grew up in too hot to handle. She broke my parents' hearts. And if she can, she's going to do it again – only this time it will be worse, because everyone will remember Magdalena and the whole thing will be dragged up again.*

I looked at my mother's face, at the grief etched into every line, and I wished with all my heart that I could do something to save her from this pain. But I was not sassy like Hanna, nor arrogant like Kai von Jülich. *Fight Frau*

Kessel? How? I simply lacked the weapons for a fight.

Perhaps it was the very thought of weapons that did it. An image formed in my mind, so sharp and true it had an almost photographic quality. A dark canopy of trees, dripping wet and rotten, and under them the grey and crumbling bulk of a ruined house, its walls blotched and stained with lichen. And through the jagged holes in the walls, something briefly glimpsed, a flash of brilliant colour as vivid as flame. The red-headed witch, flitting about her former home.

I don't think my mind was entirely made up then; that didn't happen until later. But something changed all the same. Now I knew: I *did* have the weapons.

CHAPTER TWENTY-NINE

Over the next few days I thought of almost nothing else but Frau Kessel and the question of whether to curse her. The weather was bad – days on end of rain running down the bakery windows in streams – so there were few customers and plenty of time to ponder the question.

She was a thoroughly malicious old wretch, that was for certain. In small towns you expect a certain amount of gossip, but Frau Kessel took things to an entirely new level. To compare ordinary street-corner chat to her malevolent interference was like comparing a sniffle to the bubonic plague. I wondered how many other lives she had derailed with her pernicious meddling. I remembered the very first time my friends and I had been up to Gertrud's house in the woods and Max had hatched his plan to kill off Klara Klein by magic. *It'd be a public service*, Jochen had said. He had been joking, but now things were deadly serious. I thought that if someone were to make Frau Kessel vanish, it really *would* be a public service.

The compulsion to try was as strong as if Rote Gertrud herself had been standing there unseen at my side, whispering her poison into my ear. In folk tales, goodness so often goes with purity and simplicity; evil is as slippery and persuasive as a lawyer. *You can't curse people on someone else's say-so*, ran the argument. *They might be lying, or mistaken. They might have some crooked motive of their own. But you* know *Frau Kessel is a blight on the town and the lives of everyone in it. It has to be done. You know it.*

But the clincher came on Thursday night, when Hanna called. My parents had actually gone out, a relatively rare occurrence since my father was always up so early, and about half an hour after they left, Hanna dropped by.

'Hi,' she said, as I opened the street door, and I saw her gaze flicker up and down me. She was doing her best not to be obvious, but she couldn't resist looking, just as my mother hadn't been able to. It was ludicrous. Even if I had been pregnant there wouldn't be anything to see yet. I felt like screaming.

'Hi,' I said, biting my lip. I stood back to let her in.

She didn't waste any time. As soon as we were both upstairs in my parents' stuffy-looking living room, she said, 'What's going on with you and Kai?'

'There's nothing between me and Kai,' I said, sitting on the arm of the overstuffed sofa. I didn't feel like sinking back into the soft cushions. I felt safer perched up here; I could make a run for it if necessary.

Hanna leaned against the wall, staring at me through the untidy dark hair which flopped over her eyes. 'I came over to warn you,' she said eventually. 'People are saying . . .' She hesitated.

'That I'm pregnant and Kai had to leave town because of it?' I finished wearily.

Hanna nodded. 'That and . . . well, that you . . .' She

grimaced, not wanting to come out with it. 'You threw yourself at him. You did it on purpose.'

'That's a lie,' I choked out.

'Calm down,' said Hanna, pushing herself away from the wall and coming towards me slowly, as though I were a dangerous animal. In truth I felt like one: had Frau Kessel been before me at that moment I would have flown at her.

'I'm not calming down. It's Frau Kessel. *I'll kill her*. She's got away with this for too long. If it were you, you wouldn't *calm down*.'

The floodgates were open now. It all came pouring out in a tear-soaked tangle of words, half sobbed and half shouted.

When my rage had almost burned itself out, and I was beginning to sniff and hiccup, Hanna said in a quiet voice, 'Did you mean what you said? That you wanted to kill Frau Kessel?'

'You mean – hex her, like Klara Klein?' I said, despising the fake innocence I heard in my own voice – as though the same idea had not already occurred to me.

Hanna nodded. 'Why not? She deserves it.'

'If I thought it would really work . . .' I said. But I shook my head. 'This is nuts.'

'Why is it nuts?' said Hanna. 'It's always worked before – for you, anyway.'

It hasn't, I almost said. *Kai von Jülich is still wandering around out there, alive and well, after I wished death on him – at least I suppose he is*. But Hanna didn't know that; nobody else did.

'Hanna? If we do it, I don't want the others to know.'

'Why not?' she asked.

157

Because Jochen's already asked me to hex his stepfather and I said no. I chewed my lip.

'It'll be a pain getting to Gertrud's house without Max's car,' said Hanna.

'I know, I just . . . think it would be better if we didn't tell too many people.'

'Hmmm.' Hanna's voice was sceptical. 'Let's just tell Max, then. Nobody else.'

'He'll never keep his mouth shut,' I objected, but I was weakening.

'Oh yes, he will. If he thinks we're going to try to kill off Frau Kessel, he'll keep his beak shut. He won't be able to resist – just to see if it actually works.'

I thought about it for a little longer, but really it was a foregone conclusion. We were going to the witch's house once more and I was going to see for myself if the magic would really work again. I wanted Frau Kessel gone – for good.

CHAPTER THIRTY

Later that night, long after my parents had come home and taken themselves off to bed, I lay awake in my own room, thinking. I thought about Max and Hanna, and wondered whether they would really keep their mouths shut if we did go back to the ruined house and hex Frau Kessel. I thought about Frau Kessel herself, about that sweet old-ladyish face which concealed such malice within, like a ripe peach with black rot at its heart. But mostly I thought about my sister, Magdalena.

Something was bothering me about my memories of Magdalena, something which nagged away at the back of my mind like a forgotten appointment. I remembered the day we went to Rote Gertrud's house together, pushing our way uphill through overgrown vegetation. It must have been summer, then. With everything grown up so high it was not as easy to reach the ruined house as it was during the winter months, especially not if you were accompanied by an unwilling primary school child, who was probably shorter than a lot of the overhanging bushes and also very reluctant to walk so far uphill. Magdalena must really have wanted to go there. Why?

I racked my brains, trying to squeeze out every nuance

from the scant memories. But I could not remember Magdalena saying anything to me. I supposed that she would not have confided in me anyway, given that she had been old enough to vote whereas I was still running around in ankle socks.

I remembered seeing the witch's house. Magdalena had been wearing something yellow, something the bright colour of sunflower petals – a long shirt or a light rain jacket, I thought – and it had stood out brilliantly against the dingy grey of the walls. I remembered standing just outside the house, looking in, as my sister moved about inside it. I hadn't noticed the scrawled writing on the walls then, or if I had it had interested me so little that I had forgotten it.

What had she been doing? I turned over restlessly in my bed. Trying to pick out anything useful from the memory was like watching a scrap of old film over and over again, hoping to see something new in it in spite of the blurs and the scratches. I had a vague feeling that Magdalena had been in the far corner, the furthest one from the jagged hole which now represented the door of the house. What she had been doing, or why, escaped me.

Why does anyone go there? I asked myself, and then the answer popped into my head, so simple and obvious that I wondered why I had never seen it before. Why did anyone go up to Gertrud's house? Magdalena had been making a wish.

I wondered whether she too had had the idea of taking her revenge on Frau Kessel, or indeed on anyone else – the father of the unwanted baby, perhaps. But now I was speculating; as far as Magdalena's intentions went, my memory was an utter blank. There was not even the ghost of a recollection.

I rolled on to my back again and gazed up into the dark, eyes wide open but not seeing, watching instead the memory of a decade ago, of bright yellow and mouldering grey. *I'll look*, I told myself. *When I go back to Gertrud's house with Max and Hanna, I'll go to that corner and look.*

CHAPTER THIRTY-ONE

This time I insisted on going to Rote Gertrud's house in broad daylight, which meant waiting for Sunday afternoon. Max was not happy; being his usual impulsive self, he would have preferred to go as soon as Hanna had called him on Thursday evening, regardless of the oncoming night. Then he argued for Saturday, but Hanna couldn't come that day, and I wasn't prepared to go alone with Max. Since the incident with Kai I had been prey to all sorts of morbid suspicions, not helped by the fact that Achim Zimmer's insinuating manner had been cranked up another notch, until he seemed marinated in his own slime like an octopus in its own ink. I was afraid that someone – and by *someone* I was thinking chiefly of Frau Kessel – would see me out and about with yet another man and draw their own conclusions.

I was also afraid of what Kai might have told Max about me. Max and I had met each other when we were both in kindergarten and in theory he should have known me well enough to realize that I was not the femme fatale of Bad Münstereifel. All the same, I remembered that look he had given me the day he saw me feeding the ducks, the broad grin showing all those gleaming white teeth, and I thought that I would not like to stake my peace of mind on it. For once I stuck to my guns and insisted on Sunday afternoon.

Two days passed between declaring my resolve to Hanna and actually going to Gertrud's house to put it into action. It was long enough for me to have changed my mind, to let common sense talk me down from the ledge I had climbed on to. But there were forces driving me towards action, as surely as a savage dog nipping at a sheep's ankles can drive it towards a cliff edge. I would be serving in the cafe and someone would come in, an old woman of Frau Kessel's age or thereabouts, and while I was serving her coffee and cakes she would be looking me up and down with a speculative eye, wondering. Or I would step outside to clear one of the tables and see a green-clad figure at the end of the street, and whether it was Frau Kessel or not my stomach would lurch horribly. Was she talking about me, even at this very minute, spreading her poison through the town like a terrorist dropping toxins into the water supply? I would glance at my mother, neat in her dirndl, and wonder if it was my imagination that she looked suddenly older, more tired.

On Saturday night there were only four of us hanging around the snack bar. Izabela and Timo had gone off somewhere together, in a break from our long-established habit. He had never done that with me, I reflected rather sadly. It was not that I envied Izabela her catch, but it was dispiriting to think that in all our three years he had never been that desperate to get *me* alone.

That left Max, Hanna, Jochen and me, and since Jochen was the only one excluded from our plans for Sunday, the evening dragged. Max, Hanna and I were unable to talk freely and Jochen was still offhand with me. It was a relief when the evening was over and I was able to go home.

The following afternoon at three we were struggling uphill through the woods once more. It had not rained again but the ground was still spongy underfoot. I was determined to keep up with Max, although his legs were longer than mine; they scissored across the rough ground with the savage speed of a tailor's shears hacking through cloth. My heart was thumping wildly and I was horribly out of breath, but I forced myself to keep pace with him. I was imagining what would happen if either he or Hanna made it into Gertrud's house before I did and opened the box first. The inevitable questions. Max's grin when he discovered my failed attempt to wipe out Kai von Jülich, which he surely would. Kai had left, not died, so I supposed my message would still be there in the box, untouched. I picked up speed.

'Whoa,' said Max, but I ignored him.

When I finally stumbled into the ruined house my lungs felt as though they were about to burst, but I didn't stop to catch my breath. I was already on my knees, fumbling the little carved box open. I thought I would grab the scrap of paper with my last wish scrawled on it and tear it into tiny pieces, or even swallow it if necessary; anything so long as Max didn't read it. I rifled through the papers, raising my eyebrows as I read Max's wish, wincing as I read Jochen's. But my wish had gone. I counted the pieces of paper and there were only five. I looked down, wondering if the sixth had fluttered out, but there was nothing to see. On that brown and mulchy floor a piece of white paper would have stood out like a patch of snow.

OK, keep calm. I counted the pieces of paper again. *Five.* I stood up, the box in my hands, and looked all around me. No paper on the floor, not unless you included a chocolate bar wrapper, torn and faded.

'What's the matter, Steffi?' asked Max, with that taunting grin on his face.

Sometimes I almost hated him. I imagined him opening his closed hand to show me that he had had the missing piece of paper all the time. I would have liked to fly at him with my nails, but instead I waited, frowning and chewing my lip. He did nothing. His hands were empty.

'What's up?' said Hanna in a more sympathetic voice, nudging my arm.

'Nothing,' I said. 'My wish has gone, that's all.' I shrugged, trying to look unconcerned.

'You got your wish,' said Hanna.

'Yes,' I said, not wanting to explain. Kai had gone, that was the main thing, and nobody needed to know that I had wished him away.

I gazed up at the sky through the open space where there had once been rafters and tiles. Far above a red kite was drifting lazily on the warm air currents, searching the ground for prey. I watched it follow a great arc across the visible sky and then disappear over the treetops to the north-east.

'Come on, then,' said Max, close to my ear.

'In a minute,' I said, still looking upwards. I was thinking that I would have liked to fly away like that. People imagined witches turning into cats or hares; I thought I would have given anything to soar away into the formless spaces of the sky, to look back over my shoulder and see my old life dwindling away in the distance.

'What's the matter?' said Max mockingly. 'You have to *feel the power* or something?'

'Shut up, Max,' said Hanna, but it was almost a reflex, like slapping a biting insect. She didn't sound interested.

I walked slowly around the interior of the house, putting a hand out so that my fingertips brushed the rough surface of the wall as I passed. I heard Max mutter something under his breath and Hanna telling him to be quiet. She sounded slightly indignant that he dared to interrupt me. *She's really getting into it*, I thought. *She thinks I'm communing with Rote Gertrud or something.* I didn't react. I walked on, stepping over a fallen chunk of masonry, kicking aside a cluster of twigs. Hanna was right in a way; I *was* looking for something, but not an ephemeral connection with the dead witch. I was looking for my sister's wish.

I knew the chances of finding it weren't good. There were so many messages scrawled on those walls and I was relying on a memory that was a decade old to tell me where to look. In some places the scratched words were easy enough to read, but in others they were smothered with lichen or moss. Even if I found Magdalena's wish, would I recognize it?

I worked my way around to the far corner. The inscriptions were well preserved here; the tottering chimney stack had offered a little protection from the corrosive effect of the elements. *S.A., come back*, I read. *D.N., love. C.L., die.* Someone had added *FUC* before giving up.

It was impossible to link any of the messages to my sister. The way the letters had to be scored into the stone meant that they were composed of little slashes, like Chinese characters. Handwriting was rendered unrecognizable. Unless

Magdalena had written an entire sentence and signed it with her full name, how would I ever know which inscription was hers? I was tempted to give up.

Then I saw it. It was almost impossible to miss: a large and deeply scored K. Whoever had scratched that on to the stone had meant it to be seen. I leaned closer, touching the wall gently with my fingers. *E.K.*, ran the inscription, *die*. And then a date, half legible, ending with *8.1998*.

Of course I knew what Frau Kessel's first name was, although I thought there was probably nobody in Bad Münstereifel who dared use it, not since Frau Kessel's great friend and ally old Frau Koch had died. If I guessed rightly, the complete message, had it been unabbreviated, would have read: *Eva Kessel, die by 31.8.1998*.

Had my sister carved these characters into the stone? Had she struggled up here to the ruined house, pregnant as she was, dragging her unwilling little sister with her? It was impossible to be sure. The initials might refer to some other E.K., though in my heart of hearts I knew they didn't. Even if my sister hadn't carved these letters, there must have been so many people with cause to hate Frau Kessel, the troll who lurked at the town's heart, crunching up the raw and bloody bones of other people's lives. Someone had wished her to the Devil and now so would I.

I stood up and turned to face Max.

'Let's get on with it,' I said.

CHAPTER THIRTY-TWO

On Monday morning I had college again and so it must have been on Tuesday or Wednesday that I heard what had come of my wish. I was working in the bakery as usual. It was shortly after nine in the morning and there were no customers in the seating area yet, but a succession of people had dropped by to pick up filled rolls to take to school or to work with them.

Even before the police car appeared I heard the siren; it was a warm morning and the windows were open. The car came out of a side turning further up the street, blue lights flashing, and turned towards the south end of the town. A couple of middle-aged women who were standing chatting on the bridge turned to watch it go.

In that moment I knew. I took automatically the coins a customer was holding out to me; I was already moving round the counter, trying to get a better look, drawn as though by magnetism to the bakery window.

The blue lights were still visible at the far end of the street. As I watched, the police car veered to the right, vanishing behind the old brewery, and I knew that it was heading up the Orchheimer Strasse. I thought I could already detect a subtle change in the daily routine. The flow of pedestrians was moving south towards the Orchheimer Tor, the great gate set in the medieval walls which surrounded the town, instead of northwards towards the railway station. Something was happening.

I wove my way through the tables to the bakery door, which was propped open, and stepped out into the street.

Slow down, I told myself. *Don't make people look at you. Don't give anyone a reason to suspect.* My heart was thumping so wildly that I was afraid I might faint. I forced myself to walk slowly.

When I reached the Salzmarkt, where the Orchheimer Strasse began, I saw little groups of people moving up the street in the direction of Frau Kessel's house. Some of them went hesitantly, as though ashamed to be seen nose-poking; others were openly hurrying to get a better view. I could see only one person who was coming the other way, striding out against the flow: *Hanna*. She saw me and speeded up. When she reached me, she swung around, taking my arm, and began to walk with me, back the way she had come. She leaned over and spoke into my ear in a rapid whisper.

'You're unbelievable, Steffi. You've done it. You've actually done it. I just can't believe it.'

Her words confirmed what I had already guessed, that Frau Kessel was dead, that someone had discovered her body. All the same I felt a dizzying lurch in my stomach. The skin on my face and my bare arms felt hot. As I let Hanna lead me up the street I was expecting people to turn and stare at me, to point the finger. *There she goes, she's the one . . .*

But nobody took the slightest notice. When we got to the top of the street they were standing there in a ragged semi-circle by the police car, their faces turned to the front of a building we all knew well: Frau Kessel's house. On one of the wooden timbers which ran horizontally across the front of the house were the words *God protect this house from evil*, picked out in white paint. The irony of this was wasted on the onlookers, whose gaze was riveted to the policeman who stood, grim-faced, by the open front door.

The mood was sombre. I can't believe that there were many in the town who had any affection for Frau Kessel, but everyone knew her. No doubt if they examined their consciences quite a few of her fellow citizens had wished her dead on any number of occasions. But to wish it was one thing; to see the wish translated into reality was quite another. Whispered rumours rippled through the crowd like seismic shocks. I could pick out isolated words. *Dead*, said someone. *Murder*, said someone else.

I was beginning to feel very hot indeed, as though I was running a temperature. The atmosphere suddenly seemed suffocating. I was breathing in as hard as I could, sucking in the warm air, but I didn't seem to be getting enough oxygen. The edges of my vision were dappled with little dark spots. I swayed on my feet.

'Steffi?' said Hanna's voice close by. I felt her hauling on my arm.

There was a little pavement cafe close to Frau Kessel's house. Hanna dragged me over to one of the metal chairs and made me sit down. I put my elbows on the tabletop and rested my head in my hands.

'Are you OK?' asked Hanna in a low voice. I felt her hand touch my shoulder. 'Steffi?'

I shook my head, hiding behind the strands of fair hair which fell across my face. I didn't want to look her in the eye, not yet. I knew what she was thinking, I could hear it in the urgent tone of her voice. She was afraid that I was going to give something away, that someone would notice me collapsing and get suspicious. I thought that if I managed to keep looking down at the pattern of scratches on the tabletop and avoided everyone's eyes I had a better chance of holding myself together.

Eventually I began to feel a little calmer. I thought I might not faint after all, although I still had a slightly queasy feeling in the pit of my stomach. Hearing the sound of an engine, I looked up in time to see a car with fluorescent stripes down the sides and the word *Notarzt* emblazoned on the bonnet edging slowly through the Orchheimer Tor. The emergency doctor had arrived.

The crowd parted to let him through. I sat and watched him enter the house, without sharing any of the sense of anticipation that hung over the assembled watchers. I knew that there was nothing he could do for Frau Kessel apart from issue a death certificate. Still, I watched and waited like everyone else, feeling nauseous and guilty and strangely triumphant, and then guilty again, because I was pleased that someone had died.

Not *died*, I reminded myself. She had been *killed*. I fought down that sick feeling, a sensation which threatened to turn itself into actual vomiting. The unpleasant thought occurred to me that if I actually threw up here, in the street, on this bright sunny morning, it would only confirm the rumours about me. Frau Kessel didn't need to be here in person, catching people's sleeves and muttering in their ears; *morning sickness*, people would say to each other with significant looks.

A ripple ran through the crowd as the emergency doctor reappeared at the front door. He was a stolid-looking man, robust and square-shouldered, with a heavy-featured face that revealed little emotion. I guessed that whatever he had seen in the house, he had seen the like a thousand times before. He spoke quietly to the policeman, and his gaze flickered over the little groups of onlookers assembled outside the house, but he was giving nothing away. He went back to his car and got inside. Then, with the doors safely closed, he began to speak to someone on a mobile phone. An almost audible sigh of disappointment ran through the crowd.

I did not trust myself to stand up yet, so I stayed where I was and did my best to look as though I was not fighting to keep my breakfast down. The policeman standing outside Frau Kessel's house was Herr Wachtmeister Schumacher, I saw. His partner, Herr Wachtmeister Tondorf, was still recuperating after the heart attack he had had at Klara Klein's house. Herr Tondorf had a certain authority about him, despite his age, and if there was something he thought you didn't need to know he would have you turned around and walking off down the street with an amiable goodbye on your lips before you even realized you had been dismissed. Schumacher, on the other hand, was well known as a spineless creature. Frau Kessel, when she was alive, could have extracted information from him as easily as scooping a Weinberg snail out of its shell with a sharp-pronged fork. People were starting to converge on him and already his hands were up in a helpless *don't ask me* gesture. I felt almost sorry for him, in spite of my own preoccupations.

'*Scheisse*,' said Hanna close by my ear, and I looked around.

Julius Rensinghof was coming across the street towards me. The sunshine turned his hair into a blaze. Despite the early summer warmth he was wearing a long black coat which only accentuated his lanky build. His face was serious.

'What do we need *him* for?' muttered Hanna. She had been leaning over me, but now she straightened up and turned away, as though she did not want to face him.

I sighed, wishing that I could have turned away myself, but not daring to. Innocence has no reason to hide its face. I did my best to look him in the eyes.

'Steffi, are you OK?' was the first thing he said.

'Yes,' I said, trying to sound nonchalant. 'Why?'

'You don't look so good.'

'I'm . . . fine,' I said. 'It's just . . .'

'This?' He cocked his head towards the crowd standing outside Frau Kessel's house.

'No,' I said, too quickly and a little too loudly. 'I had to get up really early, that's all. Dad needed me to help in the bakery. I only had about three hours' sleep – I probably look like death.'

Shut up, I warned myself. *You're babbling*. I lapsed into silence, which was just as bad. It stretched out between us, a gulf ready to be filled by any number of interpretations.

Julius leaned down towards me, ignoring Hanna. 'Are you sure you're OK?'

I knew there was no way I could tell him what I had done, what had been going on. And yet I very nearly did. It was the way he asked me. He didn't speak to me as though I were still ten years old, as my parents so often seemed to do. He didn't speak to me as though I were a hopeless innocent either, as Max always did. And somehow I had the feeling that if I told him what the matter really was, if I told him about the witch's house and the curses and the fact that it was my fault that Little Klara had died with her face in a plate of cherry streusel, he wouldn't look at me the way Hanna did, as though the whole thing was some kind of gripping soap opera. Julius sounded as though he genuinely wanted to be sure that I was all right.

But there was something about Julius that made me feel even sicker about Frau Kessel's death than I already did. It wasn't just that he sounded as though he genuinely cared. It was the fact that he always seemed to see the best in me, to see something which others missed altogether. He remembered me singing at school and he thought there was a real possibility that I might stand up in front of strangers and sing to them too. He believed in me more than I believed in myself. I thought that when Julius looked at me he saw my better self, saw all that I could be.

But I knew that better self didn't exist, didn't I? I wasn't the person he thought I was, the shy girl trying to work up the courage to do what she wanted to do. I was a person who lurked about in the dank ruins of a place that no one in their right mind would visit, putting curses on people. I was either mad or dangerous, and I wasn't even sure which myself.

I ignored the sick feeling in the pit of my stomach. I made myself look at Julius, made myself look straight into his brown eyes and hold his gaze.

'I'm fine,' I lied. 'There's nothing wrong at all.'

CHAPTER THIRTY-THREE

When I cursed Frau Kessel, I really thought I wanted her to die. But within a week I was sorrier than I would ever have imagined possible.

In one sense the old woman's end made my burden lighter as it put an immediate stop to all the gossip about Steffi Nett, the baker's daughter who was cooking up something of her own beneath her dirndl apron. *That* little affair was swamped under the tsunami of talk about Frau Kessel's death, all other lesser topics being swept away like so much matchwood before the flood. When I slipped into a pew at the back of Sts Chrysanthus and Daria alongside my parents for Frau Kessel's funeral mass, nobody even gave me a second look.

I hadn't wanted to go to the mass. It seemed horribly hypocritical, since I had wished death on the old woman. The fact that this gave me something in common with perhaps ninety per cent of the other mourners was no consolation. But I could not get out of going without making a stand, which was alien to my nature, and drawing a lot of attention to myself, which was the last thing I wanted to do. I was the instigator of Frau Kessel's death, after all, and like all killers I was obliged to cover my tracks.

Like all killers. I supposed that, if you took Klara Klein's demise into account, I was now a serial killer. The thought was at once horrific and utterly unreal, and it was with me night and day, like a witch's familiar, keeping pace with me wherever I went, marking me out from other people. I would be standing behind the counter in the bakery, bagging up half a dozen rolls for a customer, and I would lose an entire minute, my consciousness dragged away to that ruined house in the woods and its unseen inhabitant. I would come back to myself to find the customer demanding their change for the third or fourth time, their expression indignant, or my mother elbowing past me to take charge.

More than once I thought I saw Frau Kessel in the street. I would gaze out of the bakery's side window and see someone fifty or a hundred metres away, an old woman with a fluff of bright white hair or someone dressed in that particular shade of dark green that Frau Kessel had always favoured, and I would feel a thrill of fear thinking that it was her. No wonder that so many legends told of murderers being haunted by their victims, I thought, wondering if I would go on seeing Frau Kessel for the rest of my life.

I hadn't expected the guilt. Frau Kessel was a menace, I told myself. Getting her out of the way was like putting down a dangerous dog before it could maul anyone else. And besides, it wasn't as though I had gone to her house with a shotgun and blasted her into eternity, edelweiss brooch and all. I had simply put in writing a wish that half the town must have made in their hearts at some time or another. None of this made me feel any better. I had wished someone dead and they had died. It was not as though I could claim to be shocked. It had worked with Klara Klein, hadn't it? It wasn't as though I could tell myself that the curse on Frau Kessel had just been a bit of fun. I had *expected* it to work.

My one comfort was the fact that it was now beyond Frau Kessel's power to hurt my family ever again, or to ruin any other lives. Now that that poisonous tongue was stilled forever, I thought the bounce might come back into my mother's step, my father might devote himself to his art in peace. What had been done to Magdalena could not be undone, but even if she never returned to the town for a single day, at least her ghost would not be dragged through the streets in disgrace.

I went into the room that had been Magdalena's and hid the five hundred euros in a slender-necked vase with an ugly orange glaze. It gave me some consolation to imagine 'discovering' the money very soon and giving it to my parents. There must be something good, I thought, in being able to offer them this small pleasure. And yet there was some indefinable barrier between us now, unseen and yet present. I had done things I could not tell them about – or at least wished them.

The details of Frau Kessel's death soon percolated throughout the town, in spite of the fact that a major junction box on the gossip network had been removed. There was a good deal of speculation and fantasy mixed in with the reports of what the police had found. The old woman had been found at the bottom of the staircase in her house. She had died of head injuries, presumably sustained in a fall from the top of the stairs. It was rumoured that she had been discovered in a great pool of blood. Some said that she had tried to write the name of her killer with it, but had expired after completing the first letter, which was variously reported as J, K and (bizarrely) X.

Nobody seemed to know for sure whether it really was murder or simply an accident, although Timo's aunt, who also lived in the Orchheimer Strasse, reported that the police had been in and out a number of times. On the last occasion they had been accompanied by a couple of men in plain clothes who might have been members of the *Kriminalpolizei*, come to investigate a crime scene. Of course, they might also have been relatives of Frau Kessel's, come to look over their inheritance, or estate agents come to value the dead woman's property. That was the trouble with getting your information from someone's aunt or cousin or best friend's cleaning lady's sister: it was well-nigh impossible to distinguish fact from fabrication.

As I moved listlessly around the cafe, setting down cups of coffee and slices of cheesecake in front of the customers, I heard a good deal of talk about it. I wondered what they would say if I suddenly blurted out the truth, although I knew I would never do it. Nobody would believe me. They would think I was mad, imagining some connection to a long-dead witch.

The guilt was bad enough. Far worse was the reaction from Max and the others.

I was alone in the flat, curled up on the sofa, when the phone rang. I picked it up and heard an all-too-familiar voice.

'Steffi?'

Jochen. My heart sank. 'Hi, Jochen. I can't really . . .' I was going to say, *I can't really talk now. I'm very busy*, but he interrupted me.

'I need to talk to you.'

'OK, but I really –'

'You killed Frau Kessel.'

'Shhhh!' I almost shrieked. 'Shut up.' My knuckles were white around the receiver, my mouth suddenly dry. 'Who told you that?'

'Who do you think? Max. You think you can keep something like that quiet for long?'

'He wasn't –' I was about to say, *He wasn't supposed to tell*, but I stopped short, realizing how that was going to sound. 'Look,' I said desperately, 'you can't talk about it. Someone might hear. Is there anyone else there?'

'No.' He sounded impatient. 'So how come you wouldn't do anything for me and now you've done this?'

'Listen, Jochen . . .'

'No, *you* listen, Steffi. You told me you wouldn't help me get rid of Udo. So what's this crap? It's OK to get rid of Frau Kessel, because she's pissed you off a few times, but you won't do anything about Udo?'

I didn't listen to any more. I didn't want to hang up only to have Jochen ring back two minutes later, even angrier, but I couldn't listen to his ranting either. I laid the receiver down next to the phone. I sat on the sofa, pulling my knees up so that I was almost curled into a ball, hugging myself, shivering. I put my fingers in my ears, so that my head was filled with the rushing of my own blood, but still I thought I could hear Jochen's shouting, as though he were drowning in it, being carried far away on its dark currents.

The next day it was Izabela. She didn't try ringing; perhaps she had heard how little success Jochen had had with that strategy. She turned up at the flat in the afternoon when

I was there on my own. As soon as I opened the front door I knew I was in trouble. There was the same old Izabela, with her pale clear skin and her dark hair falling across her face, but there was a strange intense look in her eyes, as though she had suddenly caught religion of a deeply evangelical brand. Before she was halfway into the flat she was speaking in a voice so fierce and rapid that it was like having a waterfall breaking over your head. *Just this one thing, Steffi*, she was saying, *just this one thing*, and I picked out from the torrent of words something about an elderly relative who was in such terrible pain, it would be a mercy to put them out of it, it would be a kind of release . . . In a way it was more horrible than Jochen's request that I kill off Udo, because perhaps it really would have been a merciful release for whoever it was, but I was hardly the person to decide, and besides, there are many reasons for wanting elderly relatives dead, not all of them kind ones. When I said no, Izabela was almost as angry as Jochen had been. After she had gone, I was terribly shaken. I had begun to realize my position. Now that I had finally and irrefutably proved my power the others wanted me to use it for them. They were no longer really interested in Rote Gertrud; now *I* was the witch.

Soon they were badgering me night and day. Timo called, Max called, both of them with *just one thing* they wanted me to wish for. Hanna hadn't asked for anything yet but it could only be a matter of time. She phoned twice and dropped in once too, seemingly just to chat, and I strongly suspected that she was simply adopting the more cautious strategy of gauging the right time to make her request. I began to feel trapped. They came to the bakery at all hours and on any excuse. If they couldn't come in person they telephoned, and if I didn't answer the landline they sent me texts. I switched my mobile phone off and put it at the bottom of a drawer, under stacks of T-shirts, but that didn't solve the problem. Now I would get home from college in Kall to find a cluster of tersely worded messages jotted down by my mother, and she began to nag me to call them back, just to stop them ringing the bakery.

'It's nice to be popular,' she said to me in a heavily ironic tone as she delivered another scrawled note.

Popular? I thought bitterly as I watched her bustle away. I had never felt so alone.

CHAPTER THIRTY-FOUR

Frau Kessel's death put an end to the gossip about me, but I had not quite heard the last of the affair with Kai von Jülich. On the whole I was relieved that Kai had left the town. In a way my wish had been granted; I had wished him away and he had gone. He would no longer be able to propagate his own repulsive version of events, while I was spared the embarrassment of running into him and perhaps provoking an ugly scene. I was not particularly interested in *where* Kai had gone, just as long as he stayed away. All the same, I should have realized that not everyone would feel the way I did.

One morning, about a week after Frau Kessel's funeral, I was clearing a table at the front of the cafe when I became aware that there was someone standing on the other side of the big plate-glass window, looking in. We were so close that if there had been no glass between us, we could have reached out and shaken hands. For a split second, when all I had taken in was a tall shape with bright sunlight behind it, I thought it might be Jochen or one of the others come to confront me with their demands. I jumped and knocked over a coffee cup, spilling dark dregs on to the tablecloth. While I was blotting the mess with a napkin I hazarded another glance at the person outside the window and this time I recognized her.

It was Frau von Jülich, Kai's mother. As far as I could recall, she had never set foot inside the bakery in her life, but still I would have known her anywhere. She was distinctively tall, with the same dazzlingly blonde hair and high cheekbones as her son, the same brilliant blue eyes, although hers were framed with a network of very fine lines. As usual she was dressed like a visiting countess, in a dark woollen suit which had probably cost more than my mother's entire wardrobe. I was just as surprised to see her peering through the bakery window as if Max's wish had come true and Heidi Klum really had turned up in Bad Münstereifel with a beseeching look on her face. I could not help glancing around to see what it was that had caught her interest, but there was nobody else around. My mother had vanished into the kitchen and I was alone in the bakery.

A minute later the bell jingled as Frau von Jülich entered the cafe, pausing for a moment on the threshold with the cautious air of a pedigree cat about to cross a farmyard.

I abandoned the table I had been clearing.

'*Guten Morgen*,' I said as politely as I could, although I had a sinking feeling.

Frau von Jülich did not look like the sort of person who pops into the local bakery for a cheese and ham roll in a paper bag. I guessed that she had other business here, either with myself or with my parents, and it was hard to say which was the worse option.

'*Guten Morgen*,' returned Frau von Jülich. She stood before the counter, not making any move towards a table.

For what seemed like a very long time she simply studied me. Then she said, 'Are you Stefanie Nett?'

There was no point in prevaricating. 'Yes,' I said.

Frau von Jülich glanced around her, as though she were looking for something. Her manner was oddly uncertain, considering her formidable appearance. Then she tried a smile.

'May we sit down for a moment?' she asked.

It was the first time a customer had ever asked me to sit with them. I was nonplussed.

'Would you like a cup of coffee?' I asked.

She shook her head. 'No – thank you.' She put a slender hand on the back of one of the chairs at the nearest table. 'Shall we sit here?'

I was beginning to feel very uncomfortable. I wished with all my heart that my mother would reappear from the kitchen and rescue me, but there was no sign of her. Reluctantly I took my place at the little table, sitting ramrod-straight, my hands clasped in my lap, where the folds of my apron hid their nervous twisting.

'I'm not really supposed to sit down,' I stammered rather idiotically.

The carefully plucked eyebrows rose just a fraction, although the faint smile was still on her lips. 'I'm sure you can spare two minutes from your work,' she said.

Since the cafe was deserted apart from the pair of us, this was undeniably true. I said nothing.

'I have something to ask you,' said Frau von Jülich, and now she really was smiling at me, all her perfect white teeth showing, although there was something in her eyes which told me that the smile was put on. She was anxious about something – perhaps even as nervous as I was. 'You are a friend of Kai's, aren't you? My son, Kai?'

A friend? I stared at her.

'Not really,' I said, and since something more seemed to be called for, I added reluctantly, 'I know Kai, though. Sort of.'

She leaned forward. 'You met Kai once or twice, didn't you?'

'Once,' I said. 'We went out once but . . . it didn't really work out.' *That's an understatement*, I told myself, recalling Kai's handsome face distorted with fury and the shower of gravel as he had driven past me in the Eschweiler Tal. All the same, I didn't have the nerve to tell his mother the truth, that her son was a brute, a peacock with the soul of a pig. Probably she would not even believe me.

'I'm sorry,' she said, although I was not sure what she was sorry about: for asking me something personal or for my ill luck at not managing to net such a prize.

I said nothing. There was nothing I could possibly think of to say to Kai's mother. The moment of silence stretched out between us.

Suddenly she put out one hand and touched me lightly on the shoulder. 'Please,' she said, and with astonishment I realized that she was near to tears, 'if you know where Kai has gone, or why, please tell me.' Her brittle manner was cracking like a thin veneer. In spite of her perfectly coiffed hair and expensive clothes she was still just someone's mother, worrying about her child.

I hated to be blunt, especially to this sophisticated woman, who would probably think me a guttersnipe once she had calmed down. I saw, however, that I would have to speak plainly.

'Frau von Jülich, I know what people are saying.' I was conscious of the gaze of those blue eyes, so like Kai's. I swallowed and made myself go on. 'That I'm – pregnant. And that Kai had to leave because of it.' I couldn't look at her. Instead I studied my clasped hands with their white knuckles. 'It's absolutely not true. We just went out once and –' I winced – 'nothing happened. I don't know where he is and I haven't heard from him. I swear it.'

Silence. I wondered whether Frau von Jülich had finally succumbed to tears and risked a glance at her face, but she simply looked tired, very tired.

'I'm really sorry,' I added.

'No,' she said, turning that vivid blue gaze on me. 'There's nothing to be sorry for. Thank you for being frank.'

She stood up and I rose too.

'Frau von Jülich?' It seemed too brazen to ask, but I had to know. 'Have you heard anything from Kai?'

She nodded wearily. 'He texted his father. He says he's not coming back – but he doesn't say why, or where he is.'

I could not ask her anything else. I stood at the door of the bakery and watched her walk away up the street, a slim, elegant figure who could have passed for much younger than her fifty years, head held high in spite of her burden of worry. I wondered what she would say if she knew I had wished her son dead.

CHAPTER THIRTY-FIVE

That year, in early summer, the Grim Reaper was very active in Bad Münstereifel. The mounds of flowers which fans had heaped on Klara Klein's elegant pink marble slab had barely begun to wither before another plot was opened to receive the earthly remains of Eva Kessel. And then my father felt the Reaper pass by, too close for comfort.

It was a Tuesday morning and both my mother and I were serving in the café. My father was alone in the kitchen as Achim Zimmer had taken a week off. This meant respite from Achim's insinuating glances and clammy hands but rather slower progress than usual with the morning's baking. A large group had come in very early in the day and not all the cakes and pastries were ready. My mother was waiting impatiently for a cherry streusel that would have to be served still soft and crumbling from the oven. When the streusel failed to appear and she had twice been summoned back to the table where two irritable customers were waiting, she went into the kitchen to investigate.

A moment later she came out again at top speed and ran straight to the telephone which hung on the wall near the coffee machine.

'Mum?' I said uncertainly as she punched numbers in. 'What's happened?'

'Your father's ill,' she said over her shoulder. 'Hello?' she said into the receiver.

I listened to her speaking for a couple of seconds, then I ran for the door to the kitchen.

My father, clad in his baker's whites, was sitting on a stool between two of the big metal units which stood against the kitchen wall. He was leaning against the wall, his face greyish and clammy-looking. His right hand fumbled at his left arm, as though he were trying to feel for a wound.

'Dad?'

His eyes turned to me, but he said nothing. I heard my mother come running back into the kitchen and turned a stricken face towards her.

'He's not answering me,' I said. 'What's the matter with him?'

'I think he's having a heart attack,' said my mother.

She had a strange, blank look on her face, one I had never seen before. It took me several moments to realize that she was terribly frightened.

CHAPTER THIRTY-SIX

The *Notarzt* came in a fluorescent orange car with a revolving light flashing away on top of it and parked right outside the bakery. When he arrived I was standing at the front door, taping a handwritten sign, CLOSED DUE TO ILL HEALTH, on to the glass. At the sight of the emergency vehicle I felt a chilling lurch in my stomach, as though I had stumbled on a flight of stairs. I recalled that other morning when I had stood outside Frau Kessel's house, watching a similar vehicle nudging its way under the Orchheimer Tor and waiting for them to confirm that she was dead.

Not my father, I thought. *Please, not my father.*

My father was not dead. The Reaper had broken his stride as he passed the bakery, but in the end he had shouldered his scythe and gone on his way, empty-handed. All the same, our lives could not go on unaffected. From the moment the ambulance doors closed on my father and bore him off to the hospital in Kall, the bakery was without a baker. My mother went with my father, still dressed in her green dirndl. The last thing she said to me before she climbed into the ambulance was, 'Call Achim Zimmer.'

I stood on the cobblestones in front of the bakery, doing

my best to ignore the whispers of the bystanders who had been drawn, as people always are, to the scene of the emergency. I watched the ambulance drive up the street and heard the siren go on as it rounded the corner, ushering some dawdling drivers out of the way. I turned back to the bakery and went inside, fumbling for the door handle as though I had been suddenly struck blind. *Dad*, I was thinking. *Don't die. Please, don't die.*

I closed the door behind me and locked it. Dully I surveyed the cafe. Six of the tables needed clearing. There were cups and glasses and plates smeared with cream or jam or jellied fruit. The cloths needed straightening and the chairs would have to be put back neatly under the tables. In their haste to depart, someone had knocked over what appeared to be a nearly full cup of coffee, which had stained the tablecloth and was still dripping on to the tiled floor.

Before I could even get started on any of that, there were rolls which needed to be taken out of the oven and probably loaves in the big ovens at the back of the kitchen too. I began to feel like the girl in the story of Frau Holle, besieged at every turn with jobs which needed doing, the apple tree crying, 'Shake me, shake me,' and the bread in the oven crying, 'Pull me out, lest I burn.' Suddenly the cafe was blurry, seen through the tears which had sprung to my eyes. I wanted to be with my father, not here in the bakery. But that was not an option; right now this was the best thing I could do for my parents.

The bakery was shut for now, but I couldn't turn the customers away indefinitely or we would lose the business. Tomorrow morning there must be fresh bread, cakes and pastries; there must be filled rolls and the aroma of freshly made coffee on the air. I thought that if I telephoned everyone, the regular waitresses and the ones who came in occasionally when we needed an extra pair of hands, I could get enough people to staff the counter and serve the cafe customers. But I could not run the dough mixing machines and the big ovens all by myself; for that I needed Achim.

I wiped my eyes and went to the telephone.

CHAPTER THIRTY-SEVEN

On the second ring Achim picked up the phone.

'Zimmer.'

I rested my forehead on the cool wall of the cafe.

'It's Stefanie Nett, from the bakery.'

I did my best not to listen to the slimy outpourings that this provoked. The worst thing about dealing with Achim was that he always managed to make me feel that I was inviting his lascivious glances, as though he were a prim curate with his hands folded and his gaze turned down, and I some mincing vixen. Useless to try to keep the conversation neutral and businesslike; from the insinuating tone in his voice you would have thought that I had somehow engineered my own father's heart attack in order to get Achim alone.

Eventually I extracted his agreement to come to the bakery early the following morning. He would have prolonged our conversation, which he seemed to be enjoying immensely, but I muttered something about having to go because we had customers coming in and hung up.

After I had finished speaking to Achim, I telephoned two of the other girls who worked part-time in the cafe and asked them to work extra hours. If I were going to be stuck in the kitchen with Achim most of the time, we would need additional help in the cafe. More than that, I thought there was safety in numbers. Eventually I hung up and went back to clearing the tables. As I stacked cups and plates and mopped up the spilt coffee, I thought about the days and weeks ahead. I could not face the idea that my father might not recover. To think that he might pass away believing that his second and final child was about to turn her back on the business that lay so close to his heart was more than I could bear. If I could have been with him at that moment, I would have fallen to my knees on the hospital linoleum and promised to carry on at the bakery for the rest of my working life. All the same, I was only a bakery student, nowhere near qualified. Even with Achim's help I was not sure how long I could keep the bakery running.

I finally went to bed at eleven o'clock that night. After setting my little alarm clock for two thirty, I lay staring at the ceiling and willing sleep to come. I seemed to lie there for ages, and when I did eventually drop off I was sure only moments had passed before the shrill call of the alarm woke me. I crept into the bathroom, where I hung on to the washbasin, trying to repress the waves of nausea which came from wrenching myself into wakefulness after so little sleep. I hardly recognized the person staring back at me from the mirror like a drowned face drifting to the surface of a limpid pond. Under the tangled fair hair the eyes were as dull as stones, the features drawn. It was a shocking preview of the way I might look in another forty years after shovelling another few million loaves in and out of the ovens.

I shrugged on the white baker's jacket with my sister's name on it and with a heavy heart, I went downstairs.

'*Steffi*,' said Achim insinuatingly when he saw me come into the kitchen. He had his own key and had evidently been there for some time already, as one of the big mixing machines was running.

I frowned. He said my name the way a gourmet might say *foie gras*, as though the very word lingered luxuriantly on his tongue.

'*Morgen*,' I replied curtly.

I didn't look at Achim. I thought that if I saw the faux hurt on his face, the repulsive aping of wounded feelings, I would be sick. I pointedly went over to the other side of the kitchen to consult the schedule for the day.

Achim said nothing. To my relief he seemed too busy with the morning's work to plague me. There was a great deal to be done. We had malted *Kosakenbrot* to make in tins, oval loaves of *Bauernbrot* which had to be dusted with flour and *Kyllburger* bread with a row of diagonal slits along the top of each loaf. There was every conceivable type of seeded loaf: *Mohnbrot* with poppy seeds, *Sonnenkorn* with sunflower seeds and half a dozen others. Achim decided that we should also prepare *Sauerteig*, a type of dough which kept longer than the others and did not have to be made every day. As I would be at college tomorrow the kitchen would be short-staffed, so that seemed sensible.

We moved back and forth across the kitchen, each on our own track like the little figures in a weather-house. As the morning progressed I began to feel very warm. Opening the ovens to slide loaves in and out was like hanging over a furnace. All the same I kept my white jacket tightly buttoned up to the neck, not wanting to give Achim the slightest excuse to ogle me.

Now and again I would turn around, expecting to see him standing nearby, leaning against one of the metal counters with that insinuating look on his face. I brushed my elbow against something while carrying a tray of rolls across the kitchen to the cold store and jumped like a cat, thinking he had sneaked up on me.

Get a grip, I told myself, leaning against the door of the cold store with my hands over my face. *You can't carry on like this. You might be working alone with him for a month, or longer. You have to stand up to him.*

I was tempted to linger there among the metal trolleys, with their shelves of uncooked rolls as pale and spongy as fungi in the low light, but already I was becoming chilled. Reluctantly I carried the tray back into the main kitchen, keeping an eye open for Achim. To my relief, he was standing by the back door with his lighter and a packet of cigarettes in one beefy hand. He raised them to show me, nodded and stepped outside. With a lighter heart I went across the kitchen and set the rolls down. I hoped Achim would take a good long cigarette break. In fact, in spite of my objections to the habit, I hoped he would stay outside and smoke the entire packet. Perhaps he might immolate himself, I thought; there was always hope.

An hour later I began to feel a slight twinge of guilt for wishing him ill. Achim had not directed so much as a single inappropriate glance at me and his comments had been confined to the topics of dough mixing and baking. Perhaps he had decided to leave off tormenting me in deference to my father's situation, or perhaps he had got the message and decided to stop altogether. Later on I was to regret this naivety, but of course by then it was too late; a butterfly crushed in the jaws of a toad might just as well have wished itself out again.

It was not until the very end of the morning shift that Achim made his move. My mother telephoned at ten. My father's condition was stable but she didn't want to leave the hospital, so she wouldn't be coming back before the evening. At eleven o'clock we finished work and there was a break until three. I felt that we had completed a Herculean task that morning. Achim knew the bakery routine well and I had worked in the kitchen once or twice a week since I started my training, but still it was my father who normally led the day's work. However, here we were at the end of the shift with everything produced to order. None of our regular customers had had to do without their favourite *Nussecke* or *Speckstange*, nothing had burned or sagged in the middle, and, what's more, Achim's behaviour towards me had been nothing other than gentlemanly. In spite of the dark clouds that hung over me, I felt a sudden blooming of pride. We had done the best we could for my father; we had run his kitchen like clockwork. In an uncharacteristic burst of camaraderie I went over to Achim and held out my hand.

Achim held out his hand too, but not to shake mine. His big fingers, as thick and fleshy as *Knackwurst*, closed around my wrist. He reeled me in like a fish. I saw what was coming and wrenched my head around, so that the slobbering kiss that was aimed at me with the soggy gracelessness of a water bomb landed not on my lips but somewhere in the region of my ear. I tried to drag my hand out of Achim's grasp but he was not finished yet. He was leaning towards me, fumbling for my other hand, trying to back me up against the kitchen wall, and now, revoltingly, his tongue was actually exploring my ear. I reacted as though someone had tried to feed a live snake into it, struggling frantically, but it was no good. Achim was not particularly fit – most of his bulk was fat – but his sheer size and weight made him impossible to throw off. I felt as though I had walked through the back room in a butcher's shop and a whole side of beef had fallen off its hook and landed on me.

I was revolted – and furious. Furious at myself for being such a fool, for thinking that it would ever be possible to treat Achim like an ordinary, decent human being. Furious at Achim for what he was trying to do. When Kai had put his hands all over me in his car, I had been panicky and shocked, desperate only to put as much space between us as was humanly possible. Even when I had written out the curse against him, I had felt numb, with no other thought than to protect myself from my tormentor, to put him away from me forever. Now all the suppressed rage of that moment came boiling up inside me like a geyser, scaldingly hot and stinking of brimstone.

I felt around with my free hand, groping for something to use as a weapon. It was lucky for Achim that my father was a baker and not a butcher. At that moment I was so angry that if I had laid hands on a meat cleaver I doubt I would have hesitated to use it. My fingers closed over an enamel mixing bowl and, grasping it as firmly as I could, I brought it down on the side of Achim's head with a *clang* like the note of a single cracked bell. The grip of those sausage-like fingers slackened for an instant and I wrenched myself free.

I was sorely tempted to aim another blow at Achim, but even though I was beside myself with rage, I knew better than to tangle with him again. His skin, normally as pale as a corpse's under its sprinkling of freckles, had turned an ugly shade of red, signalling his state of mind as clearly as the ruff of a frill-necked lizard.

'Don't play games with me,' he growled.

I backed away, still clutching the enamel bowl. I dared not take my eyes off Achim to look at the bowl, but I sincerely hoped there was a large dent in it.

'Leave me alone,' I said, wishing that my voice sounded strong and confident like Hanna's, instead of tremulous.

'There's no point acting the innocent,' Achim spat. His face twisted unpleasantly. 'What's the matter? An honest working man not good enough for you now you've been with Herr High-and-Mighty von Jülich?'

How I wished at that moment that I had a searing retort on my lips, some remark so flayingly acidic that Achim would shrivel under it like a salted slug. All that I could manage was a pitifully childish, 'I hate you.'

'Oh no. No, you don't,' said Achim with repulsive emphasis. I heard him breathing heavily through his nose and thought that he reminded me of nothing so much as a great flabby boar. 'You're going to like me a lot. You'll see.' He stared at me with those boiled-lobster eyes.

I'll never like you a lot, or even a little, I wanted to say. *You could be the last man alive on earth and I'd spend my whole life running from place to place rather than spend two minutes in your company. I'd rather fall naked into a pit of black mambas than touch even your little finger. And I'd rather eat my own weight in festering maggots than ever let you touch me.*

As usual, however, these words were trapped inside my

head, like the silent screams of recalcitrant spinsters walled up in a nunnery. I backed away from Achim, still holding the enamel bowl in one hand and wiping my other hand, the one he had grasped, on my white coat, as though trying to scrape off a coating of slime. It took every ounce of self-control I had to walk calmly towards the door without breaking and making a run for it.

Once I had made it into the passageway and the door had swung shut behind me, I sagged against the wall and put a hand over my face. I was trembling all over. I knew that I ought to go upstairs to the apartment before Achim had a chance to follow me out of the kitchen, but at that moment I doubted my legs would carry me.

What am I going to do? I asked myself silently.

I was still standing there leaning on the wall when I heard a door open. My head jerked up and my whole body tensed as I prepared to run for it, but then I saw that it was not the kitchen door that had opened but the one leading to the cafe. A waitress was standing there with a coffee pot in her hand. I recognized her as Bianca Müller, a fair-haired, slender girl a year or two older than I was. Bianca had always struck me as a little stand-offish and normally I would have made some excuse to scurry off rather than expose a display of raw emotion to her superior gaze. Now, however, I was simply glad to see someone other than Achim. I didn't care if she noticed my flushed face and trembling limbs.

'Stefanie?' She looked at me uncertainly. 'Are you OK?'

'No,' I told her succinctly.

She took a couple of steps towards me. 'What's the matter?'

I meant to blurt the whole thing out, to say *Achim Zimmer tried to kiss me, or possibly worse*. But when I opened my mouth, all that came out was, 'Achim Zimmer.'

We had never been at all close, Bianca and I, and somehow I expected her to brush this off. But instead she came right into the corridor, letting the door swing shut behind her.

'You too?' she said.

CHAPTER THIRTY-EIGHT

After I had finished speaking to Bianca I went upstairs to the flat and locked the door behind me. I put my baker's whites into the washing machine and sat down at the kitchen table to think. I had made myself a sandwich but I couldn't face eating it. The moist pink slice of ham in the middle of it reminded me irresistibly of Achim's face, flushed with unspeakable ardour. After that thought had occurred to me I couldn't even look at it any more. I got up and tipped the whole lot into the bin.

It's not just me, I thought. If what Bianca said was true, Achim was systematically harassing every single one of the girls in the bakery. I had got off lightly so far, it appeared, probably because I was the boss's daughter. On one occasion when Bianca had gone into the kitchen when Achim was alone there, he had put both of his repulsively clammy hands right down the front of her blouse. Now that my father was out of the picture altogether for some time to come, there was no knowing what he might try.

But that was not all. Bianca told me that Achim had the unpleasant habit of relieving some of the girls of their day's tips. Even before she had finished describing what he did, I could very well imagine it: the slimy remarks sliding inexorably towards implied threats and finally outright bullying. She had ended by warning me to keep a close eye on the takings. Now that both my parents were absent, she thought there was no knowing what Achim would do.

The question was, what was *I* going to do about it?

Think, think, I told myself. I tried to consider all the options again, mentally spreading them out before me like a deck of cards. It was really impossible to consider speaking to my parents, a fact that Achim was no doubt depending on. Could I talk to Max? I quickly rejected that notion. If I approached Max for anything he would be bound to use it as a bargaining chip to try to get me to wish something for him in return. Julius? I dismissed that idea too. Assuming that I could get over the awkwardness between us, I was quite sure that Julius would want to help, but I had the instinctive feeling that he would suggest something honest and reasonable, like *talking* to Achim, which I knew perfectly well would do no good at all. I had to act *now*, or the next attempt he made would be worse. I didn't want to think what might happen next; my imagination simply shied away from it.

In the end there was really only one answer and it lay hidden in the woods to the north of the town, a grey and crumbling bulk whose walls were carved with silent screams of hate and fury. I thought about Kai, his handsome face twisted with anger into an ugly gargoyle. I thought about Achim Zimmer saying, *You're going to like me a lot. You'll see*. And I thought about Rote Gertrud, dragged out of her house by a shrieking mob. I supposed most of them had been men too. I wondered if the accusations of child murder had been true. Perhaps they simply couldn't stand the fact that a woman was living there alone, independent of any of them. Perhaps she had turned some of them down, laughed at them even, tossing her gleaming red hair. So they had burned her, working their own brutal magic, turning living flesh into ashes and sticks, a heap of black cinders to be torn away by the wind, up into an empty sky.

Why me? I thought. *Why does the magic work for me and only me?*

In stories, heroes and heroines always discover that the reason why strange things happen around them is that they are marked out in some way, that something sets them apart from other people: elvish blood, for example, or special powers handed down from father to son. I couldn't think of a single thing that set me apart from anyone else. I was an ordinary girl, with an average education and possibly the most uninspiring prospects in the world. I wasn't a mysterious orphan, nor even the eldest child; in fact, I strongly suspected that I had been an accident and wasn't even supposed to be here at all. There was nothing I could see that would single me out for the witch's blessing – or curse.

But I had wished Frau Kessel dead and she died.

There was no escaping from that. However I looked at it, the thing was too much of a coincidence, especially when you considered that my malign powers had apparently wiped out Klara Klein too.

My mind skipped back to the ruined house in the wood, to the day my sister had taken me there. Magdalena had wished Frau Kessel dead too, but it hadn't worked for her. So it wasn't just the house and it wasn't something to do with my family. It was *me*. I was the focus for whatever was happening. There was no point in saying that I had never asked for this ability; it seemed I simply had it. I was like the shard of glass lying in a dry summer meadow that refracts the sun's rays and causes the fire that ravages the field, turning the gold to black.

The question remained: was I going to curse Achim Zimmer? I stared down at my own hands, clasped as tightly as claws on the tabletop in front of me, and wondered why I even bothered asking the question.

CHAPTER THIRTY-NINE

I telephoned Hanna. I had not wanted to involve her while I still thought I might avoid the Achim problem; I knew she would push me to curse him. Now, however, that I had made up my own mind to do it I needed help. With my extra workload, it was not going to be easy to get away from the bakery for the hours it would take me to reach Gertrud's house on foot. The only person I could think of who had their own car was Max, but I didn't want to tell him what I was going to do. It would almost certainly lead to him making demands of his own and, worse, he would tell Jochen. I couldn't face Jochen if he found out what I was up to; in fact, in truth I was a little afraid of what he might do. That was what Rote Gertrud's magic had done for all of us: it had granted my wishes, but it had crept into the spaces between us like a weed thrusting itself up between stones and forced us apart. The only one of my friends who hadn't demanded anything for themselves so far was Hanna and even then I suspected she was simply biding her time. My options were running out, though.

At any rate Hanna had a driver's licence, even though she didn't have her own car. I prayed she would be able to arrange something.

'The bastard,' was the first thing she said when I told her what Achim had done. The second was: 'You've got to hex him.'

It was a relief in a way that she suggested it before I did, but all the same I felt a twinge of conscience. I knew Hanna was fascinated with what had been happening since that first night in the woods and also that there was something unhealthy about her fascination. I had seen it in the gleam in her eyes, the enigmatic smile on her lips. Involving her in this made me feel as though I was encouraging someone to do something they had better have left alone, like trying a dangerous drug or playing chicken on a railway line. Yet there was no other option, was there? I closed my eyes, my knuckles white around the telephone receiver.

'I know. But Hanna, it has to be now. I can't carry on like this.' My voice was rising. 'I need to get to – you know – *there*. But it takes hours to walk.'

'We'll ask Max.'

'No!' I almost shouted. With an effort I made myself calm down. 'Not Max. Not anybody else. It has to be a secret.'

There was a pause. 'OK. Give me some time. I'll be over later with a car.'

'Not Max's,' I said. 'He'll know we're up to something.'

'Not Max's,' she agreed, and hung up.

I went into my bedroom and rummaged through the drawer of the desk I had used for homework years ago. I found a small notepad and a couple of pens. I tested the pens on a piece of paper to check that they both worked. I wasn't taking any chances; I was going to do this properly. I glanced around the room, at the fading posters and the discarded dolls propped up on a high shelf, at the slippery pile of magazines on the floor. An unlikely lair for a witch. I shut the desk drawer, a little too hard, and ran from the room.

Downstairs in the bakery all hell had broken loose. It looked as though a large coach party had turned up unannounced. Every table was crowded with customers. Some of them had already been served, but the majority were still waiting, some with arms crossed and furrowed brows. Bianca Müller and another waitress were moving about among them with harried expressions, like relief workers at an overcrowded refugee camp. As soon as I came in, their eyes turned towards me and I could read the message in them as clearly as if they had shouted it across the room: *Where are you going? You should be helping us.*

It was quite plain that I could not afford to leave the bakery for long. I could sense the querulous demands of the impatient customers and the harassed staff as powerfully as if they had been grabbing at me with their hands, trying to hold me fast. The short walk to the front door felt like running the gauntlet. I dared not stop to ask either of the waitresses whether they needed anything, or to tell them that I would not be long. It would be akin to steering a boat into the heart of a whirlpool: I would never manage to extricate myself once I was dragged in. I stepped out on to the doorstep, praying that Hanna would come soon, before someone – probably Bianca, who had looked thoroughly irked – had the idea of coming after me. I did my best to position myself at the corner of the bakery, out of sight of both the windows. I felt horribly guilty, but I told myself there was nothing for it. I *had* to get to the ruined house in the Eschweiler Tal; I *had* to do something about Achim. I knew that time was running out, like a gladiator who is astonished to find himself alive at the end of a bloody combat, but knows that tomorrow the beasts will have him for sure. If Achim were removed, I would be faced with the immediate problem of how to keep the kitchen running without him. If he stayed, with one hand on other people's money and the other trying to worm its way down the front of their clothes, there would be no staff and no business left at all within a very short time. *It has to work*, I thought.

CHAPTER FORTY

I had been waiting for about ten minutes when a car came nosing up the cobbled street. I gave it a glance, but then looked away, disappointed. It was a silver-grey Mercedes saloon. I had faith in Hanna's ability to borrow a vehicle, but she was not going to come up with anything like *that*.

The driver sounded the horn twice, impatiently, and I looked again. To my astonishment, it *was* Hanna behind the wheel – and not a moment too soon. As I pushed myself away from the wall and started towards the car, the front door opened and Bianca Müller flounced out, with an expression on her face that would have soured every cream cake in the bakery.

'*Tschüss*,' I said over my shoulder as I ran for the Mercedes's passenger door. I knew I was going to pay for it later, but at that moment my only concern was to get away before she caught me.

I slid into the seat, pulled the door shut and clipped on my seat belt. I had a strange sense of déjà vu as the car pulled away from the bakery, Bianca vanishing behind us just as Frau Kessel had done the day Kai had picked me up. It seemed that wherever I went, I left a trail of irritated people behind me.

As we rounded the corner I said, 'Where did you get this car?'

'It's my father's,' said Hanna.

'And he let you borrow it?' I asked incredulously.

Hanna didn't take her eyes off the road. 'Yes.'

I could smell clean leather and some sort of fresh smell like pine, as though someone had cleaned the dashboard recently. Herr Landberg was a prize pedant and ferociously status-conscious. A king of the local shooting club, he liked nothing better than to parade around in hunting green, looking as though his silver buttons would barely do up over the swell of his own self-importance. I couldn't imagine him allowing his teenage daughter to take out a treasure like this.

'Did you take it without asking him?'

She shrugged. 'He's OK with it.'

I didn't believe that for a minute, but I didn't contradict her. I felt suddenly overwhelmed. Hanna was the only one of my supposed friends who wasn't pestering me half to death to wish things for her. And now she was risking her neck for me, risking a row of truly titanic proportions if her parents found out what she had done. Tears were suddenly pricking at my eyes. I had not expected this feeling of relief. It was as though a limb made numb by perishing cold was suddenly coming back to life before the warmth of a blazing hearth. I had known I was alone, but I had not realized how terribly I had felt it until this moment. If Hanna had not been driving, I would have hugged her.

'Steffi?' she said suddenly, interrupting my thoughts. 'Look, if you're going to curse Achim . . .'

Oh no. Here it comes. Now Hanna's going to ask me to

wish just one thing *for her*. But to my surprise, she didn't.

'Why don't you wish for something else – something for yourself?'

'I don't know,' I said. I raked my fingers through my hair. 'I just want Achim gone,' I said.

'Well, look, we could . . .' She paused. 'You could wish for *anything*.' She glanced over at me. 'Steffi, what do you need?'

'I don't know,' I said stupidly.

'Something?' asked Hanna. Her voice was very low and there was a curious edge to it. '*Someone?*' she said.

I thought briefly of Kai von Jülich, how I had wished for him. I didn't know whether it was the taint of the witch's influence or whether he had always hidden his cloven hooves under the cloak of those golden good looks, but I thought I would never wish for anyone's affections again. I would take my chances with love like everyone else, and if I ended up alone, so be it. I shook my head.

Then it came to me. I had no idea how I was going to keep the bakery kitchen running if Achim really disappeared. My mother might help, but that depended on whether she felt able to leave my father. If the bakery had to close for a while, it would be catastrophic. If we couldn't afford a new coffee machine, we certainly couldn't afford to lose our entire revenue for weeks. But if we suddenly had a lot of money . . . It would be even harder to explain to my mother than the five hundred euros that were still stuffed in a vase in my sister's room, but this was an emergency.

'Money,' I said suddenly. 'To keep the bakery afloat.'

'Money for the bakery,' said Hanna flatly.

I thought I knew what she was thinking: *What a drag.*

The chance of unlimited power and she's thinking about the stupid bakery.

'Yes,' I said simply. 'Look,' I added, seeing the dubious look on her face, 'I don't want to ask for anything else. Other things – they seem to go wrong.'

I was thinking of the disastrous date with Kai von Jülich. Also, I was thinking of Jochen and the day he had visited me while my parents were at mass. If Hanna had some grudge like Jochen's, I hoped and prayed that she would not share it. I supposed that this was the moment when I should ask her whether there was anything *she* wanted me to wish for, but I couldn't bring myself to do it. Once the offer was made, I could hardly rescind it, and yet I could not face the thought of asking the question as casually as though I were asking if she wanted me to bring something back from the shops for her.

She didn't ask for anything for herself, though, and when she spoke again I felt instantly guilty.

'The money,' she said. 'How much would you need?'

CHAPTER FORTY-ONE

The ritual itself was quickly done. Afterwards, as we picked our way down the hill from the ruined house, I felt suddenly tired. It should have been easier going downhill, but I found myself stumbling over roots and stones, my shoes sliding on the steeper patches, dusty earth crumbling under my feet. *She doesn't want to let us go,* I thought, and couldn't resist shooting a backward glance over my shoulder towards the ruins of Gertrud's house. Then I missed my footing completely and went down, with a painful wrench to my right ankle.

'Scheisse.'

I sat in the dirt and nursed my leg. I didn't think anything was broken, but the sudden sharp pain had brought tears to my eyes. I didn't want to get up until it had passed.

'Are you OK?' asked Hanna, stopping beside me.

I nodded, biting my lip.

'Can you move it?'

'Yes . . . I just want to sit here for a minute, though. Shit.' I flexed the ankle and then wished I hadn't.

Hanna sank to her haunches and then slid into a sitting position next to me. 'Maybe you've torn something.'

I shook my head. 'I've just wrenched it. It'll be all right in a minute.'

We sat side by side for a while in companionable silence, while I rubbed the offending ankle with my fingers. The pain was subsiding. I thought there was no real damage done, although I was not in a hurry to get up and start walking again. It was peaceful here and now that we were a safe distance from Gertrud's house I felt a certain sense of calm which was sure to end the moment we drove back into town. I would have to face Bianca Müller and Hanna would have to face her father. Far better to sit here a little longer, safe in the knowledge that nobody knew where we were.

Now that the crunching of our footsteps had been stilled and our breathing had quietened, I was able to hear the subtle sounds of the forest quite clearly. A light breeze rustled in the bright green summer leaves. Birds were singing in the treetops. An insect buzzed past me, sawing through the air on its own unknowable business. And then, suddenly and quite distinctly, I heard wood snapping.

I didn't need to turn my head to know that it came from behind us. From further up the hill. From the direction of Gertrud's house. I felt sure that the hairs on the back of my neck were standing up; I could feel the skin tingling. My mind was summoning up pictures, pictures so clear that they had a photographic quality to them. Someone stepping out of the ruined doorway of the witch's house, someone with a face that might be the colour of milk or the colour of ashes under a mane of flaming hair. Feet moving swiftly over the uneven ground. The witch. Following me. *Me*. The one whose wishes had drawn her power, as a lightning rod draws down the fury of the storm.

I grasped Hanna's wrist, but I needn't have bothered as

she had heard it too. We stared at each other with open mouths and round eyes.

A rabbit, she mouthed at me, but she looked just as shocked as I did. Neither of us moved a muscle and in the stillness we heard a second *snap* as someone – or something – put their weight on a dry stick.

I couldn't release my grip on Hanna's arm. My mouth was dry. I dared not make a sound. Slowly, with infinite care, I turned to look up the slope behind us.

There was nothing to see – not as yet – but as I listened I heard it again, the sound of dry wood breaking under the weight of someone's passing.

Stupid, I chided myself. *It's a deer. Or maybe it's some kid who was hanging about up there.* Then: *The note. The note with the curse on it. If someone had followed us, had they read it?*

But it wasn't a kid, nor was it a deer. As I sat there on the dry earth, with my fingernails digging into Hanna's arm, I saw it. A dark flicker of movement, far off among the trees, and suddenly the bright gleam of flaming red hair.

I scrambled to my feet, heedless of my throbbing ankle, and fled down the hillside, with Hanna at my heels.

CHAPTER FORTY-TWO

We reached the car red-faced and panting, almost choking with the exertion of running down the hill. My ankle was flaring with pain and Hanna had a long scratch on one forearm from running into a sharp twig. I sagged against the side of the Mercedes but dared not sink to the ground. It seemed to me that as soon as Hanna could unlock the car we should get away, putting as much space as we could between ourselves and whatever we had seen. I didn't even like to say the name aloud, though it was hammering in my head like a painful drumbeat. *Rote Gertrud.* We had seen the witch, actually *seen* her, walking in the woods. I yanked on the car door, willing it to open, but Hanna was still fumbling with the keys.

Finally I heard the central locking click. I tore the door open, almost fell over myself in my haste to get inside, slammed the door and sat shivering in the passenger seat. I glanced out of the window at the shadowy border of the woods, willing there to be no sign of the black-clad figure, then squeezed my eyes shut, unable to bear the tension of looking. I heard Hanna getting into the driver's seat and the door closing.

'Go,' I said. 'Drive.' My teeth were chattering.

The engine roared into life. There was another hail of gravel on the bodywork as the car pulled away; another focus for Herr Landberg's fury when Hanna got the car home. At that moment, however, I couldn't have cared less. Herr Landberg might ground Hanna for taking the car; he might ask both of us for a month's wages to repair the bodywork. But I could not begin to imagine what Gertrud Vorn might want from us in exchange for granting our wishes.

Why now? I asked myself as I clung to the door handle, lurching from side to side as Hanna did a rough three-point turn and then roared back down the track. *Why did she appear today and not before?* But I remembered the first time we had been at the ruined house, all six of us. We had heard something then and tried to dismiss it as an animal – a deer or a wild pig. Perhaps even then the witch's eyes had been upon us. Perhaps she would have approached us before, if we had stayed a little longer.

Perhaps it's payback time, I thought, and my stomach seemed to turn over, nauseatingly, as though I had stumbled at the head of a flight of stairs. *Guess who she's coming for?*

CHAPTER FORTY-THREE

I got back to the bakery to find that I was too late. The front door was locked, the lights were out and the sign hanging in the front window was turned to CLOSED. I thought of my mother perhaps coming back from the hospital and finding the bakery had shut early. I had no great love for the bakery, conceiving it as something akin to the cage in the ginger-bread house in which the wicked witch kept Hänsel and Gretel, but all the same I suffered a massive twinge of conscience at the forlorn look of the place. A hundred metres up the street the pavement seating of a rival bakery was packed, so there was no need to ask where all the customers had gone.

I let myself in, pausing in the dim and empty cafe area to listen for signs of anyone moving around. There was nothing. Emboldened, I peeped into the kitchen. It was deserted, the stainless-steel surfaces gleaming grey and sterile. Evidently Achim Zimmer had departed for the day too. I was alone.

Bianca and the other waitress had carried all the dirty crockery into the kitchen and filled the big industrial dishwasher, and they had wiped down all the tables, but they had forgotten to switch off the coffee machine. I didn't really like coffee but I poured myself a cup anyway and put three teaspoons of sugar into it, with some vague idea that it would counteract the feeling of shock which still perco-lated through me like slow poison. I took a sip. It was much too strong, tasting like ashes.

After a moment I put the cup down again and went over to the front door. I rattled the handle up and down, check-ing that I had locked the door behind me when I came in. It was absolutely fast, but I was not reassured. A solid dead-bolt might keep out casual thieves and vandals, but it would present no barrier at all to the thing I most feared. I sat down again, with my eyes on the door.

There is no way that Rote Gertrud is going to walk up to that door, I told myself. *It's broad daylight. We're not in the woods any more. There are* people *around.*

I watched the door, the cup of coffee cooling in my hands.

What about tonight? said a voice at the back of my mind. *Bad Münstereifel is deserted after dark. Satan himself could stroll down the Werther Strasse with all his horned minions cavorting around him and nobody would see him.*

I shivered. *Oh, God, I wish I didn't have to stay here alone.* My mind kept sliding back to the figure we had seen in the woods – the dark form, the fiery hair.

You called her, I reminded myself. *If she's walking, it's your fault.*

I sat there until the coffee, acrid to begin with, was com-pletely undrinkable. Then I limped upstairs to the flat, my ankle aching with the persistence of a rotten tooth. Sitting in the café area with windows and glass-fronted doors on all sides was making me jumpy. Every time anyone passed by I found my eyes drawn to them, my flesh creeping: a figure in a long summer dress made of some dark material which fluttered around her calves; a teenage girl with hair dyed a startling shade of red. I would catch a glimpse out of the corner of my eye and feel a sickening lurch in my stomach before realizing that it was just another overdressed tourist, just another schoolkid.

Upstairs, the flat had an abandoned feel. Plates were piled up in the kitchen sink. I opened the dishwasher and slotted them into the rack. I pressed the button to start the machine and the sound was loud in the silence. In the bathroom, the glass-fronted cabinet still stood open after my mother had frantically emptied out the things she thought my father would need: his razor, his toothbrush, his comb. I pushed the cabinet door shut, but when my reflection slid into view I turned away. I didn't need to study it to know that I looked terrible.

I went through into the living room and sat on the overstuffed sofa. There was a copy of *Das Goldene Blatt* on the coffee table, with the singing star Heino on the cover. I picked it up, hoping to distract myself from the worries running incessantly around inside my head, but when I opened it I found myself looking at a double-page spread about Klara Klein. Hastily I put the magazine down again.

At half past five my mother telephoned.

'Steffi?'

Her voice was barely recognizable. She sounded like an old woman of ninety, hoarse and frail. My father was alive – just – but from what my mother said, his grip on life was slowly peeling away, finger by finger, the drop into the void only a faltering heartbeat away. As I listened, guilt descended on me in a smothering cloud. I felt responsible. Had my intent to abandon the bakery contributed to his heart attack? I imagined him worrying about it, fretting while he worked, the anxiety creating just enough additional pressure to make the whole boiler blow up. Suppose he died thinking that the business he had nurtured so lovingly for decades was going to collapse because I wasn't prepared to take it over?

I felt as though I had taken a false step on unknown ground and fallen down a well, the darkness closing in on me as I screamed past the encircling walls, the light disappearing to a faint circle overhead. Singing with Julius's band, studying music, leaving the bakery – all of it seemed like a beguiling chimera that I had utterly failed to resist. If I had been at my father's bedside at that moment, I really would have taken that cold hand in mine and promised to work at the bakery, carry on at college, consecrate the rest of my existence to *Florentiner* and cherry streusel, if only he would stay with us, get better, not *die*.

'Mum?' I said. 'I want to come and see him.' I tried to sound firm but my voice was wavering.

There was a short silence, during which I heard something on the other end of the line which might have been a sigh.

'Yes,' she said eventually. 'I think you should come.'

Conscience pricked me. 'Mum, I don't know who's going to look after the bakery. Bianca and Doris came in today, but they might not . . . I mean, I'm not sure I can get them to come back tomorrow. And Achim . . .'

My voice trailed off. I was not sure what I wanted to say about Achim.

'Tell Achim not to come in tomorrow,' said my mother's

voice, and the tightness in it was audible even over the telephone line. I thought she was trying to stop herself crying. She coughed a little. 'We'll close the bakery for . . . a day or two.'

My God, I thought. *He's really dying.*

I said goodbye and hung up the phone. I would have to make some calls, find someone who would drive me over to Mechernich hospital, pack myself a few things in case I was there all night. I ought to get moving, but still I sat there with my hand on the telephone receiver, gazing into space.

I wished I didn't have to stay here alone, I thought. *And now I don't.*

At last I put my head in my hands and wept.

Chapter Forty-four

When I was done with crying, I picked up the telephone again and called Max. In truth, bold ebullient Max was the last person I felt like seeing, but I could think of no one else. I imagined that Hanna was at home by now, standing with her head down like someone walking through a storm, listening to her father ranting and raving about her having taken his Mercedes. Possibly he wouldn't let me speak to her if I did ring up. Even if I had felt like relying on our past closeness, there was no point phoning Timo as he didn't have a car, and nor did Izabela.

Oddly, I found myself thinking of Julius. I knew he would come if I asked him. I knew he was not just interested in me as a stopgap for his band. I could call him and he would come round as soon as I gave the word, with that quizzical look on his face, the one that said there was something here that he found deeply interesting, something hidden that was worth trying to draw out.

But Julius didn't have a car either. He went around on foot or on a bicycle so disreputable-looking that it was a wonder it hadn't already fallen to pieces. The band's equipment was carried around by someone who had a van, but I didn't know him at all, didn't even know his name.

In the end Max was the only option. I would just have to trust that the seriousness of the situation would put a temporary stop to his requests for me to wish things. I steeled myself and dialled his number.

'Steffi,' he said with relish, and I heard that syrupy innuendo in his voice again.

'Can you drive me to Mechernich hospital?' I said, and all of a sudden I was crying. 'Max, I think my father is dying.'

For once even Max was shocked into seriousness. I listened to him changing gear, slipping into concerned mode, promising to be at the bakery within twenty minutes. I thanked him briefly and put down the phone.

I was outside the bakery a full ten minutes before Max arrived in the ageing Opel that had taken us on our previous excursions to the Eschweiler Tal. As I went to open the passenger door, it occurred to me that if anyone – Frau Kessel, for example – were watching, they would be treated to the sight of Steffi Nett with yet another young man. But Frau Kessel wasn't watching, was she? Frau Kessel was dead. I got into the car.

As we drove out of the town, I caught Max looking at me speculatively. I glared at him, but said nothing. What was there to say? I did not know what specific charges Kai had laid against me, but I had no desire to refute them one by one. Max's gaze shifted back to the road.

For a while we drove in silence. We passed the car park near the Hirnberg, where a track led into the woods and over the hill to the Eschweiler Tal. I was as acutely aware of the location as if it had been a lighthouse blinking its light into the darkness of a storm. Perhaps the same thoughts were passing through Max's mind, because suddenly he said, 'Why don't you wish for your father to recover?'

I stared at Max with my mouth open. It was so blindingly obvious that I couldn't believe I hadn't thought of it myself. *Why shouldn't it work?* I thought. Everything else I had asked for had happened, apart from the removal of Achim Zimmer, and it was still early days for *that*. I had a vague feeling that perhaps asking for benevolent things, such as the healing of a loved one, would not be as successful as asking for malign ones, but if my father were close to death I had nothing to lose by trying. I thought too that asking for his survival might somehow even the balance, which was currently tipped right down in favour of death and disappearance. I didn't like to see myself as some kind of lens refracting the dark forces all about me, spreading their black rot across everything. If I really did have some sort of power, I wanted it to be for good.

'I could drive you up there,' offered Max.

I looked at him sharply, wondering whether he was going to add a little codicil: *I'll drive you if you wish this one thing for me* . . . But he was looking innocently at the road ahead.

'OK,' I said, and lapsed into silence.

At the hospital Max settled himself in the waiting area in Reception, while I went to the ward where my father lay. My mother was sitting by the bed. I was aware of her standing up as I approached, but I only had eyes for my father. Under all the tubes and wires he seemed somehow diminished, as though his body were a contraption almost too rickety to continue functioning, which I supposed in fact it was. The hands which had kneaded a thousand loaves and pressed cherries into the tops of his beloved *Florentiner* biscuits were limp and still. His eyes were closed.

I felt my mother's hand on my shoulder. Silently I turned to her and she put her arms around me. I had thought she meant to comfort me, but after a while I felt her shaking with silent tears and realized that she was the one who needed comforting. I looked over her shoulder at the silent figure in the bed and felt a misery so vast that it was numbing; it was like drowning.

'Steffi,' said my mother close to my ear. 'Don't leave the bakery. Promise you won't leave. Your father needs you.'

The silence in the room was so intense that it sounded in my ear like the inaudible scream of a bat. Then I heard the slow painful rasp of my father taking a breath.

'I promise,' I said.

CHAPTER FORTY-FIVE

They wouldn't let me stay at the hospital overnight. My mother would have to leave for a while too, to change her clothes and snatch some sleep, but she had a friend who lived in Mechernich who had offered to let her stay there rather than going back to Bad Münstereifel. I knew that when my mother accepted the offer she was thinking that it would be best if she were close by, so that if the call came, the one that said that my father was leaving us, she might be there in time to bid him farewell.

When I went back to Reception, Max was still waiting for me. He was leafing through a motorcycle magazine that looked as though it had been printed in 1970, but when he saw me coming he dropped it on the seat beside him and stood up.

I was afraid that he would try to embrace me, so I stood a little distance away, holding myself stiffly as though waiting for an attack.

'Will you take me home, please?' I said.

I was fighting the urge to burst into tears. I saw him step towards me and I brushed past him, heading for the door.

When we got to the car I huddled in the passenger seat, with the side of my face pressed to the cool window, keeping myself as far away from Max as possible. I squeezed my eyes shut, but tears were leaking out of the corners.

For a while Max said nothing. I guessed there was nothing he *could* say. Virtually nothing ever emerged from his lips that was not loud, confident or facetious. Asking him to come up with something quiet and comforting was like expecting someone to play a minuet on the bagpipes.

I was silent for a while too, but eventually I couldn't help it. The crying burst out in a sharp sound like a stifled cough, but then I simply wailed through bared teeth, resting my head on the glass.

'Steffi . . .' began Max, but I shook my head blindly.

It was late by now and the evening traffic had thinned out. It didn't take long to drive back to Bad Münstereifel. As we headed down the steep hill which led into the east side of the town, I felt as though I were being sucked down into the depths of a pit. I wondered if I would ever see my father again. I wondered if he would live long enough to see me fulfil the promise I had made. I wondered how I would keep that promise if Achim weren't there to help. But I dreaded even one more day alone with him in the kitchen; I lacked the strength for the fight.

I forced myself to stop crying. In truth, that numb feeling was coming over me again, a sense of dislocation that was worse than actual unhappiness.

When the car pulled up outside the bakery Max got out with me.

'We can go to the Tal tomorrow if you want,' he said, and I thought I could detect a note of eagerness in his voice.

'Yes,' I said. 'I'll phone.'

I fumbled for my keys in my pocket. Dropping them on the cobbles, I cursed and reached down for them. Max was quicker. He scooped them up and handed them to me.

'Do you want me to come in?' he said.

He might have been genuinely concerned for my well-being, but I didn't wait to find out.

'No,' I said, sliding the key into the lock. The door opened. 'I'm fine,' I lied, then slipped inside and closed the door in his face.

There was no need to set the alarm clock that night. The bakery would be closed tomorrow and all the regular customers would be buying their breakfast rolls and taking their morning coffee in the cafe up the street. I phoned Achim Zimmer and told him not to come in. To my relief the call was brief and businesslike. Perhaps even his troll's conscience was stirred by the imminence of death, though I didn't stay on the line to find out.

I hadn't had any dinner, but I didn't really feel hungry. I checked all the doors and windows one last time, then went to bed. I had been up early for the morning shift in the bakery and had not slept since. Now it was like falling into a black and soundless void. I was aware of nothing at all until 2.03 a.m., when I awoke with a start.

The illuminated numerals on my alarm clock floated in the darkness. Still night; nowhere near time to get up. What had woken me? I lay in bed listening, my body tense. Although all was silent, I had the impression that it was a sound that had startled me and that it had come from nearby. For a long time I stared into the darkness, until at last I began to relax, my body's craving for sleep taking over. I had almost drifted off again when I heard it.

A sharp, metallic *clank*. It might have been the sound of

a utensil striking one of the metal surfaces in the bakery kitchen, or of someone stumbling into one of the big dough-mixing machines. The kitchen was directly below my room and I was pretty sure the sound had come from there. In fact, I was 100 per cent sure; the certainty ran through me with the thumping of my heart and the quickening of my breath.

There's someone downstairs.

Could Achim possibly have come in anyway? I didn't think so. I had spoken to him personally and he knew he wasn't wanted. Besides, he was not due in for another half-hour even on his earliest shift.

I sat up, pushing the duvet aside, even before I had started considering what I should do. Then I listened again. For about a minute there was nothing at all. Then I heard a slapping sound, as though a gate were swinging shut in the wind.

The kitchen window.

But I checked it.

I slid out of bed and stood there in my nightdress in the middle of the darkened room, my heart thudding.

Who's down there?

Unbidden, an image came into my mind. A dark cloak, the hem trailing on the tiled floor. A long slim hand, white as milk, touching the smooth metal work surface, savouring the coolness of it. A bright fall of copper-coloured hair covering the face and then the head turning, slowly, very slowly, until suddenly I could see –

No.

I put my hands to my face, as though I could somehow shield myself from the thought.

It can't be Gertrud Vorn down there. It can't be. That's impossible.

Suddenly I couldn't bear the darkness a moment longer. I flew to the bedside table and switched on the lamp, filling the room with golden light. Then I slid open a drawer, fumbled for a T-shirt, grabbed my jeans from the chair. I wasn't going to confront the witch of Schönau – if she really was down there – dressed in a cotton jersey nightdress with a rabbit embroidered on the front of it.

This is insane, I thought as I pulled on my clothes. All the same, I had to do something. The thought of sitting there alone in my room, waiting for the stealthy tread on the stairs outside the flat, the rattle of the door handle turning slowly from the outside, the pad of soft feet outside my room – it was too horrible to contemplate.

I didn't put shoes on. My only ally was silence, so I opted for bare feet, but it wasn't the coldness of the tiles in the hallway that made me shiver as I made my way carefully to the door of the flat, pulling my cardigan tightly around my body. I stood there for a while listening. I could hear no further sounds from the kitchens below. I leaned close to the door and pressed my ear to the wood.

All I could hear was the rushing of blood in my ear. Otherwise there was silence.

Where is she?

Before the thought had even half crossed my mind I was seized with the conviction that Rote Gertrud was on the other side of the door, as close to the panels as I was, standing still and quiet on the little landing, waiting. Only a few centimetres of flimsy wood separated us.

Fear welled up in me, threatening to split me open like

ice in a pipe. It took all of my fraying self-control not to run away from the door, barricade myself in my room. But I thought that hiding in there without knowing whether it was my imagination running wild or there really was someone standing silently outside the flat, waiting to make her move, would send me mad. I bit my lip, screwing up the shreds of my courage, and reached for the key which was still in the lock.

One quick sharp turn and I was able to fling the door open.

Oh, my God, please don't let there be –

The little landing was empty.

I waited for my heart rate and breathing to steady themselves, until I felt as though I could move again without gasping like a fish out of water. I gazed down the stairs. In the light spilling from the flat I could see that there was nobody there. Emboldened, I started to go down the stairs, treading as softly as I could.

I had just reached the second-to-bottom step when I heard that slapping sound again. I froze. I thought I heard something else too, a scratching or skittering, as though something were scuttling away to hide. Then silence once more.

When I reached the door to the kitchen I realized my mistake: the key was still upstairs in the flat. I tried the door but, as expected, it was locked. For a moment I stood there irresolutely. There was no sound of anything moving in the kitchen.

In the morning, I said to myself. I pushed at the door again, but it held fast. *I'll check in the morning.*

CHAPTER FORTY-SIX

The next morning I awoke late, the first time in years on a weekday. I felt disorientated and a little guilty sitting in the sunny kitchen eating breakfast, while downstairs the bakery was as silent and still as a funeral parlour. I should have been at college that morning. Instead I phoned the secretariat and told them my father was ill and that I wouldn't be coming in. Later I would go to the Eschweiler Tal with Max to see whether the unseen power that had brought money to me and death to Klara Klein could bring health back to my father. First, however, I had something else to do.

After breakfast I went downstairs and unlocked the door to the kitchen. It was broad daylight now, but still I felt a faint echo of the fear that had infected me the night before as I pushed the door open. The kitchen was dim without the fluorescent lighting switched on and unusually cool since the ovens were not fired up. I looked at the stainless-steel surfaces gleaming in the cold light from the little windows and thought of a mortuary. I stepped over the threshold and looked about me.

Nothing, I thought. I went cautiously towards the middle of the room and stopped. Leaned to the right; twisted to look behind me. No sign of anyone and no sign of anything having been disturbed. A whisk was lying on one of the metal surfaces; perhaps it had fallen from the hook above. Was that the metallic sound I had heard in the night? I went over and picked it up, replaced it on its hook. Then I resumed my silent inspection of the kitchen.

I paused at the door to the cold store. As usual, it was tightly closed. There was no reason to think that it had been disturbed in any way. *Who's going to steal fifty uncooked bread rolls?* All the same, I thought I should check inside. The cold store was big enough to walk right into, easily big enough for someone to hide in, assuming they could stand the low temperature.

I curled my fingers around the heavy door handle, pushed down and pulled the door towards me. It released with a visible puff of freezing air. I peered inside. Everything seemed to be in order, with the shelves neatly stacked and the rolling rack of uncooked dough neatly pushed against the back wall. All the same, I had the strangest feeling that someone had been in here. Was it my imagination or was the store a little colder than normal?

I backed out and looked at the dial on the wall outside. Yes. The cold store was always kept at the same temperature, close to zero. Over time the front of the dial had become discoloured and I could see a faint pale triangle where the tip of the pointer always was. Now it was pointing a few degrees lower than normal.

Funny.

I moved the pointer back to its accustomed place. Had someone been playing around with the temperature control? It was hard to see why. Perhaps Achim had turned it down, though I couldn't think of a good reason for that either.

I closed the cold store door with a prickle of unease and glanced around the kitchen again. There was really nothing out of place and yet I felt deeply uncomfortable, as though I was treading on hostile territory. Yet this was the bakery, the familiar, dull, stultifying environment in which I had passed so many of my days.

I went to the back of the kitchen and tried the door. It was locked fast. Then I went to the window. It was closed too and I was turning away when I heard a very faint sound, a tap or a click. I turned back.

There was wind outside, and I watched as the window moved almost imperceptibly back and forth in its frame. The catch was undone.

Didn't I check this window? I thought I had, but I had been in a state of nervous anxiety. I might have missed something. From a distance it was difficult to tell whether the catch was properly done up, or simply lying against the wood. I fumbled with the catch with trembling fingers, forcing it shut. Then I pushed at the window, testing it. It was absolutely shut fast now.

That's probably what you heard, I told myself. *The window banging. Nothing else. Nobody's been in here.*

I backed away from the window. If someone had been in the kitchens, wouldn't they have done something – stolen something or thrown a few things around if they couldn't find anything to steal? It didn't make any sense, someone just climbing in to look around.

Rote Gertrud, I thought, and a chill went through me. But that didn't make any sense either, even assuming you expected there to be any logic in a world where long-dead witches could prowl through the town, hunting out their victims. If Red Gertrud were abroad, there had been such a breach of natural law that the presence of a barrier such as a window or a door would hardly be sufficient to keep her out, and its being open would hardly be necessary to let her in.

In spite of the cool emptiness of the kitchen, I was beginning to feel a stifling sense of oppression. I went hastily out of the kitchen, not forgetting to lock the door behind me, and into the cafe.

It had a forlorn air, with the blinds down and the glass-fronted cabinet standing empty. Normally the air would have been fragrant with the smell of baking and freshly made filter coffee. Today I could smell the underlying scent of the citrus surface cleaner that Bianca Müller had used on the tables and counter. It was a depressing reminder of the bakery's moribund condition; it made me think of a bed in a hospital room, the sheets and blankets removed, the mattress clean and blank where a few hours before someone had lain. Then I thought of my father and my stomach tightened.

I had heard nothing from my mother and I supposed that was good news. If my father had taken a turn for the worse (I avoided thinking about what *that* meant) she would have phoned. I looked around me, at the tables spread out like an archipelago through which I threaded my way every day of my working life. *I have* promised *to stay here*, I said to myself.

I went to the front door, meaning to look out at the street, as though it might offer some small promise of freedom. I was about to step on to the doormat when I realized there was something lying on it.

It was an envelope – an utterly nondescript envelope, but one in a style that I recognized. Plain white, with a typed address label on the front and no return details. *Steffi Nett*, said the direction. The envelope was fat, as though tightly stuffed.

I stooped and picked it up. Suddenly my heart was racing. Until that moment I had hardly given another thought to the second wish we had made, Hanna and I, the day I cursed Achim Zimmer. Money, enough of it to cover the bakery's immediate losses. Of course I hadn't wished for enough to last forever; if it worked there would be an unending supply anyway. I had wished for ten thousand and cast the wish out like bait. Since then I had been preoccupied with other things, but now I found myself wondering whether it could possibly have come true. If there were really ten thousand euros in that envelope, I thought it would prove irrevocably and forever that it was not one of my friends messing around. None of them had ten thousand to give me – probably not even Max had ever seen that much cash.

I turned the envelope over in my hands, strangely reluctant to open it. It was going to clear things up either way, wasn't it? Either there would be ten thousand euros packed into it or there would be a heap of useless paper and a note reading, *Ha ha, fooled you*, followed by a name.

Open it, I urged myself, and tugged at the tightly sealed flap. I tugged a little too hard and the envelope tore. I had most of the envelope in my left hand and a ragged scrap in my right, but I was not looking at either of them. I was looking at the banknotes which were fluttering to the tiled floor, which were bulging out of the rip in the envelope. I didn't need to count the money to know.

Ten thousand euros.

CHAPTER FORTY-SEVEN

I was still standing there, open-mouthed, looking down at the banknotes which were falling like autumn leaves on to my shoes, when the bakery telephone rang. It sounded unnaturally loud in the still and empty cafe area, and I actually jumped.

I glanced at the door and windows. There was nobody about, no nosy passers-by getting too close to the glass. I picked up as many of the notes as I could in one hand and went for the phone with the other. It was surreal, standing there with the receiver in my hand and the greater part of ten thousand euros in banknotes in the other – I felt a slightly hysterical urge to laugh.

'Nett?'

'Steffi?' It was Hanna.

It occurred to me that the caller could have been my mother, with unwelcome news, and suddenly the situation felt less hilarious.

'Yes,' I said.

'Max told me . . . you know . . . about your father,' she said. 'I'm sorry. We all are.'

I couldn't think of much to say. 'Thanks,' I settled on lamely, rubbing my forehead with the back of a hand that was gripping a great wad of banknotes.

'Max says . . .' Hanna paused. 'He says you want to go up to Gertrud's house. To wish your father better.'

'Yes,' I said, and I thought, *It's worked again. Another wish granted.* The only one which hadn't been was the one about Achim Zimmer, but that might be only a matter of time. *I could cure my father,* I thought with a sudden exhilarating sense of power. *I could really do it.*

'Max has called everyone,' said Hanna's voice in my ear. 'Izabela can't get away, but the rest of us are coming. Jochen told his boss he had diarrhoea.'

She was trying to make me laugh, lighten my mood, but the moment she mentioned Jochen and the others I felt apprehension fasten on to me again like a leech.

'Hanna . . .' I began, but she swept on.

'We're coming round as soon as Max has picked everyone up, OK? The bakery is shut, right? So you don't have to be there or anything?'

'No,' I said. 'But Hanna –'

'It's OK,' she said, as though I had thanked her. 'See you in maybe half an hour.' And she rang off.

I held the lifeless receiver in my hand and grimaced at it. I thought about ringing her back and saying I couldn't go, that I had to go to the hospital instead. In fact, my mother would be expecting me. I should be getting my things together and catching the bus, not chasing off to the Eschweiler Tal with Max and the others.

This might be Dad's best chance.

That was the thing: I could decide between visiting my father, who probably hadn't even known I was there the day before, and going to Rote Gertrud's house to do something I now believed would save him. I thought about it

240

for a while, but the decision had already been made.

When Max sounded his car horn outside the bakery door thirty minutes later, I ran out without a second glance. As I was locking the door behind me, I heard the phone ringing again in the deserted bakery. I paused for a moment and then let it ring. I pocketed the key and got into the car.

CHAPTER FORTY-EIGHT

I found myself sitting next to Hanna, with Timo on the other side of her. He was looking directly at me, the first time he had looked at me with interest since he had taken up with Izabela, though I didn't think romance had anything to do with it. Both of them were looking at me, in fact, as though I were some celebrity landed among them, as though I were really Max's wish about Heidi Klum made flesh. If it had not been for the driving desire to wish for my father's recovery I would have got straight back out of the car again and fled, because the way they were eyeing me made my skin crawl.

Jochen was in the seat next to Max, I noted with relief. He had flipped down the sunshade and I saw that he was watching me in the vanity mirror. The expression in his eyes was unreadable. I looked away.

As I settled back in the seat I could feel the bulk of the envelope and the money stuffed inside my jacket. I had not dared leave the money anywhere, so I had decided to carry it with me.

All the same, I wished I had not had to do so. I was as conscious of it as if I had been carrying a concealed weapon. If the others discovered I had ten thousand euros in cash in my inside pocket there would be a hailstorm of questions, of pleas, of begging. *Do this for me now, Steffi. Just do this. Just do this one thing.* I rubbed the front of my jacket with my hand, feeling the hidden bulk, but I said nothing.

I huddled in my corner of the seat, my face turned to the window, and brooded. The outskirts of the town flashed past, then the road which led to the Eschweiler Tal. We left tarmac and began to bounce along the gravel track which led into the heart of the Tal. I said nothing and the others were silent too. I could feel the tension in the way Hanna held herself on the seat next to me.

We rumbled along until we reached the spot where Max always left the car. While he was applying the handbrake I had already opened the door and was climbing out. I looked at the blue skies, and the flourishing green of the wooded hillside. I did my best not to look at my friends, though I was aware of their gaze on me.

'C'mon,' I muttered, and made for the trees.

As we struggled our way uphill through the undergrowth, I could almost *hear* the others' thoughts, their unspoken urge to ask me for things, held back only by their respect for my father's situation. *They don't think of asking Rote Gertrud for anything any more*, I realized. *I'm the witch now.* I wondered what they would say if they knew what I had in my inside pocket.

The climb uphill was warm work and we were all perspiring by the time we reached the ruined house. Hanna entered first and as I climbed over the stones which littered the entrance I could see she already had the carved box in her hands and was holding it out to me.

I took it in my own hands and opened the lid. The curse

on Achim Zimmer had gone. *Of course*, I thought. I had spoken to Achim the day before. So far as I knew, nemesis had not fallen upon him and ended his slimy existence, but I supposed that his days were numbered. *No way to take back the curse.* In spite of all Achim had done, of all I feared he would do, it was still somehow shocking. *Self-defence*, I told myself. *There was no other way.*

Someone pushed a pen and paper into my hands. No one said a word, but I could feel them all hanging over me with expectation as I carefully lettered my wish. There was absolute silence as I finished writing, folded the paper very carefully and placed it in the box, placed the box on the ground.

Then it all fell apart.

Max – I should have known it, as Max could never suppress his own impulses for more than about half a minute – was the first. Bringing out another piece of paper, holding out the pen again, wheedling, blustering, his mouth grinning but his eyes serious.

They must have taken my silence for acceptance because the next moment they were all clustering around me, blurting out their wishes, trying to attract my attention. Still, I might have pushed them away, simply refused, pleading upset over my father's condition – if Jochen hadn't lost his head and grabbed my jacket.

I think he only meant to make me listen, but as I pulled away the lining parted and the envelope fell out, scattering banknotes.

There was a stunned silence. Then: 'What's this?' That was Max, of course. I snatched up the envelope and the loose notes, cramming them back inside my jacket, but it was too late.

'The other wish – it worked,' said Hanna, and all eyes momentarily turned to her.

'What other wish?' said Timo incredulously. His eyes were round, his gaze fixed on my hand as it disappeared into my jacket with the money.

'Ten thousand euros,' said Hanna, and a shockwave ran through the group.

I heard a collective intake of breath and it was the sharp ebb of the tide that precedes a tsunami. The next instant they were all over me, clamouring, almost shouting in my face in their excitement, hands grabbing at the front of my jacket, at my sleeve: *Steffi, you've got to – Steffi, please – Steffi – Steffi – Steffi –*

I was suffocating, surrounded by jostling bodies, the faces of my friends turned to gargoyles by avarice and cupidity. I tried to push them away, but they came crowding back. Max was waving a piece of paper at me. Someone else nearly had my eye out with a pen they were flourishing in my face. I began to panic, thinking I would be stifled in the crush, the way that Gertrud Vorn had been stifled all those years ago by the choking smoke of her own burning.

I gave a hoarse scream, struck out, and then I was stumbling back, turning, out of the ruined house, flinging myself into the undergrowth, running downhill faster than I would ever had dared, had not utter panic lent wings to my feet.

The others would come after me, I knew – ostensibly to comfort me, to calm me down, but all the while throbbing with the need to get back to the nub of things, which was the overwhelming urgency for me to gratify their desires, to make their wishes for them. And their curses.

I could hear Hanna calling me. I dodged to the right and

cut away through the trees, stooping low. In my dark jacket and jeans I would be hard to spot, or so I hoped. My breath was ragged, my heart thumping wildly. The overhanging branches seemed to loom at me, trying to grab me with jagged talons of twigs. I skidded to avoid them, then stumbled onwards, swiping at them with my arms.

I was not following any particular course, driven simply by the blind desire to put space between myself and the others, but all of a sudden I burst out of the undergrowth on to a narrow path. At the same moment I realized that there was someone standing on the path with their back to me: a tall, lean figure in black.

My crashing exit from the undergrowth did not go unmarked. A second before I would have thundered into it, the figure turned and I saw a face I knew. I was practically in his arms before I could stop myself.

'Oh, my God,' I said. 'Julius.'

CHAPTER FORTY-NINE

Our faces were ten centimetres apart. I stared into Julius's brown eyes, saw him blink, surprised. No time to think about what it meant, meeting him here. Already I was struggling to get away, pushing him away from me.

'Let me go,' I panted, though in truth he wasn't holding me back at all.

'Steffi, what –' he began, and then we both heard it.

Someone was crashing down the hill after me; perhaps more than one of them. I panicked, looking wildly about me for a means of escape. By the sound of it, I would be in their sights in less than half a minute.

'I've got to get away,' I choked out, but I was deluding myself. I was shuddering with the exertion of my headlong flight and the ankle I had hurt before was aching alarmingly. I had no hope of outrunning four determined pursuers, two of them much taller and more powerful than I was.

Julius didn't waste time asking me what was going on. He could hear the others' approach as clearly as I could. He looked at my anguished face and made a snap decision.

'Come with me,' he said, and grabbed my wrist.

For an instant I almost resisted, but I was at the end of my strength. I let him lead me off the path, stumbling as I tried to keep up with him. About three metres away from the track was a fallen tree. It had crashed down, tearing itself right out of the ground as it did so, leaving a hollow shielded by the earth-clogged roots. Julius half dragged me into the hollow and threw himself down beside me.

While we cowered in the hole I heard someone panting as they fought their way through the undergrowth on to the path.

'Steffi?' said a voice. It was Jochen.

I cringed. Out of all of them, Jochen was the one I really didn't want to face. He had been angry with me before, so how would he be now, when he knew that I had made another wish for myself and that it had come true again? I realized that I was actually afraid.

'Steffi?' he said again, dropping his voice in an attempt to sound coaxing. Something rustled underfoot and I guessed that he was moving about, peering into the thick vegetation that covered the ground, hoping to catch a glimpse of me, or a sign of the route I had taken. 'Steff-ee . . .'

Now there was definite menace in his tone. I pressed my hands over my mouth, as though words might leak out unbidden and reveal our position. I felt my strength draining out of me, running out of every limb and vanishing down some dark sinkhole. I guessed the colour was vanishing from my face, because I saw Julius telegraph his concern to me, his eyebrows drawn together, his gaze pregnant with warning. I could not even shake my head. I just stared back at him, my eyes wide with horror.

'Ste-ff-ee . . .' called Jochen again.

After a moment's silence I heard him cursing. A little later the bushes rustled as he went back the way he had come.

I had been rigid with tension; now I was faint with relief. I slumped there in the earthy hollow and felt the hot tears begin to come.

Julius looked at me and then leaned towards me. When he put a hand on my shoulder, his grip held both comfort and a warning. He raised the other hand, putting a finger to his lips. Once he saw that I had understood, he risked raising himself up and looking over the top of the fallen tree.

A few seconds later he was back at my side. 'I think they've gone,' he said, 'but we should wait.'

'I can't run anyway,' I said in a hoarse whisper. 'I'm going to be sick if I do.'

'Hmm.' He put his head on one side. 'What's going on? Was that Jochen Meyer?'

I nodded.

'I thought he was a friend of yours.'

'He is,' I managed, and then wondered if that was actually true – if it had ever been true.

'OK,' said Julius patiently. 'Do you want to tell me why he's chasing you around the woods?'

'It's not just him,' I said. 'There are others. Hanna and Timo and Max.'

Julius looked at me for a moment. 'All of them were chasing you?'

I nodded, rubbing my face with the back of my hand.

'Why?'

He kept coming back to that simple question.

'It's complicated,' I said, and then surprised myself with a shaky laugh. *Complicated*. That was the understatement of the year. Of the decade. Of the *century* maybe.

Julius didn't say anything. He just waited for me to go on.

'We went up to – well, there's this place – up there, up the hill in the trees.'

'You mean Rote Gertrud's house?'

'Yes.' I shouldn't have been surprised. Gerd's house was hardly a secret. Half the town had been up there at one time or another, judging by the extensive hieroglyphics on the battered walls.

'And?' persisted Julius.

'And . . . they think – the others, I mean – that . . .'

I faltered to a stop. It was going to sound so stupid if I put it into words. *They think I have the power to do magic.* It sounded ridiculous, even to me.

Julius was looking at me with his eyebrows raised, his brown eyes quizzical.

'It was Max's idea,' I blurted out eventually, and instantly felt even sillier. I was admitting that Max had led me by the nose.

'What was?'

'Cursing people,' I said.

'Ah.' Julius looked reflective, and I guessed he was wondering how this piece of infantile foolishness had translated itself into my four friends hunting me down the hill like a frightened deer. 'Whom did you curse?' he asked.

'Klara Klein.'

Julius gave a low whistle.

'Don't,' I said crossly.

'How long before . . .' he asked me.

'Right before,' I said.

There was a silence. 'So why are the others chasing you?'

I gave a heavy sigh. 'They think I'm the one who's doing it. Making it come true.'

He looked at me incredulously. 'So what were they doing? Trying to lynch the witch or something?'

'Don't call me that,' I said. I shook my head. 'They weren't trying to lynch me.' I wasn't so sure that was true of Jochen, but I let that go. 'They wanted me to *wish* stuff for them.'

'That's crazy, you know,' said Julius.

I shrugged. I knew it was crazy too, but it worked.

'Klara Klein was ancient,' he said. 'She probably would have bitten the dust some time soon anyway.'

'I know, but . . .'

'*Other* stuff came true?' said Julius, marvelling. 'What did you wish for?'

I could see an absorbed look in his eyes. He was already imagining what it might have been, what he would have wished for in my place. A terrible certainty gripped me: if I let him pursue his train of thought he would realize that I had wished for Kai von Jülich.

'Money,' I said firmly. I didn't say how much.

'And it worked?'

I nodded.

'And they think you're the one who's doing it?'

I sighed. 'It only works when it's me who wishes.'

'That's insane.'

'I know. Julius, we didn't take it seriously at the beginning . . . we were just messing around. But then it worked. It actually worked . . . Well, it does if *I* do it.'

We looked at each other.

'But Steffi . . .'

I could see where this was going. If I didn't put a stop to it now, Julius wouldn't rest until he had the whole sorry story out of me. I felt a distinct thrill of fear at the thought. It was bad enough that my five friends knew about Klara Klein and Frau Kessel; if people outside our circle came to know about it, where would it end? I imagined what would happen if it got out that I had cursed Kai von Jülich. His mother would be back again and this time she wouldn't be nice about it. I imagined her putting those beautifully manicured fingers around my throat and trying to choke the truth out of me. *What have you done with my son?*

I shuddered.

'Julius.' I looked him levelly in the eyes. 'OK. You're right. It's insane. It was probably just a coincidence, Klara Klein dying like that, and the other stuff too. It just got out of hand. Max is an idiot.'

I struggled to get to my feet. My jacket and jeans were covered in earth, but I didn't care. I wanted to end this conversation before the pair of us strayed into areas that were best fenced off – better still, not just fenced off but surrounded by razor wire and KEEP OUT signs. I tested my ankle. I could put my weight on it, but that deep warning ache was still there in the joint. I didn't think I should attempt to walk home on it.

There was no sign of the others now. The shouting had ceased. Perhaps they had calmed down. They might have gone down to the car, to see if I was there. There was probably time to follow them. I could try yelling, in case anyone was still within earshot. But then I thought of sitting inside Max's Opel, crushed up against Hanna and Timo, with Max in front of me and Jochen glaring at me from the passenger seat. I could almost feel the atmosphere, the choking *pressure* of it, like hanging over the rim of a smoking volcano. How long would it be before they lost control again, before someone grabbed me by the lapels and shook me like a terrier shaking a rat? Before all of them tried to grab me? *Do this for me – just do this for me – just this one thing –*

I turned reluctantly back to Julius. 'I don't think I can get home on my own.'

'Do you want me to find your friends?' He sounded dubious.

'No!' I said immediately. 'Just . . . can't you take me?'

'I suppose so.' He was staring at me appraisingly. 'Steffi, this thing up at Rote Gertrud's house . . .'

'It was just some stupid game,' I said swiftly. 'Forget I said anything.'

'But your friends were trying to hunt you.'

'I told you,' I said. 'Max is an idiot.' I shook back my hair. 'Now, can we go?'

We made slow progress down the hill, with me trying not to put too much strain on my aching ankle in spite of the steep gradient, and afraid to make too much noise in case any of the others were still lurking there in the shadows under the trees.

Julius came over and offered me his arm. After a while he put his arm right around me. I stiffened, thinking that perhaps he was going to try something, but he simply carried on walking with me, supporting me as we made our way over the rough ground and through the tangled undergrowth.

I began to relax. Julius said very little as we went along

253

and I hoped that the subject of our visits to Rote Gertrud's house had been dropped. It all sounded ridiculously childish when you thought about it in the light of day, the sort of thing a bunch of fifth-graders would do. Perhaps he had decided that I was joking. Perhaps he despised me for such a stupid escapade. I shot a glance at his face, those angular features with their sprinkling of freckles. As far as I could tell, Julius was deep in thought. Were it not for the warmth of his arm around me, I would have said he had forgotten I was there.

And why were you *there?* I asked myself suddenly. Everyone in the town knew about the house in the woods. The messages scratched on to the walls proved that it had been visited countless times. Even so, I could hardly believe it was coincidence that Julius of all people was there on the same day as we were, at the same time.

Are you following me? I wondered with dismay. I did not want to contemplate the idea that in addition to my other woes I had someone following me around, checking to see where I went, stalking me . . . The thought chilled me. If I had not needed the support of Julius's arm I would have pushed him away.

I began to feel very weary, too weary to think straight. When we finally emerged from the woods on to the track which led through the Eschweiler Tal, I barely had the energy to put one foot in front of another. There was no sign of Max's Opel. I could pick out the spot where he always parked; there was nothing there. Clearly the others had given up and left me. Nor was there any sign of another car. How had Julius got here?

He was already disengaging himself from me. 'Stay there,'

he said, striding on his long legs towards a clump of bushes.

I stood in the middle of the track, keeping my weight on my good leg, and watched as he came out from behind the bushes, wheeling his ancient bicycle.

'Oh, crap,' I said.

CHAPTER FIFTY

If my flight down the hill had been ignominious, it was a thousand times worse riding back to Bad Münstereifel on the back of Julius's boneshaker. I had to sit sideways on the rack at the back, hanging on to Julius to stop myself falling off whenever the bike went over a bump. At the Werther Tor I had to dismount, as two of us riding over the cobblestones would have been too much for the aged machine. I walked the last few hundred metres, muttered my thanks to Julius and vanished into the bakery before he could say anything.

The light on the answering machine was blinking. I pressed the button and listened to my mother's exasperated voice asking where I was. At least she sounded irritated and not upset, I thought; that boded well for my father. I slipped my mobile out of my pocket and realized that it was turned off. No wonder she sounded annoyed. I went slowly upstairs, hanging on to the banister.

The very first thing I did when I got inside the flat was call my mother, willing the news to be good. She told me that my father was a little better, that the doctors were cautiously optimistic that he would pull through after all. 'No thanks to you,' she added tartly. 'Disappearing like that.'

I remembered my wish, written out carefully under the others' watchful eyes, and thought that perhaps she was wrong, but I did not react. Instead I said that I would take the bus to the hospital as soon as I could and rang off.

Then I went into my room and looked for somewhere to hide the torn envelope with its precious contents. In the end I stuffed it under my pillow. After that I went into the kitchen and poured myself a tall glass of mineral water. My flight down the hill and the uncomfortable ride home had left me hot and thirsty.

I raised the glass to my lips and, as I savoured the coolness of the water, my mind slid back to the ruin in the woods, to the urgent, distorted faces of my friends, to the moment I had burst out of the undergrowth on to the path and almost run right into the figure standing there. Julius. I stopped drinking, almost choking on the water. Drops ran down my chin. My stomach seemed to do a lazy roll, as though I were in an aircraft that had banked suddenly.

Why hadn't I seen it before? In that moment, when I had recognized Julius, all I had had on my mind was the driving need to push past him, to escape. I hadn't thought about what I was seeing. A tall, dark figure with a shock of flaming red hair.

I recalled the day Hanna and I had visited the witch's house – the panic we had felt at the glimpse of someone moving among the distant trees, someone with that unmistakable bright coppery hair like the flame at the end of a torch. *Panic*, that was the word. We had looked, we had *assumed*, we hadn't waited for a chance to see the figure more closely. We had run for it, as though the Devil himself had been at our heels. Now I put a new interpretation on what we had glimpsed. We had seen Julius that day, not Rote Gertrud. Which meant . . .

It really wasn't coincidence I ran into him. He goes up there a lot.

It made sense, in a horrible kind of way. What else was there to see on that side of the valley? Walkers kept to the main track. The diehard local-history freaks might seek out the *Teufelsloch*, the cave they called the Devil's Hole, but that was on the other side of the river. I knew from talk in the town that there was even a gruesome kind of tourism associated with the cave, thrill-seekers wanting to see the place where the last victim of the town's one and only serial killer had been found. But there was no reason for anyone to go into the woods on the *other* side of the valley, not unless they were looking for Gertrud's house. Ergo, Julius had been on a similar mission to our own, and it was simply down to luck that we had not met each other at the ruins themselves.

There's only one reason anyone goes there, I thought, and then came a second thought hard on the heels of the first: *Unless . . . he hasn't been making his own wishes at all, he's been reading mine.*

I put the glass down on the draining board, not trusting myself to hold it for another moment. In the two seconds it took me to cross the kitchen my legs felt as though I were walking on spindly stilts and my injured ankle threatened to buckle. I dropped into a chair and put my head in my hands, as though trying to ward off a fainting fit.

No, I thought. *Not possible.* But already my imagination was streaking ahead like a greyhound pursuing a hare. I saw Julius walking through the forest – perhaps the first time he really *had* just been out for a walk – and coming on the ruined house. I saw him stepping inside, over the jumble of broken stones and rusting beer cans and mossy branches. Surveying the scarred walls. His gaze falling upon something half concealed in the drift of leaves on the floor. The carved box. I saw him pick it up, his face creased with curiosity, and open the lid.

OK, I told myself. *It's possible that he has read every one of your wishes*. I clenched my fingers in my hair, grimacing at the thought. *It's even possible that he was the one who took your wishes out of the box . . . assuming he recognized your handwriting. But* – and this was the nub of it – *he can't have made them all come true. It's impossible*.

I thought about Klara Klein, lying dead in her locked house. *Heart attack*, everyone said. There was no sign of anyone breaking and entering, at least not until Herr Wacht-meister Schumacher broke down the door.

Maybe someone scared her to death. She was old, she was titanically fat, she was all alone in the house. What would it take? A few raps on the window – a threatening phone call?

Stop it, I told myself. *This is ridiculous.*

Julius's face came into my mind, the sharp cheekbones, the dappling of freckles, the warm brown eyes with an eternal question in them. I tried to imagine him terrorizing someone to death, or pushing an old woman downstairs, and I simply couldn't do it. All the same, I mistrusted myself. Killers didn't get away with things by being obvious maniacs; they were plausible, likeable even. That was how they got away with it.

There's no way Julius has ten thousand euros to give away. There was no denying that; if he had, he wouldn't still have been going about on that decrepit old bicycle.

No matter how much I thought about things, I could make no sense of them. I could dream up some tortuous route by which someone – Julius – might have made one or other of my hastily scrawled desires come true, but then the sheer impossibility of anyone granting all of them would hit me. I recalled the moment when Kai von Jülich had strolled into the bakery, with all the easy arrogance of wealth and good looks, and leaned towards me over the counter, relishing my name in his mouth like some gorgeous delicacy. There was no way anyone else could have made that happen.

I might have sat there all afternoon, going over every eventuality with the feverish persistence of a cryptographer trying to crack a particularly labyrinthine code, had the shrill ringing of the telephone not interrupted me. It was my mother, contrarily asking me to bring a change of clothes for her and whether I had left yet.

Packing my mother's things for her did me good. The moving about brought me back to myself, as stamping brings life back to feet numb with cold. I looked at my watch and realized that the bus would be leaving from the station in fifteen minutes. As I locked the front door behind me and went downstairs with the bag, my head was full of my father and how I would find him. When I let myself out into the street I was calculating whether there was time to stop off at the florist's.

Julius and the many masks he might be wearing had not gone from my mind; rather, it was as though I could hear a muffled conversation in the room next door: *Could he possibly . . . How could he have . . .*

I looked at my watch and began to walk, the ache in my ankle a distant nagging.

CHAPTER FIFTY-ONE

I returned in the middle of the evening, as dark was falling. Against all expectations, my father's condition had stabilized, and now my mother was beginning to talk about the bakery reopening in a couple of days.

'You had better call Achim,' she said to me. 'Make sure he doesn't go off anywhere.'

Privately I wished Achim *would* go off somewhere, the further the better.

All the same, I was faced with a new and unpleasant dilemma. If Julius had *really* had something to do with the gratification of my wishes, I could not let him attack Achim, however richly Achim might deserve it. I thought it might make me an actual accessory to murder if I stood by and let it happen, knowing whose hand was going to strike the blow. This was irrational, I acknowledged. If I was prepared to accept the death and disappearance of three other people by magic, why was I so squeamish when it came to this? But the fact remained that I was. I realized that I *liked* – that I *had* liked – Julius, not in the yearning-for-the-moon way I had cared for Kai von Jülich, but I liked him all the same. I had thought he was a good person, a little too good in some ways. If he had done things – terrible things, perhaps – because of

262

me, I would be horribly, shockingly responsible. Which meant I would have to do everything in my power to make him stop.

As I let myself into the bakery and trudged painfully back up the stairs, I made a decision. I would try to take back the curse on Achim, though how I would do this I was not sure. The original curse had vanished from the house in the woods, but maybe I could undo it with a new wish. If necessary, I would confront Julius, but I hoped that would be the last resort. If my suspicions were wrong I would look idiotic; if they were right I could not imagine what reaction a confrontation might provoke.

I let myself into the flat, which was dark and uninviting, and deadlocked the door behind me. I realized that I had hardly eaten that day, but I was too tired to care. I cleaned my teeth, dragged a brush through my hair and fell into bed. I lay on my side in the dark and slid a hand under the pillow to touch the envelope containing the banknotes. *How could Julius possibly have laid hands on so much money?* I asked myself, and there was no good answer, nothing that did not mean dishonesty, treachery and lies. I could no more sleep with that ominous bundle under my pillow than the princess in the story could sleep with a pea under her mattress. In the end I shoved it into the drawer of my bedside table and fell into an uneasy sleep.

This time it was 2.15 a.m. when I woke up. There was something sickening about being woken at that time of night, when I should have been in slumber so deep that it was like death. I turned on to my side and waited for the nauseating feeling of shock to subside, listening to my own rapid breathing.

I had no idea what had woken me, and for a moment I wondered whether I had simply had a bad dream, although I had no memory of one. I lay there and watched the glowing digits on the alarm clock change to 2.16. I listened. Silence.

Then I heard it, very distinctly. A crisp *bang*: the unmistakable sound of the kitchen door swinging shut. I knew that sound, because I heard it a dozen times a day, whenever a delivery was made to the back door or Achim stepped outside to have a cigarette. The door was heavy and it had a self-closing mechanism. You couldn't fail to recognize that irritating smacking sound. It didn't irritate me now, though. I was paralysed with shock, swept away on its icy flood, my feet no longer able to touch solid ground.

I lay in bed with my eyes wide, staring into the formless dark, and my heart thumping. There was no doubt about it this time. There was definitely someone downstairs. The old fears began to creep back, as stealthy and as ugly as trolls. I thought of footsteps, fleet and soundless, crossing the tiled floor of the bakery kitchen. Hands, slender and white, or perhaps – grisly thought – mere blackened sticks, clutching at the banisters leading to the flat. I thought of a thin silent figure, wrapped in black, standing motionless on the other side of the door, waiting. What would I see, I wondered, if I looked into the face hidden by the bright hair?

The hand I stretched out to switch on the bedside lamp was trembling. I sat up and listened with strained attention for any sounds from below. Nothing. I felt my nails digging into my palms and realized that I had balled my hands into fists. I made myself relax.

Calm down, I said to myself. *Maybe it's a burglar. A real, flesh-and-blood burglar – or at any rate, some stupid kid messing around, someone who doesn't realize the most valuable thing in those kitchens is Dad's secret Florentiner recipe.*

I got out of bed as silently as I could and padded over to the bedroom door. *It's the same time as before*, said an insidious little voice at the back of my mind. *Just past two.* I glanced back at the digital clock, which read 2.18. *It's not kids. You know it isn't.*

I paused, irresolute. I could call the police; that was the logical thing to do if you thought you had a break-in downstairs. But suppose it wasn't a burglar? Suppose I called out the police and there was nothing to see in the kitchen, because the person who was down there, the person who was *haunting* me, couldn't possibly exist at all? In that case I would be better off calling old Father Arnold and telling him to come round with his Bible and a bottle of holy water.

I opened the bedroom door. The hallway light was off, but the light spilling from my room was sufficient for me to pick my way to the front door without bumping into anything.

Check the door is locked. I knew I had locked it, I could *remember* doing it, and yet I still had a paranoid fear that it was *unlocked*. I put out a hand and tested the door handle very carefully, anxious to avoid making any sound that might draw attention to me. The door was locked fast. I drew the keys out of the lock, wincing at the rattle they made, and held them in my closed fist, as though there were some danger of them springing out of my hand and reopening the door by themselves. Then I listened again.

There had been nothing since that distinctive sound of

the kitchen door closing. Now I began to doubt myself. Had I heard something else – a car backfiring on the distant bypass, a neighbour slamming a bedroom window shut? I hesitated, then made up my mind. If there was anything to see downstairs, I would find it in the morning. Doubtless there would be nothing, or perhaps simply a utensil that had fallen from its hook again, like last time. I turned to go back to my room, taking the keys with me, and it was then that I heard it.

Down below, in the dark of the bakery kitchen, someone laughed.

CHAPTER FIFTY-TWO

I thought I would never sleep again after hearing that laugh: high, wild, exulting, less an expression of mirth than the cry of some predatory thing. I huddled in my bed with the light on and my mobile phone clutched in one hand, though I did not know whom I would ring, even if the thing that shrieked out its horrid glee were to pound on the door of the flat, seeking entrance. I listened, wide-eyed, and I whispered half-forgotten prayers, but I never heard the voice a second time, though the expectation of hearing it was almost more than I could bear. At length the sustained tension petrified me as effectively as a Gorgon's glare and I fell asleep in spite of myself.

When I awoke it was seven o'clock and someone was sounding a horn in the street outside the bakery with irritable insistence. I was debating whether to put my head underneath the pillow and try to get back to sleep when I heard the doorbell.

'*Scheisse*,' I said crossly to thin air, and threw off the duvet.

I had no intention of going down and opening the street door in my nightclothes. Instead I went into the living room, opened the window and peered out.

I thought I would find some irate deliveryman standing on the doorstep below, but the first thing I saw was a car parked in the street outside the bakery. It was a battered-looking white Audi, a vehicle I recognized as belonging to Achim Zimmer. My heart sank. He must have jumped the gun and turned up for work without being asked. I wondered why he had left his car there, though. In the next few hours the street would be busy with delivery vans. In fact, there was one behind the car already and, as I gazed down at it, the horn sounded again.

Someone stepped back from the bakery doorway and looked up at me. I saw that it was Herr Hack from one of the shops further down the street.

'Hey,' he shouted up. 'You need to get that car moved.'

'It's not mine,' I tried to say, but he was already pressing the buzzer again.

I closed the window and went to the bedroom, where I hastily dressed. I was not sure what was going on downstairs, but clearly there was going to be no peace until Achim had moved his car. I didn't bother brushing my hair or cleaning my teeth. I would gladly have gone downstairs looking like a bag lady if it kept Achim at arm's length.

When I got to the street door, Herr Hack's face was beginning to assume an alarming hue. He left off pressing the buzzer when he saw me coming and started to tap on the glass door with a fleshy forefinger, as though he would have liked to poke me in the eye with it. The first thing he said when I opened the door was, 'I should call the police. It's an obstruction.'

'It's not my car,' I said.

'It's parked outside your bakery.'

'It's Herr Zimmer's,' I said. 'My father's assistant.' Indignation made me bold. I looked him in the eyes. '*I* didn't park it there.'

'Move it,' he said.

'I can't,' I pointed out. 'I don't have the keys.'

'Where is Herr Zimmer?' demanded Herr Hack. He peered over my shoulder, as though Achim might somehow have concealed his substantial bulk behind me.

I shrugged. 'He isn't supposed to be here today.'

'The car must be moved,' said Herr Hack with relentless persistence. 'I need that delivery.'

As if on cue, the horn sounded again behind us.

'I can't carry all those boxes up the street myself,' Herr Hack told me truculently.

'I didn't ask you to,' I said under my breath.

'What did you say?'

But I had already turned to go into the bakery. Achim would certainly be in the kitchen, so let him come out and deal with this in person. To my annoyance I heard Herr Hack follow me inside, huffing and puffing with indignation as though he had been required to climb the foothills of the Himalayas with a twenty-kilo pack. I pretended not to notice and went to the door which led to the kitchen, hand outstretched to pull it open.

It was locked. That pulled me up sharply. I pressed down the handle and yanked at it again, but it was absolutely fast. *Funny.* I supposed that Achim had used the back door as usual, but even so he normally unlocked the door to the cafe area. Perhaps he hadn't come in to work; perhaps he had just come in to pick something up.

Why is his car abandoned outside, then?

269

There was no answer to that. I turned on my heel, brushed past Herr Hack and went back to the street door to collect my bunch of keys, which was still hanging in the inside lock. I found the kitchen door key, fumbled it into the lock and pulled the door open.

The kitchen was cool and empty. The fluorescent lights were off and the light which came through the frosted windows was flat and grey. The habitual aroma of baking had faded to a stale memory. I thought of crumbs and dust settling.

I cleared my throat. 'Achim?' I said, moving further into the kitchen. There was no reply. Now I had a view of the back door, I could see that it was closed. There were no keys in it.

Where is he?

I was aware of Herr Hack's stout figure in the kitchen doorway. His outrage was not sufficient to carry him over the threshold of that holy of holies, but all the same he was almost visibly throbbing with the desire to give Achim a piece of his mind. I was not sorry that he was here. Herr Hack was profoundly irritating, with his red face and his jabbing forefinger, but for some reason I was glad not to be alone. I had an uneasy feeling, a swarming sensation in my gut which recalled the frantic and miniature activity of an overturned ant heap.

Something's wrong.

I rounded the end of one of the metal units and something caught my eye, a flash of colour against the dull grey of stainless steel. There was a tall clear bottle with a bright crimson label standing on the metal surface. *Vodka. What's that doing here?* I stretched out my hand to pick it up, but then I thought better of it. Without thinking, I rubbed my hand on the leg of my jeans, as though I had sullied it simply by reaching for the bottle.

There was *someone in here last night*, I thought, but the realization gave me no relief. If someone had broken in for the hell of it, intent on a little drunken mayhem, they wouldn't have left the place in this pristine condition; things would be broken or disarrayed. I shivered, remembering the wild laughter I had heard in the darkness of the small hours. I could make no sense of it, but I was beginning to be afraid.

I continued my cautious exploration of the kitchen, all the time acutely conscious of that incongruous bottle standing there like a sentinel. What did it mean? I had my eyes on the far end of the kitchen, scanning it for anything which might give me a clue. I wasn't looking down and so I almost stumbled over something that was lying in the middle of the tiled floor. I looked down and then I stared.

It was a shirt. I was pretty sure it was a man's shirt and, as I looked at it lying there, with the arms pulled inside out as though someone had tugged it off in a hurry, I recognized it as one I had seen Achim wearing. It wasn't a work shirt, it was a loathsome patterned thing that even a clothing bank would have spat out.

So Achim has *been here*, I told myself. *So what? Maybe he came in, changed into his baker's whites and then . . . disappeared?* It didn't make sense.

'Hurry up,' grunted Herr Hack from the doorway, as though finding Achim and getting him to move the car were simply a matter of increased effort on my part.

Now I was moving about the kitchens more quickly, my glance darting from the bare worktops to the tiled floor and back again. There was something else on the floor, half hidden behind the leg of one of the units. A man's shoe, lying on its side. I stopped, gazed down at it and felt a cold prickle of apprehension.

Achim might have changed his shirt here and forgotten the old one, but he wouldn't leave one shoe behind.

Suddenly I understood, quite clearly, that Achim was dead. The curse had fallen upon him, just as I had wished. Except that now I would dearly have loved to have taken it back. Klara Klein dropping dead of a weak heart in her villa up in Mahlberg or Kai von Jülich vanishing into thin air, that was one thing. Hunting for a corpse in the very building where I lived and worked was quite another.

Dread welled up inside me, black and suffocating. Every pace which took me further through the kitchen might reveal something that I desperately didn't want to see. I remembered tales I had heard from the other girls who worked in the bakery, and from students at the college: the man who had committed suicide when drunk by plunging himself head first into one of the industrial mixers, the body that had been found charred to the bone in an oven. I cringed at the thought of having to see anything like that, of being the one who found it, and yet I kept on moving. How could I explain to Herr Hack that I thought Achim was lying here dead somewhere, because I had wished it? Sick with apprehension, I pushed myself on. There was nothing to do but keep looking.

I thought that the shelves of the big oven were too low for a person of Achim's bulk to be squeezed inside, and besides, when I laid a trembling hand on the door, it was absolutely cold. Still, it was only the consciousness of Herr Hack's accusatory gaze fixed on my back that made me open it. I looked at the empty shelves and bit my knuckle to stop myself from crying out.

'What are you looking in there for?' called out Herr Hack irritably. 'How could he be in there?'

I said nothing. I closed the door again.

My own footsteps sounded unnaturally loud as I continued my tour of the kitchen. I looked at the great bowl of the dough mixer and knew that I must peer inside. I clasped my hands tight across my stomach as I went to it, as though I could hold back the nauseating fear which roiled in my gut. I was thinking about what would happen if you really did put someone inside it, and whether it would be possible to make the kitchen as clean and sterile again afterwards as it now was. Wouldn't the walls and the ceiling be painted red, or drying brown, with the blood that sprayed out of it? You could spend not hours but *days* trying to clean it all up, to find every tiny drop and spurt that had splattered everything around it. It would probably get into all the tiny places in the machinery, glue up the mechanism. A tiny strangled noise came from my throat. I went right up to the mixer and forced myself to look inside.

Nothing. The interior was clean and dry, as though it had never been used. There was not so much as a sprinkling of flour in it. I realized I had been holding my breath and let it all out in a sigh.

'What are you doing?' demanded Herr Hack impatiently. 'Is he here or isn't he?'

'I don't think so,' I said in a tight voice.

I swung around to face him, a stout, florid, double-chinned bully, inflated to bursting point with his own righteous indignation. Framed in the doorway at the other end of the kitchen, he might have been a million miles away. He still thought this was about a parked car obstructing the street. I knew it was about murder.

Outside the bakery, the delivery truck driver began to sound the horn again, repeated blasts that would soon have everyone on the street out of doors and looking for the source of the noise. I imagined them all cramming themselves into the kitchen doorway alongside Herr Hack and realized that I had to do something. I began to walk back towards him, trying to form the right words in my head before I tackled him. Achim clearly wasn't here, I would say, so it was not the bakery's problem. Or . . .

As I passed the thick metal door which led into the cold store I suddenly stopped walking. It was only a tiny thing and I might not have noticed it had my nerves not already been in a state of painful sensitivity. The pointer on the temperature dial outside the cold store had been moved. That faint pale triangle was visible again at the top of the dial, where the tip of the pointer normally was, and the pointer itself was in the six o'clock position.

I caught my breath. I had *never* seen the pointer in that position before. Theoretically the temperature in the cold store could be lowered right down to minus thirty degrees centigrade, but we never needed to store anything at that sort of temperature, and as far as I knew, we had never tried putting the setting down that low. I stepped up close to the dial and saw that it was indeed set to minus thirty.

No, I thought. I looked at the door, which was at least four centimetres thick, and suddenly it looked less like the anonymous door of a cold store than the entrance to a mausoleum. I reached for the handle, then hesitated.

There's an emergency release inside, I thought. *It's not possible to get trapped in there.* I grasped the handle, turned and pulled. Ponderously, the door swung open, revealing the interior.

The side walls of the cold store were lined with metal racks, which were stacked with trays of uncooked rolls, cartons containing pots of fresh cream and other perishables. The back wall was bare and propped up against it was Achim. He was stark naked. The skin which was normally pink and white was now so pale that it had assumed a greyish tint. His head was thrown back, resting in the angle between the rack and the wall, and his mouth gaped open as though one final scream had escaped with the curl of mist that had been his last breath. I thought there were clusters of ice crystals around his mouth, but I did not want to look more closely. The great pallid, hairless bulk of the body reminded me of nothing so much as the bloodless carcass of a slaughtered pig.

Little incoherent sounds were coming from my throat. I wanted to look away, to shut out the sight of the body sprawled there, but my treacherous eyes were taking in every detail, storing them in whatever mental catacombs served as the repository for nightmares. The bluish lips. The way the body was huddled, as though Achim had tried vainly to preserve the last warmth that was fading with the ebbing of his life. The white hand, rigid and inert as a clump of coral.

There was another bottle on the floor of the cold store, I noticed: the same type as the one on the surface in the kitchen. Clear glass, red label. And there was the other shoe, wedged underneath one of the metal racks.

'What's going on there?' said Herr Hack's voice close behind me. His impatience had finally overridden his qualms about trespassing.

I turned a stricken face to him, but I could find no words to describe what was inside the cold store. I simply stood back to let him see. He shot me a glance that plainly showed that he thought I was a fool and then he looked into the cold store.

'*Lieber Gott!*' said Herr Hack.

CHAPTER FIFTY-THREE

Herr Wachtmeister Schumacher arrived, his indefinite face swimming before my eyes like a wraith, his voice a distant echo in my ears. Herr Hack hauled me back out into the cafe area and I sat at one of the tables, as though nursing the vain hope that the cold coffee machine and empty cabinet would yield forth a hot sweet drink and a slice of cherry streusel. After a while another police officer came, this time a woman, and she asked me some questions. Some time after that my mother arrived, torn from my father's side. I had no idea what had happened about the delivery van, but the horn was no longer sounding. Perhaps the driver had reversed the entire way back down the Werther Strasse, like a genie disappearing back into its bottle. I wished that time could be rewound that easily. I would have gone back, not to the moment when I had cursed Achim, but to that evening in the snack bar when I had agreed to go to the witch's house with the others. I would have gone anywhere else, done anything else, gone home to bed even.

In spite of the interminable questions that pattered down on me like a relentless drizzling rain, nobody seemed to be giving any consideration to the idea that I might have had anything to do with Achim's death. They wanted to know whether I had heard anything during the night and whether Achim had made a habit of drinking in the bakery, and they asked both my mother and myself whether he had had a history of depression and suicidal tendencies. I was unable to formulate a reply; I was remembering the laugh I had heard in the small hours, the moment I had seen the dial turned down to minus thirty and the sight of the body propped there against the wall like the hefty carcass of a slain animal. I could no more explain what I thought had happened to Achim than the fly that is struggling in a cocoon of stifling cobwebs can free itself from its gluey shroud. The more I tried to rationalize it, the more entangled my thoughts became.

Seeing that there was nothing that could be done for Achim, the emergency doctor who had arrived with the police turned his attention to me and pronounced me to be suffering from shock. The questions ceased, although I knew that this was just the ebbing of the tide; they would be back in full flood at the earliest opportunity. My mother took me upstairs, away from the cafe, whose windows were dark with the ranks of concerned citizens clustering there like the hungry dead in a zombie movie.

She saw me shivering and fetched a blanket to put around my shoulders. Then she made me sit on the sofa while she went to make me some cocoa. She was all brisk efficiency, although I suspected that this was just her way of coping. She had not seen Achim's body. She showed no desire to see it and indeed appeared to be taking refuge in treating him as though he were still alive and had committed some highly reprehensible act.

'Why did he have to do it *here*, of all places?' I heard her grumble, as she stood at the stove watching the pan of milk. 'This will be the end of the bakery.'

Privately I doubted that. I had seen the ghoulish interest the discovery of Achim's body had aroused and thought that as soon as we had the bakery open again people would come in droves to see the place where the death had occurred. I said nothing, however. I just pulled the blanket closer around my shoulders and stared at the floor.

That afternoon Hanna came to the flat. My mother had had to go back to the hospital, but she didn't want to leave me alone. She didn't ask me beforehand whether I would like someone to stay with me, or indeed whether that someone should be Hanna; if she had, I would have strenuously resisted. Instead, looking at my pale face and preoccupied expression, she made the decision for me, not wanting to give me the opportunity to say that I preferred to be alone. Perhaps she called Izzi first, but more likely she picked on Hanna because she thought that Hanna would take charge and look after me properly. Hanna always gave that impression.

When my mother showed her into the living room, however, I thought that Hanna looked a little less sure of herself than usual, as well she might. I had not forgotten the scene at the ruined house, nor my panicked flight down the hill through the woods, with my erstwhile friends in noisy pursuit. I was not going to make a fuss in front of my mother, but as soon as she had safely departed for Mechernich I intended to throw Hanna out of the flat.

The instant I heard the street door close downstairs I stood up, looked straight at Hanna and said, 'I want you to go. Now.'

'Steffi –'

'I don't want to see you. Or the others.'

'What have *I* done?' asked Hanna in an injured tone, quite unlike her normal confident manner.

I looked at her in disbelief. 'How can you say that? After what happened in Rote Gertrud's place?'

'But Steffi –'

I wasn't going to let her finish. 'I nearly broke my ankle running down that bloody hill. I'm never going up there again and I'm never having anything to do with – with any of *that* again. So you needn't come here and ask me to wish stuff for you, because I'm not going to – not ever again. And I want you to go now.'

Hanna was looking bewildered. 'I didn't come to ask you to wish anything for me. Your mother asked me to come.'

My conscience pricked me a little at that, but I was too angry to listen to it. 'I don't care. Just go.'

'All right,' said Hanna. She paused. 'If you want me to go, I'll go. But I didn't do anything. It wasn't *me* who chased you down the hill. It was Jochen and Timo and Max. I *called* you. I tried to find you, to help you.'

'Really?' I said with spiteful irony. 'And what about up at Gertrud's house? I thought you lot were going to tear me to pieces.'

'That was the others,' said Hanna. She looked stricken, as though I had perpetrated some terrible injustice against her.

In spite of myself, I found my resolve weakening. It was Hanna, after all, who had risked a major row with her control freak of a father by borrowing his car to take me to the Eschweiler Tal that time; Hanna who had crouched with me in the undergrowth, praying that the figure we saw flitting through the dank woods would not see us hiding there.

'I didn't join in,' Hanna pleaded. 'Don't you remember? I was trying to stop them hassling you. I tried to pull Max off you. I grabbed Jochen's arm and he nearly pushed me over. It was them – Max and Jochen and Timo. I didn't do anything. I was trying to *help* you.'

I looked at Hanna, at her pale, earnest face, and I cast my mind back to that afternoon at the house in the woods. The whole incident was a blur in my memory, a tangle of thrusting hands and grabbing fists and insistent voices. I could distinctly recall Timo taking hold of my jacket again, as though he thought there might be another envelope stuffed with euro notes hidden somewhere inside it, and I remembered Jochen's face, close to mine and distorted with ugly emotion. But what had Hanna been doing at the time? She had been there, I knew that, and she had been shouting as loudly as the rest of them, but what had she been saying? I thought she had been somewhere there in the fray, pushing and tugging, but she might have been trying to get the others off me, as she claimed. I really wasn't sure any more.

I didn't say anything, but I had stopped ordering Hanna out of the flat. She studied my face and I saw her features relax as she sensed that I was no longer sure of my ground.

'Honestly, Steffi,' she said, 'I wanted to help. I would have stopped them if I could. But you know what Max is like.'

I did know what Max was like, although frankly I was more nervous of Jochen, whose anger seemed ready to spill over into actual manhandling at any moment. I shrugged non-committally.

'It's all finished anyway,' I said. 'I'm not going up there ever again. Not for Max, not for anyone.'

'I'm not asking you to,' said Hanna.

She put out a hand and touched my shoulder. I didn't shake her off, but neither did I react. Part of me felt as cold and immovable as marble, and I wanted her to sense that. I wondered whether she would say anything about the money, which was still stuffed into the drawer in my bedroom, hidden and unlooked at, like the guilty evidence of a crime.

'Please,' said Hanna at last, 'don't be mad at me.'

I looked at the floor and sighed. Then I looked back at Hanna and said, 'OK.' I saw her start to smile tentatively, felt that she was about to step towards me, and I held up a hand as though to ward her off. 'But I'm not wishing anything for anyone else, not even you.'

I sat back down on the sofa, all my anger draining out of me. It was exhausting being that furious with someone; my body felt as though it had been working as hard as if it were fighting off a virus.

After a moment Hanna sat down too, on one of my father's overstuffed armchairs. For a little while neither of us said anything. I thought about Hanna, about the things she had risked for me, and why she had done them, and I thought about the curses I had made against people, people who were now dead. I thought about Achim and his threat to make me 'like' him, about Frau Kessel and Klara Klein, and about my sister, Magdalena, and my mother telling me I would break my father's heart. I felt like a drowning person, drawn deep into the depths of a whirlpool. I no longer knew which way was up, which way went towards the airy light and which towards the darkness that meant the end of everything. I leaned forward and put my head in my hands.

The armchair creaked as Hanna got up. A moment later I felt a light touch on my back.

'Are you OK?' she asked.

'I don't know,' I managed to say.

Through the curtain of light hair falling over my face I could see Hanna squatting in front of me.

'Was it you who found Achim?' she asked in a low voice.

'Yes,' I said.

'And he was . . . already dead?'

'Totally,' I said, and found myself stifling a nervous urge to laugh. 'He was . . . frozen. I think he was frozen *solid*, actually. Like a leg of lamb or something.' My stomach lurched queasily at that. 'He was definitely . . . dead.'

'What did the police say?'

'Oh.' I shook my head restlessly. 'They asked me about a million questions. Like, was Achim depressed or had he ever threatened to kill himself? Had I heard anything during the night?'

'What did you tell them?' asked Hanna.

'I didn't tell them anything.' I shook back my hair and glanced at her. 'I wasn't going to tell them we hexed Achim, was I?'

'No,' she said quietly. Her eyes met mine. 'What do *you* think happened to Achim?'

'I don't think he killed himself,' I said. I remembered the sound I had heard, muffled but audible enough, the sound that had sent me scurrying back to bed, where I had pulled the covers over my head to block it out. The wild laughter, harsh and unrestrained as the howl of a wolf. 'It wasn't suicide,' I said.

CHAPTER FIFTY-FOUR

The following day was Saturday. In the middle of the morning the silence in the flat was broken by the sound of the street doorbell. I was sitting at the kitchen table, drinking a glass of orange juice and staring out of the window at the brilliant crimson flowers in the window box at the side of another building. *Ten thousand euros*, I was thinking, and the enormity of it was too much to comprehend. *Ten thousand euros and a dead man in the cold store of the bakery*. It was a mystery I couldn't fathom, with no solution that I wanted.

I wasn't expecting anyone and at first when I heard the bell I was inclined to ignore it. But whoever was outside was pretty determined. The bell went again and again, an irritable buzzing that was hard to ignore. I drained the glass of juice, put it down on the table and went to investigate.

As I walked through the deserted bakery I could see the shape of someone standing at the door, the bright summer sunshine rendering them a silhouette. The buzzer sounded again, insistently, and I clicked my tongue in annoyance. I couldn't imagine what the caller wanted; the CLOSED sign was up, the lights were off and the bakery didn't just look shut, it looked positively dead, with no chance of an imminent resurrection.

I unlocked the door, pulled it open and found myself face to face with a woman perhaps ten years older than I was, with light brown hair in a short gamine crop. She was dressed a little more formally than the majority of summer visitors to the town, in a dark skirt and blouse. She looked as though she was on her way to a christening or a job interview. She was holding a bundle close to her. I looked more closely and realized that it was a baby, just a few months old, with a fluff of hair so blond that it was almost white.

The woman looked at me with an expression that was at once hopeful and curiously timid. I found my annoyance evaporating. I almost wished that I had freshly brewed coffee and apple strudel to offer her.

'I'm sorry,' I said as kindly as I could, 'but the bakery's closed until further notice.'

I would have shut the door, but the woman didn't show any sign of turning away. She just stood there, with her arms around the baby and one finger gently stroking the fluffy little head, and looked at me.

'My father's in hospital,' I said. 'There isn't anything, I'm afraid.'

'You're Stefanie Nett,' said the woman, and the way she said it made it sound as though this was a breathtaking discovery.

I didn't reply. With a sinking feeling in the pit of my stomach I wondered whether she had come, not in search of refreshment or somewhere to sit with the baby, but to see the bakery itself or, worse still, to see *me*. Like everyone else in the town, I was aware of the ghoulish tourists who came and pointed out the house where Bad Münstereifel's serial killer had lived a decade before, and who tramped up and down the Eschweiler Tal looking for *the place*. I wondered whether this innocuous-looking mother was in fact the vanguard of a new set of sensation-seekers come to gawp at *The Bakery of Horror* or even *The Girl Who Found the Body*.

'You are her, aren't you?' said the woman. 'Stefanie.'

'Yes,' I said involuntarily, and then immediately, 'No.'

I began to close the door but the woman was too quick for me. She couldn't put out a hand, because both her arms were around the baby, but she put out a foot instead and suddenly her shoe was jammed in the door. I couldn't push any harder without hurting her. For a moment I considered simply turning tail and fleeing into the back of the bakery, but then the woman spoke again.

'Don't you recognize me, Stefanie?'

'No,' I said, but the question gave me pause. I relaxed the pressure on the door and the woman pushed it open with her elbow. Once she was inside the bakery she looked at me expectantly. 'I'm sorry,' I said.

She was turning the baby around to face me. It was very drowsy; the little eyes were closed, the soft cheeks pink.

'Say hello to Auntie Stefanie, Theo.'

Still I looked at them both dumbly. *Auntie?* I was thinking. *I'm not anyone's aunt*. Maybe she was simply being twee, trying to fabricate a connection between us. Did I know her from somewhere?

Perhaps she mistook my perplexed expression for something less friendly. There was a slightly hurt tone in her voice when she said, 'This is your nephew, Theo.'

I stared at her open-mouthed, as I finally grasped what she was telling me.

'I'm Magdalena,' she said.

CHAPTER FIFTY-FIVE

I showed Magdalena into the living room; somehow I couldn't imagine taking her into the kitchen and us sitting on either side of the breakfast table with its plasticized cloth. She still didn't feel like my sister, or seem to belong to this place, despite having lived here once. I offered her coffee, which she declined, and orange juice, which she accepted, and then I sat on the edge of one of the armchairs and watched her sitting on the sofa with the baby, carefully rearranging its blanket.

'How's Papa?' asked Magdalena.

She wasn't looking at me at the time, she was looking at Theo, and that was just as well. If she had glanced at my face she might have seen the warring emotions which were passing across it, like a bloom of silt stirred up in a pond. Nobody ever called my father *Papa* except me; it sounded strange coming from this woman's lips, and I felt irrationally jealous, as though she had come to take him away from me. And then I felt both curious and awkward. She was my sister, my own flesh and blood, but when I looked at her it was hard to see the nineteen-year-old she had been; her hair had been lighter then, and she had worn it longer, and her features had been softer, more rounded. Over a decade ago, when I had last seen her, I had been a child and she had been almost grown up. Now she looked as though she had been tramping the weary ways of adulthood for years.

'He had a heart attack,' I said.

'I know. I came as soon as I could.'

'How did you find out?' I said.

As far as I was aware, neither of my parents had spoken to Magdalena in years.

'I have a friend in the town,' she said. 'She phoned me when she heard.'

I was so stunned by this piece of information that for a moment I was unable to say a thing. Magdalena still had contact with a friend in the town? I looked at her and felt the stirrings of anger. Had she no idea how our parents had suffered over the years, wondering what she was doing, whether she would ever come back? Suppose our father had died without ever knowing what had become of his eldest daughter.

'He's very ill,' I said. 'But he's still alive.'

What did you care during the last ten years? I thought resentfully. Then I relented a little. This was my sister, after all, come back from a limbo as remote as death. Whatever the repercussions, my parents could be nothing other than thrilled to see her.

'They'll be so pleased to see you,' I said impulsively. 'And the baby.'

'I hope so,' said Magdalena.

Silence as cool and deep as the soft drifting of snow fell between us again. I wondered whether I should ask to hold the baby, but in truth I had hardly ever held one in my life and I felt awkward about doing it. Instead I sat and studied my sister, wishing that I had the gift of easy conversation that everyone else seemed to have.

The hands which held the baby were ringless, I noticed.

'Are you married, then?' I asked.

'No,' said Magdalena, not looking up. 'I'm living with someone.'

'Oh.'

'You must hate me,' said Magdalena suddenly.

Now she did look at me and her face was flushed, her eyes bright and feverish.

'No –'

'You must think I'm a heartless bitch, leaving and not getting in touch all this time. Don't you?'

I just stared at her.

'It's not like I haven't thought about it,' she said passionately. 'I've been thinking about it all the time.'

'So why didn't you?' I asked her.

'Because – because I just *couldn't* come back. And if I'd stayed in touch I would have had to, sooner or later. I know Papa needed me in the bakery . . . and it would have been so much easier, that's the thing. It was really hard at first, managing on my own. Really hard.' Her voice shook. 'But I couldn't come back here. I had terrible rows with Mum, you know. She was so angry with me.'

'I know,' I said. 'She's so sorry, really she is. She still blames herself.'

'I was angry with her too,' said my sister. 'I was so angry I didn't ever want to see her again. I wanted to hurt her. That's not a good thing to have done.' Her voice broke and now I saw that she was crying. 'But it wasn't her. *She* wasn't the reason I couldn't come back. It's this town. This bloody town. Everyone knowing what had happened. Having to stand in the bakery every day when they came in, knowing what they were saying behind my back. I just couldn't stand it. All those good Catholics, all those self-righteous citizens. And Frau Kessel –'

'Frau Kessel is dead,' I said.

Magdalena stared at me. 'Thank God.'

'She was murdered,' I said, and my mouth was suddenly so dry that the words felt like ashes on my tongue. I remembered that no conclusion had been reached about the cause of death so far, not publicly anyway. 'At least, some people *think* she was murdered. It wasn't quite clear.'

'I hope she *was* murdered,' said Magdalena. 'The poisonous old witch.'

'Don't say that,' I said faintly.

'Why not?' said my sister defiantly. 'I'd have done it myself if I could.'

My mind sped back to the day, long ago, when she had taken me up to the house in the woods. *Yes*, I thought, *I suppose you would have done it. You would have done as much as I did anyway.*

I was thinking about this when Magdalena said, 'Stefanie, where is Papa? Mechernich?'

'Yes,' I said.

I noticed that she didn't use the name everyone else did – Steffi – but then why should she? She didn't know.

'We should go there,' said my sister. 'Can you come with me?'

I nodded. 'There's a bus in . . . oh, half an hour.'

'No need,' said Magdalena. 'I've brought the car.' She glanced at me. 'Let's go, right away.'

'Don't you want to finish your orange juice?'

'No,' she said. 'Thanks, but I'm not really thirsty. Anyway,' she said, getting to her feet with the baby clasped carefully to her, 'I don't have that long.'

I stared at her. 'Aren't you staying?'

She shook her head. 'It's a long drive back.'

I said nothing to that, but I could imagine the pain it would cause my mother and father. Magdalena herself didn't say another word as I led her to the front door and we went downstairs. I locked the bakery door behind us and followed her a short way up the street. There was a neat little Volkswagen parked in one of the spaces by the wall which skirted the river. Magdalena opened a rear door and began to settle Theo in his car seat. I looked at her bent back as she worked, pulling on the tiny straps and fastening the little buckle. She could have been anybody, a stranger.

She straightened up, gave me a quick glance, and then opened the passenger door for me. I looked around the familiar street, as though I were trying to impress it all upon my memory before I too set off on a long journey, then I got into the car. Magdalena was already inserting the key into the ignition. The vista of half-timbered houses and worn cobblestones seemed to hold no interest for her at all and as we drove away she didn't so much as glance in the rear-view mirror.

CHAPTER FIFTY-SIX

I had not recognized Magdalena, but my mother did at once. She gave a tiny cry at the sight of Theo and if her gaze slid to the naked ring finger, as mine had, she gave no sign of it.

'How long are you staying?' was almost the first thing she asked.

'I can't,' said my sister.

'You're not *going?*' My mother sounded aghast.

'I have to drive back this afternoon,' said Magdalena.

My father was asleep – or unconscious, I was not sure which – so the pair of them went out into the corridor to continue their discussion, my mother's voice rising in a trill of sorrow and disappointment, Magdalena's response too low for me to pick out the words.

I stood by my father's bed. I would have liked to take his hand, but I hardly dared to. He looked so old and frail, and, besides, there were tubes and wires sprouting everywhere, as though his battered heart were the junction box for some mighty network. Instead I pulled up one of the dismal grey plastic hospital chairs and sat looking at the pale face on the pillow.

Get better, I willed him silently. *Don't die.*

I thought of the times I had been up to the witch's house, the curses I had laid on people, first as a game and then in deadly earnest. I thought that if my last wish were to come true, if my father pulled through, it would somehow all be worth it. I would have repaid a debt.

The past few weeks felt like a journey through a nightmare landscape peopled with ghouls who had familiar faces and overgrown with temptations which blossomed like evil flowers. I thought of my last wish and I saw myself bursting out into open country, into clean air, into brightness and light. I could put it all behind me, like the fever dream it was. My father would be well and we would all be at home again. If Magdalena would only agree to stay . . .

I got to my feet and went to the door. My mother and Magdalena had gone, but I could see them across the corridor, through the big plate glass window of the visitors' waiting room. The thick glass deadened any sound, but I could see what was happening. My mother was holding Theo, and she was looking at his tiny face, and with one hand she was stroking his fluffy little head, but her lips were moving and she was clearly weeping.

Magdalena was crying too. I saw her put her arms around our mother, encircling her and the baby. Now I could see that she was speaking too, trying to offer words of comfort, of reconciliation. But the tears told their own story: Magdalena was going to go away again, whatever my mother said to try to make her stay. The rifts that Frau Kessel had caused in our family could not be so easily mended. My sister had a life elsewhere now, with Theo and his father, the boyfriend we had never met.

*   *   *

Magdalena spent more than an hour with my parents. She stayed for most of the day, and my father was awake and conscious for long enough to know that his prodigal daughter had returned. But she had said that she had to go, and go she did. She dropped me off at the Orchheimer Tor, the great gate at the southern end of Bad Münstereifel, and as I stood there on the cobblestones, she turned the little Volkswagen around and drove away, towards the roundabout at the end of Trier Strasse, the turning to Euskirchen and ultimately the motorway which would carry her the hundreds of kilometres to the place she now called home. I watched the car dwindling into the distance and finally disappearing around the curve of the roundabout. I wondered at Magdalena's willingness to face the prospect of driving so far with a young baby in the car and briefly I thought of the empty hours stretching ahead of her, with the Volkswagen's headlights picking out yellow tracks on the grey of the road. But Magdalena had already vanished from our lives again, just as if she had never visited at all.

I stayed where I was for another minute, staring at the distant roundabout, and then I turned and went back into the town, heading for the bakery. I passed Frau Kessel's house and then the rival bakery, where she always purchased her *Graubrot*, but there was no danger of running into her now, or ever again. I felt the fever touch of guilt and tried to turn my thoughts away from the old lady and her demise. A moment later I had rounded the corner by the old brewery and our own bakery came into view. *Home*, I said to myself, but the word gave me little comfort.

CHAPTER FIFTY-SEVEN

That night it was hard to sleep. I had spent the greater part of the day hanging around the hospital, confined in my father's room, with no further distance to roam than the vending machine in Reception. If my body was restless, my mind was worse. It ran with sickly persistence on my father's illness, on my sister's arrival and departure and on Achim's death. I reminded myself that he had figuratively and almost literally pushed me into a corner. He had forced me to hex him. If the curse had worked, and his death was not some perverse coincidence, he had only himself to blame. And yet whenever I tried to close my eyes to sleep I saw him, the great grey-white adipose bulk of him, propped up in the corner of the cold store, his skin almost the colour of the metal walls, a rime of ice crystals around his bluish lips, as though his last breath had frozen there, which I supposed it had.

The police thought it was suicide – perhaps accidental suicide – although they had carefully bagged and taken away the two bottles with their bright labels and their innocent-looking residue, as clear as water but as dangerous as poison – with that much alcohol in your blood the cold would kill you so much more rapidly than if you were sober, not to mention the fact that you would be too stupefied to think about what was happening.

Perhaps it was *suicide*, I told myself, but the idea was unconvincing. The police – certainly the *Kriminalpolizei*, who came down from Bonn – hadn't known Achim as it was my misfortune to have done. All the aggression and rapacity which had been crammed into that vast bulk, as the stuffing is crammed into a sausage skin, had been directed outwards, at others. Achim would cheerfully have tormented me until I was suicidal, but I didn't believe he would ever have taken his own life. And then there were the sounds I had heard on the night he died and the night before. I did not believe that it was Achim I had heard laughing.

Eventually I could not lie there sleeplessly any longer. I got out of bed and padded through into the kitchen to make myself a cup of fruit tea. When it was ready, I couldn't sit down at the kitchen table with it either; I was much too restless. I cradled the warm mug in my hands and went through to the living room.

The shutters and the curtains were open. If my mother had been here, she would have let down the shutters before she went to bed. It was late enough now that it was fully dark outside, and the moon was a mere sliver like a thumbnail clipping, so that the only light came from the street lamps. Bad Münstereifel is a dead town, a ghost town, at that time of night. I could see a good way up and down the street from my vantage point and nothing was moving at all, except the end of a thin white curtain at an open upstairs window in one of the houses opposite, which sucked gently in and out with the night breeze, as though the house itself were breathing deeply in its sleep.

I sipped my tea. I had forgotten to put sugar in it and it tasted bitter. I went back to the kitchen and heaped a great teaspoonful in, then I returned to the living-room window to resume my silent vigil.

I glanced up the street towards the old brewery and all was as before. Nothing moved; the street was still, with the yellow light of the street lamps picking out individual cobblestones like scales. I glanced the other way, in the direction of the Werther Tor, expecting the same unchanging tableau, and almost jumped. There was someone coming up the street.

There was no reason to think that it was anyone other than some honest citizen making their way home, even if the hour was unusually late. All the same, I had no desire to be spotted standing there in my nightclothes. I slipped behind the curtain, where I could see whoever it was approaching but could not be seen myself, or so I hoped.

He was walking quickly, whoever he was, and as he stalked along on his long legs the hem of his dark coat swirled around them. I saw one of the metal buttons on the coat wink in the light of a street lamp and even before he had come close enough for me to see the shock of red hair I knew it was Julius Rensinghof.

Some instinct made me draw even further back into the shadows. At that moment Julius glanced towards the bakery and I wondered whether he had glimpsed my sly movement. He glanced away almost immediately, however, and there was no sign that he had seen anything. Another few heartbeats and he had passed in front of the bakery itself, and I could no longer see him from where I stood. I risked moving back into the room, then slipping behind the curtain on the other side to watch him walking away up the street.

Nothing. The street was empty, the pools of yellow light under the street lamps undisturbed by his passing shadow. Unnerved, I stood there for a second wondering what to do, and then cautiously I approached the window. If I stood a metre or two away from the glass, all I could see were the opposite side of the street, the wall which bounded the river and the houses on the other side. If I wanted to look at the spot just below, I would have to go right up to the window and risk being seen.

I moved as quietly as I could, though I knew I was wasting my time. Julius wasn't likely to hear me moving about, although if he looked up he would see me. I went to the window and peered out.

He's not there, was my first thought. The street outside the bakery was completely empty. For a second I entertained the chilling idea that Julius had somehow vanished altogether, but a moment later I saw him step back into view and I felt another chill of an entirely different nature. Clearly he had been on the actual doorstep of the bakery, hidden from my sight by the little porch over the door.

What the hell was he doing? But I didn't need to ask that question; I knew the answer already. He had been standing on the doorstep, his nose almost touching the glass panel set into the door, staring into the bakery's dark interior. Now he was lingering in front of the step. In a moment or two he would probably glance upwards and unless I moved very quickly he would spot me staring down at him. Already

I could see his head turning as he looked around him. Any second now he would look up.

Now was the time to slip back into the shadows, to duck behind the curtain. Instead, I made my hand into a fist and knocked as hard as I could on the glass with my knuckles.

CHAPTER FIFTY-EIGHT

Julius's head snapped back as abruptly as if someone had fastened their fingers in his mop of fiery hair and yanked it backwards. I saw his angular face, the features made even sharper by the yellow lamplight, turned up towards me; his brown eyes gazed straight into mine.

For a moment I almost faltered. Then I was fumbling with the window catch. I prayed that Julius would not take off while I was trying to get the window open. Finally I managed it. The next second I was leaning out, the night air cool on my face and the bare skin of my arms. Julius was still looking up at me. He had not moved at all and showed no sign of bolting.

'Stay there,' I said, pointing a finger at him.

I waited for an instant to be sure that he really *was* going to stay there, then I was running for the door of the flat. I paused for long enough to grab my robe from the back of my bedroom door. I didn't like the idea of confronting anyone dressed only in my nightclothes, even if it was only Julius. I unlocked the front door and thundered down the stairs, pushing my arms into the sleeves of the robe. Then I went through the cafe area, sorting through the keys as I went, looking for the right one.

I wondered whether Julius might have taken the opportunity to make his escape, but he was still there; I could see his dark silhouette outside the front door. I wrenched it open and cannoned out into the street.

'What –' I began, and then made an effort to lower my voice. If I didn't take care we would have every single person on the street throwing up their windows and looking out. 'What are you *doing* here?' I demanded in a furious whisper.

Julius had opened his mouth to say something when we both heard the unmistakable sound of a window opening. It was simply the sound of a catch rattling and the scraping of a casement being pushed outwards, but as far as I was concerned it might as well have been the gates of Tartarus yawning wide to belch forth all its fiends. Before I had time to consider what I was doing, I had grabbed Julius by the lapels of his black coat and was dragging him into the bakery.

As we stood on the threshold, both of us breathing fast and Julius staring at me in frank astonishment, we heard an indignant voice saying, 'Who's there?' In the cool night air sound travelled well; I could have sworn I heard the voice's owner breathing heavily as she surveyed the silent street. It made me think of some flat-nosed dog, a French bulldog perhaps, panting. It was not until we had both heard the sound of the window shutting again that I dared even close the bakery door. Then I turned my back on it and fixed Julius with my gaze.

'Julius Rensinghof,' I said, 'what the hell do you think you are doing?'

'I'm –'

I didn't let him finish. 'You were staring in through the bakery window. It's –' I glanced at my wrist but of course I had no watch on; it was lying on my bedside table upstairs. 'It's past midnight,' I said. 'What did you think you were going to see?'

'Nothing,' he said, but I caught the nanosecond of hesitation in his voice.

'The bakery's shut,' I said. 'My dad's in hospital and . . .' *Achim's dead*, I had been about to say, but I thought better of it. 'Nobody's working tonight.'

'I know.'

'Then why did you come?' I demanded.

'I was passing,' said Julius defensively.

'At *this* time of night?'

'We had a gig.'

'Where's your stuff, then?'

'Felix took it in the van.'

We looked at each other.

'Where was the gig?' I asked him.

'Look, what does it matter?' said Julius shortly. 'I was just passing, OK? And I looked in to . . .' He stopped.

'To *what*?'

'To see that you were OK.'

'Why wouldn't I be?'

Julius didn't answer. I looked into those brown eyes and there was an unreadable message in them. We might have been two travellers meeting in some strange place, with no common language, no way to communicate but guesswork.

What is he not telling me?

'Julius,' I said slowly, 'do you pass by here often at night? This late, I mean – or even later?'

He didn't answer for a moment and I had the impression he was deliberating.

'Yes,' he said eventually, watching me as narrowly as I was watching him.

I was beginning to feel acutely conscious of the fact that we were alone in the bakery. My skin was prickling and I did not think it was the result of my brief foray out into the cool night. *He had the opportunity*, I was thinking. *He probably passes the bakery in the small hours a dozen times a month, after gigs and practice sessions. People who live on this street are probably used to seeing him, if any of them are up that late. Nobody would think anything of it, if they saw him passing by on a particular night.*

The more I thought about it, the more my unpleasant suspicions hardened into certainty. It was like looking at the pattern in the wallpaper when you were feverish; you began to see shapes in it – people, animals – and once you had seen them, you couldn't *unsee* them again. They would cavort up and down the walls of your sickroom until you closed your eyes just to shut out the nauseating sight of them.

But how could he have done it? I asked myself. *There were no signs of a struggle. If he shut Achim in the cold store, he – Achim – could have used the emergency release inside to let himself out afterwards.* Memory struggled to reassert itself: the sight of the great pallid bulk of Achim's body flashed before my mental eye – the scum of ice crystals at the mouth, the stiff white hand. I did my best to beat it down. *Who cares how he did it?* I thought. *Worry about that later. Right now you have other things to worry about, like the fact that it's the middle of the night and you're alone in here with him.*

Julius was still looking at me and still he said nothing. I knew that the most sensible, *safest* thing to do would be to end the conversation now – encourage him to leave. I could pretend I was tired, sick, anything. I could discuss it with Hanna in the cold light of day and we could decide between us what to do about Julius.

I knew what was sensible and yet I found myself saying, 'Did you pass by the night it happened?'

'The night what happened?' said Julius automatically.

'The night Achim died.'

Julius took a step towards me and I found myself involuntarily backing away. There was that same strange look on his face again, as though he wanted to say something but lacked the words.

'Are you sure you want me to answer that?' he said.

The street door was at my back. It opened inwards and I wondered how long it would take me to turn, pull it open, stumble outside into the street. Longer than it would take Julius to cross the space between us, that was for certain.

'Yes,' I said, marvelling at the conviction in my voice.

'All right,' said Julius.

In the dim yellowish light coming through the windows from the street lamp his face was all angles and hard lines; he might have been a figure in a medieval sculpture, hewn from the solid stone. I was painfully conscious of the fact that he was a head taller than I was. I felt like a supplicant before some looming statue.

'I *was* here,' he said. 'The night Achim died.'

Oh, Julius.

For a moment I was struck as dumb as I had ever been as a shy little girl, fighting for the right words. I was horrified, and not a little afraid, and part of me was even *relieved*, because there was an explanation that was not utterly insane, but most of all I was sad. There had been a time when I thought Julius was a good person, when I had shied away from telling him the worst about myself because I thought he had seen something better in me and I couldn't bear to destroy that. Now I thought that the darkness came from Julius, and that it was far worse than anything I had seen in myself, because I had merely *wished* death on Klara Klein and Frau Kessel and Achim Zimmer, but Julius's hands had been the ones which somehow struck them down.

I felt all of this and I could express none of it. I looked at Julius's face in the amber light and I knew it but did not know it. I simply said, 'Why?'

'Because of you,' he said. Another step closer and he had taken me by the shoulders, as though he wanted to hold me there, at arm's length, and study me. 'Don't you know that?' he asked me.

I had a terrible feeling that he was about to try to kiss me. There was a time, not so very long before, when I might have welcomed it, but now I felt as though I would be pressing my lips to the bloodstained maw of a vampire. I pulled away, but gently, afraid to provoke him.

'I didn't want any of this,' I said.

'Didn't you?' said Julius with emphasis.

He had me literally backed into a corner, I realized. I had the glass-fronted display cabinet to my right, a table to my left and the door at my back.

No, I wanted to say, but I knew it would be a lie. Klara Klein – I had had nothing against her, but as for Frau Kessel and Achim Zimmer, I had wanted both of them out of the way. There was no denying it. If Julius had done the deeds, I had supplied the volition.

'What are you going to do?' I asked him.

In spite of my fear, I recognized my own role in the sorry events that had brought us to this pass. I recognized the *rightness* of whatever retribution hovered above my own head.

'Do?' repeated Julius, as though the question gave him pause. 'I'm not going to *do* anything.'

'It was murder,' I said bluntly.

I thought I saw him flinch. I was deliberately brutal; let the consequences be damned. Julius would do whatever he wanted, follow whatever strange impulse had led him to kill to gratify someone else's wish. What I said now was probably irrelevant, but I was determined to tell the truth.

He didn't erupt into a savage rage or try to deny it. He said, 'I think about it all the time. It's not murder if it's self-defence.'

Self-defence? I stared at him. Achim Zimmer must have weighed about 110 kilos, much of it fat, but solid all the same. If it came to an honest fight between him and Julius, I supposed that every blow Julius struck would be self-defence. But Julius should not have been inside the bakery the night Achim died; he had been trespassing. And then it had hardly been an honest fight, had it? – shutting someone who was drunk inside a cold store, assuming that was what he had done.

'You should go to the police,' I said.

'Should I?' asked Julius, as though it were a rhetorical question. The remoteness of his tone sent a chill through me.

'Putting it off will only make things worse,' I said. I tried to sound reasonable, as though we were discussing something trivial like a dentist's appointment, but I could hear the waver in my own voice. 'You should go to them – now.'

'Isn't that up to you?' said Julius. He didn't try to touch me again, but I knew he was watching me, observing my face.

Was I imagining it or was there a threat in his words? Suppose I said, *Yes, I'm going to the police, right now. I'm going to go upstairs and dial 112 and when they get here I'm going to tell them who murdered Achim Zimmer and Frau Kessel and Klara Klein?* What then? What would he do?

'I'm not going to tell them anything,' I said, as firmly as I could.

'You're sure?'

If I'm not?

'I'm sure,' I said, and looked straight at him with as much conviction as I could muster. 'I'm not going to tell anyone anything.'

In the moment of silence that followed, I could feel the future – my immediate future – flickering between two possibilities, as clearly as if it were a weathercock, creaking back and forth in opposing gusts of wind. I held my breath.

Finally Julius said, 'It's over, then.'

'Yes,' I said.

He stepped closer to me again and I wondered whether I had misread the situation, whether he had not decided to trust me after all. Before I could react, his arms were around me. He didn't try to kiss me; he didn't say a word. He hugged me tightly, fiercely, as though he was trying to hold on to me forever, and I just stood there, motionless, barely daring to breathe, as though a carnivorous animal, a wolf or tiger, had me between its paws.

I don't know how long we might have stayed like that, a frozen tableau, looking for all the world like two long-parted lovers reunited, if we hadn't been interrupted. A car was coming up the Werther Strasse, the bright beams of the headlights wavering as it rumbled over the cobblestones. The lights washed over the wall by the river and the empty tables outside the bakery. I hazarded a look.

'Police,' I said.

I could have tried to get the door open at that moment – run out into the street waving my arms – but I hesitated. I still didn't fancy my chances of managing it before Julius grabbed me, and if I didn't make it, what then? We would be alone again and this time Julius would have no reason to trust me.

I was standing there irresolutely when Julius dragged me away from the door, back into the shadows. His hand was still gripping my upper arm as I watched the car go by, its blue and silver livery turned dull in the lamplight. The blue light was switched off. I couldn't see who was at the wheel. Herr Wachtmeister Schumacher was sitting in the passenger seat, but he seemed half asleep. At any rate, he didn't even glance at the bakery as the car went past. If he had turned his head even a fraction he might have seen two faces staring at him from the shadows: the killer and his muse, returned to the scene of the crime. Instead he yawned and was borne onwards, unheeding.

'I should go,' said Julius, when the police car had turned the corner at the end of the street and vanished from sight. 'If anyone sees us, they'll ask questions.'

He sounded utterly calm and might have been speaking

about the weather. I simply nodded. If he wanted to go, I dared not say anything which might make him change his mind. I opened the door and looked out. The street was deserted once again. A moment later Julius pushed past me and was gone, with one backward glance which I did my best not to meet.

I closed the front door very quietly and locked it. There were bolts at the top and bottom, which we rarely ever used, but now I slid them both home. I was afraid to look out through the glass panel at the street beyond and yet afraid not to. I thought that Julius might change his mind and come back to the bakery. I imagined looking up and seeing his face staring at me from the other side of the glass, skin sallow in the lamplight, eyes glaring with savage intensity. I tried the door handle to check that I had really locked it and saw that my hands were trembling.

I took the keys and went back upstairs to the flat, where I locked myself in, taking care to close the deadlock. Then I went around and let down all the shutters. I closed the ones overlooking the street last, so I could check that there was nobody there, no figure clad in a long dark coat with winking metal buttons standing under the street lamp or lurking in the shadows. *Julius*, I thought dismally. *How is this possible?* If Julius were capable of murder, I would never be able to trust anyone again; my mother might be a poisoner, slipping hemlock into the *Sahnetorte*, or my father the Lothario of the town, harbouring more sinister passions than his avowed dedication to *Florentiner* biscuits. The people I saw every day on the street and in the cafe, was their respectability just a veneer, were they all harbouring noxious secrets?

From my vantage point at the window I could see the empty space on the cobblestones where my sister, Magdalena, had parked her car earlier in the day. It was as easy as that for her; she had just slipped behind the wheel and driven away.

I let down the last shutter and blocked Bad Münstereifel from sight.

CHAPTER FIFTY-NINE

At seven o'clock the next morning I called Hanna. I had been awake since five, my mind racing with the sick intensity of a fever dream. I had to speak to *someone*. I was no longer sure of the truth of what had happened that last afternoon at Rote Gertrud's house. It was a jumble in my mind, a tangle of grabbing hands and insistent voices. Perhaps Hanna's had been among them; perhaps she had tried to defend me, as she claimed. I couldn't say. One thing was clear, though: it was not a good thing to be the person who stood between a killer and discovery. Julius claimed he had done it all for me, a concept I was not ready to examine in detail – it made me feel like the unwitting carrier of a disgusting disease. But although I could not follow his mind down the labyrinthine route that had led him to murder, I still did not trust the monster at the heart of the maze not to turn on me too.

I tried Hanna's mobile phone first, but it was switched off. After some deliberation, I called the landline. I could not imagine what Frau or Herr Landberg would say if either of them picked up the phone after being roused at this appallingly early hour, but I almost didn't care, so long as they let me speak to Hanna.

The phone rang twelve times and then Hanna picked it up. I didn't bother with a preamble.

'Something's happened. Can I come over? I need to talk to you.'

'No!' Hanna sounded aghast. 'No way.'

'Why not? Please, Hanna, it's important. I wouldn't ask if it wasn't.'

'My parents,' said Hanna. 'They're in bed.'

I noticed she didn't say, *They're asleep.* I wondered whether Frau and Herr Landberg were sitting up and sipping cups of coffee with their ears twitching. Perhaps Hanna was on an upstairs extension and they were two metres away, she in her knitted bedjacket and he in a pair of striped pyjamas, scanning the airwaves with the efficiency of a military defence system while pretending to study the pattern on their cups.

'Can you come here, then?'

I was amazing myself with my own persistence. This was what I had needed to bring me out of my shell, I thought wryly: three deaths, a disappearance and a serial killer with a crush on me.

There was a second's silence. I listened to the faint crackling on the line and waited for Hanna's reply.

'Of course I'll come,' she said, and broke the connection.

Fifteen minutes later the street doorbell rang. I went to the front window and looked out before I went down. I wanted to be sure that it was really Hanna and not Julius. As soon as I caught sight of her unruly dark head I left the window and went downstairs.

'What's up?' was the first thing she said when I opened the door.

'Julius Rensinghof,' I said succinctly.

As soon as she was inside, I closed the door again, locked and bolted it. Hanna watched me do this in astonishment.

'Julius Rensinghof?' she said. 'That loser?'

I opened my mouth to retort, and then shut it again. Killing three people and running a fourth out of town didn't make Julius a winner, but I wasn't sure whether it made him a loser either. It wasn't something you'd dare to say to his face anyway.

'We should go upstairs,' I said, testing the door.

Hanna was at my elbow. 'What's going on?' she said.

There was an edge to her voice. When I turned, the keys in my hand, she was so close to me that I had to stifle an impulse to push her away.

'He killed Achim Zimmer,' I told her.

'*What?*' The expression of shock on Hanna's face might have been comical under different circumstances.

'And Frau Kessel and Klara Klein,' I added for good measure. 'I don't know how he got Kai von Jülich to leave town, but . . .'

'He *didn't*,' said Hanna incredulously.

'He did,' I said grimly.

Hanna followed me as I made for the door which led to the stairs. 'He can't have,' she said.

'Oh yes, he can,' I retorted. 'He told me himself.'

'He *confessed*?'

'Last night,' I said, as we went upstairs. 'Right here, in the bakery.'

'What was he doing here?'

'I didn't *invite* him,' I said. 'He was just passing by, or so he said.' I unlocked the door. 'I asked him if he was here on the night Achim died and he said yes.'

'*Scheisse*.' Hanna sounded stunned. 'Did he say what happened?'

'Not really,' I said, as we went into the flat. 'He said he did it for me.' I saw the expression on her face, the horrified incredulity. I wondered how much of that horror was for me, the killer's genius. 'Look,' I said. 'I didn't ask him for the details. I didn't know what he was going to do – I just wanted him out. He's dangerous. He's off his head.'

We went into the living room. I sat on the couch but Hanna remained standing, as tense as a pointer dog.

'Have you called the police?' she asked me.

I shook my head.

'Why not?'

'I don't know what I'll say. I can't prove anything. It's his word against mine. Anyway,' I said, 'what about when they ask *why*? If I tell them I wrote it all down on scraps of paper up at the witch's house, either they'll think I'm crazy or they'll think I put him up to it, that I'm his accomplice. I wrote it down and he did it, as though I was giving him orders or something.'

I put my head in my hands. The more I thought about it, the worse it got. What about the money upstairs? How would I explain that? There was no way anyone would believe I wasn't involved. I *was* involved. I groaned aloud.

'He didn't do it,' said Hanna stubbornly. She sounded almost angry. 'A loser like him – he couldn't plan anything like that and carry it out.'

'He confessed,' I said.

'He's trying to make himself look big.'

'That's crazy,' I said.

I was beginning to feel a little angry myself. I didn't know how or why we were arguing about it. I simply needed Hanna to believe me, because right now I felt as exposed as a goat tethered for bait in a jungle clearing. I had no idea what was going through Julius's mind at that instant, wherever he was, but I knew it would be a mistake to assume that he would let things lie. Suppose he really did think that he was protecting me in some twisted way – what if he decided for himself that someone was a threat? What if he turned on *me*?

Hanna fell silent for a moment. Then she said, 'What are you going to do?'

What are you going to do? It was the very same question I had asked Julius. It was the nub of the matter. Up until that moment, the answer had not crystallized inside my brain, although I supposed it had flitted silently, a night bird, in the dark shadows at the edges of my conscious mind. Now it came to me, and before I even had time to think about it I had opened my mouth and said, 'I'm going to hex him.'

CHAPTER SIXTY

Julius Rensinghof. I sat on the overstuffed sofa with a note-pad on my lap and a ballpoint pen in my hand, staring at the name on the page.

Hexing Julius would be justice. I imagined him snooping about in the woods, maybe even following us deliberately. I supposed that if so, he had been following *me*, and I cringed inside. He had been in a place where he should not have been, pawing through scrawled messages that should never have been written, and he had decided to turn those out-pourings of anger and fear into reality, as though they had been evil spells inked on the yellowing pages of a grimoire, and he the demon who performed them.

'Die,' said Hanna, leaning over my shoulder. She nudged me. 'Write it. He deserves it.'

Reluctantly I put the pen to the paper again and experimentally wrote *die* after Julius's name. I wanted to see how I felt when I saw that word, whether it could possibly seem right.

What would he do if he unfolded that message and found his own name on it? I wondered. Would he accept that this was the end of the game? The chilling idea occurred to me that he might think I was telling him to turn his hand against himself. I found *that* idea intolerable. I thought I was at least partly responsible for what he had done, if he thought in his twisted way that he had been doing it for me. The game had to end, but not like that.

'No.'

I ripped the top sheet off the pad, crumpled it into a ball and dropped it on to the floor. I put the nib of the pen to the paper again.

Julius Rensinghof, vanish, I wrote. Almost immediately I tore the sheet off and screwed it up into a ball like the first one. *Vanish,* that could mean anything. Bad Münstereifel had had its own history of disappearances, and everyone in the town knew how it had ended for those who had vanished.

Why was it so difficult to do this? The killings *had* to end, I knew that.

I began again. *Julius Rensinghof, leave Bad Münstereifel forever*, I wrote. I read the line and reread it. *If only it were possible to wish that none of this had ever happened*, I thought. But it was far too late for that. This seemed to be the only solution. Swiftly I folded the paper once, twice, until it was a compact square.

'Are you sure you can get the car?' I asked Hanna.

I couldn't imagine what the pompous Herr Landberg would do if he discovered his daughter had borrowed his precious Mercedes for the second time and driven it up the Eschweiler Tal, with its bodywork-flaying carpet of small sharp stones.

'Yes,' said Hanna. 'Don't worry. My parents aren't even going to notice it's gone.'

She smiled at me slyly and for a moment I thought I saw a flicker of that excitement I had seen on her face when she and Max were urging me to write down another of those cursed wishes. Hanna *wanted* to do this; she desired it with the compulsion of a gambler hanging on the roll of the dice. Even now that we both knew who and what were at work, now we knew that there was no magic in it except the dark sorcery which turns twisted thoughts into deeds, she still could not resist the lure of it.

I began to think that I should not have asked her for help, that I was dragging her back into something as unhealthy as a drug habit. I should have gone to Rote Gertrud's house myself, even if it took me half a day to walk there and back. *But what if* he's *there?* I thought of the lonely hours it would take me to trudge the length of the Eschweiler Tal and back, and the tangled undergrowth I would have to force my way through to get to the ruined house. I imagined myself jumping at every tiny snap and rustle among the undergrowth, turning with my heart in my mouth every time the wind moved the branches. And I would be right to do so, because there was nothing to say that Julius was not up there in the woods at this very moment, waiting for me. I thought that I would feel so much better if Hanna were with me and we had the reassuring solidity and speed of Herr Landberg's Mercedes to carry us to and from the Eschweiler Tal.

'When do you think we can go?' I asked her.

She looked at her watch. 'Might as well go as soon as possible. There aren't many people around this early.'

'Shall I come with you?'

'No,' said Hanna. 'I'll bring the car here, OK? Just wait. I'll sound the horn – no, we'll have everyone looking out if we do that. I'll phone. Have you got your phone?'

I went off to my room to fetch it. When I came back, Hanna was just emerging from the living room. It was not until later that day – very much later – that I asked myself what she had been doing in the twenty seconds she was alone.

CHAPTER SIXTY-ONE

Hanna returned with the car more quickly than I had expected. I slid into the passenger seat with a feeling of déjà vu. The last time I was in Herr Landberg's car, I had been on my way to curse Achim Zimmer, my mind a maelstrom of disgust and anger and dread, my only coherent thought the desire to stop Achim. The remembrance made me sick at heart. How many times had I been up to the ruined house in the woods impelled by reasons that had seemed incontrovertible, impulses that had felt irresistible, swearing each time that this would be the last? *Give me this one last thing and I'll never ask for anything again . . .* But I had kept on asking and my wishes had been fulfilled. I leaned my head against the car window and tried to blot out the memory of Julius's face the night before in the bakery, the way he had tried to telegraph some unspoken message to me, his features sharp and intense. How was it possible that he had done all this and for *me*? I shuddered at the idea.

The streets of Bad Münstereifel were deserted at this early hour of Sunday morning and we made rapid progress. Within a couple of minutes we had passed through the gate in the medieval wall and were heading towards the Eschweiler Tal. I had travelled this same route with Kai von

Jülich, in that gleaming red car of his, which it was commonly supposed had carried him to some more exotic location than Bad Münstereifel. I supposed that Julius must know where Kai was. If my plan worked and Julius really did leave the town, Frau von Jülich might never know the answer to her questions. I wondered whether the truth was something she would really want to know. I could not think of any benevolent means by which Julius, who was so badly off that he went about on a rattletrap bike, could influence someone as rich and self-assured as Kai von Jülich to desert his comfortable life and take off somewhere without telling anyone.

How did he get Kai to ask you out, then? came the uncomfortable reply. The more I thought about it, the more questions began to arise, nibbling at the edges of my certainty like a shoal of sharp-toothed fish. I realized with despair that there were no answers to any of them. Unless I was prepared to confront Julius, I would probably never know the truth. *He confessed*, I reminded myself. That was the fact of the matter. Julius had confessed and there had to be an end to it, here and now.

I kept that thought in my mind as we parked the car and made our way up the hillside, forcing our way through brambles and ferns under the shadows of the trees. *The last time ever*, I promised myself, as the grey bulk of Gertrud's house came indistinctly into view, its crumbling walls merging into the dank vegetation around it. I tried to think of the task as a necessary evil, something to be carried out as dispassionately as a surgical procedure, and yet still as I stepped through the doorway into the shell of the house I felt like putting my hands over my eyes to blot out the sight of the scrawled messages on the walls, each one of them a silent scream.

Hanna stood beside me, scanning the mutilated walls. She said nothing, but simply waited while I retrieved the carved box from the floor. It lay on its side, propped against a chunk of masonry. It looked as though it had been kicked there, which I supposed it had, when I had struggled with the others. I saw that the catch had burst. The scraps of paper which had been inside were scattered on the ground. There seemed no point in checking whether the one wishing for my father's recovery had gone or not. I didn't think Julius could have any influence over *that*.

I dug the folded paper from my pocket and put it into the box. The lid wouldn't shut properly any more, I noticed; the hinges were bent too. Probably Max or Jochen had actually trodden on it. I put the box on the ground and placed a stone on top of it to keep the lid down. Then I turned and, picking my way over the broken stones which lay every-where, left the ruined house.

It was only once I got outside that I realized Hanna wasn't with me. I waited for a moment and then I went back, but she came out to meet me.

'Let's go,' she said, and we set off down the hill.

CHAPTER SIXTY-TWO

When Hanna dropped me off at the Werther Tor, the town was beginning to come to life. People were moving about the cobbled streets, on their way to mass at the church of Sts Chrysanthus and Daria or to one of the open bakeries for their morning rolls. It would simply be too conspicuous to drive up the Werther Strasse in Herr Landberg's Mercedes, and hardly worth the risk, since I had only a few hundred metres to walk to reach home.

We had not spoken much on the way back to the town. I had half expected Hanna to ask me about the money, which was still crammed into the little drawer of my bedside table. Either I had misjudged her, however, or she had other things on her mind. She didn't mention it at all and was preoccupied for most of the drive. When she let me out at the Werther Tor I thought she seemed to be on the point of saying something, but there was another car close behind us and she had to pull away immediately, leaving me standing alone in the shadow of the great stone gate.

I walked up the street, doing my best to look as though I had been up to nothing more suspicious than taking an early-morning stroll. Although there was a freshness in the air, the sky was a clear bright blue. I thought it was going to be a fine summer's day. The waitress at the Italian ice cream parlour was opening up the striped awning in front of the shop. She nodded and smiled at me as I passed and, in spite of myself, I felt my spirits begin to lift. Up there in the woods, in the mouldering wreckage of a dead woman's house, the world seemed bleak and menacing, a tortured labyrinth of winding corridors and dead ends leading inexorably to confusion and darkness. In the bright sunshine, however, the memory of the ruined house and what we had done there seemed unreal. Even the fear of running into Julius was diminished. This was broad daylight, after all, and I knew nearly every one of the people gazing out from shop doorways or strolling past with paper bags of bread rolls tucked under their arms. I even knew the sleek ebony cat that lay sunning himself on the cobbles, descendant of the inky-black tomcat who had terrorized the town's lapdogs when I was a child. *Perhaps*, I thought, *perhaps it really is possible to put it all behind me. Perhaps this is the end of it.*

I followed the bend in the street and I was within a hundred metres of the bakery's front door when I saw it. I don't suppose anyone else would have recognized it: just an old black bicycle, flaking rust, so battered that the owner hadn't even bothered to chain it up to anything. It was leaning against the wall by the river. There was no sign of Julius anywhere near it, but I knew better than to think that he had abandoned it. He must be somewhere very close by. I didn't bother to scrutinize the street ahead. Heart pounding, I turned on my heel and walked back the way I had come, doing my best to look nonchalant, although my cheeks were burning and I was sure that the shock I felt must be evident from my face.

Damn you, I thought sickly. *I can't even go in and out of my own front door in broad daylight.*

I could outfox him, though. The bakery's back door was accessible via a little alley which ran behind the building. If I went in that way, I could be through the kitchen and upstairs with all the doors locked before Julius even realized that I was home.

Then what? I asked myself. *You can't hide forever.*

I turned off the Werther Strasse, half ran up the side street to Alte Gasse, then slowed my pace. I risked a glance over my shoulder, aware of how furtive my behaviour must look. The street was deserted; no sign of anyone following me. I reached the alley and looked back again, but still there was no one. Fumbling for my keys, I slipped into the alley. It was short, a bottleneck leading to a small yard where Achim Zimmer had habitually smoked his cigarettes. I actually had the back door of the bakery in my sights, was within a couple of seconds of reaching it, the keys in my outstretched hand, when it all went wrong.

Even if my nerves had not been strained to the extent that I was almost humming like an electrical wire, I would have jumped. All I was aware of was a movement glimpsed out of the corner of my eye and then, before I had time to think of turning, of trying to escape, I was struggling in his grasp. I didn't need to look up into his face to know who it was. Julius had found me.

CHAPTER SIXTY-THREE

For a moment I was too shocked to make any sound at all, but then I opened my mouth to scream and suddenly Julius's hand was over it. Panicking, I tried to bite him, twisting in his grip but unable to free myself.

'Shhhh,' he said.

I kicked him as hard as I could by way of answer, but at close quarters it was hard to do any damage.

'Steffi, *stop it*,' he said.

I had no intention of stopping. I had no idea what Julius had in mind, but the mere fact that he had lurked here unseen, waiting to waylay me, said that it could not be anything good. Julius couldn't hold both of my arms while keeping a hand clamped over my mouth. I managed to get the hand holding the keys free and tried to hit him with it, using the keys as a weapon. He saw the blow coming and took his hand away from my mouth for long enough to pluck the keys right out of my grasp. I drew breath to yell for help and found myself pushed back against the wall of the yard, with Julius's face just centimetres from my own.

'Don't,' he said.

I eyed him, ready to make a break for it the instant the opportunity presented itself.

Julius must have read my intention in my eyes. He held the keys up in front of my face. He saw me flinch back and rolled his eyes.

'Calm down.'

He might just as well have been an executioner telling a condemned person to put their neck on the block. My pulse accelerated until I could feel the blood pounding thunderously in my head, a drumming that threatened to split my skull apart.

'Look,' said Julius, and his voice seemed to be coming from a long way away, muffled as though I were hearing him underwater. The pressure that was holding me against the wall slackened but he still had my arm in a steely grip. He was pulling me towards the back door of the bakery, my keys in his free hand. 'I'm going to unlock the door, OK? Can you please not scream?'

I would have screamed anyway, but looking wildly around the bare yard I wondered who would hear me. Alte Gasse was deserted and none of the neighbours had a view into the yard. The kitchens might be a better bet – I'd spent half my life in there and knew where everything was: the heavy rolling pin, the knives, all the things that could be used as weapons. *Julius knows them too*, I realized with sudden horror. Julius was dragging me to the bakery door and if he got me inside, where my screams would be muffled, I was staking my life on the fact that I knew the place better than he did.

It was no use. The door was open and Julius was pulling me after him. I did my best to resist, bracing myself in the door frame, but the old stone threshold was worn smooth and my shoes just slid across its shiny surface. With horrible inevitability, my fingers unpeeled from the frame.

As soon as he had me inside, Julius closed the door and locked it. I looked around for another escape route, but he still had my keys clasped in his fist. There was no way to open the door connecting to the cafeteria area. I backed away from him, wanting to put as much distance between us as possible, to try to judge his moves before he made them.

'Steffi,' said Julius, 'calm down, OK? I'm not threatening you.'

He took a step towards me and I slipped around the corner of one of the stainless-steel units, putting its reassuring solidity between the two of us.

Pull yourself together, I told myself as I faced him across the dull metal surface. *There has to be a way out of this. Think*.

Julius put his hands up in a conciliatory *look I have no weapons* sort of way, then took a step closer. I moved along the side of the metal unit, ready to round another corner if he tried to come any closer. I had a sudden vision, vivid and absurd, of Julius chasing me around the kitchen, brandishing some bakery implement, a palette knife or an egg whisk, the pair of us running round in circles until one of us was too exhausted to run any more. I looked at Julius, at his superior height and long legs, and knew that he would be the winner in *that* race. There was no other option than to try to talk to him, to persuade him back from the brink of whatever he was planning.

I willed myself to calm down. It would be impossible to say a word, let alone convince him of anything, while my heart was thumping and my breath was coming in short and painful gasps as though I had tried to sprint uphill.

'I . . .' I began, and swallowed. I tried again. 'Julius, whatever you're planning, you don't have to do it. I haven't told anyone anything. I'm not *going* to tell anyone anything.'

He paused in his stealthy approach and I saw a momentary look of confusion on his face.

'We can forget it, we can bury the whole thing,' I said, then winced inwardly at my choice of words. *Stay off burying and death, you idiot*, I scolded myself.

'I thought that too,' said Julius. There was a tinge of sadness in his voice which was chilling. It seemed to me to hold all the spurious regret of the sociopath who says, *Now look what you made me do*. 'But I don't think we can just leave it there,' he said.

'Why not?' I said, forcing myself to speak out boldly. 'It's finished. No one apart from the two of us needs to know anything about it.'

'Steffi . . .' Julius seemed about to say something, then thought better of it. He studied me for a moment. 'We've been friends for ages, haven't we?' he said.

I nodded. I had no intention of contradicting him, though I wondered whether it was possible to consider yourself someone's friend if so much of them was hidden from you, so much could not be understood.

'I thought at one point we might be more than friends,' said Julius. He sighed. 'I just want to know – I *need* to know – why did you do it?'

I stared at him. 'Why did I do *what*?'

He rubbed his angular face with one hand. 'Achim Zimmer. Why did you do it?' He shook his head. 'If I could just understand . . .'

I began to see light. 'Why did I –' I couldn't bring myself

to say, *Why did I curse him?* It sounded too melodramatic. 'Why did I want him dead, you mean?'

Julius nodded. I thought that now he didn't look regretful, but actually unhappy, and for a moment I was thrown off balance. I couldn't map the uncharted places of his mind, couldn't guess what he wanted me to say. Was he blaming me for something he now regretted? Did he think in some twisted way that if he understood my reasons it would justify what he had done?

'I had to,' I said. 'He was . . . threatening me.' I found I didn't want to describe what Achim had been threatening me with – it made me feel tainted, disgusting, as though I had fallen into a stinking pit of slime. Still Julius was looking at me hungrily, as though he expected – needed – to hear more. 'It wasn't just me,' I said at last. 'It was – it was the other girls at the bakery too.' I willed him to understand without my spelling it out. 'And he's been taking money. I couldn't see where it was going to end. It just seemed the only way out. My dad's in hospital, so I couldn't go to him. Anyway, Achim wasn't as bad when he was around. It was because Dad wasn't there that he was . . .'

I couldn't bring myself to say it. I even felt a surge of resentment under the fear. Why did he have to ask me about it anyway?

'Why do you want to know why I did it?' I said. 'We agreed neither of us would go to the police.'

'I know,' said Julius. 'But I've been thinking . . . and it's a big thing, deciding not to tell anyone about something like that. Since we spoke – since I knew for sure –' distractedly, he put up a hand and clenched a handful of his flaming hair – 'I've wondered if I've done the right thing.'

'It's too late to worry about that now,' I said. 'We can't change it, either of us.'

'Can't we?' He tried to approach me again, his face so regretful that for a moment I almost let him get close to me. I realized what he was about to do and moved as quickly as I could, putting the metal unit between us again.

Julius stopped, but he put his hands palm down on the stainless-steel surface and leaned towards me. 'You could still talk to the police,' he said in a quiet voice.

I looked at him and wondered whether this was a ruse. Was he trying to gauge whether I would really keep his secret? Was he pushing me to see how easily I would cave in under pressure? And if I did . . .

'I'm never going to do that,' I said.

'Then help me understand,' said Julius.

We faced each other across the metal unit.

'It was Max's idea,' I said at last. 'Klara Klein, I mean. I didn't have anything against her. It was just – I don't know – we thought it would be funny . . .'

'Max is involved? Max Müller?' Julius interrupted me.

'Well, of course he is. You know he is.' I was beginning to feel disorientated. Were we talking at cross-purposes? My mind skipped back to that day in the woods, when Max and the others had chased me down the hill and Julius had helped me hide. I had told Julius about the curse on Klara Klein; he *knew* my friends were involved.

'*Scheisse.*' To my amazement, Julius slumped back against the kitchen wall and put his hands over his face. All the fight seemed to have gone out of him. He looked like someone who had just received a catastrophic piece of news.

I could have chosen that moment to make a break for it, to try to grab the keys from him, or seize the rolling pin, or go for the telephone extension on the wall by the door. But it was beginning to dawn on me that there was something here I had failed to grasp, something small but absolutely fundamental as the axle-head on which the whole wheel turns. I was still wary, but more than anything I was curious.

'Julius?'

I saw him react to his name, but he didn't look at me.

'You *know* Max was involved. Max and the others. The curses – the one on Klara Klein and the one on Achim and the other ones – you know about them, don't you?'

Julius put his hands down and the face he turned towards me was fierce and haggard.

'"Max and the others"? You mean Jochen and Timo?'

'. . . and Izabela and Hanna,' I supplied.

'*All of you?*' he said, and his voice was thick with horror. '*All of you* were involved?'

I stared at him. 'Julius . . .'

'Six of you,' he said. 'Six. It was hardly self-defence, was it?' He shook his head. 'I'm sorry, Steffi, this changes everything.'

'I don't understand,' I said.

'I said I wouldn't talk to the police,' said Julius. 'I said it was up to you. But I thought it was just you – just you against Achim. I knew what he was like. I could see that it could be self-defence. But six of you . . .' He looked away, as though the sight of me was contaminating his eyes. 'Six against one really *is* murder.' He put up a hand to rub the side of his face and I saw that it was trembling. 'Steffi, I would have kept your secret forever if it had been only you. You know that. But not if it's Max Müller's secret too – and all the rest of them.'

'Julius, it was a stupid game,' I said. 'At least it was at the beginning.'

'A game? It was murder.'

'Maybe it was,' I said. 'But I didn't do it.' I took a deep breath. 'Look, I know I have to take some of the responsibility. I wrote those things. I should have stopped when the first one worked.' I shook my head. 'No, I shouldn't even have written the first one. I should have told Max to write it himself if he really wanted to hex someone. But it's not like I actually killed anyone myself with my own hands.'

There was a silence. Then Julius said slowly, 'You're telling me you didn't kill Achim? But you said you had to. He was threatening you and the other girls. You said you were desperate.'

'He was threatening me,' I said. 'So I wished him dead. I hexed him, like Klara Klein and –' I was going to add, *Frau Kessel*, but I thought better of it. 'He died,' I finished. 'Just like she did. Only I didn't actually *kill* either of them.'

'You were admitting you hexed him,' said Julius, more to himself than to me.

'Yes.'

'Then who actually killed him?'

'I . . .' I wondered if it would be wise to say what I had thought or not, and decided to go ahead anyway. 'I thought it was you.'

'*Me?*' Now Julius looked stunned. The shock on his face was so undeniably real that I began to feel that I had done something incredibly stupid.

'Yes,' I said. 'You confessed. Last night. You said it was you.'

'I didn't,' he said, frowning.

'You did. I asked you if you had been here that night and you said yes. And I asked you why you did it and you said – you did it for me.'

'I can't have said that,' said Julius. Then it dawned upon him and he put his hands to his head, clutching at his hair. 'I meant I was *there* because of you. I was passing and I just wanted to check everything was OK.'

I stared at Julius with what I eventually realized must have been an expression of almost idiotic open-mouthed astonishment. I shut my mouth, but still I couldn't stop staring at him. *He really didn't do it*, I thought, and on the heels of this thought, like a dog nipping at the ankles of a sheep, came the question, *Who* did *do it, then?*

'You were there that night but you didn't do it,' I said wonderingly. 'Did you see anything?'

Julius shook his head. 'I didn't see who was in there, at the back of the bakery. I saw Achim's car parked out in front. It seemed a bit odd, with the bakery being closed, but I thought maybe it was going to open in the morning after all, maybe he had come in to work.'

'Was that all?'

'No. I heard someone – well, it sounded like laughing, but it was out of control. Hysterical, perhaps, I don't know.' Julius looked a little embarrassed. 'I thought it might have been you. So . . .' He hesitated. 'I went round the back. I swear I wasn't going to eavesdrop. I just wanted to be sure you were OK.'

Now I went around the stainless-steel unit, went right up to Julius, and clutched his arm.

'Did you see who it was, the person who laughed?'

He shook his head. 'No. The window at the back has frosted glass, doesn't it? I couldn't make anyone out.'

'Are you sure it couldn't have been Achim laughing?' I knew the answer to that one already. I had heard the laugh myself and I was ready to swear on my parents' lives that it had not come from Achim Zimmer's throat.

'Absolutely. And it definitely wasn't you?'

'I swear it wasn't,' I told him. I pushed my hair back from my face and gazed up at him, willing him to believe me. 'Look, I heard it too.'

'Who did you think it was?'

'I don't know.'

I couldn't bring myself to tell him the truth, that I had actually entertained the insane idea that it might have been some sort of manifestation of Rote Gertrud, the long-dead witch of Schönau. All the same, the thought kept nagging away at the back of my mind: *If it wasn't Julius and it wasn't me, who was it?*

'We ought to tell the police about this,' said Julius.

He was looking at me carefully and I guessed that this was a final test to see what I would do. If I had been the one who was closeted in the kitchen that night with Achim, I wouldn't want the police involved.

'Yes,' I said firmly. 'Only we'll have to explain why we didn't go to them before.'

Julius considered. 'We can tell them the truth, that I thought maybe it was you, and it wasn't until we talked that I realized it wasn't.'

'Yes,' I agreed, but suddenly I wasn't thinking about what happened the night Achim died or when we should talk to the police. An ugly thought was burgeoning in my mind like a grotesque weed.

I've cursed Julius. I've cursed him – and he didn't do it.

'. . . Steffi?'

I realized Julius was speaking to me.

'What?'

'Do you want to go to the police station now?'

'I . . .' I knew that my hesitation was quite likely to arouse doubts in Julius's mind again, but I couldn't help that. All I could think about was calling Hanna and somehow getting back to the witch's house, removing that piece of paper with *Julius Rensinghof, leave Bad Münstereifel forever* inked on it. Because if it wasn't Julius who had been carrying out the scrawled wishes and curses I had left in Rote Gertrud's house, that meant someone else altogether was doing it – and that meant . . .

He's in danger.

Briefly I considered putting the whole matter before him, begging him for help. But that would mean telling him what I had done, that I had cursed him, too. No time now to think about all the implications, to think about the fact that now we both knew each other's innocence there was nothing to stop us picking up where we had left off, with something as yet undefined between us. I had to get back to Gertrud's house and I had to do it immediately. I thought quickly and opted for a lie.

'I promised my mother I'd go to the hospital.' The lie gave me a pang. 'I could call you when I get back. We could go then.'

I could hardly conceal my impatience as Julius agreed to wait for my call, then took his leave. He paused for a moment as he stood in the doorway. I was standing with my fingers on the door handle, dying to close and lock it behind him, but not daring to show it too obviously. He looked at me in silence, and I thought he had something important he wanted to say, but then he simply muttered, 'See you later,' and was gone.

CHAPTER SIXTY-FOUR

As soon as I had locked the back door I unlocked the one which led to the corridor and ran upstairs, taking the steps two at a time. Once inside the flat, I went straight into the kitchen, picked up the phone and called Hanna's home number.

There was no reply. I let the phone ring twenty-one times and then hung up. I tried Hanna's mobile and it was switched off. The impatience which had tortured me while I was waiting for Julius to leave was now a full-blown sense of throbbing urgency, infecting every cell of my body like a high fever, the Ebola virus of anxiety. *Where is Hanna?* I paced around the flat, hugging myself, fretting. I went up and down the hallway twice, and then into the living room, where Hanna and I had plotted to hex Julius.

The notepad was still on the coffee table and next to it the ballpoint pen I had used to write the message. I thought of the abortive attempts I had made, the one ordering Julius to die and the other telling him to vanish. I had screwed them up and simply thrown them on to the floor. I should pick them up. My mother wasn't expected home but I couldn't leave them lying around until she did come. I went over to the table and looked for them.

Nothing. They should have stood out like snowballs in a

coalhole, crumpled white balls of paper against the dark red and brown shades of the rug. But there was nothing there. I got down on my hands and knees and peered underneath the coffee table with a rising feeling of unease. There was nothing there, nor was there anything under the sofa as far as I could tell. I stood up and began to pull the cushions off the sofa, although I did not really expect to find anything – there was no logical way two balls of paper could have found their own way up from the floor and burrowed into the crevices of the sofa. All the same, I checked it thoroughly and afterwards I pulled it away from the wall and looked behind. Still nothing.

Did I throw them away and forget? I asked myself. I made myself stand still for a moment, panting and surrounded by upended sofa cushions. I thought back to that morning, when Hanna and I had been sitting here, and I had written those messages. I was almost certain that I had simply thrown the discarded ones on the floor and left them there, intending to clear them away later. And then, when I had written the final one, Hanna had asked me if I had my phone on me and I had gone off to fetch it. I had come back with the phone and Hanna had left to get the car. While I was waiting, I had drunk a glass of tap water and found a pair of sturdy shoes for walking up the hill, and I had kept checking my mobile phone for missed calls. But I didn't remember going back into the living room to clear up those balls of paper. As far as I could see, there was only one explanation. In the twenty seconds it had taken me to find my mobile phone, Hanna had picked them up. *But why would she do that?*

I had a horrible feeling I knew the answer.

CHAPTER SIXTY-FIVE

This time I didn't give up when Hanna let the phone ring at her end. I listened to twenty rings, then I hung up and dialled again. I heard the phone ringing at the other end, the receiver clutched in my left hand as I punched out her mobile number on my mobile with my right. It went immediately to the message service again. I pressed the red button and redialled.

I was calling the landline for the sixth time when Hanna picked it up.

'Landberg.' She didn't sound at all flustered.

'Hanna, it's me, Steffi. I've been calling and calling you.' I suspected she knew this perfectly well, but she simply said, 'I was in the garden.'

I didn't bother with any further preamble. 'Those pieces of paper, the ones I wrote on. What have you done with them?'

'I've burned one of them,' she said calmly.

'Which one?'

'"Julius Rensinghof, vanish."'

'And the other one?' I didn't even like to speak those words out loud: *Julius Rensinghof, die.*

'In the box in Gertrud's house.'

Even though I had known that was what she would say, I still felt a thrill of shock. '*Why?*' I said. 'For God's sake, *why*, Hanna?'

'Because you need him out of your life for good.'

'He didn't do it, Hanna.' My voice was rising wildly. 'It wasn't him. It was someone else. I don't know who it was, but it wasn't Julius.'

There was a long pause. 'He's a loser,' said Hanna eventually. 'You don't need him, Steffi.'

'Hanna.' I was clutching the receiver so tightly that my knuckles were white. 'He didn't do it. I can't hex someone who didn't do anything.'

'You already have,' said Hanna, and hung up.

CHAPTER SIXTY-SIX

I tried to call Hanna back on the landline, but either she was on another call or she had deliberately taken the phone off the hook. Her mobile was still diverting to the answering service.

I didn't bother swearing or throwing the phone around. A feeling of appalling dread was welling up inside me, rising like bread dough, seeming to fill every available space until my whole body was taut with it. My head was full of images, real and imagined: Klara Klein, her immense bulk precipitated headfirst into the cherry streusel; Kai von Jülich's mother, her handsome looks made haggard with anxiety, pleading for information about her son; Achim Zimmer, blue-lipped and rimed with ice crystals, frozen in the corner of the cold store. And Julius, how would it end for him if I couldn't remove the curse? I tried and failed not to think of it – blood drying on skin dappled with freckles, the sharp angles of cheekbones and jaw dented and wrecked, brown eyes fixed in a final unseeing and reproachful stare.

I was thinking about something else too. My friend Hanna and her part in what was happening. Dumpy, sensible, assertive Hanna, who could always be relied on in a crisis. Except that now I sensed she was playing quite another role and she was closer to the eye of the storm than I could ever have imagined.

I remembered her peculiar eagerness for me to hex Frau Kessel, the brightness in her eyes when we had talked about it. At this very moment I had in my possession just over ten thousand euros in cash and it had been Hanna who had urged me to wish for it. Now she had wrested control from me altogether. She was the one who wanted Julius dead, even if it was my handwriting on the death warrant. Did she know something that I didn't? I wondered whether it would achieve anything if I returned to the ruined house in the wood to take back the curse. But would I need Hanna to take it back too? Hanna who wouldn't answer my calls . . .

Think, I told myself. *You have to do something. If you don't, what's going to happen to Julius?*

I did think. How long would it take me to get to Hanna's? It was a shorter distance on foot than by car. The Landbergs lived in a large detached house on a single-track road which ran along the side of the hill skirting the town. Narrow and steep, petering into a forest track at the far end, it was not the sort of road anyone drove up for pleasure and was all but impassable in winter. However, there was a footpath running directly to it from the town centre. If I took that I could be there in less than a quarter of an hour, ten minutes if I was quick about it and even less if I ran.

I was downstairs, out of the bakery and running up the street before I had time to question the wisdom of what I was doing. There were many more people out and about now. The other bakeries and the tourist shops were all open.

'*Vorsicht!*' screeched somebody as I nearly cannoned into them. I shook my head and ran on.

I can still save this situation, I told myself. *I just have to get there in time.*

CHAPTER SIXTY-SEVEN

I had only ever been to the Landbergs' house a handful of times in all the years I had known Hanna. I remembered it as a gloomily impressive place, like an exhibition crammed with the most expensive and monstrously ugly pieces of furniture the world's most deluded carpenter could dream of. It also seemed to be much further away than I remembered. I laboured up the footpath with my lungs bursting and my heart thumping. It was a sunny day and pretty soon I was perspiring. Worse, the footpath was overhung with unkempt summer grasses and I guessed that they would be alive with blood-sucking ticks. There was nothing for it, though. If I went round by the road it would take four times as long to reach Hanna's place. I emerged on to the single-track road which led to the house, ineffectually brushing at my arms and legs, gulped in a great breath of air which seemed disgustingly tepid, and ran on, my shoes slapping on the worn tarmac.

The house was right at the end of the road, just before it petered out into an overgrown forest track that was blocked off by a heavy wooden barrier. I stood by one of the stone pillars which flanked the gate and tried to catch my breath. The gate itself was closed and probably locked, but I thought I could climb over it without too much difficulty. There was a buzzer on one of the pillars next to the letter box, but I didn't bother pressing it. If Hanna wasn't answering the phone it was unlikely she would simply open the gate.

Peering over the gate, I could see that the drive was empty. There was no sign of Herr Landberg's Mercedes, though I was not sure what this meant. Had Hanna taken it out again, trying to avoid me? If so, how had she settled it with her parents? It was inconceivable that she could keep borrowing the car right under Herr Landberg's large aquiline nose. Perhaps the Landbergs were away. Certainly the garden looked as though it had not been tended for a while; the tubs of flowers outside the house were dead from lack of watering. When I had called her about Julius, she had told me they were there, in bed, but now I wondered.

I took hold of the gate, stuck the toe of my shoe into one of the gaps in the ornate metalwork and swung myself up on top. From my vantage point I stared at the front of the house, but there was no sign of movement anywhere. I dropped down on to the Landbergs' driveway, horribly conscious of the crunching sound my feet made as they landed on the gravel. Then I walked right up to the front door.

I didn't really expect to find it unlocked but I tried the handle anyway. Then I lifted the old-fashioned knocker and let it fall once, twice. I listened but I could hear nothing inside – no footsteps hurrying towards the door, not even the furtive sound of someone creeping away to hide. I stepped back and looked up at the front of the house. The shutters were down on some of the windows but not all of them. For a moment I thought I glimpsed movement at one of the upstairs windows, but then I realized it was only sun-light flashing on the panes.

The sun was full on the front of the house and it was ter-ribly hot now. My throat was dry and there was a sour taste in my mouth. Worse, there was a detectable tang in the air, sweetish and foul, the scent of something putrefying in the heat. I guessed that it must come from the Landbergs' dust-bins, unemptied and festering in the summer weather. Doing my best to breathe through my mouth, I knocked on the door again, three times, willing Hanna to open up.

You can't avoid me forever.

Still nothing. I gazed at the neatly painted wooden panels that presented such an impenetrable barrier. Should I try breaking in? I could imagine the state of apoplexy into which Herr Landberg would certainly be catapulted if I dared to break one of his windows. Should I give up the venture and try to make my own way to the Eschweiler Tal? I was already tired, thirsty and half sick with the heat.

With a sudden overwhelming feeling of frustration I seized the knocker again and hammered at the door, send-ing a series of sharp *cracks* reverberating through the house like thunder. In the silence that followed I listened, ears straining for the slightest sound. There was nothing. If Hanna was inside listening to my frenzied knocking, she was a cooler hand than I was, staying still and silent. I could hear nothing but my own ragged breathing.

Try the back door.

I stepped away from the house and looked up again, hoping to see someone behind one of those windows. I turned my head and it was then that I noticed the up-and-over door of the double garage. It was open – not wide open, but the lower edge was perhaps four centimetres from the ground, as though someone had intended to close it but had not quite succeeded. From a distance you could barely see that the door was not closed. There was just enough clearance that a rat might have crept in underneath, but that was all.

Now I found myself looking up at the windows again, this time praying that nobody was looking out. If I could get into the garage, there was probably a connecting door to the house and that one might not be locked.

Instinctively I kept close to the wall, so that anybody who happened to look out of the upper windows would be unable to see me. As I approached the garage door I realized that I was involuntarily holding my breath. There was that smell again, sickly sweet and cloyingly pervasive, the ripe scent of rotting organic matter. As I tried to suck in a shallow breath through gritted teeth, it was disgusting. I imagined bin bags filled with stinking food remains piled up inside the garage, the seams splitting to release their noisome contents. What on earth had been happening here?

I pinched my nostrils shut with one hand, then grasped the bottom edge of the garage door with the other and heaved. The door moved up and over, sliding into place above my head. The vile stench burst forth like a poisonous cloud, but that was not the thing that made me stand there with my eyes wide and my hands clamped to my mouth as though trying to smother a scream.

The Landbergs' silver-grey Mercedes was parked in there, all right. And next to it was Kai von Jülich's red sports car.

CHAPTER SIXTY-EIGHT

I stared at Kai's car, feeling as though my eyes must start from their sockets and my brain turn to mush in my head. I could make no sense of what I was seeing. For a while Kai von Jülich's departure from the town had been the main topic of conversation in Bad Münstereifel. His own mother had come to see me to ask if I knew where he had gone. How was it possible that his car had been parked here all the time?

That smell seemed to be closing in on me, huddling against me with insinuating warmth, pressing itself greasily into my eyes and nose and mouth. I bit my knuckle, willing myself not to gag. All the time my gaze was flickering back and forth over the red sports car and I was noticing things that I would really rather not have noticed. The scarlet bodywork was as perfect as ever, although the layer of dust on it suggested that the car had not been taken out for weeks, but the windscreen was a mass of streaks and smears. It looked as though something had exploded inside the car, something wet and soupy, with little chunks of unidentifiable matter in it, and it had all dried on the inside of the glass.

There was something else too, barely visible through the

filthy windscreen. Something hunched and slumped and topped with a tangle of what might have been yellow straw.

Somewhere deep inside me there might have been a rational train of thought telling me to call the police and let someone else deal with this, to back away and run, run, *run*. But it was lost, like a tiny figure waving in a desolate landscape glimpsed from a plane a thousand metres above. As though from a vast distance, I watched my own right hand reach out, grasp the handle of the driver's door and pull.

The door opened easily and that smell roiled out, a thick stink of garbage and cheese which brought the bile up into my mouth. I looked at what was sitting behind the wheel of the sports car, then I turned away and really did throw up, every breath sucking in more of that disgusting smell, the stink of corruption, until I had vomited up everything in my stomach and was simply heaving uselessly in great cramping spasms.

The thing that had been Kai von Jülich was slumped over, what was left of the face mercifully hidden against the dashboard of the car. I saw one dark and mottled hand, the bones threatening to break through what remained of the flesh like the peaks of stones breaking through cracked earth, and I had no desire to look any further. What I wanted most of all was to shut the car door again, to get rid of the stench, that terrible, clinging, gut-wrenching stench.

My hand was on the door, groping for the handle, when I saw it. A crumpled sheet of paper, closely covered with handwriting, stuffed down the side of the bucket seat. *Suicide note? Confession?* I might not have touched it – I quailed at the thought of touching *anything* in that stinking sarcophagus – but something caught my eye. At the corner of the paper was a logo I recognized. Before I had fully thought about what I was doing, I reached out and grabbed it. Then I did close the door and stumbled back out of the garage, sucking in the clean air in great gasps, trying not to think about what I had been breathing when I was in there, the tiny molecules of unspeakable matter that must be tainting the atmosphere. If I thought about that I would throw up again and my stomach was already a taut band of pain.

Driven like a threatened animal by some instinctive need to hide, I staggered around the corner of the house and there I sagged against the wall, turning my face to the cool stone. *Dead, dead*, I thought. The full horror of it was only now bursting in on me. Even when I had seen Achim Zimmer's body, vast and greying, propped against the rear wall of the cold store, it had been nothing like this. Achim had still looked like a person, whereas Kai – I didn't want to think what he looked like. This was no longer a game; it had never been a game. We had been messing about with things we had not begun to comprehend, like children swinging on the gate that opens into the blackness of eternity.

I slid down the wall and hugged myself. I put my head on my knees and clasped handfuls of my hair in my fingers. I shut my eyes and all I could see was Kai von Jülich's body slumped behind the wheel of his sports car. I opened them again and that was better, but I could still smell a memory of that unspeakable odour on my clothing.

I sat there for a long while without any coherent thoughts about what to do. I felt in my pocket for my mobile phone but it wasn't there. I supposed it was lying somewhere on the footpath which led up to the house or perhaps on the gravel by the gate. There was nothing in my pocket except a twenty-cent piece and the crumpled sheet of paper I had taken from the car, now scrunched into a ball. I smoothed it out against the knee of my jeans, although I didn't expect it to tell me anything useful. There were no words that could change what I had just seen slumped behind the wheel of the car, nothing that could change the brutal reality of it.

I did not recognize the handwriting, but there was something else, something I knew well. The logo I had glimpsed showed an angel holding out a slice of cake. The note was written on paper headed *Konditorei Nett*. My gaze slid from the angel's chummily smiling face to the words written below in black ink.

Dearest Kai . . .

I began to feel as though I were going mad. Who at the bakery could possibly be writing letters to Kai von Jülich on our official headed paper? The paper was closely covered with handwriting on both sides. I turned it over to see whether there was any signature. There was, but although I read it several times still my brain was having problems processing what my eyes were taking in.

Steffi Nett.

I flipped the paper over and then back again. *Dearest Kai . . . Steffi Nett.* I was apparently holding in my hands a letter from myself to Kai von Jülich; a letter written in a handwriting that was not my own and that I had no memory of writing.

Am I losing my mind?

I stared at the signature until it ceased to have any meaning at all and was just a group of syllables spilling across the page. *Steffi Nett. Steffi Nett.* Finally I pulled myself together, turned back to the other side and began to read.

Dearest Kai, you may be surprised to get this letter from me. Well, don't be . . .

The tone of the first few lines was familiar – more familiar than I would ever have dared to be in the days before Kai had asked me out. In fact it was positively flirtatious. I imagined Kai reading this and my face began to tingle with hot embarrassment. Then I read on and embarrassment turned to sickening horror. Whoever had penned this letter in the guise of Steffi Nett had gone on from coquettish opening phrases to offer herself – myself – to Kai in such blatant terms that it turned my stomach to read it. No wonder it had brought Kai running; I thought that even old Father Arnold himself would have been knocking on the bakery door looking for more than a ham and egg roll if he had received a letter like this one. It didn't just suggest what we might do together; it described everything in meticulous detail. The last paragraph was a revolting exhortation to Kai to come to the bakery and make a date with me if he wanted to put these suggestions into action. *And don't tell anyone*, the writer had added. *Not if you want the time of your life.* There was a nauseatingly saccharine sign-off – 'little kisses and love' – and underneath that, in the same black ink, my name.

I didn't want to read the letter through again, as it made me feel sick. I wished I had not even read it the first time. It was disgusting and all the worse because there was a basic lack of honesty to it. It wasn't a declaration of love. It wasn't even a declaration of desire. It was a lure baited with the grossest suggestions that the writer could come up with. I was angry with the writer for putting my name to it and I was angry with Kai for believing in it. Were there no brains

354

at all in that gilded head of his? Then I thought again about the thing in the car, and the smears and blotches on the inside of the windscreen, and I gave a great groan of horror, squeezing my eyes tight shut to try to block out the memory.

It wouldn't go away, though. I suspected it would never go away, that I would never be able to lie down to sleep at night again without fearing that the awful thing that Kai had become would be waiting in my dreams, the terrible ruin of his face turned to me in reproach.

I was far from understanding what had taken place here, but there was no sorcery in what had happened to Kai, nothing but the brutal finality of a butcher's cleaver descending. And yet somehow I was at the centre of this, with the curses I had scrawled like a signature on a death warrant. It was my name at the end of the letter I had found in Kai's car, even if the handwriting was not my own.

In the end there was only one decision to be made. I dragged myself up on legs that felt rubbery with shock and staggered around the corner of the house. The thought of re-entering the garage was appalling. I looked at the front gate and told myself that I could cross the gravel drive, climb over it and walk back to the town. I could call the police and let them break into the house. But even before I had started moving towards the open garage, pulling the hem of my shirt out of my jeans so that I could press it over my mouth and nose, I knew that I was going to look for myself. Whatever had happened, it was about me and I was not going to walk away.

CHAPTER SIXTY-NINE

I slipped into the garage between the silver Mercedes and the wall, keeping as much distance as possible between myself and the red sports car. I could see almost at once that there was a door at the back that led to the house. I thought that I could make myself cross the few metres to that door and try the handle. I pressed the cloth of my shirt tightly to my nose, moving as quickly as I could and praying that I would not throw up again. I reached the door, pressed the handle down and rather to my surprise it opened easily.

The interior of the house was dark. I stepped inside and closed the door behind me, thankful to have its wooden panels between me and the garage with its expensive sarcophagus. I stood where I was for perhaps half a minute, letting my eyes adjust to the dimness, and I became aware that the air in the house had a taint that was all too familiar. I listened too and once I heard something in the distant reaches of the house, perhaps in the attic or cellar, that might have been a scuffle or a creak, but that was all. It could have been something or nothing. If Hanna was inside the house she was keeping very quiet.

I was in a hallway, I now saw. I began to move cautiously down it, slowing to peer through each open doorway. There was no sign of any living thing in the house, nothing to suggest any immediate threat, and yet everything I saw impressed me with a sense of wrongness. I noticed an ugly little telephone table piled high with unopened mail. I passed the Landbergs' large kitchen with its brown wooden fittings. The shutters were only half down and in the half-light I could see that every work surface was cluttered with dirty crockery, cartons and jars. I went into the living room and found a pair of neatly folded reading glasses lying on the glass-topped coffee table next to a copy of the *Kölner Stadt-Anzeiger* that was weeks old.

I went back into the hallway. Once again I stood and listened, but all I could hear was a faint ticking, the sound of some household appliance crooning to itself. I looked up the stairs at the dim reaches of the landing. I was aware of that smell again, the one that was always there in the background. After a while you got used to it, but sometimes you'd catch a whiff of it again and realize it was still there, sweet and ripe and foul, as though the whole house were some gigantic diseased lung exhaling rot with every breath.

Reluctantly I set my foot on the bottom stair. There was a faint creak as I put my weight on it. Then I climbed slowly up, stopping on every third step to listen. The house seemed to be empty, so why did I have that feeling of strained expectancy, as though someone or something was up there waiting for me? It was a relief when the first-floor landing finally came into view and I could see that it was empty.

The air was fouler up here. All the doors on the landing were closed, so the only light came from a little glass panel overhead. In spite of the expensive decor – the thick patterned rug, the paintings on the walls, the large Chinese vases full of dried flowers – the upper floor was a comfortless place. The sprays of desiccated flowers made me think of a funeral parlour.

I noticed almost immediately that one of the bedroom doors had been efficiently if crudely sealed with strips of silvery duct tape which ran along all the door frame. There was no key on the outside. I tried the handle but the door wouldn't budge.

Some small and animal part of my brain was telling me that I didn't want to go in there anyway, that I didn't want to see what was in the room, that I definitely didn't want to know what was making that smell which clung greasily to everything. In defiance of its increasingly urgent voice, I made myself check the door again, but it really was locked.

I went to the next one, and tried the handle; it opened easily. Inside, the shutters were up and the room was full of light. This was clearly Herr Landberg's study; it had his heavy personality stamped all over it. There was a very large desk, as solid and unfashionable-looking as its owner, with an expensive padded leather office chair behind it and a grey metal filing cabinet to one side. The walls were adorned with photographs of Herr Landberg and his shooting-club friends, all stoutly upholstered in hunting green and baring their teeth at the camera, and little wooden shields with the body parts of animals attached to them: horns and skulls and the occasional stuffed head, the eyes staring glassily across the room. I took all of this in at a glance, but the thing that really caught my attention was the metal gun locker bolted to the wall. It was wide open, as though inviting passers-by to help themselves to one of Herr Landberg's well-maintained rifles as casually as taking a cigarette from the pewter box on his desk.

The other thing I noticed was the second door to my right, a door which almost certainly connected with the sealed room. The door was standing open and from this angle all I could see was a strip of flowered wallpaper and the heavy folds of curtains. Judging by the deep shadows, the shutters were most of the way down. I stepped a little closer and now I could see that all around the door frame was the same silvery duct tape, only it was puckered here and there where the door had been wrenched open.

The sickening smell of decay that pervaded the house was boiling out of the sealed room in waves. This was the putrid core of it. I knew what I would see – what I had to see – before I went to the bedroom door, but still the sight of it almost rendered me incapable of action. Both of them were in there, in bed. Frau Landberg – recognizable by the dry nest that was what remained of her bouffant dyed black hair and the frilled nightdress she wore – was lying on her back under a counterpane that was a Rorschach pattern of dark and sinister stains. I thought that she had probably died there where she lay, with her eyes staring up at the glass chandelier until they filmed over and finally sank back into her head. Herr Landberg, however, appeared to have put up a fight. There were splashes and streaks of dried matter all over the floor on his side of the bed. I suspected he had managed to get out of bed before he was struck down and had lain on the parquet floor, gazing up at his destroyer, as the life pumped out of him. Then the killer had heaved the corpse back into the bed and pulled the covers up to his chest, leaving the two of them surrounded by the trappings of their affluence, like an entombed Pharaoh and his queen.

I had known that the house must contain a chamber of horrors like this one ever since I saw Kai von Jülich's car in the garage, but it was still a paralysing shock to see the two bodies lying there in their miasma of tainted air. A terrible sound escaped me, the dusty sound of the last strut supporting known reality giving way. I heard an answering groan and it was then that I realized for the first time that I was not alone.

CHAPTER SEVENTY

She was sitting on the floor on the far side of the bed with her back to the wall and her knees up. I couldn't see her hands.

'Hanna,' I said.

Her face was a pale shape in the gloom. 'You shouldn't have come here,' she said.

I made no reply. I was afraid to look at the things in the bed again and afraid to draw another breath of that thick and poisonous atmosphere. Abruptly I turned and stumbled out of the room. When I got to the landing I took great gulping breaths; in comparison with the tainted air in the bedroom, it was sweet and clear here. I staggered to the head of the stairs but I didn't trust my legs to carry me down them. I sank on to the top step and put my head in my hands.

After perhaps half a minute I heard Hanna's footsteps behind me and then I felt a hand on my shoulder.

'I'm sorry you had to see that,' she said.

She might have been talking about something mildly unpleasant, something squashed on the road. I didn't look at her.

'What happened?' I managed to ask eventually, still

clinging to the faint hope that there might be some explanation for what I had just seen other than the obvious one – the one that wasn't just staring me in the face but actually had me by the lapels and was shaking me.

'You did,' said Hanna simply.

I felt her sit down beside me.

'No,' I whispered into my hands. 'That – in there – I never wished for that.'

I heard Hanna sigh. 'You didn't always know what to wish for,' she said. Her hand on my shoulder moved to the side of my neck and I could feel her fingertips on my skin, almost caressing me. 'You still don't. You don't know what you need, Steffi. It was me from the start, taking the papers, the ones with your wishes on.'

'You?' I said.

The silence between us stretched out so long that when she finally spoke it almost made me jump.

'There's no magic,' she said suddenly. 'Just like there's no God. Nobody's handing out favours to people like you and me. The shy one and the fat plain one. People like my parents and yours, they go to church and pray and think that someone's listening. Nobody's listening. There's only one thing that matters, one thing that can make any difference, and that's wanting something yourself badly enough. You understand that. I saw it when I saw you making those wishes. I knew you understood.'

I remembered the way Hanna had seemed so excited, the way her eyes had shone, how she had licked her lips so that they gleamed. I had thought it was the thrill of the game, even that it was some twisted dynamic between her and Max. Was it possible that it had really been all about *me*?

362

Hanna moved closer to me and I felt her hand on my wrist, as light and deadly as the touch of a venomous spider. It was all I could do not to flinch away.

'It doesn't really matter that you didn't guess,' said Hanna, 'because now you know. I did everything you wished for, didn't I?'

She waited.

'Yes,' I croaked.

'Almost everything anyway,' she said musingly. 'I didn't have to do anything to Klara Klein. That just happened. Or if you want to believe in magic, that was it. That was fate. Klara Klein dying, that was what gave me the idea.'

Now her hand slipped right over my hand and she entwined her fingers with mine. I was too shocked by her words to react to her touch. I was thinking that if she said she had done everything I wished, everything except Klara Klein . . .

Hanna was a little closer to me now. Our shoulders weren't just touching; I could feel the pressure as she leaned against me.

'You wished for Klara Klein to die,' she said, 'and she did. No magic, just a fat old bag who couldn't stop stuffing herself with cherry streusel. The only miracle is that she lasted so long. But Max and Jochen and the rest of them . . . the looks on their faces, the things they said when they thought you'd done it with the curse you wrote. The power to make things happen, that's the real magic. I saw it and I know you saw it too, because otherwise you wouldn't have kept on wishing.'

Oh, God, I thought. I was remembering the moment at Rote Gertrud's house when I had scribbled Kai von Jülich's name on a piece of paper, my heart thumping with guilty excitement. I had made sure that none of the others saw what I had written because I thought they'd laugh at me. Shy little Steffi with her unrequited crush. And yet my secrecy had been entirely in vain. It had been one of my own friends who plucked the wish from the box and read the secret of my heart.

'You wrote the letter to Kai,' I said. 'How could you do that?'

I felt her shift slightly. 'You wished for him,' she said. 'Didn't you? I told you, the power to make things happen, that's the magic.'

'Not like that,' I told her.

In spite of my shock I felt actual anger. I remembered Kai's face looming at me in the car, the way I had hit my head on the glass as I tried to escape his embrace, the painful impact with the ground when I fell out of the car. I had heard the roar of the engine, the sound of gravel thrown up by the tyres, as I had flung myself, bruised and shocked, into the undergrowth, desperate to get away. *He's a pig*, I had told Hanna afterwards, and I supposed he really had been: too stupid to question the contents of the note and too brutish to accept that no meant no, whatever had gone before. All the same, it needn't have happened, that scene in the Tal. We could have carried on with our separate lives, with me yearning hopelessly until he found himself some girl like himself, well-off and arrogant. I need never have stumbled to the witch's house to curse him, have limped home with my bruises and my torn shirt, to be confronted by Frau Kessel, who had drawn her own monstrous conclusions. It had all started there, with that cursed letter.

'I didn't want it to be like that,' I repeated.

'It couldn't have been any other way,' said Hanna. 'You needed to see what he was really like.'

'*Why?*' I almost shrieked. '*Why* did I need to see?' I pulled away from her, pulled my hand from hers. 'He nearly raped me, Hanna. I thought we were going on a date and then he just went mad. He *hurt* me.'

'He paid for it,' said Hanna. 'He cried, you know. He got into that stupid car of his late one night and I was already in the back seat, waiting for him with my dad's Arminius revolver. He thought I was mad at him for what he did to you. He started saying he was sorry and he didn't mean it and all this other crap. I made him drive up here and back into the garage, and when he put the handbrake on I let him have it in the back of the head.'

'*No,*' I said, but in spite of my horrified incredulity I knew she was telling the truth. I had seen the evidence with my own eyes.

'He deserved it,' said Hanna, as though those three words justified everything. 'All of them did. Frau Kessel and that fat pig Achim Zimmer. You can't tell me the town isn't a better place without them.'

'You can't just go –' I began, but she interrupted me.

'I did what half the people in this town would have done if they had the guts. When Frau Kessel died, how many of those hypocrites sitting in the church afterwards really felt sorry? They were probably glad their secrets were safe at last.'

I remembered Hanna coming down the Orchheimer Strasse towards me the day they found Frau Kessel. I remembered her taking my arm and saying, *You're unbelievable, Steffi. You've done it. You've actually done it.*

'You made me think I'd done it,' I said.

'*We* did it,' she said. She looked at me and her eyes were shining, the way they had that time up at the ruined house. I had thought that look was for Max, but it was not. 'You wished it and I made it real. Nothing happens without someone wanting it to happen.'

The positive thinking of serial killing, I thought, and for a moment a hysterical laugh threatened to burst out of me. I looked around me at the expensive dullness of the Landbergs' house and the normality of it seemed more surreal than what I had seen in the master bedroom. I could not imagine how life would ever return to its normal flow after this.

'What did you do to Frau Kessel?' I said.

'I got into her house through the yard at the back. She heard me and came down with a candlestick in her skinny claw, like she was going to brain me with it or something. She said, "Hanna Landberg, what do you think you are doing in my house?" So I showed her the gun and she put the candlestick down, but it didn't shut her up.' Hanna shook her head. 'All the way up the stairs she kept on at me – did my father know I had his hunting revolver, what made me think I could get away with it and a lot more like that. I told her to shut up, but she wouldn't.'

This didn't surprise me. I doubted Satan himself and all his minions could have got Frau Kessel to shut up.

'So when we got to the top I told her to jump over the banisters. It's a long drop down the stairwell in her house – it would have done the job. But she looked at me and said, "Why don't you shoot me, Hanna Landberg?" I told her, "It's going to look like an accident." So she said, "Well, you

366

can shoot me if you like, but I'm not jumping." So I pushed her. She screamed, but the moment she hit the floor it stopped. I went down to check, but she was dead.'

The matter-of-factness in Hanna's voice chilled me to the core. Any desire to laugh hysterically passed away as rapidly as if I had had a bucket of icy water thrown over me.

'Hanna,' I said. 'Achim Zimmer – that was you too?'

'Of course it was.' She frowned. 'I can't believe you ever thought it was that loser Julius Rensinghof. He's not capable of planning anything like that. He's too stupid.' She sounded offended. 'He wouldn't have had the guts either. Two nights I had to come to the bakery. The first time was to see how it could be done.'

I recalled the sounds I had heard downstairs that night after Max had run me to the hospital to see my father. The clank, the slapping sound and then silence. I had noticed that the dial on the cold store had been moved when I went down the next morning, but I hadn't known *why*. That had been Hanna, laying her plans and having a trial run.

'How did you get him to come to the bakery?' I asked her.

She shrugged. 'How do you think? Men only think about one thing. If they get a sniff of it, they'll go anywhere, do anything. I just rang Achim up and offered him a private party in the bakery kitchen. He couldn't wait to get there, couldn't even wait long enough to park the car off the street.' Her lip curled. 'He really was a disgusting pig. And stupid. It wasn't difficult to get him drunk. Just a shame it took him so long to become incapable.'

I did my best not to think about it, about how Hanna had persuaded Achim to take his clothes off, had kept on

367

pouring out the vodka until he could no longer put his ugly desires into practice, couldn't ward off drowsiness, couldn't find the cold store's emergency door release. Had it been sufficient for Hanna to leave the cold store and close the door with Achim inside, then turn the dial to its lowest setting, or had she had to lean on the door, listening to his feeble thumps, his muffled calls for help growing fainter and fainter?

'Oh, God,' I said.

I was sick with horror, but Hanna looked at me and saw squeamishness.

'He got what he deserved, Steffi,' she said, and there was a gentleness to her tone that was worse than the venom I had heard in it before. It was the blandness of milk laced with a tasteless poison. She moved closer to me and her hand was on my shoulder again, as though she wanted to reassure me. 'Why do you feel bad about it? He deserved it.' Her hand moved to my hair, stroked it. 'You're so . . .' She stopped, and I thought that she had been going to say *weak* but decided that it was too harsh a word.

She said nothing more, but she put her arm around me. For a moment I thought confusedly that she was trying to comfort me, or seek comfort herself. Then I felt her face against mine and realized that she was not trying to comfort me, that this was not the reassuring embrace of a friend with a friend.

I was not so green as to die of shock at the idea of being kissed by another girl, but I knew now what Hanna had done and I would as soon have let myself be sucked dry by leeches. The hands which were clasping me had pushed Frau Kessel to her death; the lips which were seeking mine had lured Achim to his end. *She's the witch*, I thought, and I put up my hands and pushed her away.

'Don't,' I said.

'We belong together, Steffi,' said Hanna. Her eyes were gleaming.

'No.'

'Why not?' Hanna's face contorted into a scowl. 'Julius Rensinghof? Is that why?' She reached for me again, trying to grasp my shoulders as though she wanted to shake some sense into me. 'I told you, he's a loser. Why do you still think you need him?'

I looked at Hanna, at the ugly expression on her face, and at last I understood. *Jealousy*. What she felt about Julius had nothing to do with him being a loser and everything to do with him being a rival.

'I know better than you do what you need, Steffi,' said Hanna. 'You don't need him.'

'You can't make me wish him dead by putting a piece of paper in a box in Gertrud's house,' I told her.

'You wrote it,' she said.

'I wished for him to leave.'

'You wished him dead first.'

'I thought he was the one doing everything. I just wanted him to stop.'

'He wouldn't do all the things I did for you, Steffi,' said Hanna. She was trembling. 'I did everything you asked. Everything.'

'I didn't want this!' I shouted. 'What about your parents, back there?' I pointed wildly at the bedroom door. 'I didn't wish them dead. I didn't even *know* them, Hanna!'

'They were in the way. They've *always* been in the way. I

369

couldn't do anything, living here in one crappy room and doing a crappy job. They had money and the big house and the car and they never did anything with it. My dad just paraded around in his stupid hunting gear and my mother, God, she spent all her time cleaning the house. She did the inside of the shutters with a *toothbrush*, can you believe that? I was such a disappointment to them. Nothing better than a *Hauptschule* qualification, nothing to boast about with their friends from the shooting club. They never gave me anything. It was like starving, spending my whole life like that. And then that night we all went up to Rote Gertrud's house for the first time . . . You wished for something and it came true, and I saw the power that you had, the way it changed how we all looked at you. We're two halves of one whole, Steffi, two sides of one coin. That's the magic, not some rubbish in a ruined house in the woods full of beer cans and piss.'

Hanna turned her eyes towards me and they were full of savage brightness. I was terribly afraid that she would try to kiss me again. The stink of death hung over her. I would as soon have pressed my face to the bloody remnants on a butcher's block. I began to think too that perhaps my situation here was precarious. Someone who could talk so calmly of killing people she had known for most of her life was not the sort of person you wanted to be shut up in a lonely house with, whether they said they had done it all for you or not. I was well and truly in the labyrinth now, and the question was whether the monster at the centre would let me leave.

We did it, Hanna had said, with her eyes shining, and that, I thought with a sick feeling, was the crux of it. Hanna saw us as *we*, not as two separate people, *she* and *I*. If I broke away, told her I didn't want any part of the offerings she had brought me with bloody hands, it would be as bad as a hare breaking cover and darting in front of a greyhound. Still, it was not possible to turn to her and say, *It was a good thing that you did*, even as a lie. All my life I had been shy. People had talked for me and at me. They had made assumptions about what I wanted, even from my own life. I was sick of it, sick of being a blank screen on to which other people projected their thoughts, their dreams, their own capering demons. I shook off Hanna's clutching hands.

'No,' I said.

CHAPTER SEVENTY-ONE

I saw the emotions struggling for dominance in Hanna's face, denial and anger, like oil and vinegar swirling in a bottle.

'No, no,' I said, and already I was on my feet, ready to shove her away if she tried to get near me again. I retreated down a couple of stairs, clinging to the banister. I dared not turn my back on her.

'Don't say no, Steffi,' said Hanna.

She was on her feet too now. I saw her expression and backed down another step.

'It was wrong,' I told her. 'All of it. I was wrong to wish those things. It was just a stupid game at the start and it shouldn't have gone any further. It was wrong, Hanna. *Wrong.*'

'What's the use of saying that?' she said angrily. 'You can't take it back, Steffi.'

'I would if I could.'

'Why? Because it's *wrong*?' sneered Hanna. 'Then tell me what's right with a life where people who are half dead already tell you what to do, where it's all mapped out like a prison sentence, unending nothingness. What, are you going to go back and spend fifty years making *Florentiners* to your dad's secret recipe?' She was shouting now. 'What's – the – fucking – *point*?'

'I don't know what I'm going to do!' I shouted back. 'But I'm making up my own mind. Maybe I will make bloody *Florentiners* forever, I don't know. But *I'm* deciding. Not my parents. Not you. *I* am.'

'You can't leave,' said Hanna, and her voice was suddenly cold.

'Yes, I can,' I said, and I withdrew another step, watching her all the time in case she made a move towards me.

'You can't tell anyone. You're in this just as much as I am.'

'I didn't shoot anyone in their bed or push anyone downstairs, Hanna.'

'You told me to,' she retorted. 'I've got every single one of your notes proving it. You're in it up to the neck.'

'I don't care,' I said. 'I'll take my chances.'

'Then you're stupid. Just as stupid as the rest of them.'

'Maybe,' I said, and went down another step.

'Look, it doesn't have to be like this. Forget Julius Rensinghof. It can end here.'

'How can it end?' I asked her incredulously. 'There's a corpse in the garage and two bodies upstairs in bed. You think that's all just going to go away?'

'I have money,' said Hanna. 'Thousands of euros in my dad's safe. There's the Mercedes. We can go anywhere we want, do anything we want.' She gazed down at me and her dark eyes were as cold and hard as chips of haematite. 'It's your last chance. Stay with me.'

'No.'

I expected her to lunge at me, maybe try to get her hands

around my throat, or shove me down the stairs. I was waiting for that, holding on to the banister, ready for the assault
that never came.

Instead Hanna turned on her heel and marched away up
the landing.

Where's she going? I thought to myself, and then suddenly
I knew. It came into my head as clear as day: Herr Landberg's
study, with the shooting-club photos and the dead animals'
heads on the walls and the open gun locker. Hanna was not
going to let me leave. She wasn't going to bother with anything as unreliable as a shove from the middle of the staircase.
She was going to her father's study to fetch something that
would send a message screaming down the hallway after me,
a deadly message that could travel faster than I could run, the
kind marked *no response required*.

I thundered down the rest of the stairs as fast as I could,
paused for a dangerous second at the bottom, looking
wildly for a way out, and then I was running across the parquet floor, making for the front door. I thought I could hear
movement on the upstairs landing as I reached the door and
grabbed the handle.

Open, open, I thought as I wrenched uselessly at it. I
looked for a key, but there wasn't one in the inside lock. I
glanced up and down; there were no bolts either. Hanna
must have locked it and taken the key away altogether.

I heard the top stair creak as Hanna put her weight on it.
She wasn't bothering to run now; she knew she had the
means to drop me even if I had a good head start on her. She
had probably heard me rattling the front door too, so she
knew exactly where I was. Sick and light-headed with fear,
I ran towards the nearest open door. I glanced in and saw

that it was the kitchen, with its subsiding landscape of used cartons and jars spread over every surface like the remains of a bombed city. There was no second door out of the kitchen, I saw. If I hid in here and Hanna found me, I would be trapped.

Sick fear had laid its hand heavily on me and for a moment I almost ran back the way I had come, blind and unreasoning in panic. Then I saw the telephone table with its stack of unopened letters and I remembered that I had come into the house this way. I was within a few footsteps of the door leading to the garage. My heart thumping wildly, I opened the door. It occurred to me that it would have been a good idea to open another door in the hallway, to confuse the trail, but there was no time for that now. I could hear the rapid thuds of Hanna's feet on the stairs. She had decided to dispense with the sporting head start. I slipped through the door and closed it behind me as quietly as I could.

I looked out through the open garage door and for a moment I considered hiding inside. The distance to the gate or the shrubs bordering the garden seemed immense. I was not confident of crossing it before Hanna burst out through the door behind me and took aim. I glanced at the concrete floor, calculating whether there would be sufficient clearance for me to wriggle underneath Herr Landberg's Mercedes. Some deeply ingrained animal instinct warned me against the idea. Hanna might not think to look there, but if she did I was all out of options. If the Mercedes ever went in for another service the mechanic would be cleaning my brains from the pipework underneath. I went for the open door.

Now I was on the gravel drive and the gate was a million kilometres away. I took a split-second decision and, instead of running towards it, I ran in the other direction, towards the corner of the house. I heard the front door slam as Hanna came racing out with such force that it swung shut behind her. She had foreseen that I would go for the gate and was determined to head me off. I glanced back and saw her standing there on the gravel, chest heaving, eyes scanning the drive for signs of me. At the very instant that I reached the corner, her head turned and our eyes met. I saw the revolver in her hand and my heart seemed to give a mighty kick inside my chest, like a bucking horse. Galvanized by terror, I flung myself around the corner, my feet skidding on the gravel, desperate to put the solidity of a stone wall between myself and the gun. A split second later I heard a single harsh report which echoed off the hillside so that for a moment it seemed that the air was full of the sound, like deadly rain.

Then I was pelting the length of the wall, passing the neatly stacked log pile that Herr Landberg would not be needing next winter. The crunching of gravel under my feet and my own ragged breathing were loud in my ears, but still I was listening with fearful intensity for Hanna's footsteps and for the second report, the one that would bring death speeding towards me. I thought I could hear the sound of her approach already on the gravel as I turned the far corner, my lungs burning and my heart thumping.

At the rear of the house was a large conservatory, utterly useless to hide behind, and around it an expanse of lawn edged with shrubs and trees. I was running out of options. I circled the conservatory, hoping that it might provide a little cover for my flight, even for an instant, then made for the shelter of the trees. As I ran I sent up a silent prayer of thanks for the long dry summer. Since Herr Landberg had clearly not been in a position to mow the lawn for some weeks, only the searing heat had kept the grass short and dry. If it had been wet my footprints would have shown up as clearly as a neon sign saying *She went this way*. I dived between two large overhanging shrubs, jarring my knees and elbows painfully on the hard earth. Then I lay there in the shadows, trying desperately to stifle my own gasps of exertion and terror.

Had Hanna seen me? I dared not look out in case she saw me, but my ears strained for every sound. I heard running footsteps, then they were muffled and I guessed that she was crossing the grass. I bit my lip in an agony of terror but dared not move a muscle.

'Steffi?'

Hanna's voice sounded so calm, so reasonable. If I had not seen the gun in her hand for myself, if I had not heard its deadly report, I might have been tempted to come out. I caught the sound of something – a dried leaf, a tuft of baked grass – whispering under her feet and then a rustling. Judging that it was far enough from where I lay that she would not detect a very stealthy movement, I edged far enough forward to peep out from my hiding place.

On the other side of the lawn, Hanna was searching the bushes, thrusting them aside with the hand that still grasped the revolver. With a thrill of horror I realized that she was conducting a search and that sooner or later she would work her way over to the spot where I lay hidden. I had to move and the sooner the better, before she got close enough to spot me.

Trying desperately not to make a sound, I wormed my way backwards, deeper into the shelter of the overhanging vegetation. And at last luck was with me. I was right at the border of the garden, where it backed on to the forest. There was a wire fence separating the two, but even Herr Landberg's fastidiousness had not extended to fighting his way through the shrubbery to maintain it. A long section was torn and curling upwards. I ducked my head and wriggled underneath, shrinking as low as I could, aware that to catch my clothing on the wire now was to sign my own death warrant.

I emerged on the other side, dusty and scratched but in one piece. I paused for a second, listening, and I heard my name hanging on the air, ragged as the cry of a lynx. Then I was scrambling up through brambles and saplings and the dry summer vegetation, until I found myself on a proper forest path and could break into a run.

CHAPTER SEVENTY-TWO

It took me a little over twenty minutes to run the length of the path, which ran high along the side of the hill and came out at the edge of the old town. By then I knew that no one was following me, but I was so exhausted that each breath I took seared my lungs like smoke. Brown with dust and bleeding from a dozen tiny scratches, I limped back into the town and made my way to the police station. The town was heaving with tourists, as it always was on hot summer days, but there were also a good many locals on the streets, plenty to turn and watch Steffi Nett of the *Konditorei Nett* struggle her way up the front steps of the police station, looking as though she had been in some kind of brawl.

It took me some time to convince the policeman on duty that my story was a serious one, which was no surprise. When he had understood the bit about a young woman armed with a hunting revolver and possibly a couple of rifles, he began to make some phone calls, but I could see that that favourite parental expression *You've got a lot of explaining to do, young lady* was going to be applied pretty rigorously once the situation had been defused. It was more than a rural police station could deal with, so reinforcements had to be sent for. In all it must have been at least an hour, perhaps longer, before anyone ventured cautiously up the road to the Landbergs' house.

Hanna had no intention of being hunted down and tried by the twin courts of law and public opinion. All the same, I think she waited to see whether I would change my mind and come back, take up her offer of carousing among the bones of her victims. It was not until the police actually approached the house that a single sharp *crack* was heard. When they finally got inside, Hanna had put herself out of their reach forever.

CHAPTER SEVENTY-THREE

The explanations were not so easily evaded. Weary days were spent relating my side of the story to the *Kriminalpolizei*. More weary weeks and months lie ahead while every aspect of the sorry story is investigated and examined. So far as I know, Hanna lied about keeping my notes. Certainly, to date, nobody has confronted me with a single one of them. At the same time, a document was discovered that nobody was expecting, least of all myself: a will written by Hanna leaving everything she owned to me. Under German law it is almost impossible to leave everything away from your family, but Hanna's parents were both dead and she had no other relatives that have been traced yet. And then there was the envelope with the ten thousand euros in it. I handed it over to the police with every single note intact, but I had to admit that it had arrived anonymously and that there was only the word of a dead girl to say where it had come from. It is possible that a very great deal of money will come to me – and my family – one day, and it is equally possible that none of it will come at all. As long as the bakery stays afloat, and with it my parents' dreams, I can truthfully say that I do not care which of these two possibilities comes to pass.

Assuming that there are no legal consequences for me – and there are those in the town, such as Frau von Jülich, who would like to see somebody pay – I shall have to leave Bad Münstereifel for the foreseeable future. It is not comfortable to think of running into Kai's parents or Frau Kessel's cronies. I am not the only one who feels this way: Max's uncle has been persuaded to offer him a job in Frankfurt; Izabela has gone to stay with relatives in her mother's homeland. So I am escaping from Bad Münstereifel, although not in a way or for reasons I would ever have hoped for. If you make a bargain with the Devil you must be very careful what you wish for.

The day my father came home from hospital was cool and overcast, with a hint of the coming autumn in the air. By the time he arrived at the bakery, a small crowd of interested citizens had gathered. My mother had not advertised the fact that he was coming home, and the bakery was still closed, but word had a way of getting around in Bad Münstereifel, as we knew well. I should dearly have loved to run downstairs and greet my father, but seeing the little gathering below I thought better of it and stayed at the upstairs front window instead.

My mother got out of the car first and bustled round to my father's side to open the door. My father emerged, holding on to the car door, thinner and paler than he had been when he had started his last working day at the bakery, but still recognizably himself. My mother fussed around, fetching his bags for him and trying to take his arm, as though he was too terribly frail to take a single step on his own. He waved her off. Then he drew himself upright, let go of the car door and surveyed the little crowd of his fellow citizens.

'*Guten Morgen zusammen,*' he said.

There was a moment's pause before someone said, '*Guten Morgen,*' and then others followed suit.

The crowd parted as my father made his way slowly and carefully but unaided towards the door of the bakery, my mother following with the bags. He had reached the front step and my mother was fumbling for the key when someone stepped forward.

It should have been perfectly plain from the beginning that Udo Meyer would never let a situation like this one pass by without sticking his oar in. 'Herr Nett,' he said, in that droning voice that made you want to put your fingers in your ears or else take a swing at him, 'is the bakery going to close for good?'

My father stopped and turned to face Udo, with his back to the bakery's open door. He spent perhaps a quarter of a minute looking Udo up and down, as though he were some highly perplexing object, then he said, 'The bakery will be reopening as soon as possible and remaining open.'

He turned to go inside, but Udo was not finished yet.

'Herr Nett, what about your daughter?' he asked.

My father had one foot on the doorstep, but now he paused and looked Udo in the eyes. By neither the slightest change of expression nor an infinitesimal sigh did he betray what everyone knew, which was that Udo – as the self-elected representative of the town – wanted to find out whether my father was going to disown me, as he properly should. The stare my father gave Udo was absolutely level and he held Udo's gaze so long that the other man began to fidget visibly.

'*Both* my daughters are well, thank you,' said my father at last, very deliberately. Then finally he took my mother's proffered arm, stepped into the bakery and closed the door.

CHAPTER SEVENTY-FOUR

Yesterday afternoon, when I was alone in the flat, there was a knock on the front door. My parents were both downstairs in the bakery with the new baker's assistant – someone from out of town, recently qualified, keen and energetic and with absolutely no prior knowledge of Bad Münstereifel gossip.

I was surprised and a little apprehensive to hear the knock. There were very few people I wanted to see. I dreaded the thought of having to rehash what had happened at the Landbergs' house or, just as bad, having to converse with someone without referring to it, while knowing full well that that was the only thing on their mind, that they were studying me the whole time with speculation in their eyes. Still, I presumed that my parents had not allowed whomever it was upstairs without a reason. Reluctantly I went and opened the door.

A familiar figure was standing there: tall, slim, with the collar of his tatty black coat turned up and his shock of coppery hair standing up like a corona of flame as usual.

'Julius,' I said.

'Can I come in?' he asked.

Of course I stood back to let him in, but as he passed me

I bit my lip. I was not sure what reason Julius could have for coming. If he was going to berate me for lying to him so that I could go off to Hanna's alone I didn't think I could stand it.

He paused to look at me.

'We can go into the kitchen,' I said, indicating the way.

I had a feeling that it would be awkward in the living room, each of us sitting on one of my parents' overstuffed armchairs, looking at each other across the expanse of coffee table. At least in the kitchen I could stay on my feet and busy myself making tea or something.

Julius sat at the kitchen table, his long legs sprawled out in front of him. I didn't sit; somehow I felt safer on my feet, as though I could bolt like a startled animal if need be. Instead I leaned against the kitchen units.

'Do you want anything?' I said. 'Tea, or . . .'

'A glass of water maybe,' he said.

I turned away and reached for a glass from the shelf. Then I picked up a bottle of mineral water that was standing on the work surface and began to undo the cap. It was a new bottle and the cap was very tight. As I struggled with it I kept my back turned to Julius.

'Steffi,' he said into the silence between us, 'is it true that you're leaving Bad Münstereifel?'

'Yes,' I said, without turning round.

I expected a hail of questions. Everyone else around here would have wanted to know all the details. But maybe he knew them already from the town's extensive gossip network, because all he said was, 'I'm sorry.'

I managed to get the cap off the bottle and began to pour water into the glass, but I seemed unusually clumsy. Water cascaded over the side of the glass and on to the worktop. I put the bottle down and reached for a cloth.

'Are you coming back?' he asked.

I didn't reply for a few moments. It was not a question I had even begun to answer for myself.

'I don't know,' I said in the end.

'Well, can we keep in touch?'

'Of course,' I said, rubbing at the wet work surface, not daring to turn round.

'The band still needs a singer,' he said. There was a pause and I imagined him sitting there with his head to one side, thinking. 'We don't only do gigs in Bad Münstereifel, you know.'

'The band,' I repeated. I suddenly felt chilled, as though the cold of the water I was mopping from the worktop were leaching into my skin, making my fingers clumsy and my hands tremble. 'You're always thinking of that band of yours. You never give up, do you?'

I heard the sound of chair legs scraping on the tiles as Julius stood up.

'No, I don't,' he said, and this time his voice was right behind me, centimetres away.

I put down the cloth. Still I did not dare to look at him. How could I tell him what I felt if I wasn't even sure myself? Sometimes he mesmerized me; sometimes he infuriated me. I had wished for things I now deeply regretted and I was not proud of that. I feared to share those things with someone who had always seemed to think well of me. I had lied to Julius and I had suspected him. Would it ever be possible to get past those things, to start again?

I didn't jump when Julius put his hand on my shoulder.

He made me turn towards him. He touched my face and made me look at him.

I let him put his arms around me, but when he bent to try to kiss me I had to turn my head. His lips brushed my cheek instead. He held me very close.

'Is this *No*?' said his voice in my ear.

I held on to him, feeling the rough wool of his coat under my fingers.

'It's *Maybe*,' I said.

So here I am, sitting by the window in the flat above the bakery that I am soon to leave, looking down at the street below – such a familiar street – and wondering whether I shall see someone tall and red-headed striding down it towards me today or not. When I think of the coming days and weeks and months, and what they will bring, it is like looking at a deck of tarot cards spread out in a fan before me. A whole host of possible futures.

Where it will go with Julius I still cannot say, nor whether it will survive my leaving Bad Münstereifel. But Julius is determined and I have discovered that I am more resourceful than I ever suspected. If we want to make it work, we will.

As for the rest of it, well, I could go back to my bakery studies and return to the town one day when the wounds have healed, to see my name painted in next to my father's on the front of the bakery. Or I could follow my dream of studying music, and starve, or perhaps just about get by, or perhaps be rich.

It is for me to decide.

GLOSSARY

Abitur	Final exams taken at the end of secondary education; a prerequisite for entrance to university in Germany
Arschloch	Arsehole
Bauernbrot	Literally 'farmer's bread'; a typical German rye bread
Bienenstich	Literally 'bee sting cake', which consists of a sweet bread filled with vanilla custard and topped with honeyed almonds
Currywurst	Fast-food snack of German sausage with curry sauce
Das Goldene Blatt	'The Golden Leaf' is a weekly tabloid magazine
Dinner for One	Originally a 1920s comedy sketch by British author Lauri Wylie for the theatre, the 1963 English-language TV recording of this is very popular in Germany

Florentiner	Florentines are baked sweet biscuits made with almonds, orange peel and honey; they're traditional Christmas sweets in south Germany
Freizeit Revue	'Freetime Review' is a weekly entertainment magazine
Graubrot	Literally 'grey bread'; a bread made with sourdough, rye and wholegrain wheat, making it lighter than typical rye bread
Guten Morgen	Good morning
Guten Tag	Good day (standard greeting, like 'hello')
Gymnasium	Equivalent to a grammar school in the UK
Hauptschule	Least academic type of German secondary school; graduates would still need to attend further education to gain the *Abitur* in order to attend university
Karneval	Festive season which takes place just before Lent; usually involves a parade or public celebration
Knackwurst	Typically a short, plump sausage; *knack* (German for 'to crack') refers to the sound made when the skin of the sausage is pierced after cooking
Kölner Stadt-Anzeiger	Popular daily newspaper published in Cologne

Konditorei	Little cafe with a bakery/patisserie
Kosakenbrot	Literally 'Cossack bread'; a rye bread made with sourdough, typically with a cross-hatch pattern on the upper crust
Kriminalpolizei	Criminal investigation agency of the German police force
Kyllburger	Relating to the town of Kyllburg, which is situated on the river Kyll in the Eifel region of Germany
Mohnbrot	Poppy-seed bread
Notarzt	Emergency doctor
Nussecke	Literally 'nut corner'; wedge-shaped nut-filled pastry, which is often coated or edged with chocolate
Nuss-striezel	Plaited nut-filled Danish pastry
Plunderteilchen	Danish pastries
Rathaus	Townhall
Realschule	Type of secondary school in Germany, ranked between *Hauptschule* and *Gymnasium*
Sahnetorte	Cream cake
Sauerteig	Sourdough
Scheisse	Shit
Sekt	Good-quality sparkling wine
Sonnenkorn	Sunflower-seed bread made with wholemeal oats and also linseed
Speckstange	Rye bread made with bacon
Tschüss	Bye (informal)
Vorsicht!	Careful!
Wurst	German sausage

ACKNOWLEDGEMENTS

As ever, I would like to thank Camilla Wray of the Darley Anderson Agency for her enthusiasm and energy. I would also like to thank Amanda Punter, Editorial Director at Puffin, and everyone at Puffin and Penguin for their continuing support and encouragement.

Special thanks are due to Frau Hildegard Quasten of Bäckerei Cafe Quasten in Mechernich-Kommern, and to Herr Nipp and the team at the Erft-Café and the Café am Salzmarkt in Bad Münstereifel, for their advice about the running of a German bakery and German bakery products. Any inaccuracies are entirely mine.

Last but definitely not least, I would like to thank my husband Gordon for his unflagging support.

GET INSIDE YOUR FAVOURITE BOOK

spinebreakers.co.uk

spinebreaker (n)

story-surfer, word-lover, day-dreamer,
reader/ writer/ artist/ thinker